"Me?"

The startled squeak of Sheryl's voice echoed off the walls of the little-used office.

"You," Harry confirmed, pulling a folded document out of his coat pocket. "This authorizes an indefinite detail. You're on my team, effective immediately."

"Hey, hang on here," Sheryl protested. "I'm not sure I want to be assigned to a fugitive apprehension task force, indefinitely or otherwise. Before I agree to anything like this, I want to know what's required of me."

"Basically, I want your exclusive time and attention for as long as it takes to extract every bit of information I can."

Sheryl stared at him. "Exclusive time and attention? You mean, like all day?"

Harry forced his expression to stay neutral as he answered, "And all night, if necessary."

Dear Reader,

This is it, the final month of our wonderful three-month celebration of Intimate Moments' fifteenth anniversary. It's been quite a ride, but it's not over yet. For one thing, look who's leading off the month: Rachel Lee, with *Cowboy Comes Home,* the latest fabulous title in her irresistible CONARD COUNTY miniseries. This one has everything you could possibly want in a book, including all the deep emotion Rachel is known for. Don't miss it.

And the rest of the month lives up to that wonderful beginning, with books from both old favorites and new names sure to become favorites. Merline Lovelace's *Return to Sender* will have you longing to work at the post office (I'm not kidding!), while Marilyn Tracy returns to the wonderful (but fictional, darn it!) town of Almost, Texas, with *Almost Remembered.* Look for our TRY TO REMEMBER flash to guide you to Leann Harris's *Trusting a Texan,* a terrific amnesia book, and the EXPECTANTLY YOURS flash marking Raina Lynn's second book, *Partners in Parenthood.* And finally, don't miss *A Hard-Hearted Man,* by brand-new author Melanie Craft. *Your* heart will melt—guaranteed.

And that's not all. Because we're not stopping with the fifteen years behind us. There are that many—and more!—in our future, and I know you'll want to be here for every one. So come back next month, when the excitement and the passion continue, right here in Silhouette Intimate Moments.

Yours,

Leslie J. Wainger
Executive Senior Editor

Please address questions and book requests to:
Silhouette Reader Service
U.S.: 3010 Walden Ave., P.O. Box 1325, Buffalo, NY 14269
Canadian: P.O. Box 609, Fort Erie, Ont. L2A 5X3

RETURN TO
SENDER

MERLINE
LOVELACE

Published by Silhouette Books

America's Publisher of Contemporary Romance

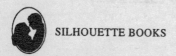

SILHOUETTE BOOKS

ISBN 0-373-07866-8

RETURN TO SENDER

MERLINE LOVELACE

After twenty-three exciting years as an officer in the United States Air Force, Merline Lovelace hung up her uniform and started writing romances. She's now written more than twenty sizzling contemporary and historical novels and is thoroughly enjoying her new profession. When not glued to the keyboard, she and her handsome hero, Al, enjoy golf, traveling and gourmet meals in fine restaurants—not necessarily in that order!

Merline can be reached at P.O. Box 892717, Oklahoma City, OK 73189.

Watch for her next book, *If a Man Answers,* coming from Silhouette Intimate Moments in September 1998.

This one's for Sherrill and Elisha and Peggy and all the folks at the S. Penn Post Office—thanks for your friendly smiles when I show up all drawn and haggard to put a finished manuscript in the mail. Thanks, too, for your cheerful professionalism. You're outstanding representatives of the finest postal system in the world!

Chapter 1

Rio de Janeiro.

Mount Sugarloaf rising majestically above the city.

Streets crowded with revelers in costumes of bright greens and yellows and reds.

The glossy postcard leaped out at Sheryl Hancock from the thick sheaf of mail. Her hand stilled its task of sorting and stuffing post office boxes. The familiar early-morning sounds of co-workers grumbling and letters whooshing into metal boxes faded. For the briefest moment, she caught a faint calypso beat in the rattle of a passing mail cart and heard the laughter of Carnival.

"Is that another postcard from Paul-boy?"

With a small jolt, Sheryl left the South America festival and returned to the Albuquerque post office where she'd worked for the past twelve years. Smiling at the woman standing a few feet away, she nodded.

"Yes. This one's from Rio."

"Rio? The guy sure gets around, doesn't he?"

Elise Hart eased her bulk around a bank of opened postal boxes to peer at the postcard in Sheryl's hand. From the expression in Elise's brown eyes, it was obvious that she, too, was feeling the momentary magic of faraway places.

"What does this one say?"

Sheryl flipped the card over. "'Hi to my favorite aunt. I've been dancing in the streets for the past four days. Wish you were here.'"

Sighing, Elise gazed at the slick card. "What I wouldn't give to dump my two boys with my mother and fly down to Rio for Carnival."

"Oh, sure. I can just see you dancing through the streets, eight months pregnant yet."

"Eight months, one week, two days and counting," the redhead replied with a grimace. "I'd put on my dancing shoes for a hunk like Mrs. Gunderson's nephew, though."

"You'd better not put on dancing shoes! I'm your birthing partner, remember? I don't want you going into premature labor on me. Besides," Sheryl tacked on, "we only have Mrs. Gunderson's word for it that her nephew qualifies as a hunk."

"According to his doting aunt, Paul-boy sports a thick mustache, specializes in tight jeans and rates about 112 on the gorgeous scale." Elise waggled her dark-red brows in an exaggerated leer. "That's qualification enough in my book."

"Paul-boy, as you insist on calling him, is also pushing forty."

"So?"

So Sheryl didn't have a whole lot of respect for jet-setting playboys who refused to grow up or grow into their responsibilities. Her father had been a pharmaceutical salesman by profession and a wanderer by nature. He'd drifted in and out of her life for short periods during her youth, until her mother's loneliness and bitter nagging had made him disappear altogether. Sheryl didn't blame him, exactly. More often than not, she herself had to grit her teeth when her mother called in one of her complaining moods. But neither did she like to talk about her absent parent.

Instead, she teased Elise about her fascination with the man they both heard about every time the frail, white-haired woman who'd moved to Albuquerque some four months ago came in to collect her mail.

"Don't you think Mrs. Gunderson might be just a bit prejudiced about this nephew of hers?"

"Maybe. He still sounds yummy." Sighing, Elise rested a hand on her high, rounded stomach. "You'd think I would have learned my lesson once and for all. My ex broke the gorgeous scale, too."

Sheryl had bitten down hard on her lip too many times in the past to keep from criticizing her friend's husband. Since their divorce seven months ago, she felt no such restraints.

"Rick also weighed in as a total loser."

"True," Elise agreed. "He was, is and always will be a jerk." She traced a few absent circles on her tummy. "We can't all find men like Brian, Sher."

At the mention of her almost-fiancé, Sheryl banished any lingering thoughts of Elise's ex, Latin

American carnivals and the globe-trotting Paul Gunderson. In their place came the easy slide of contentment that always accompanied any thought of Brian Mitchell.

"No, we can't," she confirmed.

"So have you two set a date yet?"

"We're talking about an engagement at the end of the year."

"You're engaged to get engaged." Her friend's brown eyes twinkled. "That's so...so Brian."

"I know."

Actually, the measured pace of Sheryl's relationship with the Albuquerque real estate agent satisfied her almost as much as it did him. After dating for nearly a year, they'd just started talking about the next step. They'd announce an engagement when the time was right, quite possibly at Christmas, and set a firm date for the wedding when they'd saved up enough to purchase a house. Brian was sure interest rates would drop another few points in the next year or so. Before they took the plunge into matrimony, he wanted to be in a position to buy down their monthly house payments so they could live comfortably on her salary and his commissions.

"I think that's what I like most about him," Sheryl confided. "His dependability and careful planning and—"

"Not to mention his cute buns."

"Well..."

"Ha! Don't give me that Little Miss Innocent look. I know you, girl. Under that sunshine-and-summer exterior, you crave excitement and passion as much as the next woman. Even fat, prego ones.''

''What I crave,'' Sheryl replied, laughing, ''is for you to get back to work. We've only got ten minutes until opening, and I don't want to face the hordes lined up in the lobby by myself.''

Elise made a face and dipped into the cardboard tray in front of her for another stack of letters. She and Sheryl had come in early to help throw the postal box mail, since the clerk who regularly handled it was on vacation. They'd have to scramble to finish the last wall of boxes and get their cash drawers out of the vault in time to man the front counter.

Swiftly, Sheryl shuffled through the stack in her hand for the rest of Mrs. Gunderson's mail. Today's batch was mostly junk, she saw. Coupon booklets. Advertising fliers. A preprinted solicitation from the state insurance commissioner facing a special runoff election next week. And the postcard from Paul-boy, as Elise had dubbed him. With a last, fleeting glance at the colorful street scene, Sheryl bent down to stuff the mail into Mrs. Gunderson's slot.

It wouldn't stuff.

Frowning, she dropped down on her sneakered heels to examine the three-by-five-inch box. It contained at least one, maybe two days' worth of mail.

Strange. Mrs. Gunderson usually came into the post office every day to pick up her mail. More often than not, she'd pop in to chat with the employees on the counter, her yappy black-and-white shih tzu tucked under her arm. Regulations prohibited live animals in the post office except for those being shipped, but no one had the heart to tell Inga Gunderson that she couldn't bring her baby inside with her. Particularly when she also brought in homemade cookies and melt-in-your-mouth Danish spice cakes.

A niggle of worry worked into Sheryl's mind as she shoved Mrs. Gunderson's mail into her box. She hoped the woman wasn't sick or incapacitated. She'd keep an eye out for her today, just to relieve her mind that she was okay. Pushing off her heels, she finished the wall of boxes with brisk efficiency and headed for the vault. She had less than five minutes to count out her cash drawer and restock her supplies.

She managed it in four. She was at the front counter, her ready smile in place, when the branch manager unlocked the glass doors to the lobby and the first of the day's customers streamed in.

Sheryl didn't catch a glimpse of Mrs. Gunderson all morning, nor did any of her co-workers. As the day wore on, the unclaimed mail nagged at Sheryl. During her lunch break, she checked the postal box registry for the elderly renter's address and phone number.

The section of town where Inga Gunderson lived was served by another postal station much closer to her house, Sheryl noted. Wondering why the woman would choose to rent a box at a post office so far from her home, she dialed the number. The phone rang twice, then clicked to an answering machine. Since leaving a message wouldn't do anything to assure her of the woman's well-being, Sheryl hung up in the middle of the standard I-can't-come-to-the-phone-right-now recording.

Having come in at six-thirty to help "wall" the letters for the postal boxes, she got off at three. A quick check of Mrs. Gunderson's box showed it was still stuffed with unclaimed mail. Frowning, Sheryl wove her way slowly through the maze of route carriers' work areas and headed for the women's locker room at the rear of the station. After peeling off her pin-striped uniform shirt, she replaced it with a yellow tank top that brightened up the navy shorts worn by most of the postal employees in summer. A glance at the clock on the wall had her grabbing for her purse. She'd promised to meet Brian at three-thirty to look at a property he was thinking of listing.

After extracting a promise from Elise to go right home and get off her feet, Sheryl stepped outside. Hot, dry heat hit her like a slap in the face. With the sun beating down on her head and shoulders, she crossed the asphalt parking lot toward her trusty, ice-blue Camry. She opened the door and waited a moment to let the captured heat pour out. As she stood there in the hot, blazing sun, her nagging worry over Mrs. Gunderson crystallized into real concern. She'd swing by the woman's house, she decided. Just to check on her. It was a little out of her way, but Sheryl couldn't shake the fear that something had happened to the frail, white-haired customer.

With the Toyota's air conditioner doing valiant battle against the heat, she pulled out of the parking lot behind the post office and headed west on Haines, then north on Juan Tabo. Two more turns and three miles took her to the shady, residential neighborhood and Inga Gunderson's neat, two-story adobe house. She didn't see a car in the driveway, although several were parked along the street. Maybe Mrs. Gunderson's car was in the detached rear garage. Or maybe she'd gone out of town. Or maybe...

Maybe she was ill, or had fallen down the stairs and broken a leg or a hip. The woman lived alone, with only her precious Button for company. She could be lying in the house now, helpless and in pain.

More worried than ever, Sheryl pulled into the driveway and climbed out of the car. Once more the heat enveloped her. She could almost feel her hair sizzling. The thick, naturally curly mane tended to turn unmanageable at the best of times. In this soul-sucking heat, it took on a life of its own. Tucking a few wildly corkscrewing strands into the loose French braid that hung halfway down her back, Sheryl followed a pebbled walk to the front porch. A feathery Russian olive tree crowded the railed porch and provided welcome shade. Sighing in relief, she pressed the doorbell.

When the distant sound of a buzzer produced a series of high, plaintive yips and no Mrs. Gunderson, Sheryl's concern vaulted into genuine alarm. Inga Gunderson wouldn't leave town without her Button. The two were practically joined at the hip. They even looked alike, Elise had once joked, both possessing slightly pug noses, round, inquisitive eyes and hair more white than black.

Sheryl leaned on the doorbell again, and heard a

chorus of even more frantic yaps. She pulled open the screen and pounded on the door.

"Mrs. Gunderson! Are you in there?"

A long, piteous yowl answered her call. She hammered on the door in earnest, setting the frosted-glass panes to rattling.

"Mrs. Gunderson! Are you okay?"

Button howled once more, and Sheryl reached for the old fashioned iron latch. She had just closed her hand around it when the door snapped open, jerking her inside with it.

Gasping, she found herself nose to nose with a wrinkled linen sport coat and a blue cotton shirt that stretched across a broad chest. A *very* broad chest. She took a quick step back, at which point several things happened at once, none of them good from her perspective.

Her foot caught on the door mat, throwing her off balance.

A hard hand shot out and grabbed her arm, either to save her from falling or to prevent her escape.

A tiny black-and-white fury erupted from inside the house. Gums lifted, needle-sharp teeth bared, it flew through the air and fastened its jaws on the jean-clad calf of her rescuer-captor.

"Ow!"

The man danced across the porch on one booted foot, taking Sheryl with him. Cursing, he lifted his leg and shook it. The little shih tzu snarled ferociously and hung on with all the determination of the rat catcher he was originally bred to be. Snarling a little herself, Sheryl tried to shake free of the bruising hold on her arm. When the stranger didn't loosen his grip, she dug her nails into the back of his tanned hand.

"Dammit, let go!"

She didn't know if the command shouted just above her ear was directed at her or the dog, and didn't particularly care. Pure, undiluted adrenaline pumped through her veins. She had no idea who this man was or what had happened to Mrs. Gunderson, but obviously *something* had. Something Button didn't like. Sheryl's only thought was to get away, find a phone, call the police.

Her attacker gave his upraised leg another shake, and Sheryl gouged her nails deeper into his skin. When that earned her a smothered curse and a painful jerk on her arm, she took a cue from the shih tzu and bent to bite the hand that held her.

"Hey!"

Still half-bent, Sheryl felt herself spun sideways. Her captor released his grip, but before she could bolt, his arm whipped around her waist. A half second later, she thudded back into the solid wall of blue oxford.

Her breath slammed out of her lungs. The band around her middle cut off any possibility of pulling in a replacement supply. As frantic now as the dog, she kicked back. One sneakered heel connected with the man's shin.

"Oh, for...!" Lifting her off her feet, her attacker grunted in her ear. "Calm down! I won't hurt you."

"Prove...it." she panted. "Let...me...go!"

"I will, I will. Just calm down."

Sheryl calmed, for the simple reason that she

couldn't do anything else. Her ribs felt as though they'd threaded right through one another and squeezed out everything in between. Red spots danced before her eyes.

Thankfully, the excruciating pressure on her waist eased. She drew great gulps of air into her starved lungs. The sounds of another snarl and another curse battered at her ears. They were followed by a wheezy whine. When the spots in front of her eyes cleared, she turned to face a belligerent male, holding an equally belligerent shih tzu by the scruff of its neck.

For the first time, she saw the man's face. It was as hard as the rest of his long, lean body, Sheryl decided shakily. The sun had weathered his skin to dark oak. White lines fanned the corners of his eyes. They showed whiskey gold behind lashes the same dark brown as his short, straight hair and luxuriant mustache.

His mustache!

Sheryl whipped her gaze down his rangy form. Beneath the blue cotton shirt and tan jacket, his jeans molded trim hips and tight, corded thighs. She made the connection with a rush of relief.

The hunky nephew!

She'd have to tell Elise that Mrs. Gunderson wasn't all that far-off in her description. Although Sheryl wouldn't quite rate this rugged, whipcord-lean man as 112 on the gorgeous scale, he definitely scored at least an 88 or 90. Well, maybe a 99.

Wedging the yapping shih tzu under his arm like a hairy football, he gave Sheryl a narrow-eyed once-over. "Sorry about the little dance we just did. Are you all right?"

"More or less."

"Be quiet!"

She jumped at the sharp command, but realized immediately that it was aimed at Button. Thankfully, the shih tzu recognized the voice of authority. His annoying, high-pitched yelps subsided to muttered growls.

Swinging his attention back to Sheryl, Button's handler studied her with an intentness that raised little goose bumps on her arms. She couldn't remember the last time a man had looked at her like this, as though he wanted not just to see her, but into her. In fact, she couldn't remember the last time any man had *ever* looked at her like this. Brian certainly didn't. He was too considerate, too polite to make someone feel all prickly by such scrutiny.

"What can I do for you, Miss...?"

"Hancock. Sheryl Hancock. I know your aunt," she offered by way of explanation. "I just came by to check on her."

Those golden brown eyes lasered into her. "You know my aunt?"

"Yes. You're Paul Gunderson, aren't you?"

He was silent for a moment, then countered with a question of his own. "What makes you think so?"

"The mustache," she said with a tentative smile. And the thigh-hugging jeans, she added silently. "Your aunt talks about you all the time."

"Does she?"

"Yes. She's really proud of how well you're doing

in the import-export business." Belatedly, Sheryl recalled the purpose of her visit. "Is she okay? I was worried when I didn't see her for a day or two."

"Inga's fine," he replied after a small pause. "She's upstairs. Resting."

Sheryl didn't see how anyone could rest through Button's shrill yapping, but then, Mrs. Gunderson was used to it.

"Oh, good." She started for the porch steps. "Would you tell her I came by, and that I'll talk to her tomorrow or whenever?"

Paul moved to one side. It was only a half step, a casual movement, but Sheryl couldn't edge past him without crowding against the wrought-iron rail.

"Why don't you come inside for a few minutes?" he suggested. "You can give me the real lowdown on what my aunt has to say about me, and we can both get out of the heat for a few minutes."

"I wish I could, but I'm running late for an appointment."

"There's some iced tea in the fridge. And a platter of freshly baked cookies on the kitchen table."

"Well…"

The cookies decided it. And Button's pitiable little whine. Obviously unhappy at being wedged into Paul's armpit, the dog snuffled noisily through its pug nose. The rhinestone-studded, bow-shaped barrette that kept his facial fur out of his eyes had slipped to one side. His bulging black orbs beseeched Sheryl to end his indignity.

She felt sorry for him but didn't make the mistake of reaching for the little stinker. The one time she'd tried to pet him at the post office, he'd nipped her fingers. As he now tried to nip Paul's. His sharp little teeth just missed the hand that brushed a tad too close to him. With a muttered oath, Paul jerked his hand away.

"How anyone could keep a noisy, bad-tempered fur ball like this as a pet is beyond me."

Somehow, the fact that Inga Gunderson's nephew disliked his aunt's obnoxious little Button made Sheryl feel as though they were allies of sorts. Smiling, she accepted his invitation and preceded him into the house.

Cool air wrapped around her like a sponge. The rooftop swamp cooler, so necessary to combat Albuquerque's dry, high-desert air, was obviously working overtime. As Sheryl's eyes made the adjustment from blazing outside light to the shadowed interior, she looked about in some surprise. The house certainly didn't fit Mrs. Gunderson's personality. No pictures decorated the walls. No knick-knacks crowded the tables. The furniture was a sort of pseudo-Southwest, a mix of bleached wood and brown Naugahyde, and not particularly comfortable looking.

Turning, she caught a glint of sunlight on Paul's dark hair as he bent down to deposit Button on the floor. To her consternation, she also caught a glimpse of what looked very much like a shoulder holster under the tan sport coat. She must have made some startled sound, because Paul glanced up and saw the direction of her wide-eyed stare. He released the dog and straightened, rolling his shoulders so that his jacket fell in place. The leather harness disappeared from view.

Sheryl had seen it, though.

And he knew she had.

His face went tight and altogether too hard for her peace of mind. Then Button gave a shrill, piercing bark and raced across the room. With another ear-splitting yip, he disappeared up the stairs. He left behind a tense silence, broken only by the whoosh of chilled air being forced through the vents by the swamp cooler.

Sheryl swallowed a sudden lump in her throat. "Is that a gun under your jacket?"

"It is."

"I, uh, didn't know the import-export business was so risky."

"It can be."

She took a discreet step toward the door. Guns made her nervous. Very nervous. Even when carried by handsome strangers. Especially when carried by handsome strangers.

"I think I'll pass on the cookies. It's been a long day, and I'm late for an appointment. Tell your aunt that I'll see her tomorrow. Or whenever."

"I'd really like you to stay a few minutes, Miss Hancock. I'm anxious to hear what Inga has to say about her nephew."

"Some other time, maybe."

He stepped sideways, blocking her retreat as effectively as he had on the porch. But this time the movement wasn't the least casual.

"I'm afraid I'll have to insist."

Chapter 2

She knew about Inga Gunderson's nephew!

As he stared down into the blonde's wide, distinctly nervous green eyes, Deputy U.S. Marshal Harry MacMillan's pulse kicked up to twice its normal speed. He forgot about the ache in his gut, legacy of a roundhouse punch delivered by the seemingly frail, white-haired woman upstairs. He ignored the stinging little dents in his calf, courtesy of her sharp-toothed dust mop. His blood hammering, he gave the new entry onto the scene a thoroughly professional once-over.

Five-six or -seven, he guessed. A local, from her speech pattern and deep tan. As Harry had discovered in the week he'd been in Albuquerque, the sun carried twice the firepower at these mile-high elevations than it did at lower levels. It had certainly added a glow to this woman's skin. With her long, curly, corn-silk hair, tip-tilted nose and nicely proportioned set of curves, she looked more like the girl next door than the accomplice of an escaped fugitive. But Harry had been a U.S. marshal long enough to know that even the most angelic face could disguise the soul of a killer.

His jaw clenched at the memory of his friend's agonizing death. For a second or two, Harry debated whether to identify himself or milk more information from the woman first. He wasn't about to jeopardize this case, which had become a personal quest, by letting a suspect incriminate herself without Mirandizing her, but this woman wasn't a suspect. Yet.

"Tell me how you know Inga Gunderson."

Her eyes slid past him to the door. "I, uh, see her almost every day."

"Where?"

"At the branch office where I work."

"What branch office?"

She started to answer, then forced a deep, steadying breath into her lungs. "What's this all about? Is Mrs. Gunderson really all right?"

She had guts. Harry would give her that. She was obviously frightened. He could detect a faint tremor in the hands clenched at the seams of her navy shorts. Yet instead of replying to Harry's abrupt demands for information, she was throwing out a few questions of her own.

"Are you her nephew or not?"

He couldn't withhold his identity in the face of a direct question. Lifting his free hand, he reached into his coat pocket. The woman uttered a yelp every bit as piercing as the damned dog's, and jumped back.

"Relax, I'm just getting my ID."

He pulled out the worn brown-leather case containing his credentials. Flipping it open one-handed, he displayed the five-pointed gold star and a picture ID.

"Harry MacMillan, deputy U.S. marshal."

Her gaze swung from him to the badge to him and back again. Her nervousness gave way to a flash of indignation.

"Why didn't you say so?!"

"I just did." Coolly, he returned the case to his pocket. "May I see your identification, please."

"Mine? Why? I've told you my name."

Her response came out clipped and more than a little angry. That was fine with Harry. Until he discovered her exact relationship to the fugitive he'd been tracking for almost a year, he didn't mind keeping her rattled and off balance.

"I know who you said you were, Miss Hancock. I'd just like to see some confirmation."

"I left my purse in the car."

"Oh, that's smart."

The caustic comment made her stiffen, but before she could reply Harry cut back to the matter that had consumed his days and nights for so many months.

"Tell me again how you know Inga Gunderson."

Sheryl had always thought of herself as a dedicated federal employee. She enjoyed her job, and considered the service that she provided important to her community. Nor did she hesitate to volunteer her time and energies for special projects, such as selling

T-shirts to aid victims of the devastating floods last year or coordinating the Christmas Wish program that responded to some of the desperate letters to Santa Claus that came into the post office during the holidays. She'd never come close to any kind of dangerous activity or bomb threats, but she certainly would have cooperated with other federal agencies in any ongoing investigation...if asked.

What nicked the edges of her normally placid temper was that this man didn't ask. He demanded. Still, he was a federal agent. And he wanted an answer.

"Mrs. Gunderson stops in almost every day at the station where I work," she repeated.

"What station?"

"The Monzano Street post office."

"The Monzano post office." He shoved a hand through his short, cinnamon-brown hair. "Well, hell!"

Sheryl bristled at the unbridled disgust in his voice. Although her friendly personality and ready smile acted as a preventive against the verbal abuse many postal employees experienced, she'd endured her share of sneers and jokes about the post office. The slurs, even said in fun, always hurt. She took pride in her work, as did most of her co-workers. What's more, she'd chosen a demanding occupation. She'd like to see anyone, this lean, tough deputy marshal included, sling the amount of mail she did each day and still come up smiling.

"Do you have a problem with the post office?" she asked with a touch of belligerence.

"What?" The question seemed to jerk him from

his private and not very pleasant thoughts. "No. Have a seat, Miss Hancock. I'll call my contacts and verify your identity."

"Why?" she asked again.

His hawk's eyes sliced into her. "You've just walked into the middle of an ongoing investigation. You're not walking out until I ascertain that you're who you say you are…and until I understand your exact relationship with the woman who calls herself 'Mrs. Gunderson.'"

"*Calls* herself 'Inga Gunderson'?"

"Among other aliases. Sit down."

Feeling a little like Alice sliding down through the rabbit hole, Sheryl perched on the edge of the uncomfortable, sand-colored sofa. Good grief! What in the world had she stumbled into?

She found out a few moments later. Deputy U.S. Marshal MacMillan dropped the phone onto its cradle and ran a quick, assessing eye over her yellow tank top and navy shorts.

"Well, you check out. The FBI's computers have your weight at 121, but the rest of the details from your background information file substantiate your identity."

Sheryl wasn't sure which flustered her more, the fact that this man had instant access to her background file or that he'd accurately noted the few extra pounds she'd put on recently. Okay, more than a few pounds.

MacMillan's gaze swept over her once more, then settled on her face. "According to the file, you're clean. Not even a speeding ticket in the past ten years.''

From his dry tone, he didn't consider a spotless driving record a particularly meritorious achievement.

"Thank you. I think. Now will you tell me what's going on here? Is Mrs. Gunderson…or whoever she is…really all right? Why in the world is a deputy U.S. marshal checking up on that sweet, fragile lady?''

"Because we suspect that sweet, fragile lady of being involved in the illegal importation of depleted uranium.''

"Mrs. *Gunderson?*''

The marshal, Sheryl decided, had been sniffing something a lot more potent than the glue on the back of stamps!

"Let me get this straight. You think Inga Gunderson is smuggling uranium?''

"Depleted uranium," he corrected, as though she should know the difference.

She didn't.

"It's the same heavy metal that's used in the manufacture of armor-piercing artillery shells," he explained in answer to her blank look. Almost imperceptibly, his voice roughened. "Recently, it's also been used to produce new cop-killer bullets.''

Sheryl stared at him, stunned. For the life of her, she couldn't connect the tiny, chirpy woman who brought her and her co-workers mouthwatering spice cakes with a smuggling ring. A uranium smuggling ring, for heaven's sake! Of all the thoughts whirling around in her confused, chaotic mind, only one surfaced.

"I thought the Customs Service tracked down smugglers."

"They do." The planes of MacMillan's face became merciless. "We're working with Customs on this, as well as with the Nuclear Regulatory Commission, the FBI, the CIA and a whole alphabet of other agencies on this case. But the U.S. Marshals Service has a special interest in the outcome of this case. One of our deputies took a uranium-tipped bullet in the chest when he was escorting Inga Gunderson's supposed nephew to prison."

"Paul?" Sheryl gasped.

The hazy image she'd formed of a handsome, mustached jet-setter lazing on the beach at Ipanema among the bikinied Brazilians surfaced for a moment, then shattered forever.

She shook her head in dismay. She should have known better than to let herself become intrigued, even slightly, by a globe-trotting wanderer! Her father hadn't stayed in one place long enough for anyone, her mother included, to get to know him or his many varied business concerns. For all Sheryl knew, he could have been a smuggler, too. But not, she prayed, a murderer.

At the memory of her father's roving ways, she gave silent, heartfelt thanks for her steady, reliable, soon-to-be-fiancé. Sure, Brian occasionally fell asleep on the couch beside her. And once or twice he'd displayed more excitement over the prospect of closing a real estate deal than he did over their plans for the future. But Sheryl knew he would always be there for her.

As he was probably there for her right now, she realized with a start. No doubt he was waiting in the heat at the house he wanted to show her, flicking impatient little glances at his watch. She'd promised to be there by three-thirty. She snuck a quick look at her watch. It was well past that now, she saw.

"What do you know about Paul Gunderson?"

The curt question snapped her attention back to Deputy Marshal MacMillan.

"Only what Inga told me. That he's a sales rep for an international firm and that he travels a lot. From his postcards, it looks like his company sends him to some pretty exotic locales."

MacMillan dropped his hands from his hips. His well-muscled body seemed to torque to an even higher degree of tension.

"Postcards?" he asked softly.

"He sends her bright, cheery cards from the various places he travels to. They come to her box at the Monzano branch. We—my friends at the post office and I—thought it was sweet the way he stayed in touch with his aunt like that."

"Yeah, real sweet." His face tight with disgust, MacMillan shook his head. "We ordered a mail cover the same day we tracked Inga Gunderson to Albuquerque. The folks at the central post office assured us they had the screen in place. Dammit, they should have caught the fact that she had another postal box."

Sheryl's defensive hackles went up on behalf of her fellow employees. "Hey, they're only human. They do their best."

The marshal didn't dignify that with a reply. He thought for a moment, his forehead furrowed.

"We didn't find any postcards here at the house. Obviously, Inga Gunderson destroyed them as soon as she retrieved them from her box. Did you happen to see the messages on the cards?"

Sheryl squirmed a bit. Technically, postal employees weren't supposed to read their patrons' mail. It was hard to abide by that rule, though. More than one of the male clerks slipped raunchy magazines out of their brown wrappers for a peek when the supervisors weren't around. *Cosmo*s and *Good Housekeeping* had been known to take a detour to the ladies' room. The glossy postcards that came from all over the world weren't wrapped, though, and even the most conscientious employee, which Sheryl considered herself, couldn't resist a peek.

"Well, I may have glanced at one or two. Like the one that arrived this morning, for instance. It—"

The marshal started. "One came in this morning?"

"Yes. From Rio."

"Damn! Wait here. I'm going to get my partner." He spun on one booted heel. His long legs ate up the distance to the hallway. "Ev! Bring the woman down!"

Sheryl heard a terse reply, followed by a series of shrill yaps. A few moments later, she recognized Mrs. Gunderson's distinctive Scandinavian accent above the dog's clamor. When she made out the specific words, Sheryl's jaw sagged. She wouldn't have imagined that her smiling, white-haired patron could know such obscenities, much less spew them out like that!

She watched, wide-eyed, as a short, stocky man hauled a handcuffed Inga Gunderson into the living room.

"Get your hands off me, you fat little turd!"

The elderly lady accompanied her strident demand with a swing of her foot. A sturdy black oxford connected with her escort's left shin. Button connected with his right.

Luckily, the newcomer was wearing slacks. As MacMillan had earlier, he took several dancing hops, shaking his leg furiously to dislodge the little dog. Button hung on like a snarling, bug-eyed demon.

The law enforcement officer sent MacMillan a look of profound disgust. "Shoot the damned thing, will you?"

"No!"

Both women uttered the protest simultaneously. As much as Sheryl disliked the spoiled, noisy shih tzu, she didn't want to see it hurt.

"Button!" she commanded. "Down, boy!"

The dog ignored Sheryl's order, but its black eyes rolled to one side at the sound of its mistress's frantic pleas.

"Let go, precious. Let go, and come to Mommy."

The warbly, pleading voice was so different from the one that had been spitting vile oaths just moments ago that both men blinked. Sheryl, who'd heard Inga Gunderson carry on lengthy, cooing conversations with her pet many times before, wasn't as surprised by the abrupt transition from vitriol to syrupy sweetness.

"Let go, sweetie-kins. Come to Mommy."

The shih tzu released its death grip on the agent's pants.

"There's a pretty Butty-boo."

With his black eyes still hostile under the lopsided rhinestone hair clip, the little dog settled on its haunches beside its mistress. In another disconcerting shift in both tone and temperament, Inga Gunderson directed her attention to Sheryl.

"What are you doing here? Don't tell me you're working with these pigs, too?"

"No. That is, I just stopped by to make sure you were all right and I—"

"She's been telling us about some postcards," MacMillan interrupted ruthlessly.

Inga's seamed face contorted. Fury blazed in her black eyes. "You just waltzed in here and started spilling your guts to these jerks? Is that the thanks I get for baking all those damn cookies for you and the other idiots at the post office, so you wouldn't lose my mail like you do everyone else's?"

Shocked, Sheryl had no reply. Even Button seemed taken aback by his mistress's venom. He gave an uncertain whine, as if unsure whom he should attack this time. Before he could decide, MacMillan reached down and once again scooped the dog into the tight, restraining pocket of his arm.

"Get her out of here," he ordered his partner curtly. "Call for backup and wait in the car until it arrives. I'll meet you at the detention facility when I finish with Miss Hancock."

The older woman spit out another oath as she was tugged toward the front door. "Hancock can't tell you anything. She doesn't know a thing. *I* don't know a thing! If you think you can pin a smuggling rap on me, you're pumping some of that coke you feds like to snitch whenever you seize a load."

Yipping furiously, Button tried to squirm free of the marshal's hold and go after his mistress. Mac-Millan waited until the slam of the front door cut off most of Mrs. Gunderson's angry protests before releasing the dog. Nails clicking on the wood floor, the animal dashed for the hallway. His grating, high-pitched barks rose to a crescendo as his claws scratched frantically at the door.

Sheryl shut out the dog's desperate cries and focused, instead, on the man who faced her, his eyes watchful behind their screen of gold-tipped lashes.

"She's right. I don't know anything. Nothing that pertains to uranium smuggling, anyway."

"Why don't you let me decide what is and isn't pertinent? Tell me again about these postcards."

"There's nothing to tell, really. They come in spurts, every few weeks, from different places around the world. The messages are brief—from the little I've noticed of them," Sheryl tacked on hastily.

"Can you remember dates to go with the locations?"

"Maybe. If I think about it."

"Good! I want to take a look at the card that arrived this morning. If you don't mind, we can take your car back to the branch office."

"Now?"

"Now."

"But I have an appointment."

"Cancel it."

"You don't understand. I'm supposed to meet my fiancé."

The marshal's keen gaze took in her ringless left hand, then lifted to her face.

"We're, uh, unofficially engaged," Sheryl explained for the second time that day.

"This shouldn't take long," MacMillan assured her, taking her elbow to guide her toward the door. "You can use my cell phone to call your friend."

His touch felt warm on her skin and decidedly firm. They made it to the hall before a half whine, half growl stopped them both in their tracks. The shih tzu blocked the front door, his black eyes uncertain under his silky black-and-white fur.

"We can't just leave Button," Sheryl protested.

"I'll have someone contact the animal shelter. They can pick him up."

"The shelter?" Her brows drew together. "They only keep animals for a week or so. What happens if Mrs. Gunderson isn't free to claim him within the allotted time?"

"We'll make sure they keep the mutt as long as necessary."

A touch of impatience colored MacMillan's deep voice. He reached for the door, and the dog gave another uncertain whine. Sheryl dragged her feet, worrying her lower lip with her teeth.

"He doesn't understand what's happening."

"Yeah, well, he'll figure things out soon enough if

he tries to take a chunk out of the animal control people.''

"I take it you're not a dog lover, Mr....Sheriff... Marshal MacMillan.''

"Call me 'Harry.' And, yes, I like dogs. Real dogs. Not hairy little rats wearing rhinestones. Now, if you don't mind, Miss Hancock, I'd like to get to the post office and take a look at that postcard.''

"We can't just let him be carted off to the pound.''

The marshal's jaw squared. "I don't think you understand the seriousness of this investigation. A law enforcement officer died, possibly because of Inga Gunderson's complicity in illegal activity.''

"I'm sorry," she said quietly. "But that's not Button's fault.''

"I didn't say it was.''

"We can't just leave him.''

"Yes, we can.''

With her sunny disposition and easygoing nature, Sheryl didn't find it necessary to dig in her heels very often. But when she did, they stayed dug.

"I won't leave him.''

Some moments later, Sheryl stepped out of the adobe house into the suffocating heat. A disgruntled deputy U.S. marshal trailed behind her, carrying an equally disgruntled shih tzu under his arm.

She slid into her car and winced as the oven-hot vinyl seat covers singed the backs of her thighs. Trying to keep the smallest possible portion of her anatomy in direct contact with the seat, she keyed the ignition and shoved the air-conditioning to max.

With the two males eyeing each other warily in the passenger seat, Sheryl retraced the route to the Monzano station. She was pulling into the parking lot behind the building when she realized that she'd forgotten all about Brian. She started to ask Harry MacMillan if she could use his phone, but he had already climbed out.

He came around the car in a few man-sized strides. Opening her door, he reached down a hand to help Sheryl out. The courteous gesture from the sharp-edged marshal surprised her. Tentatively, her fingers folded around MacMillan's hand. It was harder than Brian's, she thought with a little tingle of awareness that took her by surprise. Rougher. Like the man himself.

Swinging out of the car, she tugged her hand free with a small smile of thanks. "We can go in the back door. I have the combination."

Button went with them, of course. They couldn't leave him in the car. Even this late in the afternoon, heat shimmered like clear, wavery smoke above the asphalt. Stuffed once more under MacMillan's arm and distinctly unhappy about it, the little dog snuffled indignantly through his pug nose.

Sweat trickled down between Sheryl's breasts by the time she punched the combination into the cipher lock and led the way into the dim, cavernous interior. Familiar gray walls and a huge expanse of black tile outlined with bright-yellow tape to mark the work areas welcomed her. As anxious now as MacMillan to retrieve the postcard from Mrs. Gunderson's box, she wove her way among hampers stacked high with outgoing mail toward her supervisor's desk, situated strategically in the center of the work area.

"You do have a search warrant, don't you?" she asked Harry over one shoulder.

He nodded confidently. "We have authority to screen all mail sent to the address of Inga Gunderson, alias Betty Hoffman, alias Eva Jorgens."

"Her home address or her post office box?"

"Does it make a difference?"

At MacMillan's frown, Sheryl stopped. "You need specific authority to search a post office box."

"I'm sure the warrant includes that authority."

"We'll have to verify that fact."

Impatience flickered in his eyes. "Let's talk to your supervisor about it."

"We will. I'd have to get her approval before I could allow you into the box in any case."

Sheryl introduced Harry to Pat Martinez, a tall, willowy Albuquerque native with jet-black hair dramatically winged in silver. The customer service supervisor obligingly called the main post office and requested a copy of the warrant. It whirred up on the fax a few moments later.

After ripping it off the machine, Pat skimmed through it. "I'm sorry, this isn't specific enough. It only grants you authority to search mail addressed to Mrs. Gunderson's home address. It'll have to be amended to allow access to a postal box."

Sheryl politely kept any trace of "I told you so" off her face. Harry wasn't as restrained. He scowled at her boss with distinct displeasure.

"Are you sure?"

"Yes, Marshal, I'm sure," Pat drawled. With twenty-two years of service under her belt, she would be. "But you're welcome to call the postal inspector at the central office for confirmation."

He conceded defeat with a distinct lack of graciousness. "I'll take your word for it." Still scowling, he shoved Button at Sheryl. "Here, hold your friend."

He pulled a small black address book out of his pocket, then punched a number into the phone. His face tight, he asked the person who answered at the other end about the availability of a federal judge named, appropriately, Warren. He listened intently for a moment, then requested that the speaker dispatch a car and driver to the Monzano Street post office immediately.

Sheryl watched him hang up with a mixture of relief and regret. Her part in the unfolding Mrs. Gunderson drama was over. She certainly didn't want to get any more involved with smugglers and kindly old ladies who spewed obscenities, but the trip to Inga's house had certainly livened up her day. So had the broad-shouldered law enforcement officer. Sheryl couldn't wait to tell Brian and Elise about her brush with the U.S. Marshals Service.

MacMillan soon disabused her of the notion that her role in what she privately termed the post office caper had ended, however.

"I'll be back in forty-five minutes," he told her curtly. "An hour at most. I'm sorry, but I'll have to ask you to wait for me here."

"Me? Why?"

"I want you to take a look at the message on this postcard and tell me how it compares with the others."

"But I'm already late for my appointment."

He cocked his head, studying her with a glint in his eyes that Sheryl couldn't quite interpret.

"Just out of curiosity, do you always make appointments, not dates, with this guy you're sort of engaged to?"

Since the question was entirely too personal and none of his business, she ignored it. "I'm late," she repeated firmly. "I have to go."

"You're a material witness in a federal investigation, Miss Hancock. If I have to, I'll get a subpoena from Judge Warren while I'm downtown and bring you in for questioning."

She hitched Button up on her hip, eyeing MacMillan with a good deal less than friendliness.

"You know, Marshal, your bedside manner could use a little work."

"I'm a law enforcement officer, not a doctor," he reminded her. Unnecessarily, she thought. Then, to her astonishment, his mustache lifted in a quick, slashing grin.

"But this is the first time I've had any complaints about my bedside manner. Just wait for me here, okay? And don't talk about the case to anyone else until I get back.''

Sheryl was still feeling the impact of that toe-curling grin when Harry MacMillan strode out of the post office a few moments later.

Chapter 3

With only a little encouragement, the Albuquerque police officer detailed to Harry's special fugitive task force got him to the Dennis Chavez Federal Building in seventeen minutes flat. Luckily, they pushed against the rush-hour traffic streaming out of downtown Albuquerque and the huge air force base just south of I-40. The car had barely rolled to a stop at the rear entrance to the federal building before Harry had the door open.

"Thanks."

"Any time, Marshal. Always happy to help out a Wyatt Earp who's lost his horse."

Grinning at the reference to the most legendary figure of the U.S. Marshals Service, Harry tipped him a two-fingered salute. A moment later, he flashed his credentials at the courthouse security checkpoint. The guard obligingly turned off the sensors of the metal detector to accommodate his weapon and waved him through.

Harry took the stairs to the judge's private chambers two at a time. Despite his impatience over this detour downtown for another warrant, excitement whipped through him. He was close. So damned close. With a sixth sense honed by his fifteen years as a U.S. marshal, Harry could almost see the fugitive he'd been tracking for the past eleven months. Hear him panting in fear. Smell his stink.

Paul Gunderson. Aka Harvey Millard and Jacques Garone and Rafael Pasquale and a half-dozen other aliases. Harry knew him in every one of his assumed personas. The bastard had started life as Richard Johnson. Had gone all through high school and college and a good part of a government career with that identity. His performance record as an auditor for the Defense Department described him as well above average in intelligence but occasionally stubborn and difficult to supervise. So difficult, apparently, that a long string of bosses had failed to question the necessity for his frequent trips abroad.

While conducting often unnecessary audits of overseas units, Johnson had also used his string of aliases to establish a very lucrative side business as a broker for the sale and shipment of depleted uranium, a byproduct of the nuclear process. As Harry had discovered, most of the uranium Johnson illegally diverted went to arms manufacturers who used it to produce armor-piercing artillery and mortar shells for sale to third-world countries. But recently a new type of handgun ammunition had made an appearance on the black market, and the U.S. government had mounted a special task force to find its source.

When he was arrested a little over two years ago, Johnson had claimed that he didn't know the product he brokered was being used to manufacture bullets that shredded police officers' protective armor like confetti. The man who gunned down the marshals escorting Johnson to trial certainly knew, though. He left one officer writhing in agony. In the ensuing melee, Johnson finished off the other.

Harry had lost a friend that day. His best friend.

He'd been tracking Johnson ever since. After months of frustrating dead ends, chance information from a snitch had established a tenuous link between Johnson and the Gunderson woman. She'd slipped through their fingers several times before Harry finally traced her to Albuquerque. Through the damned dog yet! Harry didn't even want to think about all the calls they'd made to veterinarians and grooming parlors before they got a lead on an elderly woman with a Scandinavian accent and a black-and-white shih tzu!

They'd no sooner found her than she'd almost slipped away again. Harry had barely set up electronic surveillance of her home when the same dog groomer who IDed her alerted him that Inga Gunderson had canceled her pet's regularly scheduled appointment. She was, according to the groomer, going out of town. Harry had been forced to move in…and had gotten nothing out of the woman.

Then Sheryl Hancock had stumbled on the scene.

With her tumble of blond hair and sunshine-filled green eyes, she would have made Harry's pulse jump in the most ordinary of circumstances. The fact that she provided a definitive link to Paul Gunderson sent it shooting right off the Richter scale. He shook his head, still not quite believing that the Gundersons had been using the U.S. mail to coordinate their activities all this time.

The mail, for God's sake!

In retrospect, he supposed it made sense. Phones were too easily tapped these days. Radio and satellite communications too frequently intercepted by scanners set to random searches of the airwaves. For all the heat the postal system sometimes took, it usually delivered…which was more than could be said for a good many other institutions, private or public. The card sitting in Inga Gunderson's box right now could very well hold vital information. Every nerve in Harry's body tightened at the thought of studying its message.

He cornered the judge and did some fast talking to obtain an amended warrant. A quick call to his partner to check on Inga Gunderson's status confirmed what Harry already suspected. The woman refused to talk until her lawyer arrived. Since the man was currently cruising the interstate somewhere on the other side of Amarillo, it would be some hours yet before he arrived and they could confront the suspect.

"Everything we've got on her is circumstantial," Ev warned. "I don't know if it's enough to hold her unless we establish a hard connection between her and Richard Johnson or Paul Gunderson or whatever he's calling himself now."

"I'm working on it. Just sit on the woman as hard

as you can. Maybe she'll crack. And give me a call when her lawyer shows."

"Will do."

Harry hung up, more determined than ever to get his hands on that postcard.

"Box 89212?"

Buck Aguilar glanced from Sheryl and Pat Martinez to the man facing him across a sorting rack. Oblivious to the tension radiating from the marshal, the postal worker handed Pat back the amended warrant.

"Closed that box this afternoon."

He picked up the stack of mail he'd been working before the interruption. Letters flew in a white blur into the sorting bins.

His face a study in disbelief, Harry leaned forward. "What do you mean, you closed it?"

At the fierce demand, Buck lifted his head once again. Slowly, his gaze drifted from the marshal's face to his boots and back up again. From the expression on the mail carrier's broad, sculpted face, Sheryl could tell that he didn't take kindly to being grilled.

"Got a notice terminating the box," Buck replied in his taciturn way. "Closed it."

The clatter of wheels on concrete as another employee pushed a cart across the room drowned Harry's short, explicit reply. Sheryl caught the gist of it, though. The marshal was *not* happy. She waited for the fireworks. They weren't long in coming.

"What did you do with the contents of the box?

Or more specifically—'' Harry sent a dagger glance
at Sheryl and her supervisor ''—what did you do with
the postcard that was in there?''

"Returned to sender. Had to. BCNO."

"What the hell does that mean?"

Buck glanced at the marshal again, his eyes flat.
Spots of red rose in his cheeks, darkening the skin
he'd inherited from his Jacarillo Apache ancestors.
Sheryl and the other employees at the Monzano
branch office knew that look. Too well. It settled on
her co-worker's face whenever he was about to butt
heads with another employee or an obnoxious customer. Since Buck stood six-four and carried close to
250 pounds on his muscled frame, that didn't occur
often. But when it did, the results weren't pretty.

Pat Martinez replied for him. "*BCNO* means 'Box
closed, no order.' Without a forwarding order, we
have no choice but to return the mail to sender."

"Dammit!"

"You got a problem with that, Sheriff?"

Buck's soft query lifted the hairs on Sheryl's neck.

"Yeah, I've got a problem with that. And it's 'Marshal.'"

The two men faced each other across the bin like
characters in some B-grade Western movie. *The Law-
man and the Apache*. At any minute, Sheryl expected
them to whip out their guns and knives. Even Button
sensed the sudden tension. Poking his nose through
the straps of Sheryl's purse, he issued a low, throaty
growl.

Hastily, she stepped into the breech. "Maybe it's

not too late to retrieve the card. What time did you close the box, Buck?''

His gaze shifted once again. Infinitesimally, his expression softened. '''Bout three-thirty, Sher.''

"Oh, dear.''

Although it seemed impossible, the marshal bristled even more. "What does 'oh, dear' mean?''

She turned to him, apology spilling from her green eyes. "I'm afraid it means that the contents of Mrs. Gunderson's box went back to the Processing and Distribution Center on the four o'clock run.''

"You mean that postcard left here even before I went chasing downtown after the blasted amended warrant?''

"Well...yes.''

Harry stared at her, aggravation apparent in every line of his body. For a moment, she wasn't quite sure how he'd handle this new setback. Finally, he blew out a long, ragged breath.

"So where is this distribution center?''

"The P&DC is on Broadway, but...''

"But what?''

Sheryl shared a look with her supervisor and co-worker. They were more than willing to let her handle the thoroughly disgruntled marshal. Bracing herself, she gave him the bad news.

"But the center uses state-of-the-art, high-speed sorters. It also makes runs to the airport every half hour. Since we rent cargo space on all the commercial carriers, your postcard would have gone out—'' she glanced at the clock on the wall ''—an hour ago, at

least. Depending on how it was routed, it's halfway
to Dallas or Atlanta or New York right now.''

A muscle twitched on the side of MacMillan's jaw.
"I suppose there's no way to trace the routing?"

"Not unless it was certified, registered or sent via
Global Express, which it wasn't.''

"Great!"

A heavy silence descended, broken when Pat Martinez handed Harry his useless warrant.

"I'm sorry about sending you downtown on a wild-
goose chase, Marshal, but I won't apologize for the
fact that my employees followed regulations. If you
don't need me for anything else, I'll get back to
work.''

"No. Thanks.''

Buck moved off, too, rolling his empty hamper
away to collect a full one from the row at the back
of the box area. Sheryl and Button waited while Harry
rubbed a hand across the back of his neck, flattening
his cotton shirt against his stomach and ribs.

At the sight of those lean hollows and broad surfaces, a sudden and completely unexpected tingle of
awareness darted through Sheryl. Content with Brian,
she hadn't looked at other men in the year or so
they'd been dating. She'd certainly never let her gaze
linger on a set of washboard ribs or a flat, trim belly.
Or noticed the tight fit of a pair of jeans across muscled thighs and...

"Are you hungry?"

Sheryl jerked her gaze upward. "Excuse me?"

"Are you hungry? I skipped breakfast, and Ev and
I were too busy taking physical and verbal abuse from

the Gunderson woman to grab lunch. Why don't we have dinner while we talk about these postcards?''

"Tonight?"

The tightness left his face. A corner of his thick, luxuriant mustache tipped up in a reluctant smile. "That was the general idea. I know I made you miss your... appointment...with this guy you're sort of engaged to. Let me make it up to you by feeding you while I squeeze your brain.''

"Squeeze my brain, huh? Interesting approach. Does it get you a lot of dinner dates?''

"It never fails.'' His smile feathered closer to a grin. "Another example of my charming bedside manner, Miss Hancock. So, are you hungry?''

She was starved, Sheryl realized. She was also obligated to provide what information she could to the authorities, represented in this instance by Deputy U.S. Marshal Harry MacMillan.

Still, she hesitated. When she'd called Brian a while ago to apologize for standing him up, he'd sounded more than a little piqued. Sheryl couldn't blame him. In an attempt to soothe his ruffled feathers, she'd promised to cook his favorite chicken dish tonight. They'd fallen into the routine of eating at her apartment on Tuesdays and his on Fridays. This was supposed to have been her night. Oh, well, she'd just have to make it up to him next week.

"I need to make a phone call,'' she said, hitching her purse and its furry passenger up on her shoulder.

Graciously, MacMillan handed her his mobile phone. With both dog and man listening in, Sheryl conducted a short, uncomfortable conversation with Brian.

"I'm sorry I've kept you waiting all this time, but something's come up. I'm going to be tied up awhile longer. Yes, I know it's Tuesday night. No, I can't put this off until tomorrow."

She caught MacMillan's speculative gaze, and turned a shoulder. "Yes. Maybe. I'll phone you when I get home."

Sheryl ended the call on a small sigh. Brian's structured approach to life usually gave her such a comfortable feeling. Sometimes, though, it made things just a bit difficult.

"Trouble in almost-paradise?" Harry inquired politely, slipping his phone back into his pocket.

"Not really. Where would you like to eat?"

"You pick it. I don't know Albuquerque all that well."

She thought for a minute. "How about El Pinto? They have the best Mexican food in the city and we can get a table outside, where we can talk privately."

"Sounds good to me."

Sheryl led the way to the rear exit, absorbing the fact that he was apparently a stranger to the city.

"Where's home? Or can you say?"

As soon as she articulated the casual question, she wondered if he would...or should...answer. She had no idea what kind of security U.S. marshals operated under. He'd told her not to talk about the case. Maybe he wasn't supposed to talk about himself, either.

Evidently, that wasn't a problem.

"I'm assigned to the fugitive apprehension unit of

the Oklahoma City district office," he replied, "but I don't spend a whole lot of time there. My job keeps me on the road most of the time."

Another wanderer! They seemed to constitute half the world's population. Sheryl's minor annoyance with Brian's inflexibility vanished instantly. He, at least, wouldn't take off without warning for parts unknown. She led the way outside, blinking at the abrupt transition from dim interior to dazzling sunlight.

"I'd better meet you at the restaurant. I'll have to go by my apartment first to drop off Button. Unless you want to take him back to your place?" she finished hopefully.

"I can't," he replied without the slightest hint of regret. "I'm staying in a motel."

She sighed, resigning herself to an unplanned houseguest. "Do you know how to get to El Pinto?"

"Haven't got a clue. Just give me the address. I'll find it."

She chewed her lip, thinking perhaps she should suggest a more accessible place. "It's kind of hard to locate if you're not familiar with Albuquerque."

He sent her a look of patented amusement. "U.S. marshals have been tracking down bad guys since George Washington pinned gold stars on the original thirteen deputies. I'm pretty sure I can find this restaurant."

"I stand corrected," Sheryl said gravely.

She drove out of the parking lot a few moments later, with Button occupying the seat beside her. Harry trailed in a tan government sedan. Following her directions, he turned south at the corner of Haines and Juan Tabo, and she headed north.

By this late hour, Albuquerque's rush-hour traffic had thinned to a steady but fast-moving stream. The trip to her apartment complex took less than fifteen minutes. As always, the cream-colored adobe architecture and profusion of flowers decorating the fountain in the center of the tree-shaded complex gave her a quiet joy. Sheryl had moved into her one-bedroom apartment soon after her last promotion and loved its cool Southwestern colors and high-ceilinged rooms. It was perfect for her, but the pale-mauve carpet hadn't been pet-proofed. After unlocking the front door, she set the shih tzu down in the tiled foyer.

"We have to establish a few ground rules, fella. No yapping, or you'll get me thrown out of here. No taking bites out of me or my furniture. No accidents on the rug."

Busy sniffing out the place, Button ignored her.

"I'm serious," she warned.

Once she'd plopped her purse down on the counter separating the kitchen from the small dining area, she pulled a plastic bowl from the cupboard and filled it with water.

"It's either me or the pound, so you'd better... Hey!"

With regal indifference to her startled protest, the shih tzu lifted his raised leg another inch and sprayed the dining table.

Obviously, Button didn't believe in rules!

Sheryl went to work with paper towels, then scooped up the unrepentant dog. A moment later, she set him and the water dish down on the other side of the sliding-glass patio doors. Hands on hips, she surveyed the small, closed-in area. The leafy Chinese elm growing on the other side of the adobe wall provided plenty of shade. The few square yards of grass edging the patio tiles provided Button's other necessary commodity.

"This is your temporary residence, dog. Make yourself comfortable."

After sliding the patio door closed behind her, she heeled off her sneakers and padded into the bathroom to splash cold water on her face. Then she shucked her shorts and tank top and pulled on a gauzy sundress in a cool mint green. She had her hair unbraided and was pulling a brush through its stubborn curls when a series of high-pitched yips told her Button wanted in.

Too bad. He'd better get used to outdoor living.

She soon learned that what Button wanted, Button had his own way of getting. Within moments, the yips rose to a grating, insistent crescendo.

The brush hit the counter with a thud. Muttering, Sheryl retraced her steps and cut the dog's protests off with a stern admonition.

"I guess I didn't make myself clear. You've lost your house privileges. You're going to camp out here on the patio, Buttsy-boo, or take a trip to the pound."

Ten minutes later, Sheryl slammed the front door behind her and left a smug Button in undisputed possession of her air-conditioned apartment. It was either cave in to his hair-raising howls or risk eviction. In desperation, she'd spread a layer of newspapers over the bathroom floor. She could only hope that the dog would condescend to use them. The next few days, she thought grimly, could prove a severe strain on her benevolence toward animals in general and squish-faced lapdogs in particular.

As she shoved the car key into the ignition, a sudden thought struck her. If even half of what Harry had told her about Mrs. Gunderson's activities was true, Sheryl could be stuck with her unwanted house-guest for a lot longer than a few days.

Groaning, she backed out of the carport. No way was she keeping that mutt for more than a day or two. Harry had to have stumbled across some relative or acquaintance of Mrs. Gunderson during his investigation, someone who could take over custody of her pet. She put the issue on the table as soon as they were seated in El Pinto's shaded, colorful outdoor dining area. Harry stretched his long legs out under the tiled table and graciously refrained from pointing out that it was her insistence on taking the dog with them that had caused her dilemma in the first place.

"There's nothing I'd like better than to identify a few of Inga Gunderson's friends and acquaintances."

Sheryl had to scoot her chair closer to catch his reply over the noise of the busy restaurant. A fountain bubbled and splashed just behind them, providing a cheerful accompaniment to the mariachi trio strumming and thumping their guitars as they strolled through the patio area. Harry had chosen the table deliberately so they could talk without raising the interest of other diners. Even so, Sheryl hadn't counted on practically sitting in his lap to carry on a conversation.

"As far as we know," he continued, "Inga doesn't have any acquaintances here. She made a few calls to local businesses, but no one's phoned her or visited her." His gold-flecked eyes settled on his dinner partner. "Except you, Miss Hancock."

"'Sheryl,'" she amended absently. "So what will happen to her?"

"We have sufficient circumstantial evidence to book her on suspicion of smuggling. The charge might or might not stick, but she's not the one I really want. It's her supposed nephew I'm after."

Despite Harry's relaxed pose, Sheryl couldn't miss the utter implacability in his face. He slipped a pen and small black-leather notebook out of his jacket pocket, all business now.

"Tell me about the postcards."

She waited to reply until the waitress had placed a brimming basket of tortilla chips on the table and taken their drink orders.

"They usually come in batches," she told Harry. "Two or three will arrive within a week of each other, then a month might go by before another set comes in."

"I figured as much," the marshal said, almost to himself. "He'd have to send backups in case the first didn't arrive. Have any others come in with this one from Rio?"

"Two. The first was from Prague. The second from Pamplona."

"Pamplona?" His brow creased. "Isn't that where

they run bulls through the streets? With the locals running right ahead of them?''

"That's what the scene on the card showed.'' Sheryl hunched forward, recalling the vivid street scene with a shake of her head. "Can you imagine racing down a narrow, cobbled street a few steps ahead of thundering, black bulls?''

"I can imagine it, but it's not real high on my list of fun things to do,'' Harry admitted dryly. He loaded a chip with salsa. "How about you?''

"Me? No way! I have enough trouble staying ahead of my bills, let alone a herd of bulls. Uh, you'd better go easy on that stuff. I heard the green chili crop came in especially hot this year.''

"Not to fear, I've got a lead-lined stom— Arrggh!''

He shot up straight in his chair, grabbed his water glass and downed the entire contents in three noisy gulps. Blinking rapidly, he stared at the little dish of salsa in disbelief.

"Good Lord! Do you New Mexicans really eat this stuff?''

"Some of us do,'' Sheryl answered, laughing. "But we work up to it over a period of years.''

The waitress arrived at that moment. Harry shot her a look of profound gratitude and all but snatched the Don Miguel light he'd ordered out of her hand. The ice-cold beer, like the water, went down in a few long, gulping swallows.

The waitress turned an amused smile on Sheryl. "Didn't you warn him?''

"I tried to.''

Winking, she picked up her tray. "Another gringo bites the dust."

Sheryl eyed the marshal, not quite sure she'd agree with the waitress's assessment. His golden brown eyes watered, to be sure. A pepper-induced flush darkened his cheeks above the line of his mustache. He drained his mug with the desperation of a man who'd just crawled across a hundred miles of burning desert.

She would categorize him as down, but certainly not out. He showed too much strength in those broad shoulders. Carried himself with too much authority. Even in his boots and jeans and casual open-necked shirt, he gave the impression of a man who knew what he wanted and went after it.

For an unguarded moment, Sheryl wondered if he would pursue a woman he desired with the same single-minded determination he pursued the fugitives he hunted. He would, she decided. He'd pursue her, and when he caught her, he'd somehow manage to convince her she'd been the hunter all along. The thought sent a ripple of excitement singing through her veins. She shook her head at her own foolishness.

Still, the tingle stayed with her while Harry dragged the heel of his hand across his eyes.

"Remind me to listen to your warnings next time."

The offhand remark made Sheryl smile, until she realized that there probably wouldn't be a next time. As soon as she filled Marshal MacMillan in on the details from the postcards, he'd ride off into the sunset in pursuit of his quarry.

How stupid of her to romanticize his profession.

She'd better remember that he lived the same life-style her father had. Here today, gone tomorrow, with never a backward glance for those he left behind.

Recovering from his bout with the green chilies, Harry got back to business.

"Prague, Pamplona and Rio," he recited with just a hint of hoarseness. "We've suspected all along that our man is triangulating his shipments."

"Triangulating them?"

"Sending them through second and third countries, where they're rebundled with other products like coffee or bat guano, then smuggled into the States."

"Why in the world would someone bundle uranium with bat guano and...? Oh! To disguise the scent of the metal containers and get them past the Customs dogs, right?"

"You got it in one." He leaned forward, all business now. "Can you remember any of the words on the cards?"

"On two of them. I didn't see the one from Prague. My friend Elise described it to me, though."

"Okay, start with Rio. Give me what you can remember."

"I can give it to you exactly." She wrinkled her brow. "'Hi to my favorite aunt. I've been dancing in the streets for the past four days. Wish you were here.'"

Harry stared at her in blank astonishment. "You can recall it word for word?"

"Sure."

"How?" he shot back. "With the thousands of

pieces of mail you handle every day, how in the hell can you remember one postcard?''

"Because I handle thousands of pieces of mail every day,'' she explained patiently. "The white envelopes and brown flats—the paper-wrapped magazines and manila envelopes—all blur together. Not that many postcards come through, though, and when they do, they catch our attention immediately."

She decided not to add that the really interesting postcards got passed from employee to employee. The male workers particularly enjoyed the topless beach scenes that American tourists loved to send back to their relatives. Some cards went well beyond topless and tipped into outright obscenity. Those they were required to turn into the postal inspectors. Sheryl had long ago ceased being surprised at what people stuck stamps on and dropped in a mailbox.

Harry had her repeat the message. He copied the few sentences in his pad, then studied their content.

"I don't think this is Carnival season. I'm sure that happens right before Lent in Rio, just as it does in New Orleans."

He made another note to himself to check the dates of Rio's famous festival. Sheryl was sitting so close she could make out every stroke. His handwriting mirrored his personality, she decided. Bold. Aggressive. Impatient.

"Maybe the four days has some significance," she suggested.

"It probably does." He frowned down at his notes. "I don't know what yet, though."

"Do you want to know about the picture on the front side?" she asked after a moment.

"Later. Let's finish the back first. What else do you remember about it?"

"What do you want to start with? The handwriting? The color of ink? The stamp? The cancellation mark?"

He sat back, his eyes gleaming. He looked like a man who'd just hit a superjackpot.

"Start wherever you want."

They worked their way right through sour cream enchiladas, smoked charro beans, rice and sopapillas dripping with honey. The mariachi band came to their table and left again, richer by the generous tip Harry passed them. The tables around them emptied, refilled. They were still working the Rio postcard when Harry's phone beeped.

"MacMillan." He listened for a moment, his brow creasing. "Right. I'm on my way."

Snapping the phone shut, he rose to pull out Sheryl's chair. "I'm sorry. Inga Gunderson's lawyer just showed up and wants to see his client. We'll have to go over the rest of the cards tomorrow. I'll call you to set up a time."

A small, unexpected dart of pleasure rippled through Sheryl at the thought of continuing this discussion with Marshal MacMillan. Shrugging, she chalked it up to the fact that she still had something worthwhile to contribute to his investigation.

She drove out of the parking lot a few moments later, thinking that she'd better reschedule the last-minute layette shopping spree she and Elise had planned for tomorrow night. As determined as Harry was to extract every last bit of information from her, they might have to work late.

She couldn't know that he would walk into the post office just after nine the next morning and reschedule her entire life.

Chapter 4

"I'm sorry, sir," Sheryl repeated for the third time. "I can't hand out a DHS check over the counter. Even if I could, I wouldn't give you a check addressed to someone else."

The runny-eyed scarecrow on the other side of the counter lifted an arm and swiped it across his nose. His hand shook so badly that the tattoos decorating the inside of his wrist were a blur of red and blue.

"That's my old lady's welfare check," he whined. "I gotta have it. I want it."

Yeah, right, Sheryl thought. What he wanted was another fix, courtesy of the Department of Human Services. She wondered how many other women this creep had bullied or beaten out of their food and rent money over the years to feed his drug habit.

"I can't give it to you," she repeated.

"My old lady's moved, I'm tellin' ya, and she

didn't get her check this month. She sent me in to pick it up.''

"I'm sure someone explained to her that the post office can't forward a DHS check. We're required by regulations to deliver it to the address where she physically resides or send it back."

"Send it back? Why, dammit?"

The angry explosion turned the heads of the other customers who'd come in with the first rush of the morning. In the booth next to Sheryl's, Elise glanced up sharply from the stamps she was dealing out.

Holding on to her patience with both hands, Sheryl tried again. "We have to send the checks back to DHS because a few people abused the system by moving constantly and collecting checks from several different counties at once. Now everyone has to pay the price for their fraud."

The lank-haired junkie fixed her with a malevolent glare. "Yeah, well, I don't give a rat's ass about them other people. I just want my old lady's money. You'd better give it to me, bitch, or I'm gonna—"

"You're going to what?"

At the dangerous drawl, both Sheryl and her unpleasant customer jerked around.

The sight of Harry MacMillan's broad-shouldered form sent relief pinging through her. Relief and something else, something far too close to excitement for Sheryl's peace of mind. Swallowing, she ascribed the sudden flutter in her stomach to the fact that the marshal looked particularly intimidating this morning.

As he had yesterday, he wore jeans and a welltailored sport coat, this one a soft, lightweight, blue broadcloth. As it had yesterday, his jacket strained at the seams of his wide shoulders. Adding to his overall physical presence, his jaw had a hard edge that sent off its own silent warning. The gold in his eyes glinted hard and cold.

Sheryl could handle nasty characters like the one standing in front of her at this moment. She'd done it many times. But that didn't stop her from enjoying the pasty look that came over the druggie's face when he took in Harry's size and stance.

"Nah, no problem," he replied to Harry, but his mouth pinched when he turned back to Sheryl. "Me 'n' my old lady need that money."

"Tell her to contact DHS," She instructed once again. "They'll issue an emergency payment if necessary."

His thin, ravaged face contorted with fury and a need she could only begin to guess at. "I wouldn't be here if it wasn't necessary, you stupid—"

He broke off, slinging a sideways look at Harry.

The marshal jerked his head toward the lobby doors. "You'd better leave, pal. Now."

The watery eyes flared with reckless bravado. "You gonna make me, *pal?*"

"If I have to."

Like waves eddying around a rock, the other customers in the post office backed away from the two men. A tight, taut silence gripped the area. Sheryl's knee inched toward the silent alarm button just under her counter.

The thin, pinch-faced junkie broke the shimmering tension just before she exerted enough pressure to set off the alarm. With another spiteful glance at Sheryl, he pushed past Harry and shouldered open the glass door. A collective murmur of relief rose from the other customers as the door thumped shut behind him.

Harry didn't relax his vigilance until the departing figure had stalked to a battered motorcycle, threw a leg over the seat, jumped on the starter and roared out of the parking lot.

"Nice guy," one of the women in line murmured.

"Wonder what his problem was?" another groused.

"Do you get many customers like that?" Harry inquired, moving to Sheryl's station.

No one objected to the fact that he cut ahead of them in line, she noticed.

"Not many. What are you doing here? I thought you were going to call and set up a time for us to meet?"

"I decided to come in person, instead. Can you get someone to cover for you here? I need to talk to you privately."

"Yes, of course. Wait for me in the lobby and I'll let you in through that door to the back area."

With a nod to the other customers, Harry turned away. Elise demanded an explanation the moment the glass doors swung shut behind him.

"Who *is* that?"

"He's—"

Sheryl caught herself just in time. Harry had told her not to discuss the case with anyone other than her supervisor. She hadn't, although the restriction had resulted in another uncomfortable phone conversation with Brian after she'd driven home from El Pinto.

"He's an acquaintance," she finished lamely, if truthfully.

"Since when?"

"Since last night."

Elise's dark-red brows pulled together in a troubled frown. "Does Brian know about this new acquaintance of yours?"

"There's nothing to know." With an apologetic smile at the lined-up customers, Sheryl plopped a Closed sign in front of her station. "I'll send Peggy up to cover the counter with you."

She found the petite brunette on the outside loading dock, pulling in long, contented drags of cigarette smoke mixed with diesel fumes from the mail truck parked next to the ramp.

"I know you're on break, but something's come up. Can you cover for me out front for a few minutes?"

"Sure." Peggy took another pull, then stubbed out her cigarette in the tub of sand the irreverent carriers always referred to as the butt box. Carefully, she tucked the half-smoked cigarette into the pocket of her uniform shirt.

"I have to conserve every puff. I promised myself I'd only smoke a half a pack today."

"I thought you decided to quit completely."

"I did! I will! After this pack. Maybe." Smiling ruefully at Sheryl's grin, she strolled back into the station. "How long do you think you'll be? I'm supposed to help Pat with the vault inventory this morning.''

"Not long," Sheryl assured her. "I just need to set up an appointment."

Contrary to her expectations, she soon discovered that Harry hadn't driven to the Monzano station to make an appointment.

She stared at him, dumbfounded, while he calmly informed her and her supervisor that Albuquerque's postmaster had agreed to assign Miss Hancock to the special fugitive apprehension task force that Harry headed.

"Me?"

Sheryl's startled squeak echoed off the walls of the stationmaster's little-used private office.

"You," he confirmed, pulling a folded document out of his coat pocket. "This authorizes an indefinite detail, effective immediately."

"May I see that?" her supervisor asked.

"Of course."

Pat Martinez stuck her pencil into her upswept jet-black hair and skimmed the brief communiqué he handed her.

"Well, it looks like you're on temporary duty, Sheryl."

"Hey, hang on here," she protested. "I'm not sure I want to be assigned to a fugitive apprehension task force, indefinitely or otherwise. Before I agree to anything like this, I want to know what's required of me."

"Basically, I want your exclusive time and attention for as long it takes to extract every bit of information I can about those postcards.''

"Exclusive time and attention? You mean, like all day?"

"And all night, if necessary."

Sheryl gaped at him. "You're kidding, right?"

He didn't crack so much as a hint of a smile. "No, Miss Hancock, I'm not. My team's been at it pretty much around the clock since we tracked Inga Gunderson to Albuquerque. I won't ask that you put in twenty-four hours at a stretch, of course, but I will ask that you work with me as long as necessary and as hard as possible."

"Look, I don't mind working with you, but we're shorthanded here. The box clerk is on vacation and Elise could go out on maternity leave at any moment."

"So the postmaster indicated." Calmly, Harry nodded to the document held by Sheryl's supervisor. "We took that into consideration."

"The postmaster is sending a temp to cover your absence," Pat explained. "If Elise goes out, he'll cover that, too." Her eyes lifted to Harry. "You're thorough, MacMillan."

"I learned my lesson after the fiasco with the warrant," he admitted. "This time, I made sure we dotted every i and crossed every t."

Sheryl wasn't sure she liked being lumped in with the i's and t's, but she let it pass. Now that she'd recovered from her initial surprise, she didn't object to the detail. She just didn't care for Harry's high-handed way of arranging it.

As if realizing that he needed to mend some bridges with his new detailee, the marshal gave her a smile that tried for apologetic but fell a few degrees short. Sheryl suspected that MacMillan rarely apologized for anything.

"I didn't have time to coordinate this with you and Ms. Martinez beforehand. My partner and I were up most of the night running air routes that service Prague, Pamplona and Rio through the computers. We're convinced our man is bringing in a shipment soon, and we're not going to let it or him slip through our fingers. We've got to break the code that was on those postcards, and to do that we need your help, Sheryl."

Put like that, how could she refuse?

"Well, if you're sure someone's coming out here to cover for me..."

"The postmaster assured me that wasn't a problem."

Sheryl looked to Pat, who nodded. "We'll manage until the temp gets here. Go close down your station."

Still a little bemused by her sudden transition from postal clerk to task force augmentee, Sheryl headed for the front. Naturally, her curious co-workers peppered her with questions.

"What's going on, Sher?" Elise wanted to know. "Why are you closing out?"

Peggy grinned wickedly over the divider separating the stations. "And who's the long, tall stud with the mustache? Tell us all, girl."

"I can't right now. I'll tell you about it later."

When she could, Sheryl amended silently, hitting a

sequence of keystrokes to tally her counter transactions. The printer stuttered out a report for her abridged workday. Another quick sequence shut down the computer.

Her hand resting on her mounded tummy, Elise waited for the next customer. "Where are you going now?"

That much at least Sheryl could reveal. "Downtown. The postmaster has assigned me to a special detail."

"With the stud? No kidding?" Peggy waggled her brows. "How do I go about getting assigned to this detail?"

"By stopping by to check on little old ladies on your way home from work."

"Huh?"

"I'll tell you about it later," Sheryl repeated.

With swift efficiency, she ejected her disk from her terminal and removed her cash drawer. After stacking her stock of stamps on top of the drawer, she carried the lot to the vault. A quick inventory tallied her cash receipts with the money orders, stamps and supplies she'd sold so far this morning. She scribbled her name across the report, then left it for the T-6 clerk who had the unenviable task of reconciling all the counter clerks' reports with the master printout produced at the end of each day. That done, she hurried back to her counter to retrieve her purse and extract a promise from Elise.

"Brian's supposed to pick me up at eleven-thirty. He wanted to show me a house during lunch that he's going to list. He needs a woman's opinion about the renovations that might be necessary to the kitchen. Would you go with him? Please? You know how he always raves about what you did with your kitchen.''

Brian wasn't the only one who raved about the miracles Elise had performed with the small fixer-upper he'd found for her after her divorce. With two kids to house and a third about to make an appearance, she'd taken wallpapering and sheet curtains to a higher plane of art. She'd also turned a dilapidated kitchen into a marvel of bleached cabinets, hand-decorated tiles and artfully disguised pipes.

''I'll be happy to go with him, but...''

''Thanks! Tell him I'll call him tonight.''

Sheryl left Elise with a frown still creasing her forehead and hurried toward the back. Now that she'd gotten used to the idea, she had to admit the prospect of taking part in a criminal investigation sent a little thrill of excitement through her. The Wanted posters tacked to the bulletin board in the outer lobby and the occasional creeps who came into the post office, like the one this morning, were the closest she'd come to the dark, seamy side of life. Besides, she was only doing her civic duty by helping Harry piece together the puzzle of the postcards.

Which didn't explain the way her pulse seemed to stutter with that strange, inexplicable excitement when she saw the marshal. Hands shoved into his pockets, ankles crossed, he lounged against one of the carriers' sorting desks as though he had nothing else in the world more important to do than wait for her. The pose didn't fit his character, she now knew. Harry MacMillan was anything but patient. She'd just met

him yesterday—fallen into his arms, more correctly—
and now he'd pulled her off her job to work on his
team.

At the sound of her footsteps, he glanced up, and
Sheryl's excitement took on a deeper, keener edge.
His toffee-colored eyes swept her with the same intent
scrutiny that had raised goose bumps on her skin yesterday. Suddenly self-conscious, she glanced down at
her pin-striped shirt with its neat little cross tab tie
and her navy shorts.

"Should I change out of my uniform?"

His gaze skimmed from her nose to her knees and
back again. "You're fine."

She was a whole lot better than fine, Harry thought
as he followed her to the exit. He'd never paid much
attention to postal uniforms, but Sheryl Hancock filled
hers out nicely. Very nicely.

Her pin-striped shirt with its little red tab was in-
nocuous enough, but the long, curving stretch of leg
displayed by those navy shorts pushed his simple observation into swift, gut-level male appreciation. It
also put a knot in his belly that didn't belong there
right now.

Frowning, Harry gave himself a mental shake. He'd
better keep his mind focused on the information
Sheryl could supply, not on her tanned legs or the
seductive swing of her hips. And he'd darn well better
remember why he'd yanked her from her workplace
and put her on his team. She held the key to those
damned postcards. He felt it with every instinct he
possessed. He wasn't going to rest until he'd pulled
every scrap of information out of this woman.

Despite his stern reminder that his business with Sheryl was just that, business, his pulse tripped at the thought of the hours ahead. On the advice of her lawyer, Inga Gunderson flatly refused to talk to the investigators. Harry and Ev had spent several frustrating hours with the woman last night. Finally, they'd left her stewing in her own venom. The clerk of the court had assured them that she wouldn't get a bail hearing until late tomorrow, if then, given the overloaded court docket.

Earlier this morning, Ev had left to drive up to the labs at Los Alamos to talk to one of the government's foremost experts on the use and physical properties of depleted uranium. The New Mexico state trooper assigned to the task force was now out at the local FAA office, compiling a list of secondary airstrips within a hundred-mile radius. The Customs agent working with them on an as-needed basis had returned to his office to cull through foreign flight schedules. For the next few hours at least, Harry would have the task force headquarters—and Sheryl—to himself.

He intended to make good use of that time.

"Why don't I drive, since my vehicle is cleared for the secure parking at the Chavez Federal Building? We can come back for your car later."

"Okay. Just let me open my windows a bit to keep from baking the seats."

A moment later, Sheryl buckled herself into the blast furnace heat of the tan sedan. "So you're operating out of the downtown courthouse?"

"We've set up task force headquarters in the U.S. Marshals' offices."

Task force headquarters!

A vague image formed in her mind of a busy, high-tech command post, complete with wall-sized screen satellite maps displaying all kinds of vital information, humming computer terminals, beeping phones and a team of dedicated, intense professionals. The idea of becoming a part, however briefly, of the effort kindled a sense of adventure.

Reality came crashing down on her the moment she stepped inside the third-floor conference room in the multistory federal building in the heart of the city. Hand-scribbled paper charts decorated the nondescript tan walls. Foam coffee cups and cardboard boxes of records littered the long conference table. Wires from the phones clustered in the center of the table snaked around the cups and over the boxes like gray streamers. A faint, stale odor drifted from the crushed pizza cartons that had been stuffed into metal wastebaskets in a corner. Sheryl looked around, gulping.

"This is it? Your headquarters?"

"This is it." Harry shrugged off the clutter with the same ease he shrugged out of his jacket. "Make yourself comfortable."

She might have been able to do just that if her gaze hadn't snagged on the blue steel gun butt nestled against his left side. Even holstered, the weapon looked ugly and far too dangerous for her peace of mind.

Harry tossed his jacket over a chair back and

turned, catching her wary expression. "Don't worry. I know how to use it."

Somehow, that didn't reassure her.

"I don't like guns," she admitted, dropping her shoulder bag into a chair. "They make me nervous. Very nervous."

Calmly, he rolled up the cuffs of his white cotton shirt. "They make me nervous, too. Especially when they're loaded with uranium-tipped bullets. Ready to get to work?"

After that unsubtle reminder of the reason she was here, Sheryl could hardly say no. Pulling out one of the chairs, she rolled up to the table.

"I'm ready."

"We pretty well took apart the postcard from Rio last night. Let's start with the one from Pamplona today. We'll reverse the process and work the front side first. Can you describe the scene?"

She shot him an amused glance.

"Of course you can," he answered himself. "You talk, I'll listen."

Summoning up a mental image of the card, Sheryl painted a vivid word picture that included a narrow, cobbled street lined with two-story stone houses. Geranium-filled window boxes. White-shirted young men racing between the buildings, looking over their shoulders at the herd of black bulls just visible at a bend in the street.

Harry copied down every word, so intent on searching for similarities with the card from Rio that it was some time before he noticed the subtle difference in Sheryl's voice. It sounded softer, he realized in surprise, almost dreamy. He glanced up to find her staring at the wall, her mouth curving slightly. She'd gotten lost somewhere on a high, sunny plain in Spain's Basque province.

Harry got a little lost himself just looking at her. The faint trace of freckles across the bridge of her nose fascinated him, as did the mass of tawny hair tumbling down her back. She'd pulled the hair at her temples back and caught it in one of those plastic clips with long, dangerous-looking teeth. His hand itched to spring the clip free, to let those curls take on a life of their own.

"There was a cathedral in the background," she murmured, drawing his attention away from the curve of her cheek. "An old Gothic cathedral complete with flying buttresses and a huge rose-colored window in the south transept. One of man's finest monuments to God."

Sighing, she shifted in her seat and caught Harry staring at her. "I've read a little bit about medieval Gothic cathedrals," she confessed with an embarrassed shrug. "Some people consider them the architectural wonders of the modern world."

"Have you ever been inside one?"

"No. Have you?"

He nodded. "Notre Dame."

"In Paris?"

Her breathless awe made Harry bite back a grin. He'd visited the majestic structure on a wet, dreary spring day. All he could recall were impenetrable shadows, cold dampness and thousands of votive candles flickering in the darkness. Of course, he was a marine gunny sergeant on leave at the time, and far more interested in the *filles de joie* working the broad embankments along the Seine than in the gray stone cathedral

"Maybe your sort-of fiancé will spring for a trip to Paris for a honeymoon," he commented casually.

He saw at once that he'd said the wrong thing. The soft, faraway look disappeared from her green eyes. She sat up, a tiny frown creasing her brow.

"Brian isn't interested in traveling, any more than I am. We prefer to save our money for something more practical, like a house or a new car or the kids' college education."

Without warning, a thought rifled through Harry's mind. If he wanted to stake his claim to a woman like this one, he'd whisk her off to a deserted island, peel off her clothes and make love to her a dozen times a day before either of them started thinking about a house and a new car and the kids' college education.

His belly clenched at the image of Sheryl sprawled in the surf, her tanned body offered up to the sun like a pagan sacrifice. Her arms reached for him. Her eyes...

Dammit!

A quick shake of his head banished the crashing surf. He had to remember why he was here. And that Sheryl was spoken for...almost. Pushing aside her vague relationship with the jerk who made appointments instead of dates, he brought them both back to the matter at hand.

"Let's talk about the message on the back."

She blinked at his brusque instruction, but complied willingly enough.

"As best I recall, it was short and sweet. 'Hi, Auntie. I've spent two great...'" She paused, chewing on her lower lip. "No, it was three. 'I've spent three great days keeping a half step ahead of the bulls. See you soon, Paul.'"

"Run it through your mind again," Harry ordered. "Close your eyes. See the words. Picture the—"

One of the phones on the table shrilled. He grabbed the receiver, listened for a few minutes and hung up with a promise to call back later.

"Close your eyes, Sheryl."

Obediently, she blanked out the chart-strewn walls.

"Visualize the words. Follow every curl of every letter. Describe them to me."

Like a dutiful disciple of a master mesmerizer, she let Harry's deep, slow voice lull her into a state of near somnolence. Slowly, lines of dark swirls began to take shape.

She didn't even notice when morning faded into afternoon, or when the uninspiring conference room began to take on an aura of a real live operations center. She did note that the phones rang constantly, and that a seemingly steady stream of people popped in to talk to Harry or pass information.

Sometime around the middle of the afternoon, the short, stocky Everett Sloan returned from Los Alamos Laboratories. Sheryl soon discovered that, unlike Harry, he was assigned to the Albuquerque office of the U.S. Marshals and had been tapped as the local coordinator for the task force. Shedding his wrinkled suit jacket, Ev informed his temporary partner that he'd collected more information than he'd ever wanted to know about the properties and characteristics of the heavy metal known as U-235.

A short time later, a slender, striking brunette in the brown shirt, gray pants and Smoky the Bear hat of a New Mexico state trooper joined the group. After brief introductions, Fay Chandler tossed her hat on the table and unrolled a huge aerial map showing every airstrip, paved or otherwise, within a hundred-mile radius. The three-letter designation code for each strip had been highlighted in yellow. If their suspect intended to bring his contraband in someplace other than Albuquerque International, Fay would coordinate the local response team.

In the midst of all this activity, Harry somehow remained focused on Sheryl and the postcards. After hours of work, he reduced the sheets of information he'd pulled from her to a few key words and phrases. He repeated them now in an almost singsong mantra.

"Rio…Carnival…April…four."

Sheryl picked up the chorus. "Pamplona…bulls…July…three."

"Prague…Wenceslas Square…September…two."

MacMillan stared at the words, as though the sheer intensity of his scrutiny would solve the riddle they represented. "I know there's a pattern in there somewhere. A reverse order of numbers or letters or something!"

"Maybe the computers will find it." Ev Sloan slid his thumbs under his flashy red-and-yellow Bugs Bunny suspenders to hitch up his pants. "I'll go down to the data center and plug the key words in. The airstrip designation codes, too. Be back in a flash with the trash.''

Harry caught Sheryl's smile and put a more practical spin on Ev's blithe remark. ''You'll think it's trash, too, when you see the endless combinations the computers will kick out. It'll take us the rest of the evening, if not the night, to go over them.''

Sheryl's smile fizzled. Good grief! He hadn't been kidding about working day and night. She snuck a peek at the clock on the wall. It was after five. They'd worked right through lunch. The Diet Pepsis and bags of Krispy Korn Kurls Harry had procured from the vending machines down the hall had long since disappeared. Practical considerations such as real food and a cool shower and retrieving her car from the post office parking lot crept into Sheryl's mind.

As if to echo her thoughts, a loud, rolling growl issued from her tummy.

''I'm a creature of habit,'' she offered apologetically when Harry glanced her way. ''I tend to crave food...real food...a couple of times a day.''

He speared a look at the clock, then reached for the jacket he'd tossed over a chair back hours ago. ''Sorry. I didn't intend to starve you. There's a decent Italian sub shop across the street. Ev, Fay, you two up for another round of green peppers and sausage?''

Ev shook his head. ''I want to get the computers rolling. Bring me back a garlic sausage special.''

''I'll pass, too,'' Fay put in. ''My youngest has a T-ball game at six-thirty and I swore on his stack of

Goosebumps that I'd make this one. I'll come back here after the game's over, Harry.''

MacMillan shrugged into his jacket. "You've been at this hard for the past three days and nights. Relax and enjoy the game."

Laughing, Fay rerolled her aeronautical maps. "Your single status is showing, Marshal. Anyone with kids would know better than to advise a parent to relax at a T-ball game."

"I stand corrected."

So he was single. Without knowing why she did so, Sheryl tucked that bit of information away for future reference. She'd noticed that he didn't wear a wedding ring. A lot of men didn't, of course, but the confirmation that the marshal was neither married nor a parent added a new dimension to the man...and triggered a whole new set of questions in her mind. Was he divorced? Currently involved with someone? Seeing someone who didn't mind the fact that he spent almost all his time away from home, chasing fugitives?

Sheryl shook off her intense curiosity about the marshal with something of an effort. His personal life had nothing to do with her, she reminded herself, or with her part in his investigation. She shifted her attention to Fay, who winked and settled her hat on her sleek, dark hair.

"Some people think that high-speed chases in pursuit of fleeing suspects and cement-footed drunks are tough, but I'm here to tell you that keeping up with my four rug-rats takes a whole lot more stamina."

"I don't have any rug-rats at home, but I can

imag—'' Sheryl stopped abruptly, her eyes widening. "Oh, no! I do!"

"If you're referring to the obnoxious rodent you insisted on taking home with you," Harry drawled, "I can't think of a more perfect description."

She grabbed her purse, trying not to think of the damage the shih tzu might have done to her dining-room chairs and pale-mauve carpet during his long incarceration.

"I have to swing by the post office to get my car, then go home to let Button out," she said worriedly.

"Good enough. We can grab some dinner on the way."

The thought of sharing another meal with Harry sent a tingle of anticipation down Sheryl's spine... followed by an instant rush of guilt. Belatedly, she realized that she hadn't even thought of Brian since early morning. The marshal's forceful personality and fierce determination to bring Richard Johnson-Paul Gunderson to justice had swept her right into the stream of the investigation, to the exclusion of all else.

"I'd better pass on dinner, too," she said. "I'll grab a sandwich at home."

And call Brian.

The task force leader conceded the point with a small shrug. "Whatever works."

Just as well, Harry thought as he waited beside Sheryl for the elevator to the underground parking. This manhunt had consumed him for almost a year, yet today he'd had to fight to stay focused on the information his newest team member was providing.

Harry knew damn well that Sheryl didn't have any idea of the way his muscles had clenched every time she'd leaned over to check his notes. Or the havoc she'd caused to his concentration whenever she'd stretched out those long, tanned legs. After almost eight hours of breathing her scent and registering every nuance in her voice and body language, Harry figured he'd better put some distance between them. He needed to regain his sharp-edged sense of purpose, which was proving more difficult than he would have imagined around Sheryl.

They turned into the Monzano station well after six. To the east, the jagged Sandia Mountains were beginning to take on the watermelon-pink hue that the Spaniards had named them for. To the west, the sun blazed a fiery gold above the five volcanoes that rose from the lava fields like stubby sentinels.

The station's front parking lot had long since emptied, and a high, sliding gate blocked the entrance to the fenced-in rear lot. Rows of white Jeeps with the postal service's distinctive red-and-blue markings filled the back parking area. Sheryl spied her ice-blue Camry at the far end of the lot.

"You can let me out here," she told Harry. "I have a key card to activate the gate. I'll see you back at the courthouse in an hour or so."

"I'll wait here until you drive out."

She didn't argue. Although the station was located in a quiet, residential neighborhood, it took in large amounts of cash every day. They'd never had a robbery at the Manzano station, but postal bulletins reg-

ularly warned employees to stay alert when coming
in early or leaving late. After keying the gate, Sheryl
waited while the metal wheels rattled and bumped
across the concrete. Her footsteps made little sucking
noises as she crossed asphalt still soft from the
scorching afternoon sun.

She was almost to her car when she heard a clink
behind her. It sounded as though someone or something had bumped into a parked Jeep. Sheryl glanced
over her shoulder. Nothing moved except the elon-
gated shadow that floated at an angle behind her.
Frowning, she dug in her purse for her keys and
wound through the last row of vehicles at a brisk
pace. Relief rippled through her as she approached
her trusty little Camry. When she got her first full
look at the car, relief melted into instant dismay. The
vehicle sat low to the ground. Too low. Keys in hand,
Sheryl stood staring at its board-flat tires.

Slowly, she moved closer and bent to examine the
front tire. It hadn't just gone flat, she saw with a sudden, hollow sensation. It had been slashed. She was
still poking at the gaping wounds in the rubber with
her finger when another sound cut through the stillness like a knife.

Her heart leaping into her throat, Sheryl spun
around. The slanting rays of the sun hit her full in the
face…and blurred the dark silhouette of the figure
looming over her.

Chapter 5

"**W**hat the hell...?"

Sheryl recognized Harry's broad-shouldered form at almost the same moment his voice penetrated her sudden, paralyzing fear.

Without stopping to think, without taking a breath, she flowed toward him. She didn't expect him to curl an arm around her and draw her hard against his body, but she certainly didn't protest when he did. She closed her eyes, taking shameless comfort in his presence. It was a moment before she managed to murmur a shaky explanation.

"Someone slashed my tires."

"So I see," he rasped, his voice low and tight above her head. "I got antsy about letting you walk back here alone. Looks like I had reason to."

His muscles twisting like steel under her cheek, he

turned to survey the parking lot and the wire fence surrounding it.

"Not a security camera in sight," he muttered in disgust.

Slowly, Sheryl disengaged from his hold. She was still shaken enough to miss the security of his arms, but not so much that she didn't realize the feel of his body pressed against hers wasn't helping her regain her equilibrium. Swallowing, she tried to steady her nerves while he completed a scowling survey of the area.

The vista on the other side of the fence didn't afford him any more satisfaction than the lack of outside cameras in the parking lot. A tumbleweed-strewn field cut by a jagged arroyo separated the station from the residential area. The landscape shimmered with a silvery beauty that only someone used to New Mexico's serene, natural emptiness could appreciate. At this moment, all Sheryl could think of was how easily someone could have crossed the emptiness and scaled the wire link fence.

Echoing her thoughts, Harry scanned the residences in the distance and shook his head. "Those houses are too far away for anyone to spot a fence climber. The post office should have better security."

"That's assuming whoever cut my tires climbed the fence. He could've just walked into the lot. With all the carriers coming and going, we don't keep the gates locked during the day."

"I know."

Belatedly, she remembered that Harry had driven

in and out of those open gates with her several times. She wasn't thinking clearly, she realized.

He went down on one knee to examine the tires. "We're also assuming that an outsider caused this damage."

A new series of shocks eddied through Sheryl. "You can't think anyone at the post office would cut my tires like that."

He rose, dusting his hands. "Why not?"

"They're my friends as well as my co-workers!"

"All of them?"

"Well…"

She could name one carrier whose coarse, barroom style of humor had resulted in a couple of private and very heated discussions about what was considered acceptable language in the workplace. Then there was that temporary Christmas clerk who'd pestered her for dates long after she and Brian started seeing each other. Neither of those men had ever shown any animosity toward her, however. Certainly not the kind of animosity that would lead to something like this.

"Yes," she finished. "All of them."

Harry lifted a skeptical brow but didn't argue. "Well, I suspect you can't say the same about all of your customers."

"No." She shuddered, thinking of the thin, hostile doper who'd confronted her across the counter this morning. "I can't."

"That's why I followed you into the parking lot. I got to thinking about the crackhead who'd threatened you." He hesitated, then continued slowly. "I also got to thinking about the fact that right now you're my only link to Inga Gunderson's nephew."

Sheryl stared up at him in confusion. "What could that have to do with my slashed tires?"

"Maybe nothing," he answered, his face tight. "Maybe everything."

Before she could make any sense of that, he pulled out his phone. "Let's get the police out here to check the area before I call Ev."

Her mind whirling, Sheryl listened while he contacted the Albuquerque police and asked them to send a patrol car to the Monzano station right away. A moment later, he made a short, succinct call to his partner.

"Find out if the Gunderson woman contacted anyone other than her lawyer, or if she sent out any messages, written or otherwise. I want every second of her time accounted for since we brought her in yesterday afternoon."

Yesterday afternoon? Sheryl shook her head in disbelief. Was it only yesterday afternoon that she'd driven to Inga Gunderson's house, worried about the woman's well-being? Just a little more than twenty-four hours since she'd practically fallen into Harry MacMillan's arms? It seemed longer. A whole lot longer!

No wonder, considering all that had happened in those hours. She'd stood Brian up not once but twice. She'd gained a thoroughly obnoxious houseguest. She'd transitioned from postal clerk to task force augmentee without so much as five minutes' notice. And she'd just lost four tires that she'd planned to squeeze another thousand miles out of, despite the fact that the tread had pretty well disappeared. She was wondering if her insurance would cover the cost of replacements when she caught the tail end of Harry's conversation.

"Finish up at Miss Hancock's apartment. I'll call you when I get through." He snapped the phone shut.

"Finish up what at my apartment?"

"I'm going to follow you home after we get done here. I want to check your locks."

"Check my locks? Why?"

"Just in case the person who did this also knows where you live."

"Oh."

Harry's eyes narrowed at the sudden catch in her voice. Sliding the phone into his pocket, he nodded toward the loading dock.

"Let's wait over there, out of the heat."

Sheryl trailed beside him, but she didn't need the shade offered by the overhanging roof to cut the effects of the sun. The idea that the person responsible for the damage to her car might also know her home address had cooled her considerably. Harry's carefully neutral expression only added to that chill.

"I'm not trying to scare you," he said evenly, "but this wasn't a random act. The perpetrator didn't vandalize any of the other vehicles. Only yours."

"I noticed that."

"He could have done it out of spite." He slanted her a careful look. "Or he might have been trying to disable your car so you couldn't drive off when you came back to the post office...although there are certainly less obvious ways of doing that.''

"For someone who isn't trying to scare me, you're doing a darn good job of it!''

"Sorry.''

Blowing out a long breath, he tried to recover the ground he'd just lost.

"Look, all cops are suspicious by nature, and most of us are downright paranoid. I'm reaching here, really reaching, to even imagine a connection between this incident and the fact that Inga Gunderson knows you're providing us information about her postcards.''

"I hope so!''

The near panic in her voice brought his brows down in a quick frown. Cursing under his breath, he backpedaled even more.

"I'll wait to see if the police can lift any prints from the car before I speculate any further. In the meantime, try to think of anyone who might hold a grudge against you or want to get even over something.''

"Other than the creep this morning, I can't think of anyone. I lead a pretty quiet life aside from my work.''

"That doesn't say a lot for your fiancé,'' MacMillan offered as an aside. "Correction, sort-of fiancé.''

A tinge of heat took some of the chill from Sheryl's cheeks. "Brian and I are very comfortable together.''

His brow went up. "That says even less.''

"Yes, well, not everyone wants to go chasing all over the world after bad guys, Marshal. Some of us prefer a more settled kind of life, not to mention un-slashed tires.''

''We'll get the tires fixed and put a—''

He broke off, his head lifting at the sound of a siren in the distance. It drew closer, the wail undulating through the evening stillness. Sheryl gave a little breath of relief.

''They got here fast.''

Harry pushed away from the dock. ''That's one of the benefits of having a representative from the Albuquerque Police Department on the task force. Come on, let's go direct them to the crime scene.''

Hearing her trusty little Camry described as a ''crime scene'' didn't exactly soothe the victim's ragged nerves. She trailed after MacMillan, sincerely wishing Mrs. Inga Gunderson had never brought her melt-in-your-mouth cookies and yappy little dog into the Monzano Street station.

The reminder that the yappy little dog had no doubt spent the day demolishing Sheryl's apartment didn't particularly help matters, either.

By the time the police finished their investigation of the scene and a twenty-four-hour roadside service had replaced the Camry's tires, the spectacular light show that constituted a New Mexico sunset had begun. The entire western horizon blazed with color. Streaks of pink and turquoise layered into vibrant reds and velvet purples. The sun hovered like a shimmering gold fireball just above the Rio Grande. As Sheryl drove up the sloping rise toward her east-side apartment with Harry following close behind, the city lights twinkled like earthbound stars in her rearview mirror.

The serenity and beauty of the descending night helped loosen the tight knot of tension at the back of her neck. The police hadn't found anything that would identify the slasher. No prints, no footprints, no personal item conveniently dropped at the scene as so often occurred in movies and detective novels. The police had promised to canvas the houses that backed onto the fields around the station, but didn't hold out any more hope than Harry had that someone might have witnessed the vandalism. Tomorrow, they would interview Sheryl's co-workers. Rumors would speed like runaway roadrunners around the post office with this incident coming on top of her sudden detail. Elise must be wondering what in the world her friend had gotten herself into.

She'd call her tonight, Sheryl decided. And Brian. Despite the marshal's orders, she had to tell them something. They were her best friends.

When she caught her train of thought, Sheryl's hands tightened on the steering wheel. When had she started thinking of Brian as a friend, not a lover, for goodness' sake? And why did Harry's little editorial comments about their relationship raise her hackles?

Frowning, she waited for the easy slide of comfort that always accompanied any reminder of Brian and their future together. It came, but it brought along with it another traitorous thought. Was comfort really what she wanted in a marriage?

Oh, great! As if escaped fugitives, smuggled uranium and slashed tires weren't enough, Sheryl had to pick now of all times to question a relationship that she'd happily taken for granted until this minute.

The events of the past two days had rattled her, she decided. Both her home and her work schedule had been thrown off-kilter, as had the comfortable routine she and Brian had fallen into. As soon as she finished this detail and Harry MacMillan went chasing after his fugitive, her life would return to its normal, regular pace.

Sheryl pulled into her assigned parking slot, wondering why in the world the prospect didn't cheer her as much as it should have. A car door slammed in the area reserved for visitor parking, then Harry appeared beside the Camry. As he had before, he opened Sheryl's door and reached down a hand to help her out.

Oddly reluctant, she put her hand in his. The small electrical jolt that raced from her palm to her wrist to her elbow did *not* help resolve the confusion that welled in her mind. With a distinct lack of graciousness for the small courtesy, Sheryl yanked her hand free and led the way through the two-story adobe buildings.

While she fumbled through the keys for the one to her front door, Harry swept an appreciative eye around the tiled courtyard shared by the eight apartments in her cluster. Soft light from strategically placed luminaria bathed the little bubbling fountain and wooden benches carved with New Mexico's zia symbol. Clay pots spilled a profusion of flowers that hadn't yet folded their petals for the night. Their fragrance hung on the descending dusk like a gauzy cloud.

"This is nice," he commented. "Very nice. A place like this might tempt even me into coming home once in a while."

Once in a while.

The phrase echoed in Sheryl's head as she shoved the key into the lock. If she'd needed anything more to banish the doubts that had plagued her a few moments ago, that would have done it. She had no use for men who returned home every few weeks or months and stayed only long enough to get their laundry done.

"It's comfortable," she replied with deliberate casualness. "And I like the view. From the back patio, you can see— Oh, no!"

She halted in the entryway, aghast. Dirty laundry trailed in a colorful array from the foyer to the living room. Bras, panties, socks, tank tops and uniform shirts decorated the tiles, along with what looked like every shoe she owned.

"Button?" Harry inquired from behind her.

"No," Sheryl said in a huff. Slamming the door, she tossed her purse and her keys on the kitchen counter and bent to scoop up an armful of underwear. "This is the latest decorating scheme for working women who have to dress on the run."

"It works for me."

At his amused comment, she shot a glance over her shoulder. Her face heated when she spied the filmy, chocolate-and-ecru lace bra dangling from his hand. She'd splurged on the bra and matching panties just last week. As any woman who'd ever had to wear a uniform to work could attest, a touch of sinfully decadent silk under the standard, company-issued outer items did wonders for one's inner femininity.

"I'll take that." She snatched the bra out of his hand. "Why don't you wade through this stuff and go into the living room. Since we haven't heard a peep out of Butty-boo, he's obviously—"

"Butty-boo?"

"That's what Inga called him, among other, similarly nauseating names. He must be hiding." She started down the hall. "You check the living room. I'll check the bedroom."

She found the shih tzu stretched out in regal abandon on her bed. He'd made a nest of the handwoven Zuni blanket she used as a spread. His black-and-white fur blended in with the striking pattern on the blanket, and she might have missed him completely if he hadn't lifted his head at her entrance and given a lazy, halfhearted bark.

"That's it?" Sheryl demanded indignantly. "Two people walk into the house who could be burglars for all you know, and that's the best you can do? One little yip?"

In answer, Button yawned and plopped his head back down.

"Had a hard day, did you?"

Disgusted, she used one foot to right the overturned straw basket she used as a clothes hamper.

"Well, so did I, and I'm telling you here and now that I'd better not come home to any more messes like this one."

With that totally useless warning, Sheryl dumped her laundry in the basket and steeled herself to check the bathroom. To her surprise and considerable relief, Button had used the newspapers she'd spread across the tiles. She hoped that meant he hadn't also used the living-room carpet.

She took a few moments to swipe a little powder on her shiny nose and tuck some stray tendrils of hair back behind her ear, then headed for the living room. Button's black eyes followed her across the room. With another yawn and an elaborate stretch, he climbed out of his nest, leaped down from the bed and padded after her.

Sheryl had taken only a step or two into the living room when the dog gave a shrill bark that seemed to pierce right through her eardrums. Like a small, furry cannonball, Button launched himself across the mauve carpet at the figure jimmying the locks on the sliding-glass patio doors.

This time, Harry met the attack head-on. Jerking around, he growled at the oncoming canine.

"Take another bite out of my leg and you're history, pal!"

The shih tzu halted a few paces away, every hair bristling.

His target bristled a bit himself. "If it were up to me, you'd be chowing down at the pound right now, so back off. Back off, I said!"

Button didn't take kindly to ultimatums. His black lips drew back even farther. Bug eyes showed red with suppressed fury. The growls that came from deep in his throat grew even more menacing. Guessing that the standoff might break at any second, Sheryl hurried forward and scooped the dog into her arms.

"This is Harry, remember? He's one of the good guys. Well, not a good guy to you, since he sent your mistress off in handcuffs, but he's okay. Really."

Murmuring reassurances, she stroked the small, quivering bundle of fur.

"Helluva watchdog," the marshal muttered in disgust. "What was he doing back there, anyway? Trying on the rest of your underwear?"

Despite the fact that she herself didn't feel particularly benevolent toward the animal, Sheryl didn't have the heart to expose him to more criticism. Harry didn't need to know that Button had sprawled in indolent indifference while persons unknown had entered her apartment. Besides, the dog had leaped to the attack quickly enough once roused. Deciding to treat the marshal's question as rhetorical, she didn't bother to answer.

"How are the locks?"

"The dead bolt on the front door is sturdy enough. These patio doors are another story. If you don't mind, I'd like to get some security people up here to install a drop bar and kick lock, as well as a rudimentary alarm system. I'll have them wire your car while they're at it. They can be here in an hour or so."

"Tonight?"

"Tonight."

Sheryl's fingers curled into the dog's silky topknot. The fear that had gripped her for a few paralyzing moments in the parking lot reached out long tentacles once more. She shivered.

Harry's keen glance caught the small movement. He gave a smothered oath. "My paranoia's working overtime. The alarm probably isn't necessary, but I'd feel better with it in."

"Probably?" she repeated hollowly.

Harry cursed again and closed the short distance between them. Button issued a warning growl, which the marshal ignored. Lifting a hand, he smoothed an errant curl back from her cheek.

"I'm sorry, Sher. I didn't mean to scare you again."

The touch of his palm against her cheek startled Sheryl so much that she barely noticed his use of her nickname. She did, however, notice the tiny bits of gold warming his brown eyes. And the way his mustache thickened slightly at the corners, as if to disguise the small, curving laugh lines that appeared whenever his mouth kicked into one of his half-rogue, all-male grins.

The way it did now.

Except this grin was more rueful than roguish. It matched the look in his eyes, Sheryl thought, as his hand slid slowly from her cheek to curl back of her neck.

She shivered once more, but this time it wasn't from fear. This time, she realized with something close to dismay, it was from delight. Caught on a confusing cross of sensations, she could only stand and watch the way Harry's grin tipped from rueful into a smile that trapped her breath in the back of her throat.

He shouldn't do this! Harry's mind shouted the warning, even as his fingers got lost in the silky softness of her hair. He knew better than to mix business with personal desire. But suddenly, without the least warning, desire had grabbed hold of him and wouldn't let go.

She felt so soft. Smelled so intoxicating, a mixture of hot sun and powdery talcum, with a little shih tzu thrown in for leavening. She was also scared, Harry reminded himself savagely. Off balance from all that had happened in the past few days. Almost engaged.

Another man might have drawn back at that sobering thought. Someone else might have respected the territory this Brian character had tentatively staked out. Instead of deterring Harry, the very nebulousness of the other man's claim angered him. Any jerk who kept a woman like Sheryl dangling in some twilight never-never land didn't deserve her.

So when she didn't draw back, when her lips opened on a sigh instead of a protest, Harry bent his head and brushed them with his own. She tasted so fresh, so irresistible, that he brought his mouth back for another sample.

The kiss started out slow and soft and friendly. Within seconds, it powered up to fast and hard and well beyond friendship. A dozen different sensations exploded in Harry's chest and belly. The urge to pull Sheryl into his arms, to feel every inch of her against his length, clawed at him. He started to do just that when another, sharper sensation bit into his lower right arm.

"Dammit!"

He jumped back, almost yanking the stubby little monster locked onto his jacket sleeve out of Sheryl's arms. She caught the dog just in time and held on to it by its rear legs. It hung there between them, a growling, snarling mop with one end firmly attached to Harry's sleeve and the other to the woman who held him.

"You misbegotten, mangy little..."

"He was just trying to protect me," Sheryl got out on a gasp. "I think."

Harry thought differently, but he was too busy working his fingers onto either side of the dog's muzzle to say so at that moment. Exerting just enough pressure to spring those tiny, steel jaws open, he pulled his coat sleeve free. He then reached over and extracted the animal from Sheryl's unresisting arms.

Two long strides took him back to the sliding doors. A moment later, the glass panel slammed shut. Buggy black eyes glared at him from the outside. Ignoring the glare and the bad-tempered yips that accompanied it, Harry turned back to Sheryl.

His fierce, driving need to sweep her into his arms once more took a direct hit when he caught her expression. It held a combination of regret and guilt...and not the least hint of any invitation to continue.

Chapter 6

"**I**'m sorry."

The apology came out with a gruffer edge than Harry had intended, for the simple reason that he couldn't think of anything he felt less sorry about than taking Sheryl into his arms. Yet that kiss ranked right up there among the dumbest things he'd ever done.

That said something, considering that he'd pulled some real boners in his life. Two in particular he'd always regret. The first was succumbing to a bad case of lust and marrying too young, much too young to figure out how to get his struggling marriage through the stress of his job. The second occurred years later, when he decided to take a few long-overdue days off to go fishing in Canada. That fateful weekend his best buddy was gunned down. By the time Harry had returned and taken charge of the operation to track down Dean's killers, the trail had gone stone cold.

Now it had finally heated up, and he couldn't allow himself to get sidetracked by a moss-eyed blonde who raised his blood pressure a half-dozen points every time she glanced his way. Nor, he reminded himself with deliberate ruthlessness, could he afford to confuse her by coming on to her like this. He needed her calm and rational and able to concentrate on the task she'd been detailed to do. She still had information Harry wanted to pull out of her.

"That was out of line," he admitted, less gruffly, more firmly. "It won't happen again."

"N-no. It won't."

The guilt in her voice rubbed him raw. Cursing the predatory instincts that had driven him to poach so recklessly on another man's territory, he tried to recapture her trust.

"I guess this damned investigation has sanded away the few civilized edges I possessed."

It had sanded away a few of Sheryl's edges, too. She couldn't remember the last time a kiss had seared her like that. Dazed, she struggled to subdue the runaway fire racing through her veins. A massive dose of guilt helped speed the process considerably.

She was almost engaged, for heaven's sake! How could she have just stood there and let Harry kiss her like that? How could she have been so shallow, so disloyal to Brian? She'd never even looked at another man in all the time they'd been seeing each other. What's more, she'd certainly never dreamed that a near stranger could generate this combination of singing excitement and stinging regret with just the touch of his mouth on hers. She stared at Harry, seeing her own consternation in his frown.

"We've got a good number of hours of work ahead of us yet," he got out curtly. "You can't concentrate if you're worried that I might pounce at any minute. I won't, I promise."

A small sense of pique piled on top of Sheryl's rapidly mounting guilt. She knew darn well she was as much to blame for what had just happened as Harry. Her instinctive, uninhibited response to his touch shook her to her core, and she didn't need him to tell her it wouldn't happen again. She wouldn't do that to Brian or to herself. Still, it rankled just a bit that the marshal regretted their kiss as much as she did, if for entirely different reasons.

Feeling flustered and thoroughly off balance, Sheryl had a need to put some distance between her and Harry. She moved into the kitchen, where she snatched up Button's plastic water dish and shoved it under the faucet to rinse it out.

"Why don't you head back downtown," she suggested with what she hoped was a credible semblance of calm. "I'll follow after I feed Button, and we can put in a few more hours' work."

Harry looked as though there was nothing he'd like better than to get back to business, but he shook his head. "I'd like to stay here until the security folks arrive and do their thing, if you don't mind."

Sheryl stared at him while water ran over the sides of the dish. In the aftermath of his shattering kiss, she'd totally forgotten what had led up to it.

"No, of course I don't mind."

"I'll call them and get them on the way."

With brisk efficiency, he mobilized the necessary specialists. Another quick call alerted Ev to the fact that he'd have to scrounge his own dinner.

"I guess I could make us some sandwiches," Sheryl said slowly when he snapped the phone shut. "Or I could cook lemon chicken. I have all the fixings. We can eat and work while we wait."

The idea of preparing Brian's favorite meal for Harry disconcerted Sheryl all over again. Honestly, she had to get a grip here. Harry had certainly recovered his poise fast enough. He'd faced the awkwardness head-on and moved beyond it. She could do the same. Briskly, she swiped a paper towel around the bowl and filled it with the dried dog food she'd picked up yesterday.

"I'll feed Button and get something started."

"I have a better idea." Harry shrugged out of his coat, then rolled up his sleeves. "You feed the rodent while I pour you a glass of wine or whatever relaxes you. Then I'll cook the chicken."

"There's some wine in the fridge," Sheryl said doubtfully, "but you don't have to fix dinner."

"I don't have to, but I'd like to."

He flashed her a grin that strung her tummy into tight knots. Good grief, what in the world was the matter with her?

"Being on the road so much, I don't get to practice my culinary skills very often. But my ex-wife trained me well. She never opened a can or flipped on a burner when I was home."

"Well…"

He traded places with Sheryl, taking over the kitchen with an easy competence that put the last of her doubts to rest. A quick investigation of her cupboards and fridge produced skillet, chicken, flour, lemons, onions, cracked pepper, butter and a half-full bottle of chilled Chablis.

While Harry assembled the necessary ingredients, Sheryl fed Button. Naturally, the dog displayed his displeasure over his banishment to the patio by turning up his pug nose at the dry food. She left him and his dinner outside, then occupied one of the tall rawhide-and-rattan counter stools. Sipping slowly on the wine Harry had poured for her, she tried to understand the welter of confused emotions this man stirred in her.

She gave up after the second or third sip and contented herself with just watching. He hadn't been kidding about his culinary skills. Within moments, he had the floured chicken fillets sizzling in the skillet. While they browned, he made short work of dicing the onion. Seconds later, the onion, more butter and a generous dollop of Chablis went into the pan. Sheryl sniffed the delicious combination of scents, conscious once more of the inadequacy of the Korn Kurls she'd eaten for lunch.

"My compliments to your ex-wife," she murmured. "You really do know your way around a kitchen."

"Unfortunately, cooking is my one and only domestic skill…or so I've been told."

"How long were you married?" she asked curiously.

He squeezed a wedge of lemon over the chicken. The drops spurted and spit in the hot pan, adding their tangy scent to the aroma of butter and onions rising from the cooktop.

"Eight years by calendar reckoning. Three, maybe four, if you count the time my wife and I spent at home together. She's an account executive for a Dallas PR firm now, but when we met she was just starting in the business. Her job took her on the road as much as mine did, and..."

"And constant absences don't necessarily make the heart grow fonder," she finished slowly.

He shrugged, but Sheryl had been in this man's company enough by now to catch the tight note in his voice. Harry MacMillan didn't give up on anything easily, she now knew, whether it was a marriage or the relentless pursuit of a fugitive.

"Something like that," he concurred, sending her a keen glance through the spiraling steam. "You sound as though you've been there, too."

"In a way."

She traced a circle on the counter with her glass. She rarely spoke about the father whose absence had left such a void in her heart, but Harry's blunt honesty about his divorce invited reciprocation. Reluctantly, she shared a little of her own background.

"My father traveled a lot in his job, too. My mother stewed and fretted every minute he was gone, which didn't make for happy homecomings."

"I imagine not. Is he still on the road?"

"As far as I know. He and Mom divorced when I was six. He showed up for a Christmas or two, and we wrote each other until I was about ten. The letters got fewer and farther between after he took an overseas position. Last I heard, he was in Oman."

"Want me to track him down for you? It would only take a few calls."

He was serious, Sheryl saw with a little gulp.

"No, thanks," she said hastily. "I don't need him wandering in and out of my life anymore."

"Well, the offer stands if you change your mind," he replied, flipping the slotted wooden spoon into the air like a baton. He caught it with a smooth ripple of white shirt and lean muscle. "Do you have any rice in the cupboard? I'm even better at rice Marconi than lemon chicken."

"And so modest, too."

He grinned. "Modesty isn't one of the skills they emphasize in the academy. Relax, enjoy your wine and watch a master at work."

Maybe it was the Chablis. Or the sight of this tall, rangy man moving so matter-of-factly about her little kitchen. In any case, Sheryl relaxed, enjoyed her wine and managed to ignore the fact that the master chef sported a leather shoulder holster instead of a tall, white hat. Her prickly sense of guilt stayed with her, though, and kept her from completely enjoying the meal Harry served up with a flourish.

It also kept her on the other side of the dining-room table after they finished eating and got down to work. Button, released from his banishment, perched on the back of the sofa and watched the marshal with unblinking, unwavering hostility. With the wine and food to soothe the nerves made ragged by Harry's kiss, Sheryl was able to recall the details on several batches of postcards.

"Venice, the Antibes, Barbados." Harry tapped his pen on the tabletop. "You're sure the cards that arrived before the Rio set came from those three locations?"

"I'm sure. It's hard to mistake gondolas and canals. I remember Antibes because of the little gold emblem in the corner of the card that advertised the Côte d'Azur. And Barbados..."

Sheryl gazed at the wall, seeing in its wavy plaster a sea so polished it glittered like clear, blue topaz, and white beaches lined with banyan trees whose roots hung downward like long, scraggly beards.

"If the picture on the card came anywhere close to reality," she murmured, "Barbados must have the most beautiful beaches in the world."

Harry's pen stilled. Against his will, against his better judgment, he let his glance linger on Sheryl's face. Damn, didn't the woman have any idea what that soft, dreamy expression did to a man's concentration? Or how much of herself she revealed in these unguarded moments? Despite her assertions to the contrary, Harry suspected that the daughter had inherited more than a touch of her father's wanderlust. She tried hard to suppress it, but it slipped out in moments like this, when she mentally transported herself to a white sweep of beach.

Despite *his* intentions to the contrary, Harry mentally transported himself there with her.

The sound of a low, rumbling growl wrenched him back to Albuquerque. A quick look revealed that Button had shifted his attention from Harry to the front door. The dog's entire body quivered as he pushed up on all four paws and stared at the entryway. His gums pulled back. Another low growl rattled in his throat.

Carefully, Harry laid down his pen. "Are you expecting anyone?"

Sheryl's eyes widened at his soft query. Gulping, she shifted her gaze to the door. "No," she whispered.

"Stay here!"

Harry moved toward the door, his mind spinning with possibilities. The dog might have alerted on a neighbor arriving home. Maybe the security team was outside. Whoever it was, Harry had been a cop too long to take a chance on mights and maybes. He waited in the entryway, his every sense straining.

He heard no murmur of voices, no passing footsteps, no doorbell. Only Button's quivering growls... and a small, almost inaudible scrape.

Pulse pounding, back to the wall, Harry edged toward the door. With no side windows to peer out, he had to resort to the peephole. He made out a bent head, a pale blur of a shirt, a glint of moonlight on steel.

With a kick to his gut, he saw the dead bolt slowly twist.

His hand whipped across his chest. The Smith & Wesson came out of its leather nest with a smooth, familiar slide. He reached for the doorknob and waited until the dead bolt clicked open.

The knob moved under his palm. He exploded into action at the exact instant Button flew off the sofa, snarling, and Sheryl shouted at him.

"Harry! Wait!"

Her cry was still echoing in his ears when he yanked the door open with his free hand. A second later, the stranger standing on the other side of the door slammed up against the hallway wall. The Smith & Wesson dug into his ribs.

His cheek squashed into the plaster, the tall, slender man couldn't do much more than gape over his shoulder at his attacker.

"Wh— What's going on here?" he stuttered. "Who are you?"

In response, Harry torqued the stranger's arm up his spine another few inches. His adrenaline pumped like high-octane jet fuel. Button's high-pitched yaps scratched on his strung-tight nerves like fingernails on a chalkboard.

"You first," he countered roughly. "Who the hell are you?"

Before he got an answer, Sheryl locked both hands on his arm. "It's Brian," she shouted, yanking at his bruising hold. "Let go, Harry. It's Brian. Brian Mitchell."

Slowly, he released his grip and stepped back. Button didn't give up as readily. It took Sheryl's direct intervention before the still-snarling dog retired from the field. A good-sized strip of gray twill pants dangled from his locked jaws.

The two men faced each other, blood still up and faces flushed. Sheryl dumped the dog on the sofa and hurried back to calm the roiled waters.

"Brian, I'm so sorry! I didn't expect you, and it's been such a crazy day. Are you okay? Button didn't break the skin on your leg, did he?"

"No." Jaw clamped, the younger man watched his attacker holster his gun. "Who's this?"

"This is, er..." She turned, her face a study in frustration. "I can tell him, can't I?"

Harry took his time replying. Now that he knew the man didn't pose an immediate threat, his sharp-edged tension should have eased. Instead, Sheryl's fluttering and fussing raised his hackles all over again. It didn't take any great deductive skills to identify the man as Brian, her almost-fiancé.

Eyes glinting, he assessed the newcomer. An inch or two shorter than Harry's own six-one, he carried a good deal less weight on his trim frame. He also, the marshal noted, didn't take kindly to having his face shoved up against the wall.

"Elise said someone came into the station this morning and pulled you for a special detail. I take it this is the guy."

"Yes."

His gaze sliced from Sheryl to Harry. "Working kind of late, aren't you?"

She answered for them, a tinge of pink in her cheeks. "Yes, we are. Why don't you come in? I want to check your leg to make sure Button didn't do any serious damage."

Unmoving, Brian looked the marshal up and down.

His lip curled. "I wouldn't have picked you for a shih tzu owner."

"You got that much right, anyway," Harry replied with a careless shrug. "I would have dumped the mutt in the pound. Sher insisted on bringing it home."

He used the nickname deliberately, not exactly sure why he wanted to get a rise out of the younger man. Whatever the reason, Brian's scowl sent a spear of satisfaction through his belly.

Sheryl listened to their terse exchange with increasing consternation flavored with a pinch of irritation. They sounded like two boys baiting each other. She could understand why Brian might feel antagonistic, given Harry's rough handling and his presence in her apartment so late at night, but she could do without the marshal's deliberate provocation.

"Let's go into the living room," she said firmly. "Harry will explain what we're doing while I check your leg."

The remains of the meal still sitting on the table didn't help matters, of course. Nor did the empty wine bottle on the kitchen counter. Frowning, Brian took in the littered table, the half-empty wineglasses and the dog once more stretched along the back of the sofa, his duty done. Slowly, he turned to face Sheryl.

"My leg's fine," he said quietly, all trace of antagonism gone now. "But I can certainly use a little explaining."

Before she could reply, Harry stepped forward. The gold star gleamed from the leather credentials case lying in his palm.

"I'm Deputy U.S. Marshal Harry MacMillan.

Since Sheryl vouches for you, I'll tell you that I'm tracking a fugitive who escaped while being transported for trial a year ago. His trail led to Albuquerque and, obliquely, to the Monzano branch of the post office.''

Brian's face registered blank astonishment, followed by swift concern. "Is this fugitive dangerous?"

"He's suspected of killing the marshal escorting him to trial."

"And you pulled Sheryl into a hunt for a cop killer?"

"I requested that she be assigned to my team, yes."

"Well, you can just unrequest her," Brian declared. "I don't want her taking part in any manhunt for a cop killer."

Sheryl gave a little huff of exasperation. "Ex-cuse me. I'm getting a little tired of this two-sided conversation. In case you've forgotten, this is my apartment and my living room, and it's my decision whether or not I'm going to work on this detail."

Brian conceded her point stiffly. "Of course it's your decision, but I don't like it. Aside from the possible danger, this detail of yours has already disrupted our schedule. I waited almost an hour for you yesterday afternoon, and we missed our Tuesday night together."

As she looked up into his gray eyes, Sheryl's momentary irritation disappeared, swept away by a fresh wave of guilt. She loved Brian. She'd loved him for almost a year now. Yet she'd gotten so caught up in Harry's investigation that she hadn't spared much thought to this kind, considerate man—until the marshal kissed her.

She felt a sudden, urgent need to fold herself into Brian's arms and feel his mouth on hers. She turned, offering Harry a forced smile. "Would you keep Button entertained for a few minutes? I'm going to walk Brian to his car."

"You stay here and talk," he countered. "Much as I hate to be seen in public with this sorry excuse for a dog, he can keep me company while I reconnoiter the outside layout for the security folks."

Sheryl grabbed the leash she'd purchased when she bought the dog food and shoved it in his hand gratefully. Frowning, Brian watched the oversized marshal depart with the undersized mop of fur at the end of a bright-red lead.

"Security folks?" he echoed as the door closed. "What security folks?"

Sighing, Sheryl abandoned her need to be held in favor of Brian's need to know. Taking a seat beside him on the sofa, she tucked a foot under her and recapped the events of the past few days. When she got to the part about the slashed tires, Brian voiced his growing consternation.

"At the risk of repeating myself, I have to say I don't like this. I wish you'd take yourself off this detail."

"We don't know that my slashed tires had anything to do with my participation on the task force. Anyone could have done it, but Harry insists it's better not to take chances. He's got a team coming out to install new locks and an alarm system."

"I still don't like it," Brian repeated stubbornly.

Sheryl bit back the retort that she'd didn't particularly like that part, either. She probably should feel flattered by Brian's protective streak. Instead, she resented it just a little bit. No, more than a little bit.

Suddenly, Sheryl remembered that she'd curled into Harry's side for protection only this afternoon, without feeling the least hint of resentment.

Guilt, confusion and a desperate need to reestablish her usual sense of comfortable ease with Brian brought her forward. Sliding her arms around his neck, she smiled up at him.

"I'm sorry you don't like it, and I appreciate your concern. I want to be part of this team, though. If I have any knowledge that could lead to the capture of a murderer, I have to share it. After this detail, we'll get back to our regular routine. I promise."

Conceding with his usual good-natured grace, he bent his head and met her halfway. Their mouths fit together with practiced sureness...and none of the explosive excitement that Sheryl had experienced only a half hour ago.

Dismayed, she rose up on her knees. Her body melted against Brian's. Her fingers tunneled through his hair. Brian was more than willing to deepen the embrace. His arms went around her waist, drawing her closer.

Afterward, she could never sort out whether he pulled back first or she did. Nor would she ever forget the look in his eyes. Puzzled. Surprised. Not hurt, but close. Too close.

"I guess I'd better leave," he said slowly. "So you

and—what's his name?—Harry can get back to work.''

When his arms dropped away, her ache spread into a slow, lancing pain. Deep within her, she knew that she would never find her usual comfortable satisfaction in his embrace again. She'd changed. Somehow, she'd become a different person.

She loved Brian. She would always love him. But she knew now that she'd mistaken the nature of that love. Comfort didn't form the basis for a marriage. Security couldn't ensure happiness. For either of them.

If nothing else, Harry's searing kiss had demonstrated that. Sheryl didn't fool herself that she'd fallen in love with Harry MacMillan, or even in lust. She'd barely known the man for thirty-six hours. Yet in that brief period, he'd knocked the foundations right out from under Sheryl's nice, placid existence.

Aching, she wet her lips and tried to articulate some of her confused thoughts.

''Brian…''

He shook his head. ''I need to do some thinking. I guess you do, too. We'll talk about it when you finish this detail, Sher.''

He pushed himself off the sofa. Miserable, Sheryl followed him to the door. He paused, one hand on the knob, as reluctant to walk out as she was to let him.

''Elise said you rescheduled your shopping expedition for a bassinet for tomorrow night. You need to call her if you're going to be working late again.''

''I will.'' She grabbed at the excuse to delay his

departure for another few moments. "Or maybe you could take her?"

He nodded. "Sure, if you can't make it. And don't forget to call your mother. You know she expects to hear from you every Thursday."

"I won't."

He opened the door, and a small silence fell between them. Sheryl felt her heart splinter into tiny shards of pain when he curled a hand under her chin.

"Bye, Sher," he said softly.

"Goodbye, Brian."

He tilted her head up for a final kiss.

Harry watched from the shadows across the courtyard. He needed to see this, he thought, his jaw tight. He needed the physical evidence of Brian's claim. Of Sheryl's affection.

It made Harry's own relationship with her easier, clearer, sharper. She was part of his team.

Nothing more.

Nothing less.

Which didn't explain why he had to battle the irrational temptation to unclip Button's leash and turn the man-eating fur ball loose on Brian Mitchell again.

Chapter 7

Sheryl walked into the task force operations center twenty minutes late on Thursday morning. A taut, unsmiling Harry greeted her.

"Where the hell have you been? I was about to send a squad car up to your place to check on you."

"Button set the darn alarm off twice before I figured out how to bypass the motion detectors."

The marshal bit back what Sheryl suspected was another biting comment about hairy little rodents. Instead, he raked her with a glance that left small scorch marks everywhere it touched her skin.

"Call in the next time you have a problem."

The curt order raised her brows and her hackles. "Yes, sir!"

Harry narrowed his eyes but didn't respond.

Tossing her purse onto a chair, Sheryl headed for the coffeepot in the corner of the conference room.

She didn't know what had gotten into Harry this morning, but his uncertain mood more than matched her own. She felt grouchy and irritable and unaccountably off-kilter in the marshal's presence.

Much of her edginess she could ascribe to the fact that she hadn't gotten much sleep last night. She'd spent countless hours tossing and turning and thinking about Brian. She'd spent almost as many hours trying *not* to think about Harry's shattering kiss. She couldn't, wouldn't, allow herself to dwell on the sensations the marshal had roused in her, not when she owed Brian her loyalty.

To make matters even worse, Button had added his bit to her restless night. The mutt insisted on burrowing under the covers and curling up in the bend of her knees. Every time Sheryl had tried to straighten her legs, she'd disturbed his slumber...a move that Button didn't particularly appreciate. He'd voiced his displeasure in no uncertain terms. Between the dog's growls and her own troubled thoughts, Sheryl was sure she'd barely closed her eyes for an hour or so before the alarm went off.

Grumbling, she'd dragged out of bed, pulled on a pair of white slacks and a cool, sleeveless silk blouse in a bright ruby red, then grabbed a glass of juice and a slice of toast. She still might have made it down to the federal building by eight if she'd hadn't had to struggle with the unfamiliar alarm system. Twenty minutes and three calls to the alarm company later, she'd slammed the door behind her and headed for her car.

Her day hadn't gotten off to a good start, even before Harry's curt greeting. As she greeted the assembled team members, she guessed that it wouldn't get much better.

Crisp and professional in her New Mexico state trooper's uniform, Fay Chandler shook her head in response to Sheryl's query about her son's T-ball game.

"They got creamed," she said glumly. "I had to take the whole team for pizza to cheer them up. They perked up at the first whiff of pepperoni, but my husband was still moping when I left the house this morning. He's worse than my seven-year-old."

Folding her hands around the hot, steaming coffee, Sheryl took cautious injections of the liquid caffeine. She carried the cup with her to the conference table and greeted Everett Sloan. The poor man was almost buried behind a stack of computer printouts.

"Hi, Ev. Looks like you're hard at it already."

The short, barrel-chested deputy marshal waved a half-eaten chocolate donut. "'Hard' is the operative word. The computers crunched the numbers and words you gave us from the first set of postcards. Take a look at what they kicked out."

Sheryl's eyes widened at the row of cardboard boxes stacked along one wall, each filled with neatly folded printouts.

"Good grief! Do you have to go through all those?"

"Every one of them."

"What in the world are they?"

"We bounced the numbers and letters of the words you gave us against the known codes maintained by the FBI and Defense Intelligence Agency to see if there's a pattern. So far, no luck." Grimacing, he surveyed the boxes still awaiting his attention. "It'll take until Christmas to find a needle in that haystack...if there is one."

"We don't have until Christmas," Harry put in from the other end of the table. "We've got to break that code fast. We caught Inga Gunderson with her bags packed, remember? We have to assume the drop is scheduled for sometime soon...if it hasn't already gone down," he added grimly.

Fay hitched a hip on the edge of the conference table. "My bet is that Inga sent a message through her lawyer. She probably alerted either the sender or the receivers to the fact she's been tagged. If they didn't call off the shipment, they've no doubt diverted it to an alternate location."

Ev shook his head. "I know her lawyer. Several of us in the Albuquerque Marshals' office had to provide extra courtroom security when he defended one of his skinhead clients against a charge of communicating a threat against a federal law enforcement official. The scuzzball swore his buddies would blow up the Federal building if he was found guilty."

Since the Oklahoma City bombing, Sheryl knew, those threats were taken very, very seriously. She remembered the tension that had gripped the city during that trial.

"Don Ortega gave the guy one helluva defense," Ev continued, "but he told me afterward he fully expected to go up in smoke with his client. He's tough but straight. He wouldn't knowingly aid an escaped prisoner or contribute to the commission of a crime.''

"But he might do it unknowingly," Fay argued. "Maybe Inga and company used some kind of a coded message. They're certainly handy enough at that sort of thing."

Ev shook his head emphatically. "Not Don. He's too smart to act as a courier for a suspected felon. Besides, the supervisor of the women's detention center swears Inga hasn't made any calls to anyone other than her attorney. So the odds are that the drop is still on...for a time we've yet to determine at a place we haven't identified."

"We'll identify both," Harry swore, his face as tight and determined as his voice. "Keep working those computer reports. If you don't find anything that makes sense, run them again with the day-month combinations for the next five days."

His partner groaned. "I'm going to need more energy for this."

Polishing off his donut, Ev dug another out of the box in the center of the table. While he munched his way through the report in front of him, Harry turned to the state trooper.

"I want you to drive out to all the airports we've IDed as possible landing sites. Talk to the Customs people and airport managers personally. Ask them to info us on any flight plans with South America as originating departure point or cargo manifests showing transport from or through Rio. Also, tell them to notify us immediately of any unscheduled requests for transit servicing on aircraft large enough to carry this kind of a cargo load.''

Fay reached for her Smoky the Bear hat. ''Will do, Chief.''

Topping off his coffee, Harry walked back to his seat. ''All right, Sheryl, let's get to work.''

She shot him a quick glance as she settled in the chair next to his. He'd shed his jacket, but otherwise wore his standard uniform of boots, jeans and button-down cotton shirt, this one a soft, faded yellow. His clean-shaven jaw and neatly trimmed mustache looked crisply professional, but the lines at the corners of his eyes and mouth suggested that he'd hadn't slept much more than she had.

No doubt his investigation had kept him awake. It certainly seemed to consume him this morning. He gave no sign that he even remembered brushing a hand across her cheek last night or sending her into a shivering, shuddering nosedive with the touch of his mouth on hers. Not that Sheryl wanted him to remember, of course, any more than she wanted him to kiss her again.

Not until she'd sorted out her feelings for Brian, anyway.

''Where do you want to start?'' she asked briskly.

''Let's go over the wording from the Venice-Antibes-Barbados cards again. Start with Barbados.''

''Fine.''

They worked for several hours before Harry was satisfied that he'd extracted all the information he could on that set of postcards. After sending the key words down to the computer center for analysis, they moved on to other cards that had arrived during Inga Gunderson's four months in Albuquerque. The further back Sheryl reached into her memory, the hazier the dates and stamps and messages got. The scenes on the front side of the cards remained vivid, however.

"Give me what you can on this one from Heidelberg," Harry instructed.

"It came in early April, a week or so before the fifteenth. I remember that much, because it provided such a colorful counterpoint to all the dreary income tax returns we had to sort and process."

Harry scribbled a note. "Go on."

"It was one of my favorites. It had four different scenes on the front. One showed a fairy tale castle perched above the Neckar River. Another depicted the old bridge that spans the river. Then there was a group of university students lifting their beer steins and singing, just like Mario Lanza and his friends did in the *Student Prince.*"

At the other end of the table, Ev groaned. "Mario Lanza and the *Student Prince.* I can just imagine what the computers will do with that one!"

Harry ignored him. "What about the fourth scene?"

"That was the best." Sheryl assembled her thoughts. "It showed a monstrous wine cask in the basement of the castle. According to Paul's note, the cask holds something like fifty thousand gallons. Supposedly, the king's dwarf once drained the whole thing."

Harry stared at her. A slow, almost reluctant approval dawned in his eyes, warming them to honey brown. "Fifty thousand gallons, huh? That gives us an interesting number to work with. Good going, Sher."

For the first time that morning, Sheryl relaxed. A sense of partnership, of shared purpose, replaced her earlier irritation with Harry's brusque manner. When he wasn't glowering at her or barking out orders, the marshal had his own brand of rough-edged charm.

As she'd discovered last night.

From the other end of the table, Ev whistled softly. "How the heck can you remember that kind of detail?"

"A good memory is one of the primary qualifications for a postal worker," she replied, smiling. "Especially those of us who are scheme qualified."

"Okay, I'll bite. What's 'scheme qualified'?"

"Although I primarily work the front counter, I'm also authorized to come in early and help throw mail for the carrier runs. Everything arrives in bulk from the central distribution center, you see, then we have to sort it by zip."

"I thought you had machines to do that."

"I wish!" Sheryl laughed. "No, most of the mail is hand-thrown at the branch level. I worked at two different Albuquerque stations before I moved to the Monzano branch. I can pretty well tell you the zip for any street you pick out of the phone book," she finished smugly.

"No kidding?"

Ev looked as though he wanted to put her to the test, but Harry intervened.

"Unless they're pertinent to this investigation, I'm not interested in any zips but the ones on these postcards. Let's get back to work."

"Yes, sir!" Ev and Sheryl chorused.

Harry grilled her relentlessly, extracting every detail she could remember about Mrs. Gunderson's correspondence and then some. They worked steadily, despite constant interruptions.

The phones in the task force operations center rang frequently. In one call, the DEA advised that the informant who'd tipped them to Paul and Inga Gunderson had just come up with another name. They were working to ID the man now. Just before noon, the CIA came back with an unconfirmed field report that six canisters of depleted uranium had indeed passed through Prague four days ago. Their contact was still working Pamplona and Rio to see if he could pick up the trail. His face alive with fierce satisfaction, Harry reported the news to his small team.

"Hot damn!" Ev exclaimed. "Prague! Good going, Sheryl."

A thrill shot through her. She couldn't believe the information she'd provided only yesterday had already borne fruit. Her eyes met Harry's above his latest ream of notes.

"I owe you," he said quietly. "Big time."

Her skin tingled everywhere his gaze touched it. She smiled, and answered just as softly.

"All in the line of duty, Marshal."

The call that came in from their contact in the APD a little later took some of the edge off Sheryl's sense of satisfaction. The police hadn't turned up any leads regarding her slashed tires, nor had they located the man who'd hassled her yesterday morning over his girlfriend's welfare check. The woman had moved, and none of the neighbors knew her or her boyfriend's current address.

"They're going to keep working it," Harry advised.

"I hope so."

In addition to the many incoming calls, the task force also had a number of visitors, including the deputy U.S. district attorney working the charges against Inga Gunderson. Harry and Ev conferred with the man in private for some time. Just before noon, the three of them went downstairs for Inga Gunderson's custody hearing. The marshals returned an hour later, elated and more determined than ever. The government's lawyer had convinced the judge to hold Inga pending a grand-jury review of the charges against her, they reported. The good guys had won another two, possibly three days while the woman remained in custody.

"That's great for you," Sheryl said with a sigh, "but it looks like I've got Button for at least two, possibly three, more days."

"There's always the pound," Harry reminded her.

When she declined to reply, Ev picked up on the conversation.

"Inga's attorney asked about the dog. Said his client was worried about her precious Butty-Boo. We assured him the mutt was in good hands." His pudgy face took on a thoughtful air. "Maybe we should check the mutt out again."

Harry's head jerked up sharply. "You said you went over him while we were at Inga's house."

"I took his collar apart and searched what I could of his fur without losing all ten of my fingers. I might have missed something."

"Great."

"Or he could be carrying something internally," Ev finished with a grimace. He eyed the other marshal across the table. "I'll let you handle this one, Mac-Millan. You lugged the mutt around under your arm for most of yesterday. He knows you."

"I've done a lot of things in the pursuit of justice," Harry drawled, "but I draw the line at a body cavity search of a fuzz ball with teeth. If you don't mind giving me your house keys and the alarm code, Sheryl, I'll send a squad car out to pick him up and take him to the vet who works the drug dogs. He's got full X-ray capability."

Sheryl dug her keys out of her purse, then passed them across the table. Poor Button. She suspected he wouldn't enjoy the next hour or so. Neither would the vet.

Harry dispatched the squad car, resumed his seat next to hers and reviewed his notes. "Okay, we've got details on eight postcards now. Can you remember any more?"

Sheryl sorted through her memory. "I think there were two, perhaps three, more."

They worked steadily for another hour. A uniformed police officer returned Sheryl's keys and a report that the dog was clean. Fay Chandler called in from Farmington, where she was waiting for the manager of the local airport to make an appearance. Ev

PLAY "LUCKY 7" AND GET
THREE FREE GIFTS!

HOW TO PLAY:

1. With a coin, carefully scratch off the silver box at the right. Then check the claim chart to see what we have for you — **FREE BOOKS** and a gift — **ALL YOURS! ALL FREE!**

2. Send back this card and you'll receive brand-new Silhouette Intimate Moments® novels. These books have a cover price of $4.25 each, but they are yours to keep absolutely free.

3. There's no catch. You're under no obligation to buy anything. We charge nothing — ZERO — for your first shipment. And you don't have to make any minimum number of purchases — not even one!

4. The fact is thousands of readers enjoy receiving books by mail from the Silhouette Reader Service™ months before they're available in stores. They like the convenience of home delivery and they love our discount prices!

5. We hope that after receiving your free books you'll want to remain a subscriber. But the choice is yours — to continue or cancel, any time at all! So why not take us up on our invitation, with no risk of any kind. You'll be glad you did!

YOURS FREE!

PLAY LUCKY 7 FOR THIS EXCITING FREE GIFT!

THIS SURPRISE MYSTERY GIFT COULD BE YOURS FREE WHEN YOU PLAY

LUCKY 7!

NO COST! NO OBLIGATION TO BUY!
NO PURCHASE NECESSARY!

The Silhouette Reader Service™ — Here's how it works

Accepting free books places you under no obligation to buy anything. You may keep the books and gift and return the shipping statement marked "cancel." If you do not cancel, about a month later we'll send you 6 additional novels, and bill you just $3.57 each, plus 25¢ delivery per book and applicable sales tax, if any.* That's the complete price — and compared to cover prices of $4.25 each — quite a bargain! You may cancel at any time, but if you choose to continue, every month we'll send you 6 more books, which you may either purchase at the discount price...or return to us and cancel your subscription.

*Terms and prices subject to change without notice. Sales tax applicable in N.Y.

BUSINESS REPLY MAIL
FIRST-CLASS MAIL   PERMIT NO. 717   BUFFALO, NY

POSTAGE WILL BE PAID BY ADDRESSEE

SILHOUETTE READER SERVICE
3010 WALDEN AVE
PO BOX 1867
BUFFALO NY 14240-9952

NO POSTAGE
NECESSARY
IF MAILED
IN THE
UNITED STATES

If offer card is missing write to: Silhouette Reader Service, 3010 Walden Ave., P.O. Box 1867, Buffalo, NY 14240-1867 went downstairs to confer with his buddies in the computer center.

Finally, Harry leaned back in his chair and tapped his stub of a pencil on his notes. "Well, I guess that's it. We've covered the same ground three times now, with nothing new to add to our list of key words or numbers."

"I wish I could remember more."

"You've given us and the computer wizards downstairs enough to keep us busy the rest of the night. If we don't break whatever code these cards carried, it won't be from lack of trying."

Feeling oddly deflated now that she'd finished her task, Sheryl swept the empty conference room with a glance. After only two days, the litter of phones and maps and computerized printouts seemed as familiar to her as her own living room.

"Do you need me for anything else?"

Harry's gaze drifted over her face for a moment. "If...when...we make sense of what you've told us, I'll give you a call. We might need you to verify some detail. In the meantime, I want you to stay alert...and let me know if any more postcards show up, of course."

"Of course."

"Preferably *before* you return them to sender."

"We'll try to be less efficient," she said gravely.

A small silence gripped them, as though neither wanted to make the next move. Then Harry pushed back his chair.

"I know I've put you through the wringer for the past couple of days. I appreciate the information you've provided, Sheryl. I'll make sure the postmaster knows how much."

He held out his hand. Hers slipped into it with a warm shock that disturbed her almost as much as the realization that she might not see him again after today.

"You'll let me know when…if…Inga gets out of custody, so I can send Button back to her?"

"I will, although if I have my way, that won't occur for seven to ten years, minimum."

"Well…" She tugged her hand free of his.

"I'll walk you down to your car."

Their footsteps echoed in the tiled corridor. Side by side, they waited for the elevator.

Why couldn't he just let her go? Harry wondered. Just let her walk away? There wasn't any need to prolong the contact. He'd gotten what he wanted out of her.

No, his mind mocked, not quite all he wanted.

With every breath he drew in he caught her scent and knew he wanted more from this woman. A lot more. He'd spent most of last night thinking about the feel of her mouth under his, tasting again her wine-flavored kiss. And most of today trying not to notice how her tawny hair curled at her temples, or the way her red silk blouse showed off her golden skin.

If Harry hadn't witnessed the scene in her doorway last night, he might have come back to Albuquerque after he cornered his quarry and given this Brian character a run for his money. But the aching tenderness in Sheryl's face when she'd bid her almost-fiancé good-night had killed that half-formed idea before it really took root. His predatory instincts might allow him to challenge another male for a woman's interest, but he wouldn't loose those instincts on one so obviously in love with another man...as much as he burned to.

The elevator swooshed open, then carried them downward in a smooth, silent descent. With a smile and a nod to the guard manning the security post, Harry escorted Sheryl to the underground parking garage.

Her little Camry sat waiting in the numbered slot Harry had arranged for her. She deactivated the newly installed alarm with the remote device, unlocked the door and tossed her purse inside. Then she unclipped her temporary badge and handed it to him.

"I guess I won't need this anymore."

His hand fisted over the plastic badge. "Thanks again, Sheryl. You've given me more to work with than I've had in almost a year."

"You're welcome."

Let her go! Dammit, he had to let her go! Deliberately, he stepped back.

"I'll keep you posted on what happens," he said again, more briskly this time. "And what to do with Button."

She took the hint and slid into the car. "Thanks."

Harry closed the door for her and stood in a faint haze of exhaust while Sheryl backed out of the slot and drove up the exit ramp. Turning on one heel, he returned to the conference room.

He made a quick call to the task force's contact in the APD to confirm that they'd keep an eye on the Monzano Street station and Miss Hancock's apartment for the next few days. Then he got back to the glamorous, adventurous work of a U.S. marshal.

"All right, Ev, let me have some of those computer printouts."

* * *

They worked until well after midnight. Wire tight from the combination of long hours and a mounting frustration over his inability to break the damned code of the postcards, Harry drove to his motel just off of I-40.

The door slammed shut behind him. The chain latch rattled into place. The puny little chain and flimsy door lock wouldn't keep out a determined ten-year-old, but the .357 Magnum Harry slid out of its holster and laid on the nightstand beside his bed provided adequate backup security.

Enough light streamed in through curtains the maid had left open to show him the switches on the wall. He flicked them on, flooding the overdone South-western decor with light. The garish orange-and-red bedspread leaped out at him. Decorated with bleached cattle skulls, tall saguaro cacti and stick figures that some New York designer probably intended as Kachinas, it was almost as bad as the cheap prints on the wall. The room was clean, however, which was all Harry required.

He closed the curtains and headed for the shower, stripping as he went. Naked, he leaned back against the smooth, slick tiles and let the tepid water sluice over him.

They were close. So damned close. He and Ev had winnowed the thousands of possible combinations of letters and numbers on the postcards down to a hundred or so that made sense. Tomorrow, they'd go over those again, looking for some tie to the local area, some key to a date, a time, a set of coordinates.

They'd worked hard today. Tomorrow, they'd work even harder. The drop had to happen soon. If Paul

Gunderson had passed the stuff through Prague four days ago and was triangulating the shipment through Spain and Rio, he had to bring it into the States any day now. Any hour.

Frustration coiled like a living thing in Harry's gut. Prague. Pamploma. Rio. At last he had a track on the bastard. He wouldn't let him slip through his fingers this time.

He lifted his face to the water, willing himself to relax. He needed to clear his mind, so he could start fresh in a few hours. He needed sleep.

Not that there was much chance of that, he acknowledged, twisting the water off. If last night was any indication, he'd spend half of tonight trying not to think of Sheryl Hancock naked and heavy eyed with pleasure from his kisses, the other half thoroughly enjoying the image.

He slung a towel around his neck and padded into the bedroom. Just as well she had such an amazing memory, he thought grimly. Two days in her company had done enough damage to his concentration. Tomorrow, at least, he wouldn't have to battle the distraction of her smile and her long, endless legs.

Harry almost succeeded in putting both out of his mind. After a short night and a quick breakfast of coffee and *huevos rancheros* in the motel's restaurant, he entered the conference room just after six. Ev arrived at six-thirty, Fay a little later. They slogged through the remaining reports for a couple of hours and had just been joined by an FBI agent with a reputation as an expert in codes and signals when one of the phones rang.

Impatiently, Harry snatched it up. "MacMillan."

"This is Officer Lawrence with the APD. I have a note here to keep you advised of any unusual activity at the Monzano Street post office."

He went still. "Yes?"

"A call came into 911 a few minutes ago, requesting an ambulance at that location."

Ev's desultory conversation with the FBI agent faded into the background. Harry gripped the phone, his eyes fixed on an aeronautical map tacked to the far wall.

"For what reason?"

"I didn't get the whole story. Only that they needed an ambulance to transport a white female to the hospital immediately."

"Did you get a name?"

"No, but I understand it's one of the employees."

His pulse stopped, restarted with a sharp, agonizing kick. "What hospital?"

"University Hospital at UNM."

In one fluid motion, Harry slammed the phone down, shoved back his chair and grabbed his jacket. Throwing a terse explanation over his shoulder to the others, he raced out of the conference room.

Chapter 8

Sheryl called in to work early the next morning to let her supervisor know that Harry had released her from the special task force. Things were quiet for a Friday, Pat Martinez informed her. The temp had her counter station covered, but they could use her help throwing mail on the second shift.

Feeling an unaccountable lack of enthusiasm for a return to her everyday routine, Sheryl decided to run a few errands on her way in. She indulged Button with a supply of doggie treats and herself with a new novel by her favorite romance author before pulling into the parking lot of the Monzano Street station.

The moment she walked through the rear door and headed for the time clock, Sheryl got the immediate impression that things were anything but quiet. Tension hung over the back room, as thick and as heavy as a cloud. The mail carriers who hadn't already started their daily runs crowded around the station supervisor's desk. In the center of the throng, Pat paced back and forth with a phone glued to her ear, her face grave as she spoke to the person on the other end. Peggy, who should have been on the front counter with Elise, was hunched on a corner of Pat's desk. Even Buck Aguilar stood with arms folded and worried lines carved into his usually impassive face.

Sheryl punched in and wove her way through the work stations toward the group clustered around Pat. The station manager's worried voice carried clearly in the silence that gripped her audience.

"Yes, yes, I know. I'll try to reach her again. Just keep us posted, okay?"

The receiver clattered into its cradle.

"They don't know anything yet," she announced to the assembled crowd. "Brian's going to call us as soon as he gets word."

"Brian?" Sheryl nudged her way to the front. "What's Brian going to call about?"

"Sheryl!" Pat sprang up, relief and worry battling on her face. "I've been trying to reach you since right after you called to tell me you were coming in this morning."

"Why? What's going on?"

"Elise fell and went into labor."

"Oh, no!" A tight fist squeezed Sheryl's heart. "Is she okay? And the baby?"

"We don't know. They took her to the hospital by ambulance an hour ago. She was frantic that we get hold of you, since you're her labor coach. I tried your house, then Brian's office, thinking he might know where you were. He didn't, but he went to University Hospital to stay with Elise until we found you.''

''Get hold of Brian at the hospital,'' Sheryl called, already on the run. ''Tell him I'll be there in fifteen minutes.''

It took her a frustrating, anxious half hour.

She sped down Juan Tabo and swung onto Lomas quickly enough, only to find both westbound lanes blocked by orange barrels. A long line of earthmovers rumbled by, digging up big chunks of concrete. Dust flew everywhere, and Sheryl's anxiety mounted by the second as she waited for the last of them to pass. Even with one lane open each way, traffic crawled at a stop-and-go, five-mile-an-hour pace.

Cursing under her breath, she turned off at the next side street and cut through a sprawl of residential neighborhoods. The Camry's new tires squealed as she slowed to a rolling stop at the stop signs dotting every block, then tore across the intersections. By the time the distinctive dun-colored adobe architecture of the University of New Mexico came into view, she trembled with barely controlled panic.

Elise wasn't due for another two weeks...if then. The baby's sonogram had showed it slightly under-sized, and the obstetrician had revised the due date twice already. With the stress of her divorce coming right on top of the discovery that she was pregnant, Elise hadn't been vague about the possible date of the baby's conception. She and Rick had split up and rec-onciled twice before finally calling it quits. She could have gotten pregnant during either one of those brief, tempestuous reconciliations.

And Pat had said that Elise had fallen! Every time Sheryl thought of the hard, uncarpeted tile floors at the post office, the giant fist wrapped a little tighter around her heart. Offering up a steady litany of prayers for Elise and her baby, she squealed into the University Hospital parking lot, slammed out of the Camry, and ran for the multistory brown-stucco building.

Since she and Elise had toured the facility as part of their prenatal orientation, she didn't need to consult the directory or ask directions to the birthing rooms. The moment the elevator hummed to a stop on the third floor, she bolted out and ran for the nurses' station in the labor and delivery wing.

"Which room is Mrs. Hart in? Is she all right? I'm her birthing partner—I need to be with her."

A stubby woman in flowered scrubs held up a hand. "Whoa. Slow down and catch your breath. Mrs. Hart's had a rough time, but the hemorrhaging stopped before she went into hard labor."

"Hemorrhaging! Oh, my God!"

"She's okay, really. Last time I checked, she was about to deliver."

"Which room is she in?"

The nurse hesitated. "You'll have to scrub before you can go in, but I'm not sure it's necessary at this point. Her husband's with her. From what I saw a little while ago, he's filling in pretty well as coach."

Sheryl's brows shot up. "Rick's here?"

"I thought he said his name was Brian."

Belatedly, Sheryl remembered the hospital rule restricting attendance in the birthing room during delivery to family members and/or designated coaches.

"We, er, call him 'Rick' for short. Look, I won't burst in, I promise, but I need to be with Elise. Where can I scrub?"

"I'll show you."

A few moments later, a gowned-and-masked Sheryl entered the birthing sanctuary. Doors on either side of the long corridor revealed rooms made homelike by reclining chairs, plants, pictures and low tables littered with magazines. Most of the doors stood open. Two were shut, including Elise's. Mindful of the nurse's injunction, she approached it quietly.

An anguished moan from inside the room raised the hairs on the back of her neck. She nudged the door open an inch or two, and stopped in her tracks.

A trio of medical specialists stood at the foot of the bed, poised to receive the baby. Brian leaned over a groaning, grunting Elise. At least, she thought it was Brian. He was gowned and masked and wearing a surgical cap to keep his auburn hair out of his eyes, and she barely recognized him. She recognized his voice, though, as hoarse and ragged as it was.

"You're doing great. One more push, Elise. One more push."

Sweat glistened on his forehead. His right hand clenched the laboring woman's. With his left, he smoothed her damp hair back from her forehead.

"Breathe with me, then push!"

"I…can't."

"Yes, you can."

"The baby's crowning," the doctor said from the bottom of the bed. "We need a good push here, Mom."

"Breathe, Elise." The command came out in a desperate squeak. Brian swallowed and tried again. "Breathe, then push. Puff. Puff. Puff."

"Puff. Puf...arrrgh!" Elise lifted half off the mattress, then came down with a grunt. Limp and panting, she snarled out a fervent litany.

"Damn Rick! Damn all men! Damn every male who ever learned how to work a zipper!"

Startled, Brian drew back. Elise grabbed the front of his gown and dragged him down to her level.

"Not you! Oh, God, not you! Don't... Don't leave me, Brian. Please, don't leave me."

"I won't, I promise. Now push."

Sheryl peered through the crack in the door, her heart in her throat. After sharing the ups and downs of her friend's divorce and training with her for just this moment, she longed to rush into the room, shove Brian aside and take Elise's hand to help her through the next stage of her ordeal. But her friend's urgent plea and Brian's reply kept her rooted in place. The two of them had bonded. The drama of the baby's imminent birth had forged a link between them that Sheryl couldn't bring herself to break or even intrude on.

"The head's clear," the doctor announced calmly. "Relax a moment, Mom, then we'll work the shoulders. You're doing great. Ready? Okay, here we go."

Sheryl felt her own stomach contract painfully as Elise grunted, then gave a long, rolling moan.

"We've got him."

One of the nurses smiled at the two anxious watchers. "He's a handsome little thing! The spitting image of his dad."

Brian started, then grinned behind his mask. With a whoop of sheer exhilaration, he bent and planted a kiss on Elise's forehead.

She used her death grip on the front of his hospital gown to drag him down even farther. Awkwardly, Brian took her into his arms. She clung to him, sobbing with relief and joy. A second later, the baby gave a lusty wail.

"Don't relax yet," the doctor instructed when Elise collapsed back on the bed, wiped out from her ordeal. "We've still got some work to do here."

Elated, relieved and hugely disappointed that she hadn't participated in the intense drama except as an observer, Sheryl watched Brian smooth back Elise's hair once more. A fierce tenderness came over the part of his face that showed above the mask. The sheer intensity of his expression took Sheryl by surprise. Swiftly, she thought back through the months she and Brian had been dating. She couldn't ever remember seeing him display such raw, naked emotion.

The realization stunned her and added another layer to the wrenching turmoil that had plagued her for two nights now. If she'd had any doubts about the decision she'd made in the dark hours just before dawn this morning, she only needed to look at his face to know it was the right one.

She loved Brian, but she wasn't *in* love with him. Nor, apparently, was he in love with her. Never once had she roused that kind of intense emotion in him. Never had she caused such a display of fierce protectiveness.

Slowly, Sheryl let the door whisper shut and backed away...or tried to. A solid wall of unyielding flesh blocked her way. Turning, she found herself chest to chest with Marshal MacMillan.

"Harry!" She tugged off her face mask. "What are you doing here?"

"I got word that EMS was transporting a female employee from the Monzano Street post office to the hospital. I thought..."

A small muscle worked on one side of his jaw. He paused, then finished in a voice that sounded like glass grinding.

"I thought it might be you."

"Oh, no! Did you think the slasher had come back?"

"Among other things," he admitted, taking Sheryl's elbow to move her to one side as an orderly trundled by with a cart. "By the time EMS verified the patient's identity, I was already in the parking lot, so I came up to see what the problem was."

"Did they tell you? My friend Elise fell and went into labor."

He nodded. "They also told me you were on the way down here, so I waited. How's she doing?"

Sheryl relaxed against the hallway wall, strangely comforted by Harry's presence. "Okay, I think. She and the baby both."

"Good! The nurse said her husband was in with

her. From the glimpse I had over your shoulder a moment ago, he's certainly a proud papa.''

''Well, there's a little mix-up about that. Elise is divorced. I was supposed to act as her coach, but I didn't get here in time, so Brian filled in for me.''

''Brian?'' A puzzled frown flitted across his face. ''That was your Brian in there?''

So Harry had seen it, too. The raw emotion. The special bond Brian had forged with Elise.

Sheryl fumbled for an answer other than the one her aching heart supplied. No, he wasn't her Brian. Not any more. Maybe he never had been. But until she talked to him, she wouldn't discuss the matter with anyone else.

Thankfully, one of the nurses walked out of Elise's room at that moment and spared her the necessity of a reply. Sheryl sprang away from the wall and hurried toward her.

''Is everything okay? How are Elise and the baby?''

''Mother and son are both fine,'' she answered with a smile. ''And Dad's so proud, he's about to pop. Give them another few minutes to finish cleaning up, then you can go in.''

Their voices must have carried to the occupants of the birthing room, because Brian came charging out a second later. His dark-red hair stuck straight up in spikes. The hospital gown had twisted around his waist. Huge, wet patches darkened his underarms and arrowed down his chest. Sheryl had never seen him looking so ruffled...or so excited.

''Sher! You missed it!'' He tore off his mask. ''It

was so fantastic! Elise is wonderful. And the baby, he's…he's wonderful!''

"Yes, I…''

"Look, can you call the school? Elise is worried about the boys. Tell them I'll pick them up this afternoon and bring them down to see their new brother.''

"Sure, I—''

"Thanks! I have to go back in. The doc says it'll be a few minutes yet before you can come in. You, too…''

He blinked owlishly, as if recognizing for the first time the man who stood silently behind Sheryl. If Brian wondered why Harry had turned up at the hospital, he was too distracted to ask about it now.

"You, too, MacMillan.''

He turned away to reenter the birthing room, then spun back. "You're never going to believe it, Sher! He's got my hair. Elise's is sort of sorrel, but this little guy has a cap of dark red fuzz.'' He grinned idiotically. "Just like mine.''

"Brian!'' Sheryl caught him just before he disappeared. "Do you want me to call your office? If you're going to pick the boys up from school, should I tell your secretary to reschedule your afternoon appointments?''

He flapped a hand. "Whatever.''

The door whirred shut behind him.

"Well, well,'' Harry murmured in the small, ensuing silence. "Is that the same man who had to schedule everything, even his meetings with his almost-fiancée?''

"No," Sheryl answered with a sigh. "It isn't."

Turning, she caught a speculative gleam in the marshal's warm brown eyes. Unwilling to discuss her relationship with Brian until she'd had time to talk to him, she deliberately changed the subject.

"If you want to go in and see Elise and the baby, I'll show you where to find a gown and mask."

"I'd better pass. They don't need a stranger hovering over them right now."

"No, I guess not."

She hesitated, torn between the need to join Elise and a sudden, surging reluctance to say goodbye to Harry for the second time in as many days.

"Thanks for coming down to check on me, even if it wasn't me who needed checking."

"You're welcome."

It took some effort, but she summoned a smile. "Maybe I'll see you around."

The gleam she'd caught in his eyes a moment ago returned, deeper, more intense, like the glint of new-struck gold.

"Maybe you will."

Sheryl spent the rest of the morning and most of the afternoon at the hospital. Brian left after lunch, promising to be back within an hour with Elise's other two boys. His jubilation had subsided in the aftermath of the birth, but his eyes still lit with wonder whenever he caught a glimpse of the baby.

Lazy and at peace in the stillness of the afternoon, Elise cradled her son in her arms and smiled at the woman perched on the edge of her bed. The friendship that had stretched across years of shared work and a variety of family crises, big and small, co-cooned them.

"I'm sorry you missed your tour of duty as birthing partner, Sher. I could have used your moral support. The others were easy, but I was a little scared with this one after my fall."

"We were all scared."

Elise brushed a finger over the baby's dark-russet down. "I was going to call him Terence, after my grandfather, but I think I'll name him Brian, instead. Brian Hart. How does that sound to you, little one?"

It must have sounded pretty good, as the baby pursed its tiny lips a few times, scrunched its wrinkled face, then settled once more into sleep.

"I don't know what I would have done without Brian," Elise murmured. "He's...wonderful."

Sheryl found a smile. "He says the same thing about you and little Red here."

Her friend's gaze lifted. "I know I've told you this before, but you're so lucky to have him. There aren't many like him around."

"No, there aren't."

Sheryl's smile felt distinctly ragged about the edges. She had to talk to Brian. Soon. This burden of confusion and guilt and regret was getting too heavy to lug around much longer.

As it turned out, she didn't have to talk to Brian. He talked to her.

They met at the hospital later that evening. Elise's room overflowed with flowers and friends from the post office. Murmurs of laughter filled the small room as Peggy and Pat and even Buck Aguilar cooed and showered the new arrival with rattles and blankets and an infant-sized postal service uniform.

Deciding to give the others time and space to admire Baby Brian, Sheryl slipped out and went in search of a vending machine. A cool diet soda fizzed in her hand as she paused by a window, staring out at the golden haze of the sunset.

"Sher?"

She turned and smiled a welcome at Brian. He looked very different from the man who'd rushed out of Elise's room this morning, his face drenched with sweat and his eyes alive with exultation. Tonight, he wore what Sheryl always teasingly called his real-estate-agent's uniform—a lightweight blue seersucker jacket, white shirt, navy slacks. His conservative red tie was neatly knotted.

Leaning against the window alcove, Sheryl offered him a sip of her drink. He declined. His gaze, like hers, drifted to the glorious sunset.

"Have you been in to see Elise and the baby yet?" she asked after a moment.

He nodded. "For a few minutes. I could barely squeeze in the room."

"Did she tell you what she'd decided to name him?"

"Yes."

The single word carried such quiet, glowing pride that Sheryl's heart contracted. God, she hated to hurt this man! They'd shared so many hours, so many dreams. Caught up in her own swamping guilt and regret, she almost missed his next comment.

"I need to talk to you, Sher. I don't know if this is the right time... I don't know if there is a right time." He raked a hand through his hair. "But this morning, when I saw what Elise went through, when I was there with her, I realized what marriage is really about."

Sheryl wanted to weep. She set her drink on the window ledge and took his hands in hers.

"Oh, Brian, I..."

He gripped her fingers. "Let me say this."

"But..."

"Please!"

Miserable beyond words, she nodded.

He took a deep breath and plunged ahead. "Marriage means...should mean...sharing everything. Giving everything. Joining together and, if it's in the picture, holding on to each other at moments like the one that happened this morning."

"I know."

He swallowed, gripping her hands so tightly Sheryl thought her bones would crack. "It shouldn't be something comfortable, something easy and familiar or something we just drift into because it's the next step."

"What?"

His words were so unexpected she was sure she hadn't heard him right.

"Oh, God, Sher, I'm sorry. This hurts so much."

"What does?"

"When I was with Elise this morning, I realized that...that I love you. I'll always love you. But..."

That small "but" rang like a gong in her ears. In growing incredulity, Sheryl stared up at him.

"But what?"

"But maybe... Maybe I don't love you enough," he finished, his eyes anguished. "Maybe not the way a man who might someday stand beside you and hold your hand while you give birth to his children should. I think... I think maybe we shouldn't see each other for a while. Until I sort through this awful confusion, anyway."

Sheryl wouldn't have been human if she'd hadn't experienced a spurt of genuine hurt before her rush of relief. After all, the man she'd spent the better part of the past year with had just dumped her. But she cared for him too much to let him shoulder the entire burden of guilt.

"I love you, too, Brian. I always will. But..."

He went still. "But?"

She gave him a weak, watery smile. "But not in the way a woman who might someday cling to your hand while she gave birth to your children should."

Chapter 9

Sheryl arrived home well after nine that night. Wrung out from the long, traumatic day and her painful discussion with Brian, she dropped her uniform in the basket of dirty clothes that Button, thankfully, had left unmolested.

She thought about crawling into bed. A good cry might shake the awful, empty feeling that had dogged her since she woke up this morning. Arriving at the hospital too late to share the miracle of birth with Elise after all those months of anticipation had only added to her hollowness. The subsequent breakup with Brian had taken that lost feeling to a new low.

As if those disturbing events weren't enough, another lowering realization had hit her as she'd driven home through the dark night. Just twenty-four hours off the task force, and she missed Harry MacMillan as much as she missed her ex-almost.

eyes acted like a balm to her spirits, pulling her out of her depression like a fast-climbing roller coaster.

"What made you think I needed cheering up?" she asked curiously.

"Let's just say my cop's instincts were working overtime again. I also want to go over the info you gave us on the Rio card one more time. Even the FBI's so-called expert can't crack the damned code."

Ahhh. Now the real reason for his visit was out. She didn't mind. Working a few hours with Harry would do her more good than sobbing while Patrick Swayze tried to cross time and space to be with Demi Moore. Or lying in bed, thinking about Brian.

"Have a seat," the marshal instructed, heading for the kitchen. "I think I remember where everything is."

Button trailed at his heels, having abandoned all pride in anticipation of a late-night treat. Sheryl settled into one of the rattan-backed dining-room chairs as instructed and hooked her bare feet on the bottom rung. With a little advance notice of this visit, she might have traded her cutoffs and T-shirt for something more presentable. She might even have pulled a brush through her unruly hair. As it was, Harry would just have to put up with a face scrubbed clean of all makeup and a tumble of loose curls spilling over her shoulders.

He didn't seem to mind her casual attire when he emerged a moment later with plates, napkins and a wineglass filled with the last of the leftover Chablis. In fact, his eyes gleamed appreciatively as his gaze drifted over her.

"I like the roadrunners."

A hint of a flush rose in Sheryl's cheeks. She definitely should have changed...or at least put on a bra under the thin T-shirt.

"We have a lot of them out here," she said primly, then tried to divert his attention from the covey of birds darting across her chest. "Why do you want to go over the Rio card again?"

The glint left his eyes, and his jaw took on a hard angle that Sheryl was coming to recognize.

"I'm missing something. It's probably so simple it's staring me right in the face, but I'll be damned if I can see it."

"Maybe we'll see it tonight."

"I hope so. My gut tells me we're running out of time."

He passed her the wine and plates, then dug in his jacket pocket for a dew-streaked can of beer. The momentary tightness around his mouth eased as he popped the top and hefted the can in the air.

"Shall we toast the baby?"

"Sounds good to me."

Smiling, Sheryl chinked her wineglass against the can. She sipped slowly, her eyes on the strong column of Harry's throat as he satisfied his thirst. For the first time that day, she felt herself relax. Really relax. As much as she could in Harry's presence.

Sure enough, she enjoyed her sense of ease for ten, perhaps twenty, seconds. Then he set his beer on the table, brushed a finger across his mustache and dropped a casual bomb.

"So did you give Brian his walking papers?"

Sheryl choked. Her wineglass hit the whitewashed oak tabletop with more force than she'd intended. While she fought to clear her throat, Harry calmly served up the pizza.

"Well?"

"No, I didn't give Brian his walking papers! Not that it's any of your business."

"Why not?"

She glared at him across the pizza carton. Getting dumped by Brian was one thing. Telling Harry about it was something else again.

"What makes you think I would even want to?"

He leaned back in his chair, his expression gentle. As gentle as someone with his rugged features could manage, anyway.

"I was there, Sheryl. I saw him with Elise. I also saw your face when he went dashing back into her room."

"Oh."

A small silence spun out between them, broken only by the noisy, snuffling slurps coming from the kitchen. Button, at least, was enjoying his pizza.

Sheryl chipped at the crust with a short, polished nail. She wanted...needed...to talk to someone. Normally, she would have shared her troubled thoughts with Elise. She couldn't burden her friend with this particular problem right now, though, any more than she could call her own mother in Las Cruces to talk about it. Joan Hancock adored Brian, and had told her daughter several thousand times that she'd better latch onto him. Men that reliable, that steady, didn't grow in potato patches.

Maybe... Maybe Harry was just the confidant Sheryl needed. He knew her situation well enough to murmur sympathetically between slices of pineapple and Canadian bacon, but not so well that he'd burden her with unsolicited advice, as her mother assuredly would.

She stole a glance at him from beneath her lashes. Legs stretched, ankles crossed, he lounged in his chair. He looked so friendly, so relaxed that she couldn't quite believe this was the same man she'd almost taken a bite out of on Inga Gunderson's front porch. His air of easy companionship invited her confidence.

"Brian and I had a long talk tonight in the hospital waiting room," she said slowly. "I didn't give him his walking papers, as you put it. I, uh, didn't get the chance. He gave me mine."

A slice of pizza halted halfway to Harry's mouth. "What?"

"He said that his time with Elise this morning changed every thought, every misconception, he'd ever formed about marriage." She nudged a chunk of pineapple with the tip of her nail. "And about love. It shouldn't be easy, or comfortable, or something we just sort of drift into."

Snorting in derision, the marshal dropped his pizza onto his plate. "No kidding! He's just coming to that brilliant conclusion?"

Sheryl couldn't help smiling at the utter disgust in his voice. Harry MacMillan wouldn't drift into anything. He'd charge in, guns blazing...figuratively, she hoped!

"Don't come down on Brian so hard," she said ruefully. "It took me a while to figure it out, too."

Across the table, golden brown eyes narrowed suddenly. "Are you saying that's all this guy was to you? Someone easy and comfortable?"

"Well…"

The single, hesitant syllable curled Harry's hands into fists. At that moment he would have taken great pleasure in shoving the absent real-estate-agent's face not just into the hallway wall but through it. Hell! It didn't take a Sherlock Holmes, much less a U.S. marshal, to figure out that the jerk hadn't fully committed to Sheryl. If he'd wanted her, really wanted her, he wouldn't have moved so slowly or made any damned appointments! He would've staked his claim with a ring, or at least with a more definitive arrangement than their sort-of engagement.

But after seeing them in each other's arms the other night, Harry had assumed…had thought…

What?

That Sheryl loved the guy? That she wanted Brian Mitchell more than he showed signs of wanting her?

The idea that she might be hurting was what had brought Harry to her apartment tonight. That and the sudden lost look in her eyes when the idiot had rushed back into her friend's hospital room and left her standing there. That look had stayed with Harry all afternoon, until he'd startled Ev and Fay and the FBI expert still struggling with the key words from the postcards by calling it a night. Driven by an urge he hadn't let himself think about, he'd stopped at a pizzeria just a few blocks from Sheryl's apartment and come to comfort her.

He now recognized that urge for what it was. Two parts sympathy for someone struggling with an unraveling relationship: anyone who'd gone through a divorce could relate to that hurt. One part concern for the woman he'd worked with for two days now and had come to like and respect. And one part...

One part pure, unadulterated male lust.

Harry could admit it now. When she'd opened the door to him in those short shorts and figure-hugging T-shirt, a hot spot had ignited in his gut. He knew damned well that the slow burning had nothing to do with any desire to comfort a friend or to grill a team member yet again about the postcards.

It had taken everything he had to return her greeting and nonchalantly set about feeding her and the mutt. He couldn't come anywhere close to nonchalant now, though. Any more than he could keep his gaze from dipping to the thrust of her breasts under the thin layer of pink as she rose and shoved her hands into her back pockets.

"I don't know why I didn't see it sooner, Harry." She paced the open space between the dining and living rooms. "I loved Brian. I still do. But I wasn't *in* love with him. I guess I let myself be seduced by the comfortable routine he represented."

Thoroughly distracted by the sight of those long, tanned legs and bare toes tipped with pink nail polish, Harry forgot his self-assigned role of friend and listener.

"Comfortable routine?" He snorted again. "The man has a helluva seduction technique."

"Hey, it worked for me."

The way she kept springing to Brian's defense was starting to really irritate Harry. Almost as much as her admission that she still loved the jerk.

"Right," he drawled. "That's why you're pacing the floor and ole Bry's off on his own somewhere, pondering the meaning of life and love."

She turned, surprise and indignation sending twin flags of color into her cheeks. "Whose side are you on, anyway?"

"Yours, sweetheart."

He rose, barely noticing the way the endearment slipped out. Three strides took him to where she stood, all stiff and bristly.

"You deserve better than routine, Sheryl. You deserve a dizzy, breathless, thoroughly exhausting seduction that shakes you right out of predictable and puts you down somewhere on the other side of passion."

"Is... Is that right?"

"That's right." He stroked a knuckle down her smooth, golden cheek. "You deserve kisses that wind you up so tight it takes all night to unwind."

Harry could have fallen into the wide green eyes that stared up at him and never found his way out. Her lips opened, closed, opened again. A slow flush stole into her cheeks.

"Yes," she whispered at last. "I do."

Her breasts rose and fell under their pink covering.

A pulse pounded at the base of her throat. Slowly, so slowly, her arms lifted and slid around his neck.

"Kiss me, Harry."

He kissed her.

He didn't think twice about it. Didn't listen to any of the alarms that started pinging the instant her arms looped around his neck. Didn't even hear them.

He'd hold her for a moment only, he swore fiercely. Kiss her just once more. Show her that there was life after Brian. That life *with* Brian hadn't come close to living at all. Then his mouth came down on hers, and Sheryl showed him a few things, instead.

That her taste had lingered in his mind for two days. But not this sweet. Or this wild. Or this hot.

That her lips were softer, firmer, more seductive than he remembered.

That her body matched his perfectly. Tall enough that he didn't have to bend double to reach her. Small enough to fit into the cradle of his thighs.

At the contact, he went instantly, achingly, hard. He jerked his head up, knowing that one more breath, one more press of her breasts against his chest, would drive him to something she couldn't be ready for. Not this soon after Brian.

Or maybe she could.

Her eyes opened at his abrupt movement. Harry saw himself in the dark pupils. Saw something else, as well. The passion he'd taunted her about. It shimmered in the green irises. Showed in her heavy eyelids. Sounded in the short, choppy rush of her breath.

This time, she didn't have to ask for his kiss. This

time, he gave it, and took everything she offered in return.

By the time she dragged her mouth away, gasping, every muscle in Harry's body strained with the need to press her down on the nearest horizontal surface. With an effort that popped beads of sweat out on his forehead, he loosened his arms enough for her to draw back.

"Harry, I..."

She stopped, swiped her tongue along her lower lip. The burning need in Harry's gut needled into white, hot fingers of fire.

"You what, sweetheart?"

"I want to wind up tight," she whispered, her eyes holding his. "And take all night to unwind."

Few saints would fail to respond to that invitation, and Harry had no illusions that anyone would ever nominate him for canonization. Still, he forced himself to move slowly, giving her time to pull back at any move, any touch.

He lifted a hand to her throat and stroked the smooth skin under her chin. "I think we can manage a little winding and a lot of unwinding. If you're sure?"

A wobbly smile tugged at lips still rosy from his kiss. "Who's being cautious and careful now? What happened to breathless and dizzy and thoroughly exhausting?"

Grinning, he slid his arm under the backs of the thighs that had been driving him insane for the past half hour. Sweeping her into a tight hold, he headed for the hall.

"Breathless and dizzy coming right up, ma'am. Thoroughly exhausting to follow."

Sheryl barely heard Button's startled yip as Harry swept past with her in his arms. She didn't think about the idiocy of what she'd just asked this man to do. Tomorrow, she'd regret it. Maybe later tonight, when Harry left, as he inevitably would.

At this moment, she wanted only to end the swirling confusion he'd thrown her into the first moment he'd appeared in her life. To get past the pain of her break with Brian. To do something insane, something unplanned and unscheduled and definitely unroutine.

She buried her face in the warm skin of his neck. When he crossed the threshold to her bedroom, he twisted at the waist. With one booted heel, he kicked the door shut behind him. Sharp, annoyed yips rose from the other side.

"I might not hesitate at a little bribery," he told her, his voice a rumble in her ear, "but I draw the line at voyeurism."

"He'll bark all night," Sheryl warned, lifting her head. "Or however long it takes to unwind."

"Let him." His mustache lifted in a wicked grin. "And in case there's any doubt, it's going to take a long time. A very long time."

The husky promise sent ripples of excitement over every inch of her skin. The way he lowered her, sliding her body down his, turned those ripples into a near tidal wave. Her T-shirt snagged on his buttons. It lifted, baring her midriff. Cooled air raised goose bumps above her belly button. Harry's hard, driving kiss raised goose bumps below.

Her shirt hit the floor sometime later. His jeans and boots followed. In a tangle of arms and legs, they tumbled onto the downy black-and-white blanket that covered her bed. Gasping, Sheryl let Harry work the same magic on her breasts that he'd worked on her mouth. His soft, silky mustache teased. His fingers stroked. His tongue tasted. His teeth took her from breathless to moaning to only a kiss or two away from spinning out of control.

Sheryl wasn't exactly a passive participant in her unplanned, unroutine seduction. Her hands roamed as eagerly as his. Her tongue explored. Her body slicked and twisted and pressed everywhere it met his. She was as wet and hot and eager as he was when he finally groaned and dragged her arms down.

"Wait, sweetheart. Wait! Let me get something to protect you."

He rolled off her. Wearing only low-slung briefs and the shirt she'd tugged halfway down his back, he padded across the room to his jeans.

Sheryl flung an arm up over her head, almost as dizzy and befuddled as he'd predicted. Harry's posterior view didn't exactly unfuddle her. Lord, he was magnificent! All long, lean lines. Bronzed muscles. Tight, trim buttocks.

When he scooped up his jeans and turned, she had to admit that his front view wasn't too shabby, either. Her heart hammered as he dug out his wallet and rifled through it with an impatience that fanned the small fires he'd lit under her skin. A moment later, several packages of condoms fell onto the blanket.

Sheryl eyed the abundant supply with a raised

brow. Harry caught her look and his mustache tipped into another wicked grin.

"U.S. marshals always come prepared for extended field operations."

"So I see."

Still grinning, he sheathed himself and rejoined her on the bed. He settled between her legs smoothly, as if she were made to receive him. His weight pressed her into the blanket. With both hands, he smoothed her hair back and planted little kisses on her neck.

"I don't want to give you the wrong impression," he murmured against her throat. "Dedicated law enforcement types have all kinds of uses for those little packages."

Torn between curiosity and a wild, blazing need to arch her hips into his, Sheryl could only huff a question into his ear.

"Like…what?"

"Later," he growled, nipping the cords of her neck. "I'll tell you later."

Would they have a later? The brief thought cut through her searing, sensual haze. Then his hand found her core and there was only now. Only Harry. Only the incredible pleasure he gave her.

The pleasure spiraled, spinning tighter and tighter with each kiss, each stroke of his hand and his body. When Sheryl was sure she couldn't stand the whirling sensations a moment longer without shattering, she wrapped her legs around his and arched her hips to receive him. It might have been mere moments or a lifetime later that she exploded in a blaze of white light.

Another forever followed, then Harry thrust into her a final time. Rigid, straining, joined with her at mouth and chest and hip, he filled her body. Only later did she realize that he'd filled the newly empty place in her heart, as well.

The realization came to her as she hovered between boneless satiation and an exhausted doze. Her head cradled on Harry's shoulder, she remembered sleepily that they hadn't gotten around to the postcards. They'd get to them tomorrow, she thought, breathing in the musky scent of their lovemaking.

Tomorrow came crashing down on them far sooner than Sheryl had anticipated. She was sunk in a deep doze, her head still cradled on a warm shoulder, when the sound of a thump and a startled, pain-filled yelp pierced her somnolent semiconsciousness.

Instantly, Harry spun off the bed. Sheryl's head hit the mattress with a thump

"Wh...?"

"Stay here!"

With a pantherlike speed, he dragged on his jeans and yanked at the zipper. They rode low on his hips as he headed for the door. Gasping, Sheryl pushed herself up on one elbow. Still groggy and only half-awake, she blinked owlishly.

"What is it?"

"I don't know, and until I do, stay here, okay? No heroics and no noise."

Before his low instructions had even sunk in, he'd slipped through the door and disappeared into the shadowed hallway. Sheryl gaped at the panel for a

second or two, still in a fog. Then she threw back the
sheet and leaped out of bed. She had her panties on
and her T-shirt half over her head when the door
swung open again.

She froze, her heart in her throat.

To her infinite relief, Harry stalked in. Disgust
etched in every line of his taut body, he carried a
tomato-and-grease-smeared Button under his arm.

''The greedy little beggar climbed up onto the table. He and our half of the pizza just took a dive.''

Chapter 10

Although the little heart-shaped crystal clock on her nightstand showed just a few minutes before eleven, by the time Sheryl finished dressing she was experiencing all the awkwardness of a morning-after.

Button's noisy accident had shaken her right out of her sleepy, sensual haze. Like a splash of cold water in her face, reality now set in with a vengeance. She couldn't quite believe she'd begged Harry to kiss her like that. To seduce her, for pity's sake!

She walked down the hall to the living room, cringing inside as she realized how pathetic she must have sounded. First, by admitting that Brian had dumped her. Then, by practically demanding that the marshal take her to bed as a balm to her wounded ego. She couldn't remember when she'd ever done anything so rash. So stupid. So embarrassing to admit to after the fact.

Heat blazed in both cheeks when she found Harry in the dining room. Hunkered down on one knee, he was scrubbing at the grease stains in her carpet with a sponge and muttering imprecations at the dog that sat a few feet away, watching him with a show of blasé interest.

"You don't have to do that," Sheryl protested, her discomfiture mounting at the sight of Harry's naked chest. Had she really wrapped her arms and legs and everything else she could around his lean, powerful torso?

She had, she admitted with a new flush of heat. She could still feel the ache in her thighs, and taste him on her lips. How in the world had she lost herself like that? She hardly knew much more about this man than his name, his occupation, his marital status and the fact that he logged more travel miles in a month than most people did in two years. That alone should have stopped her from throwing herself at him the way she had! Hadn't she learned her lesson from her parents?

Obviously not. Even now, she ached to wrap her arms around him once again. Smart, Sheryl! Real smart. Dropping to her knees, she reached for the sponge.

"I'll do that while you get dressed."

He looped an arm across his bent knee and regarded her with a lazy smile.

"Unwound already, Sher? And here I promised that it would take all night."

His teasing raised the heat in her cheeks to a raging

inferno. She attacked the pizza stain, unable to meet his eyes.

"Yes, well, I know you came here to work, not to, uh, help me get past this bad patch with Brian, and you don't have all night for that."

His hand closed over her wrist, stilling her agitated movements. When she looked up, his air of lazy amusement had completely disappeared.

"Is that what you think just happened here? That I played some kind of sexual Good Samaritan by taking you to bed?"

She wouldn't have put it in quite those words, but she couldn't deny the fact that he'd done exactly that.

"Don't think that I'm not..." She swallowed. "That I'm not grateful. I needed a...a distraction tonight and you—"

With a swiftness that made her gasp, he rose, bringing her up with him. Sudden, fierce anger blazed in his brown eyes.

"A distraction?" he echoed in a tone that raised the fine hairs on the back of her neck. "You needed a distraction?"

Sheryl knew she was digging herself in deeper with every word, but she didn't have the faintest idea how to get out of this hole. She'd only wanted to let Harry know that she didn't expect him to continue the admittedly spectacular lovemaking she'd forced on him. Instead, she'd unintentionally ruffled his male ego. More embarrassed than ever, she tugged her wrist free.

"That didn't come out the way I meant it. You were more than a distraction. You were..." Her face flaming, she admitted the unvarnished truth. "You were wonderful. Thank you."

Harry stared at her, at a total loss for words for one of the few times in his life. Anger still pounded through him. Incredulity now added its own side-swiping kick. He couldn't believe that Sheryl had just *thanked* him, for God's sake! If this whole conversation didn't make him so damned furious, he might have laughed at the irony of it. He couldn't remember the last time he'd lost himself so completely, so passionately, in a woman's arms. Or the last time he'd drifted into sleep with a head nestled on his shoulder and a soft, breathy sigh warming his neck.

Harry hadn't exactly sworn off female companionship in the years since his divorce, but neither had he ignored the lessons he'd learned from that sobering experience. As long as he made his living chasing renegades, he couldn't expect any woman to put up with his here-today, gone-tonight lifestyle. Deliberately, he'd kept his friendships with women light and casual. Even more deliberately, he dated women whose own careers or interests coincided with the transitory nature of his. In any case, he sure as hell had never jeopardized an ongoing investigation by seducing one of the key players involved.

He'd broken every one of his self-imposed rules tonight. Deep in his gut, Harry knew damned well that he'd break them again if Sheryl turned her face up to his at this moment and asked him in that sweet, seductive way of hers to kiss her. Hell, he didn't need asking. Wide-awake now and still tight from the crash that had brought him springing out of bed, he had to battle the urge to sweep Sheryl into his arms and take her back to bed to show her just how much of a *distraction* he could provide. Just the thought of burying himself in her slick, satiny heat once again sent a spear of razor-sharp need through him.

With something of a shock, Harry realized that he wanted this woman even more fiercely now than he had before she'd given herself to him. And here she was, brushing him off with a polite thank-you.

Despite her red cheeks, she met his gaze with a dignity that tugged at something inside him. Something sharper than need. Deeper than desire.

"I'm sorry," she said quietly. "I didn't mean to insult you or cheapen what happened between us. It *was* wonderful, Harry. I just didn't want you to think that I want...or expect...anything more. I know why you're in Albuquerque, and that you'll be gone as soon as something breaks on your fugitive."

She had just put his own thoughts into words. Harry didn't particularly like hearing them.

"Sheryl..."

Her eyes gentled. Her hand came up to stroke his cheek. "It's all right, Marshal. Some men are wanderers by nature as much as by profession. My father was one. So, I think, are you. I understand."

Harry wasn't sure he did. He heard what she was saying. He agreed with it completely. So why did he want to—

The muted shrill of his cellular phone interrupted his chaotic thoughts. Frowning, he extracted the instrument from the jacket he'd left hanging on the back of a dining-room chair.

"MacMillan."

"Harry!" Ev's voice leaped out at him. "Where the hell are you?"

"At Sheryl's apartment." He didn't give his partner a chance to comment on that one. "Where are you?"

"Outside your motel room. I was on my way home when I got the news. I swung by your place to give you the word personally."

"What word?"

"The Santa Fe airport manager just called. He's got a small, twin-engine jet about two hours out, requesting permission to land."

Harry's gut knotted. "And?"

"And the pilot also requested that Customs be notified. He wants to off-load a cargo of Peruvian sheepskin hides destined for a factory just outside Taos that manufactures those Marlboro-man sheepskin coats. From what I'm told, the hides stink. Like you wouldn't believe. Customs isn't too happy about processing the cargo tonight."

"This could be it," his listener said softly.

"I think it is. The FAA ran a quick check on the aircraft's tail number and flight plan. This leg of the flight originated in Peru, but the aircraft is registered in Brazil, Harry. Brazil!"

"Get a helo warmed up and ready for us."

"Already done. It's on the pad at State Police headquarters. Fay's on her way there now."

"I'll meet you both in ten minutes."

Harry snapped the phone shut and jammed it into his jacket. Every sense, every instinct, pushed at him to race into the bedroom and grab his clothes. To slam out of the apartment, jump into his car and hit the street, siren wailing.

For the first time that he could remember, his cop's instincts took second place to a stronger, even more urgent demand. In answer to the question in Sheryl's wide eyes, he paused long enough to give her a swift recap.

"We've got a break, Sher. A plane registered in Brazil is coming into the Santa Fe airport in a couple of hours."

"No kidding!"

She was still standing where he'd left her when he came running back, shoving his shirttail into his jeans. He grabbed his holster and slipped into it with a roll of his shoulders. Then he snatched up his jacket and strode to where she stood. His big hands framed her face.

"I've got to go."

"I know. Be careful."

He gave himself another second to sear her eyes and her nose and the tangled silk of her hair into his memory. Then he kissed her, hard, and headed for the door.

"Harry!"

"What?"

"Come back when you can. I, uh, want to know what happens."

"I will."

The nondescript government sedan squealed out of the apartment complex. With one eye on the late-night traffic, Harry fumbled the detachable Kojak light into its mounting and flipped its switch. The rotating light slashed through the night like a sword. A half second later, he activated the siren and shoved the accelerator to the floor. The unmarked, unremarkable vehicle roared to life.

Ten minutes later, the car squealed through the gates leading to the headquarters of Troop R of the New Mexico Highway Patrol. Grabbing the duffel bag containing his field gear from the trunk, Harry raced for the helo pad. Ev and Fay met him halfway, both jubilant, both lugging their own field gear.

"Give me a rundown on who we've got playing so far," Harry shouted over the piercing whine of the helicopter's engine.

"Our Santa Fe highway patrol detachment is pulling in every trooper they've got to cordon off the airport," Fay yelled. "The Santa Fe city police have alerted their SWAT team. They'll be in place when we get there."

They ducked under the whirring rotor blades and climbed aboard through the side hatch. The copilot greeted them with a grin and directed them to the web rack that stretched behind the operators' seats.

Panting, Ev buckled himself in. "Customs has a Cessna Citation in the air tracking our boy as we speak. They've also got two Blackhawks en route from El Paso, with a four-man bust team aboard each."

Fierce satisfaction shot through Harry at the news. The huge Sikorsky UH-60 Blackhawk helicopters came equipped with an arsenal of lethal weapons and enough candlepower to light up half of New Mexico.

"Good. We might just give them a chance to show their stuff."

While the copilot buckled himself in, the pilot stretched around to show the passengers where to plug in their headsets.

"What's the flying time to Santa Fe?" Harry asked, his words tinny over the static of the radio.

"Twenty minutes, sir."

"Right. Let's do it."

The aviator gave him a thumbs-up and turned her attention to the controls. Seconds later, the chopper lifted off. It banked steeply, then zoomed north.

Harry used the short flight to coordinate the operation with the key players involved. The copilot patched him through to the Customs National Aviation Center in Oklahoma City, which was now tracking the suspect aircraft, the New Mexico state police ops center and the Santa Fe airport manager.

"Our boy is still over an hour out." he summarized for Ev and Fay. "That gives us plenty of time to familiarize ourselves with the layout of the field and get our people into position. No one moves until I give the signal. No one. Understood?"

Harry didn't want any mistakes. No John Waynes charging in ahead of the cavalry. No hotshot Rambos trying to show their stuff. If the man he'd been tracking for almost a year was flying in aboard this aircraft, the bastard wasn't going to get away. Not this time.

The short flight passed in a blur of dark mountains to their right and the sparse lights of the homes scattered along the Rio Grande valley below. The helo set down at the Santa Fe airport just long enough for Harry and the two others to jump out. Bent double, they dashed through the cloud of dust thrown up by the rotor wash. As soon as they were clear, Harry shed his coat and pulled his body armor out of his gear bag. A dark, lightweight windbreaker with "U.S. Marshal" emblazoned on the back covered the armor and identified him to the other players involved. After shoving spare ammo clips into his pockets, he checked his weapon, then went to meet the nervous airport manager waiting for him inside the distinctive New Mexico-style airport facility.

In a deliberate attempt to retain Santa Fe's unique character and limit its growth, the city planners had also limited the size of the airport that serviced it. To make access even more difficult, high mountain peaks ringed its relatively short runway. Consequently, no large-bodied jetliners landed in the city. The millions of tourists a year who poured into Santa Fe from all over the world usually flew into Albuquerque and drove the fifty-five-mile scenic route north. Even the legislators who routinely traveled to the capital to conduct their business did so by car or by small aircraft.

The inconvenient access might have constituted an annoyance for some travelers, but it added up to a major plus for Harry and the team members who gathered within minutes of his arrival. With only one north-south runway and the parallel taxiway to cover, he quickly orchestrated the disposition of his forces.

They melted into the night like dark shadows, radios muted and lights doused.

After a final visual and radar check of their hand-held secure radios, Ev headed for the tower to coordinate the final approach and takedown. Harry and Fay climbed into the airport service vehicle that would serve as their mobile command post. When the truck pulled into its customary slot beside the central hangar, Harry stared into the night.

A million stars dotted the sky above the solid blackness of the mountains. Richard Johnson, aka Paul Gunderson, was out there somewhere. With any luck, that somewhere would soon narrow down to a stretch of runway in the high New Mexico desert.

A shiver rippled along Harry's spine, part primal anticipation, part plain old-fashioned chill. Even in mid-June, Sante Fe's seven-thousand-foot elevation put a nip in the night air. He zipped his jacket, folded his arms. His eyes on the splatter of stars to the south, the hunter settled down to await his prey.

The minutes crawled by.

The secure radio cackled as Ev gave periodic updates on the aircraft's approach. Forty minutes out. Thirty. Twenty.

The Blackhawks swept over the airport, rotors thumping in the night, and touched down behind the hangars. One would move into position to block any possible takeoff attempt should anything spook the quarry once it was on the ground. The second would come in from the rear.

Quiet settled over the waiting, watching team. Even Ev's status reports were hushed.

Fifteen minutes.

Ten.

This was for Dean, Harry promised the dark, silent night. For the man who'd razzed him as a rookie, and stood beside him at the altar, and asked him to act as godfather to his son. And for Jenny, who'd cried in Harry's arms until she had no more tears left to shed. For every marshal who'd ever died in the line of duty, and every son or mother or husband or wife left behind.

Without warning, an image of Sheryl formed in Harry's mind. Her hair tumbling around her shoulders. Her eyes wide with excitement and the first, faint hint of worry on his behalf. It struck him that he'd left Sheryl, as Dean had left Jenny, to chase after Paul Gunderson.

Dean had never returned.

Harry might not, either. Dammit, he shouldn't have made that rash promise to Sheryl. Even without the hazards inherent in his job, success bred its own demands. If Gunderson stepped off an airplane in Santa Fe in the next few minutes, as Harry sincerely prayed he would, he'd climb right back on a plane, this time in handcuffs and leg irons. Harry would go with him. He wouldn't be driving back to Sheryl's place to give her a play-by-play of the night's events…or to redeem the promise of the hard, swift kiss he'd left her with.

He had no business making her any kind of promises at all, he thought soberly.

Even if he wanted to, he couldn't offer her much more than a choice between short bursts of pleasure and long stretches of loneliness. And a husband whose job might or might not leave her weeping in someone's arms, as Dean's had left Jenny.

Suddenly, the radio cackled. "He's on final approach. Check out that spot of light at one o'clock, 'bout two thousand feet up."

Harry blanked his mind of Sheryl, of Jenny, even of Dean. His eyes narrowed on the tiny speck of light slowly dropping out of the sky.

The takedown was a textbook operation.

Following the tower's directions, the twin-engine King Air rolled to a stop on the parking apron, fifty yards from where Harry waited in the service vehicle. As soon as the engines whined down and the hatch opened, the Blackhawks rose from behind the adjacent hangar like huge specters. They dropped down, their thirty-million-candlepower spotlights pinning the two figures who emerged from the King Air in a blinding haze of white light. The helo crews poured out.

Harry clicked the mike on the vehicle's loudspeaker and shouted a warning. "This is the U.S. Marshals Service. Hit the ground. Now!" He was out of the vehicle, his weapon drawn, before the echoes had stopped bouncing off the hangar walls.

The two figures took one look at the dark-suited figures converging on them from all directions and dropped like stones.

Harry reached them as they hit the pavement. Disappointment rose like bile in his throat. Even from the back, he could see that neither of the individuals spread-eagled on the concrete fit Paul Gunderson's physical description.

Ev Sloan reached the same conclusion when he panted up beside Harry a moment later.

"He's not with 'em. Damn!"

"My sentiments exactly," Harry got out through clenched jaws. Raising his voice, he issued a curt order. "All right. On your feet. We need to inspect your cargo."

A two-man Customs team went through the King Air's cargo with dogs, handheld scanners and an array of sophisticated chemical testing compounds. A second team searched the plane itself, which had been towed into a hangar for privacy.

By the time the first streaks of a golden dawn pierced the darkness of the mountain peaks outside, unbaled sheepskin hides lay strewn along one half of the hangar. Barely cured and still wearing a coat of gray, greasy wool, they gave off a stench that had emptied the contents of several team members' stomachs and put the drug dogs completely out of action.

The plane's guts lay on the other side of the hangar floor...along with a neat row of plastic bags. Even without the dogs, the stash in the concealed compartment in the plane's belly had been hard to miss.

The senior Customs agent approached Harry, grinning. Sweat streaked his face, and he carried the stink of hides with him.

"Five hundred kilos and a nice, new King Air for the Treasury Department to auction off. Not a bad haul, Marshal. Not bad at all."

"No. Just not the one we wanted."

The agent thrust out his hand. "Sorry you didn't get your man this time. Maybe next time."

"Yeah. Next time."

Leaving the other agency operatives to their prizes, Harry walked out into the slowly gathering dawn. Ev leaned against the hood of a black-and-white state police car, sipping coffee from a leaking paper cup. Then he tossed out the dregs of his coffee and crumpled the cup.

"Well, I guess it's back to the damned computer printouts and postcards. You get anything more from Sheryl when you were up at her place last night?"

"No."

And yes.

Harry had gotten far more from her than he'd planned or hoped for. The need to return to her apartment, to finish this damnable night in her arms, tore through his layers of weariness.

He thought of a thousand reasons why he shouldn't go back...and one consuming reason why he should.

Chapter 11

Sheryl curled in a loose ball on top of the black-and-white blanket. Button lay sprawled beside her. She stroked his silky fur with a slow, light touch, taking care not to wake him while he snuffled and twitched in the throes of some doggie dream. Her gaze drifted to the small crystal clock on the table beside her bed.

Five past six.

Seven hours since Harry had left. Seven hours of waiting and worrying. Of wondering when...if...he'd come back. He'd been gone for only seven hours, yet it seemed as though days had passed since he'd rolled out of this bed and raced into the kitchen in response to Button's attack on the pizza.

Until tonight, Sheryl had never really appreciated the loneliness that had turned her mother into such a bitter, unhappy woman. She'd seen it happening, of course. Even as a child, she'd recognized that her father's extended absences had leached the youth from her mother's face and carved those small, tight lines on either side of her face. Mentally, she'd braced herself every time her father walked out the door. She'd shared her mother's hurt and dissatisfaction, but she'd never *felt* the emptiness deep inside her, as she had these past hours. Never experienced this sense of being so alone.

Despite the hollow feeling in her chest, Sheryl could summon no trace of bitterness. Instead of hurt, a lingering wonder spread through her veins every time she thought of the hours together with Harry. Her breasts still tingled from his stinging kisses. One shoulder still carried a little red mark from his prickly mustache. She'd never experienced anything even remotely resembling the explosions of heat and light and skyrocketing sensation the marshal had detonated under her skin. Not once but twice.

Recalling her fumbling attempt to thank him for services rendered, Sheryl almost groaned aloud. Talk about putting her foot in it! Harry had bristled all over with male indignation. For a moment, he'd looked remarkably like Button with his fur up.

Smiling, she combed her fingers through the soft, feathery ruff decorating the paw closest to her. The shih tzu snuffled and jerked his leg away. One black eye opened and glared at her though the light of the gathering dawn.

"Sorry."

He gave a long-suffering look and rolled onto his back, all four paws sticking straight up in the air.

Sheryl speared another glance at the clock. Six-fifteen.

Too restless to even pretend sleep any longer, she tickled the dog's pink belly. "Want to get up? You can finish off the pizza for breakfast."

Black gums pulled back. A warning growl rumbled up from the furry chest. Hastily, Sheryl pulled her fingers out of reach.

"Okay, okay! You don't mind if I get up, do you?"

Silly question. Before she'd was halfway across the bedroom, Button was already sunk back into sleep.

A quick shower washed away the grittiness of her sleepless night. Since it was Saturday, Sheryl didn't even glance at the uniforms hanging neatly in her closet. Instead, she pulled out her favorite denim sundress. With its thin straps, scooped neck and loose fit, it was perfect for Albuquerque's June heat. Tiny wooden buttons marched down the front and stopped above the knee, baring a long length of leg when she walked. The stonewashed blue complemented her tan and her streaky blond hair, she knew. Now all she had to do was erase the signs of her sleepless night. Making a face at her reflection in the mirror, she applied a little blush and a swipe of lipstick. A few determined strokes with the brush subdued her hair into a semblance of order. Clipping it back with a wooden barrette that matched the buttons on the dress, she padded barefoot into the kitchen.

The first thing she saw was the pizza carton on the counter. Instantly, she started worrying and wondering again.

Where was Harry? What had happened after he'd left her last night?

Leaning a hip against the counter, she filled the automatic coffeemaker and waited while it brewed. Slowly, a rich aroma spread through the kitchen. Even more slowly, the soft, golden dawn lightened to day.

The sound of Button's nails clicking on the tiles alerted her to the fact that he'd decided to join the living. He wandered into the kitchen and gave her a disgruntled look, obviously as annoyed with her early rising as he'd been with her tossing and turning.

"Do you need to go out? Hold on a sec. I'll get the paper and pour a cup of coffee and join you on the back patio."

Sheryl flicked off the alarm and went outside to hunt down her newspaper. As usual, the deliveryman had tossed it halfway across the courtyard. She didn't realize Button had slipped out the front door with her until his piercing yip cut through the early morning quiet.

Startled, Sheryl spun around. From the corner of one eye, she saw Button charge across the courtyard toward the silver-haired Persian that had been sunning itself at the base of the small fountain. The cat went straight up in the air, hissing, and came down with claws extended.

"Oh, no!"

Oblivious to her dismayed exclamation, Button leaped to attack. His quarry decided that discretion was the better part of valor. Streaking across the tiled courtyard, it disappeared through the arched entryway that led to the parking lot. The shih tzu followed in noisy pursuit.

The darned dog was going to wake every person in the apartment complex with that shrill bark. Dropping the paper, Sheryl joined in the chase.

"Button! Here, boy! Here!"

She rounded the entryway corner just in time to see both cat and dog dart across the parking lot. Another cluster of apartments swallowed them up. Sheryl started across the rough asphalt. Suddenly, her bare heel came down on a pebble. Pain shot all the way up to the back of her knee.

"Dammit!"

Wincing, she took a few limping steps, then ran awkwardly on the ball of her injured foot. To her consternation, the noisy barking grew fainter and fainter. A moment later, it disappeared completely, swallowed up by the twisting walkways, picturesque courtyards and multistory buildings of the sprawling complex.

Seriously concerned now, Sheryl ran through archway after archway. Button would never find his way back through this maze. Stepping up the pace as much as the pain in her heel would allow, she searched the apartment grounds. Her dress skirt flapped around her knees. The wooden barrette holding her hair back snapped open and clattered to the walkway behind her. Sweat popped out on her forehead and upper lip.

"Button!" she called in gathering desperation. "Here, boy! Come to Sheryl!"

Her breath cut through her lungs like razor blades when she caught the sound of a crash, followed by a yelp. She tore down another path and through an arch-way, then came to a skidding, one-heeled halt. If she'd had any breath left, Sheryl would have gasped at the scene that greeted her. As it was, she could only pant helplessly.

An oversized clay pot had been knocked on its side. It now spilled dirt and pink geraniums onto the tiles. Beside the overturned pot lay a tipped-over sundial. Colorful fliers and sections of a newspaper littered the courtyard. In the midst of the havoc, not one but two silver Persians now stood shoulder to shoulder. Fur up, backs arched, they hissed for all they were worth. Their indignant owner stood behind them, flapping her arms furiously at the intruder. Button was belly to the ground, but hadn't given up the fight.

By the time Sheryl had scooped up the snarling shih tzu, apologized profusely to the cats' owner, offered to pay for the damages and listened to an irate discourse on dog owners who ignore leash laws, the sun had tipped over the apartment walls and heated the morning. Limping and hot and not exactly happy with her unrepentant houseguest, she lectured him sternly as she retraced her steps to her apartment. She took a wrong turn twice, which didn't improve her mood or Button's standing. Unconcerned over the fact that he was in disgrace, the dog surveyed the areas they passed through, ears up and eyes alert for his next quarry.

Sheryl was still lecturing when she rounded the corner of her building. The sight of two squad cars pulled up close to the arch leading to her courtyard stopped her in midscold. Curious and now a little

worried, she hurried through the curving entrance.
Worry turned to gulping alarm when she saw a uniformed officer standing just outside her open apartment door.

Oh, God! Something must have gone wrong last
night! Maybe Harry was hurt!

Her heart squeezed tight. So did her arms, eliciting
an indignant squawk from Button.

"Sorry!"

Easing the pressure on the little dog, she ran across
the courtyard. "What's going on? What's happened?"

"Miss Hancock?"

"Yes. Is Harry all right?"

"Harry?"

"Harry MacMillan. Marshal MacMillan."

"Oh, yeah. He's inside. He's the one who called
us when he found your front door open."

Sheryl fought down an instant rush of guilt. She'd
forgotten all about the security systems in her worry
over Button.

"Are you all right, Miss Hancock?"

"Yes, I'm fine."

"Then where the hell have you been?"

The snarl spun Sheryl around. Harry filled her
doorway, his body taut with tension and his eyes furious. Another uniformed police officer hovered at his
shoulder.

She took one look at his face and decided this
wasn't the time to tell him about the wild chase Button had led her through the apartment complex. In the

mood he was obviously in, he'd probably skin the dog whole.

"I, uh, went out to get the newspaper."

His blistering look raked her from her sweat-streaked face to her bare toes, then moved to the rolled newspaper lying a few yards away…right where Sheryl had dropped it.

"You want to run that by me one more time?"

She didn't care for his tone. Nor did she appreciate being dressed down like a recruit in front of the two police officers.

"Not particularly."

Although she wouldn't have thought it possible, his jaw tightened another notch. Turning to the police officer, he held out a hand.

"Looks like I called you out on a false alarm. Sorry."

"No problem, Marshal."

"Thanks for responding so quickly."

"Anytime."

With a nod to Sheryl and Button, the two police-men departed the scene. Harry turned to face her, his temper still obviously simmering. In no mood for a public fracas, Sheryl brushed past him and headed for the cool sanctuary of her apartment.

Harry trailed after her, scowling. "Why are you limping?"

"I stepped on a stone."

For some reason, that seemed to incense him even further. He followed her inside, lecturing her with a lot less restraint than she'd lectured Button just a few moments ago.

"That could have been glass you stepped on."

"Well, it wasn't."

"Running around barefoot is about as smart as leaving your front door wide-open! Speaking of which…"

The oak door slammed behind her, rattling the colorful Piña prints on the entryway wall.

"You want to tell me what good a security system is if you don't even bother to close the damned door?"

Enough was enough. Sheryl had run a good mile or more after the blasted mutt. She was hot and sweaty. Her hair hung in limp tendrils around her face. Her heel still hurt like hell. And she'd spent most of the night worrying about a U.S. marshal who, judging from his foul temper, obviously hadn't apprehended the fugitive he wanted.

Bending, she released the dog. Button promptly scampered off, leaving her to face the irate Harry on her own. She turned to find him standing close. Too close. She could see the stubble darkening his cheeks and chin…and the anger still simmering in his whiskey-gold eyes.

Drawing in a deep breath, she decided to go right to the source of that anger. "I take it Paul Gunderson wasn't aboard the plane you intercepted."

"No, he wasn't."

"I'm sorry."

"Yeah," he rasped. "Me, too. And it didn't exactly help matters when I arrived to find your apartment wide-open and you gone."

"Okay, that was careless."

"Careless? How about idiotic? Irresponsible?

"How about we don't get carried away here?" she snapped back.

Her spurt of defiance seemed to fuel his anger. He stepped even closer. Sheryl refused to back away, not that she could have if she'd wanted to. Her shoulder blades almost pressed against the wall as it was.

"Do you have any idea what I went through when I found the door open and you missing?"

The savagery in his voice jolted through her like an electrical shock. In another man, the suppressed violence might have frightened her. In Harry, it thrilled the tiny, adventurous corner of her soul she'd never known she possessed until he'd burst into her life.

How could she have fooled herself into believing she wanted safe and secure and comfortable? The truth hit her with devastating certainty.

She wanted the fierce emotion she saw blazing in this man's eyes.

She wanted the fire and excitement and the passion that only he had stirred in her.

She wanted Harry...however she could have him.

"No," she whispered. "I don't know what you went through. Tell me."

He buried his hands in her hair and pulled her head back. "I'll show you."

This kiss didn't even come close to resembling the ones they'd shared last night. Those were wild and tender and passionate. This one was raw. Elemental. Primitive. So powerful that Sheryl's head went back and her entire body arched into his.

Nor did Harry display any of the teasing finesse he'd used on her before. His mouth claimed hers. Rough and urgent, his hands found her hips and lifted her into him. Sweat-slick and breathless and instantly aroused, Sheryl felt him harden against her.

He dragged his head up. Nostrils flaring, he stared down at her. Raw male need stretched the skin over his cheekbones tight and turned the golden lights in his eyes to small, blazing fires.

Sheryl wasn't stupid. She knew that this barely controlled savagery sprang as much from his frustration over his failure to nab Paul Gunderson last night as from the worry and anger she'd inadvertently sparked in him this morning. She didn't care. Wherever it sprang from, it consumed her.

Wanting him every bit as fiercely as he wanted her, she slid an arm around his neck and dragged his head back down. She knew the instant his mouth covered hers that a kiss wasn't enough. She fumbled for his belt buckle. He stiffened, then attacked the wooden buttons on her denim sundress. The little fasteners went flying. They landed on the tiles with a series of sharp pops. The dress hit the floor somewhere between the entryway and the bedroom. His jeans and shirt followed.

On fire with a need that slicked her inside and out, Sheryl pushed Harry to the bed and straddled him. He was ready for her. More than ready. But when he reached for her hips to lift her onto his rigid shaft, she wiggled backward.

"Oh, no! Not this time. This time, I want to give you what you gave me last night."

"Sheryl…"

"I'm going to wind you up tight," she promised. "And leave you breathless and dizzy and wanting more."

Much more. So much more.

Her fingers combed the hair on his belly. Moved lower. At her touch, his stomach hollowed. Hot, velvety steel filled her hand. Sheryl's throat went dry. She ran her tongue over her lips.

His shaft leaped in her hand. With a wicked smile that surprised her almost as much as it did Harry, she bent and proceeded to leave him breathless and groaning and wanting more.

Much more.

She was still smiling when she and Harry both dropped into an exhausted stupor.

A bounce of the bedsprings woke her with a jerk some time later. Harry shot straight up, his face a study in sleep-hazed confusion.

"Oh, God!" she moaned. "What now?"

"Did you just—"

He broke off, his entire body stiffening. An expression of profound disgust replaced his confusion. Yanking back the rumpled black-and-white Zuni blanket, he glared at the animal wedged comfortably between their knees.

Button lifted his head and snarled, obviously as displeased at having his rest disturbed as Harry was. The two males wore such identical expressions of dislike that Sheryl fell back on the bed, giggling helplessly.

"You should see your face," she gasped.

Harry didn't share her amusement. "Yeah, well, you should try waking up to a set of claws raking down your thigh."

"I have," she told him, still giggling. "Believe me, I have."

For a moment, he looked as though he intended to take Button on for undisputed possession of the bed. Bit by bit, the light of battle went out of his eyes. Rasping a hand across his chin, he let out a long breath.

"I've got to go."

Sheryl's giggles died, but she managed to keep her smile going. "I know."

"Even though we didn't get Gunderson, we've still got some matters to clear up from last night. Ev will be waiting for me."

She nodded.

"Mind if I use your shower?"

"Be my guest," she said with deliberate nonchalance. "I've even got a razor in there. It's contoured for a woman's legs, but I think it'll scrape off everything but your mustache."

While the water pelted against the shower door, Sheryl slipped out of bed and retrieved her sundress. She wouldn't regret his leaving, she repeated over and over, as if it were a mantra. She wouldn't try to hold him.

She couldn't, even if she wanted to.

She could only keep her smile fixed firmly in place when he walked out of the shower, his chest bare above his jeans and his dark hair glistening.

He gathered his clothes. By the time he buckled on

his holster, a frown creased his brow. He crossed to where she sat on the edge of the bed.

"I'll call you."

"Ha! That's what they all say."

Her feeble attempt at humor fell flat. If anything, the line in his forehead grooved even deeper.

"I'll call you. That's all I can promise."

Sheryl sympathized with the wrenching conflict she saw in his eyes. He wanted to leave. Needed to leave. Yet something he couldn't quite articulate tugged at him. That something gave her the courage to rise slowly and lift her palms to his cheeks.

Like Harry, she'd gone through a bit of wrenching herself in the past few days. Without wanting to, without trying to, she'd slipped out of her nice, easy routine and discovered that she wanted more of life than comfort and security.

Harry had shown her what life could…should…be. He'd given her a taste of excitement, of adventure. Of something that she was beginning to recognize as love. She wasn't sure when she'd fallen for this rough-edged marshal, but she had. She suspected it had happened last night, when she'd opened the door and found him standing there with his pineapple-and-Canadian-bacon pizza. She'd known it this morning, when he pinned her against the wall and everything inside her had leaped at his touch.

She was willing to take a chance that what she felt could withstand the test of time. The trial of separation and the tears of loneliness. She wanted to believe that what she could share with Harry was special, different…unlike what her parents had shared.

He hadn't reached that point yet. She saw the hesitation in his eyes. Heard it in his voice. Maybe he'd never reach it. Maybe he'd walk out the door, get caught up in his investigation and forget her.

And maybe he wouldn't.

Sheryl would risk it.

"I didn't ask for any promises, Marshal," she said softly. "I don't need them."

Her smile gentling, she rose on tiptoe and brushed his mouth with a kiss.

"Call me when you can."

For the next few hours, she jumped every time the phone rang…which didn't make for a restful morning, considering that it rang constantly.

Elise called first. After a glowing recount of the baby's first night, she mentioned that the doctor had cleared them both to go home tomorrow.

"So soon?"

"It'll be forty-eight hours, Sher. That's long enough for either of us."

"I'll drive you."

"Thanks, but Brian said he would take us home. Do you suppose you could swing by my house to pick up some clean clothes, though? Mine got a little messed up when I fell."

"Sure." Wedging the phone between her ear and her shoulder, Sheryl reached for a pad and pen. "Tell me what you need."

She scribbled down the short list and hung up, promising to see Elise and the baby later this morning. Just seconds after that, the phone rang again. Her heart jumping, she snatched up the receiver.

It took some doing, but she finally managed to convince the telemarketer at the other end that she did *not* want to switch her long distance carrier.

The third call came shortly after that. Her mother wanted to hear about Elise's delivery.

Sheryl sank onto the sofa. This conversation would take a lot longer than the one she'd just had with the telemarketer, she knew. Scratching Button's ears absently, she told her mother what had happened at the hospital…and afterward. The news that Sheryl had failed to perform her coaching duties surprised Joan Hancock. The news of her breakup with Brian left her stuttering.

"But…but…you two were almost engaged!"

"'Almost' is the operative word, Mom."

"I don't understand. What happened?"

Sighing, Sheryl crossed her ankles on the sturdy bleached-oak plank that served as her coffee table. She'd abandoned her now almost buttonless denim dress for a cool, gauzy turquoise top and matching flowered leggings. With Button snuggled against her thighs, she tried to explain to her mother the feelings she'd only recently discovered herself.

"We decided that we wanted more than what we had together."

"You don't even know *what* you had! You'd better think twice, Sheryl Ann Hancock, before you let a man like Brian slip through your fingers."

Joan's voice took on the brittle edge her daughter

recognized all too well. Mentally, Sheryl braced herself.

"He's so nice," her mother argued. "So reliable. He'd never leave you to lie awake at night wondering where he was, or make you worry about whether he had a decent meal or remembered to take his blood pressure medicine."

Recalling the near-sleepless night she'd just spent wondering and worrying about Harry, Sheryl could only agree.

"No, he wouldn't."

"Call him," Joan urged. "Brian loves you. I know he does. Tell him you made a mistake. Tell him you want to patch things up. And I suggest you do it before that so-called friend of yours sinks her claws in him."

Sheryl blinked at the acid comment. "What are you talking about?"

"Oh, come on! I may get up to Albuquerque only a few times a month, but that's more than enough for me to see that Elise knows very well what a prize Brian is, if you don't. She's been mooning after him ever since her divorce."

Struck, Sheryl thought back over the past few months. Elise hadn't exactly mooned over Brian, but she, like Joan, was forever singing his praises. Then there was that kiss at the hospital to consider, when Elise had dragged the man down by his tie. And the substitute father's wide-eyed wonder in the baby.

A huge grin tracked across Sheryl's face. Harry had all but wiped away the ache in her heart caused by her breakup with Brian. She and the marshal might or might not ever reach the "almost" point she'd reached with Brian. Right now, though, she couldn't think of anything that would please her more than for her two best friends to find the same passion, the same wild need, that she'd discovered in Harry's arms.

She sprang up, dislodging the sleeping dog in the process. He gave her a disgusted look and plopped down again.

"I've gotta go, Mom. I have to swing by Elise's house to pick up some clothes for her. Then I'm heading for the hospital. She and I need to talk."

"Yes," her mother sniffed. "You do."

Still grinning, Sheryl hung up and headed for the bedroom. She was halfway across the room when the phone rang again. She spun around, ignoring the protest of her bruised heel, and grabbed the phone.

It had to be Harry this time!

"Miss Hancock?"

She swallowed her swift disappointment. "Yes?"

"My name is Don Ortega. I'm an attorney representing a woman you know as Mrs. Inga Gunderson."

"Oh! Yes, I think I heard your name mentioned."

"I understand from Marshal Everett Sloan that you're keeping my client's dog."

She eyed the animal sprawled in blissful abandon on her sofa.

"Well, I'm not sure who's keeping whom, but he's here. Why? Does Mrs. Gunderson want me to take him to someone else?"

She frowned, wondering why the thought of losing her uninvited houseguest didn't fill her with instant elation. The mutt had chewed up her underwear, sprayed her dining-room chair and led her on a not-so-merry chase through the apartment complex this morning. Even worse, his sharp claws had brought Harry jerking straight up this morning, as they had her more than once the past few nights. She ought to be dancing with joy at the prospect of dumping him on some other unsuspecting victim.

Instead, she breathed an inexplicable sigh of relief when the lawyer responded to her question with a negative.

"No, my client doesn't have any close friends or acquaintances in Albuquerque. She's just worried about her, er, Butty-boo. She asked me to check with you and find out if you'd given him his heartworm pill," he finished on a dry note.

"I didn't know he needed one."

"According to my client, he has to have one today. She was quite insistent about it. Evidently, her dog almost died last year when the worms got into his bloodstream and wrapped around his heart."

The gruesome description made Sheryl gulp.

"She says that he could pick up another infestation if he misses even one dose of the medication," Ortega advised her.

"So where can I get this medication?"

"If you wouldn't mind going to the pet store on Menaul, where Mrs. Gunderson does business, you can pick up the pills and charge them to her account. My client has instructed me to call ahead and authorize the expenditure."

"Well…"

She hesitated, wondering if she should contact

Harry or Ev Sloan before she acceded to the attorney's request. But Ev had vouched for the lawyer himself, she recalled, swearing that he was tough but straight. Evidently, he also cared enough about his clients to relay their concern for their pets.

"I don't mind," she told Ortega. "Give me the address of this store."

She jotted it down just below the list of items Elise had asked her to bring to the hospital.

"I was just leaving to visit a friend at University Hospital. I'll stop at the pet store on my way."

"Thank you, Miss Hancock. I'm sure my client will be most grateful."

His client, Sheryl discovered when she walked out of the pet store a little over an hour later, was more than grateful. She was lying in wait for her...in the form of two men with slicked-back hair, unsmiling eyes, shiny gray suits and black turtlenecks that must have made them miserable in Albuquerque's sweltering heat.

One of the men appeared at Sheryl's side just as she unlocked her car door. The other materialized from behind a parked car. Before she had done more than glance at them, before she could grasp their intent, before she could scream or even try to twist away, the shorter of the men slapped a folded handkerchief over her mouth.

She fought for two or three seconds. Two or three breaths. Then the street and the car and the gray suits tilted crazily. Another breath, and they disappeared in a haze of blackness.

Chapter 12

"Dammit, where is she?"

Harry paced the task force operations center like a caged, hungry and very irritated panther. He'd been trying to reach Sheryl since just after ten, and it was now almost three.

Ev Sloan leaned back in his chair and watched his partner's restless prowling. Like Harry's, his face showed the effects of his previous long night in the tired lines and gray shadows under his eyes.

"Want me to call central dispatch and have them put out an APB?"

Harry shoved his hands in his pockets and jiggled his loose change. His gut urged him to agree to the all-points bulletin, but this morning's fiasco held him back. He didn't want to use up any more chits with the Albuquerque police than he already had. Sheryl was probably out shopping or visiting friends. A patrol car had already swung by her apartment and verified that her car wasn't in its assigned slot…and the door to her place was shut!

"We'll hold off on the APB," he growled.

"Whatever you say." Ev scraped a hand across the stubble on his chin. "I'm getting too old for this kind of work. I used to get an adrenaline fix from a take-down like last night's that would last me for weeks. Now all I want to do is to nail this bastard Gunderson, go home, kick off my shoes and grab the remote."

"I'll settle for seeing my son's T-ball team bring in just one run," Fay put in with a smile.

The other two men at the conference table took up the refrain. They'd joined the team this morning, each an expert in his own field. While they tossed desultory comments about the best way to ease the strain that gripped them all, Harry paced the length of the room again, his change jingling.

Why the hell couldn't he shake this edgy, unfinished feeling that had been with him almost since he'd left Sheryl this morning?

Because he'd left Sheryl this morning.

He had to face the truth. The way he'd walked out of her arms and her apartment was eating at him from the inside out. It didn't do any good to remind himself that he'd had to get back to the command center and attend to the up-channel reports from the drug bust last night. Or that he'd wanted another go at Inga Gunderson. The blasted woman still refused to talk, except to pester Harry and Ev and her lawyer, Don Ortega, with repeated instructions on the care and feeding of her precious Button. Harry had come out of this morning's session at the detention center so tight jawed with frustration that his back teeth ached.

A flash message from the CIA with the news that they'd traced the six canisters of depleted uranium to Rio de Janeiro had only added to his mounting tension. The shipment had to be heading for the States any day now.

Any hour.

As a result of that message, the task force had redoubled its efforts. Fay had asked the FAA to send out an alert to every airport manager in the four-state area, then contacted her highway patrol counterparts. Ev had pulled in two more deputy marshals from the Albuquerque office. The added personnel were following up every lead, however tenuous, including an unconfirmed report of a visit to the city by two thugs who supposedly strong-armed for a known illegal arms dealer.

Harry had plenty to occupy his mind…yet he'd interrupted his work a half-dozen times in the past five hours to call Sheryl. Between calls, he'd find himself thinking of her at every unguarded moment.

His fists closed around the loose coins. He shouldn't have just walked out like that. After what they'd shared, his refusal to make any promises must have hit her like a slap in the face.

What the hell kind of promises could he make? he thought savagely. That he'd return to her apartment tonight? Tomorrow night? For however long he was in town? That he'd swing through Albuquerque every few months and take her up on the offer that shimmered in her green eyes when he'd left this morning?

That he'd ask her to share his life…or at least the few weeks of relatively normal life he enjoyed before he hit the road again?

The thought of sharing any kind of a life with Sheryl grabbed at Harry with a force that sucked the air right out of his lungs. He stared at the wall, the edge of the coins cutting into his palm. For a moment, he let himself contemplate a future that included nights like last night. Mornings like the one he'd woken up to today.

He wouldn't even mind the hairy little mutt digging his claws into his groin again just to hear Sheryl's laughter. His throat closed at the memory of those helpless giggles and the way she'd fallen back on the bed, her hair spilling across the blanket and her rosy-tipped breasts peaking in the cool air-conditioning.

Angrily, he shook his head to clear the erotic image. Why in the world was he putting himself through this? He'd learned the hard way that fugitive operations and a stable home life didn't make for a compatible mix. Sheryl, too, had seen firsthand her parents' inability to sustain a long-distance marriage. Harry had damned well better stop thinking about impossible futures and concentrate on right here, right now.

Which brought him back full circle to the question of where Sheryl was at this moment. More irritable and edgy than ever, he strode back to the conference table and reached for the phone.

"Maybe her friend in the hospital knows where she is," he said curtly in answer to Ev's quizzical look. "I'll make one more call, then we need to go over today's scheduled flights into every major airport in the four-state area. I want copies of all passenger lists and cargo manifests as soon as they're filed.''

The operator patched him though to University Hospital, which in turn connected him with Elise Hart's room. Harry recognized instantly the male voice that answered on the second ring. What did Sheryl's former boyfriend do—live at the damned hospital?

Curtly, he identified himself. ''This is Harry Mac-Millan. I'm trying to reach Sheryl.''

Just as curtly, Brian Mitchell responded. ''She's not here.''

''Do you know where she is?''

''No.'' Mitchell hesitated, then continued in a less abrupt tone. ''As a matter of fact, I was thinking of calling you, Marshal. Sheryl told Elise that she'd swing by her house to pick up some clean clothes before she came to the hospital this morning. She hasn't shown up and doesn't answer her phone.''

Harry stiffened. The prickly sixth sense that had been nagging at him all day vaulted into full-fledged alarm.

''We're a little worried about her,'' Brian finished.

A little worried! Christ!

''I'll check it out.''

The real-estate-agent's voice sharpened once again. ''She's okay, isn't she? This manhunt you pulled her into hasn't put her in danger.''

''I'll check it out.''

''I want you to notify me immediately when you find her!''

Yeah, right. Harry palmed him off with a half promise and slammed the phone down. Then he snatched his jacket off the back of a chair and headed for the door.

"Call the APD, Ev. Ask them to put out that all-points. And ask them to have their locksmith meet me at Sheryl's apartment."

Ev took one look at his partner's face and grabbed for the phone. "Right away!"

Harry wheeled the souped-up sedan out of the underground parking garage. The tires whined on the hot asphalt. Merging the vehicle into the light weekend traffic flow, he willed himself into a state of rigid control. He'd carried a five-pointed gold star too long to give in to the concern churning like bile in his belly.

Adobe-fronted strip malls and tree-shaded residences whizzed by. Ahead, the Sandia Mountains loomed brownish gray against an endless blue sky. The stutter of a jackhammer cut through the heat of the afternoon.

The sights and sounds registered on Harry's consciousness, but didn't penetrate. His mind was spinning with possibilities. Sheryl could have gone in to work. No one had answered at the Monzano Branch when he'd called earlier, but they might not answer the phones during off-hours.

She could be running errands. The time could have slipped away from her, and she'd forgotten her promise to stop by the hospital this morning.

Or she might have taken off on another jaunt with that damned dog. Hell, she'd chased him barefoot around the whole complex only this morning and left her door open to all comers.

His hands fisted on the steering wheel. He'd strangle her! If she'd ignored all security measures again and scared the hell out of him like this, he'd strangle her...right after he locked the door behind them, tumbled her onto the bed and told her just how much he'd hated leaving her this morning!

Assuming, a small, cold corner of his mind countered, that Sheryl was in any state to hear him.

At that moment, she wasn't.

Her stomach swirled with nausea. Her throat burned. Black spots danced under her closed lids.

In a desperate effort to clear her blurred vision, Sheryl lifted her head an inch or two. Even that slight movement brought an acrid taste into her dry, parched throat and made her senses swim. Moaning, she let her head fall. It hit the bare mattress with a soft plop, raising a musty cloud of dust motes.

"Ya back with us, sweetheart?"

The thin, nasal voice drifted through the sickening haze. Sheryl's clogged mind had barely separated the words enough to make sense of them when a deeper, almost rasping voice came from somewhere above and behind her.

"The next time you do a broad, you idiot, cut the dosage."

"Hey, enough already! You been on my back for hours about that."

"Yeah?"

The vicious snarl scraped across Sheryl's skin like

a dull knife. "Who do you think is gonna be on our backs if we miss this drop?"

"She's coming 'round, ain't she?"

"It's about damn time."

Without warning, a palm cracked against Sheryl's cheek.

"Come on, wake up."

Gasping at the pain that splintered across her face, she fought to bring the figure bending over her into focus. A greasy shine appeared...black hair, slicked back, reflecting the light of the single overhead bulb.

She blinked. Her lids gritted like sandpaper against her eyes. Slowly, she made out a wide, unshaven jaw above a black turtleneck. A pair of unsmiling eyes in a face some people might have considered handsome.

"We ain't gonna hurt you."

"You..." She swiped her tongue around her cottony mouth. "You...just...did."

"That little love tap?" The stranger snorted and dug a hand into her armpit. "Come on, sit up and take a drink. We gotta talk."

The mists fogging Sheryl's mind shredded enough for her to grasp the fact that her wrists were tied behind her. Fear spurted like ice water through her veins. Her feet dropped to the floor with a thump, first one, then the other. She swayed, dizzy and confused and more scared than she'd ever been before. The grip on her arm held her upright.

Another figure appeared from the dimness to her side, holding a glass. When he shoved it at her lips, Sheryl shrank away. A fist buried itself in her hair, yanked her head back.

"It's just water. Drink it."

With the glass chinking against her teeth, she didn't have a whole lot of choice. Most of the tepid liquid ran down her chin, but enough got through her teeth to satisfy the pourer.

The fist loosened. Sheryl brought her head up and eased the ache in her neck. Gradually, the black swirls in front of her eyes subsided

"Wh...? Where am I?"

The words came out in a croak, but Slick Hair understood them. He flicked an impatient hand.

"It don't matter where you are. What matters is where you're going."

She swallowed painfully. Her heart thumping with fear, she met her kidnapper's unsmiling gaze.

"Where am I going?"

A snigger sounded beside her. "That's what you're gonna tell us, sweetheart."

She swung her head toward the second man. Like Slick Hair, this one also wore a black turtleneck and a shiny gray suit. It must be some kind of uniform, she thought with a touch of hysteria. He had small, pinched eyes and a nasal pitch that grated on her ears. He came from somewhere east of New Mexico, obviously. Or maybe he owed that whine to the fact that someone or something had flattened his nose against his face.

Slick Hair scraped a chair across the bare wood floor, twisted it around and straddled the seat. With Broken Nose hovering at his shoulder, he smiled thinly.

"We need to have us a little chat, Sheryl." At her

start of surprise, his smile took on a sadistic edge. "What? You don't think we know your name? Of course we know it. We got it from Inga this morning."

Despite her fear and the pain lancing through her face and wrists, her head had cleared enough by now for her to grasp that the men confronting her had some connection to Harry's investigation. She just hadn't expected them to admit it so readily.

"How...?" She swallowed. "How did you talk to Inga? She's in..."

"In jail?" Slick Hair waved a hand, dismissing the small irritation of police custody. "Those bastards at the detention center wouldn't allow her more than her one damn call to her lawyer, but Inga's a shrewd old broad. She got this Ortega guy to call the shop and let our little friend there know you were coming."

"The pet shop?"

"Yeah," Broken Nose put in. "We been hangin' out there, waiting for Inga to show. We was worried when we heard the cops snatched her, but like Big Ja—" He caught himself. "Like my friend here says, she's a smart old broad. We just waited, and sure enough, she sent you."

Slick Hair folded his forearms across the back of the chair. His eyes settled on her face.

"So, you wanna tell us about the postcard?"

She tried to bluff it out. "What postcard?"

"The one that come in from Rio, Sheryl. The one from Rio."

"I don't know what you're talking about. No one sent me any postcards, from Rio or anywhere else."

"Come on, sweetheart," Broken Nose whined. "We got contacts, ya know. It didn't take no undercover dick to find out you work at a post office. Since Inga sent you to the shop, you gotta have the information we want."

"No, I—"

In a move so swift that Sheryl didn't even see it coming, Slick Hair's arm whipped out. The backhanded blow sent her tumbling sideways onto the bare mattress. She lay there for endless seconds, biting her lip against the pinwheeling pain. She wouldn't cry! She wouldn't give in to the fear coursing through her!

Harry was looking for these men or their partner in crime. He'd soon come looking for her, too. She didn't know how long she'd been out, or where she was now, or what was going to happen next, but she just had to hold on. Find out what she could. Get word to Harry somehow.

Slowly, awkwardly, she pushed herself up on one elbow and faced her captors.

"Now, tell us about the card from Rio, Sheryl."

"Wh...?" She wet her lips. "What do you want to know?"

Slick Hair smiled again, his thin lips slicing across the strong planes of his face. "Smart girl. Just tell me what Paul wrote on the back."

Bitterly regretting that she'd ever peeked at Inga Gunderson's mail, much less harbored any concern for her welfare, Sheryl summoned a mental picture of the bright, gaudy Carnival street scene. The words on the back of the card formed, went hazy, reformed.

"'Hi to my favorite aunt,'" she recited dully.

"'I've been dancing in the streets for the past five days. Wish you were here.'"

"Five days!"

Broken Nose did a quick turn about the room. It was empty of all but a rickety table, the two chairs and the cot she sat on, Sheryl saw. A blanket covered the only window.

"Five days past the date of the last drop," the smaller man continued excitedly. "Lessee. Last time, we picked up the stuff on the third. Five days past that would make it the eighth. Tomorrow. Damn! We got another whole day to wait."

Slick Hair didn't move, didn't take his eyes off Sheryl's face. With everything in her, she tried not to flinch as he reached out and twisted a hand through her hair.

"I don't think you're giving it to us straight," he said softly, bringing her face to within inches of his own. "You sure that postcard said 'five' days, Sheryl? Think hard. Real hard."

"Yes," she gasped. "Yes, I'm sure."

Slick Hair looked into her eyes for another few moments. "Get the needle," he told his partner quietly.

She tried to jerk away. "No!"

His painful grip kept her still.

"It's just a little drug we got from a friendly doc, Sheryl. It'll help you remember. Help you get the details right."

There was no way she was going to allow these men to stick a needle in her. God only knows who had used it before or what drug they'd pump into her.

"Maybe... Maybe it said 'four days.'"

Satisfaction flared in the eyes so close to her own. "Maybe it did, Sheryl."

"Jesus!" Broken Nose thumped his fist against his shiny pantleg. "That's tonight!"

"So it is," Slick Hair mused. "That must be why Inga sent you to us, Sheryl. She was probably in a real sweat, knowin' Paul was coming in tonight and no one would be there to greet him. Well, we'll be there."

Sheryl closed her eyes in an agony of remorse. Harry! I'm sorry! I'm so sorry.

"You'll be there, too," Slick Hair finished, easing his grip on her hair. "If Paul doesn't show, we're gonna be real, real unhappy with you."

The threat should have paralyzed her with fear. Instead, it slowly penetrated her despair and lit a tiny spark of anger. She hoped Paul Gunderson *did* show. She hoped he walked off a plane tonight and found not only these creeps, but a small army of law enforcement officials waiting for him. She hoped to hell she was there to see it when Harry took Gunderson and these two goons down.

Which he would! She knew he would! These men didn't realize that Harry would tear the city apart when he discovered she was missing. He'd find her car, trace her to the pet store. It wouldn't take him long to tie that visit back to Inga Gunderson. Maybe he already had.

He'd find a way to make Inga talk.

He had to!

Chapter 13

Ev Sloan waited for Harry on the steps of the Bernalilo County Detention Center. Even though the sun had dropped behind the cluster of downtown buildings and shadows stretched across the street, sweat streaked Ev's face and plastered his shirt to his chest. As he'd told Fay just before he'd left her at the operations center, he sincerely hoped he'd never have to go through again what he'd experienced since the Albuquerque police had located Sheryl Hancock's abandoned car three hellish hours ago.

His gut had twisted at the realization that the woman he'd worked with for the past couple of days had been snatched right off the street. As deep as it went, his worry over Sheryl's status didn't begin to compare with Harry's. Not that MacMillan's wrenching desperation showed to anyone who didn't know him. Ev had worked with him long enough to rec-

ognize the signs, though. The stark fury, quickly
masked. The fear, even more quickly hidden. The
cold, implacable determination that had driven him
every minute since they'd found the car.

Thank God for the crumpled piece of paper under
the Camry's front seat. Sheryl's hand-scribbled list
had led them to the pet shop and to the nervous shop
owner, who'd IDed the two men who'd followed their
victim out of the store. The process of identifying
them might have taken a whole lot longer than it had
if Harry hadn't instantly connected them to the two
strong-arms rumored to have been sighted in Albuquerque. With the FBI's help, they now had names,
backgrounds and mug shots of both men. Through a
screening of Sheryl's phone calls this morning, they
also had a link to Don Ortega.

Attorney and client were waiting inside for them
now. Ev didn't kid himself. This interview was going
to be a rough one. He'd known that since Harry had
stalked out of the task force command center a half
hour ago, instructing Ev to meet him at the detention
center. But he didn't realize how rough until he saw
MacMillan climbing out of the sedan that squealed to
a stop in front of the steps.

Ev's eyes bugged at the bundle of black-and-white
fur wedged under his partner's arm. "Why did you
bring that thing down here?"

The car door slammed. "Everyone's got a weak
spot in their defenses. Butty-boo here is Inga's."

Spinning around, Ev followed Harry up the steps.
"Christ, MacMillan, you're not going to do some-

thing stupid like strangle the mutt in front of the old woman to get her to talk?''

"That's one possibility."

"You can't! You know you can't! Ortega will have the DA, the IG, the SPCA and everyone else he can contact down on our heads!"

"Ortega's going to have his hands full dodging a charge of accessory to a kidnapping," Harry shot back.

He shoved through the glass doors, leaving Ev to trail him into the cavernous lobby. The dog tucked under his arm looked around, black eyes bright with interest. He must have spotted something that he didn't like across the lobby because he promptly let loose with a series of shrill yips that ricocheted off the marble walls and hit Ev's eardrums like sharp, piercing arrows.

"Think, man!" he urged over the noise. "Think! You can't hurt the animal, as much as we'd both like to. You can't even threaten to hurt it. You'll jeopardize our case against both Inga and Paul Gunderson if we ever get them to court. They'll say Inga confessed under duress. That she—"

Harry swung around, his eyes blazing. "Right now, our case takes second place to Sheryl Hancock's safety."

His barely contained fury cut Button off in midbark The sudden silence pounded at all three participants in the small drama.

"I dragged her into this," Harry said savagely. "I'm damned well going to get her out."

"By strangling the mutt?"

He blew out a long breath. Some of the fury left his face, but none of the determination. His gaze dropped to the dog. Someone had drawn its facial hair up and tied it with a pink bow. Sheryl, Ev supposed. MacMillan looked about as ridiculous as a man could with the prissy thing tucked under his arm.

"I won't hurt him. I couldn't. If I did, Sheryl would be on my case worse than the old woman. Beats me what either of them sees in the little rat."

Despite his professed dislike for the creature, he knuckled the furry forehead with a gentleness that made Ev blink.

"Then why did you bring him here?"

Harry's hand stilled. When he looked up, his eyes were flat and hard once again.

"If nothing else, I'm going to make damned sure Inga Gunderson knows what happens to animals left unclaimed at the pound for more than three days."

They were heading south on I-25.

That much Sheryl could see from the back floor of the panel truck. Every so often an overhead highway sign would flash in the front windshield where her two captors sat. She'd catch just enough of it to make out a few letters and words.

She shifted on the hard floor, trying to ease the burning ache in her shoulder sockets. The movement only sharpened the pain shooting from her shoulders to her fingertips. She'd long ago given up her futile attempts to twist free of the tape that bound her wrists together behind her back.

All in all, she was more miserable and frightened

than she'd ever been in her life. She hadn't drunk anything except the water Slick Hair had poured down her throat hours ago. Hadn't eaten anything since the poppy-seed muffin she'd gulped down before heading out the door this morning. She needed to go to the bathroom, badly, but she'd swallow nails before she asked her kidnappers to stop the truck, escort her to a bathroom and pull down her flowered leggings!

Not that she could ask them even if she wanted to. The bastards had slapped a wide strip of duct tape over her mouth before hauling her outside and hustling her into the waiting truck.

Her physical discomfort sapped her strength. The constant battle to hang on to to her desperate belief that Harry would find her drained it even more.

How long had it been now? Nine hours since she'd walked out of the pet shop on Menaul Avenue? Ten?

How long since Harry had realized that she was missing?

Bright highway lights flashed by in the windshield. Sheryl tried to concentrate on them, tried to keep her mind focused on the tiny details that might help if she had to reconstruct events for Harry after this was all over.

Despite her fierce concentration, doubts and sneaking, sinking fear ate away at her. What if Harry hadn't called her, as he'd promised he would? What if he'd gotten so caught up in his investigation that he didn't have time? Oh, God, what if he didn't even know she was missing?

She closed her eyes, fighting the panic that threatened to swamp her.

He said he'd call. He'd promised he would. What Harry promised, he'd do. She'd learned that much about him in the short, intense time they'd been together. He'd called her sometime today. She knew he had. And when she hadn't answered, he'd started looking.

He'd find her.

Battling fiercely with her incipient panic, she almost missed the click of directional signals. A moment later, the truck slowed and banked into a turn. Signs flashed by overhead, but Sheryl couldn't catch the lettering.

After another mile or so, Broken Nose twisted around. "It's show time, doll. You'd better hope our star performer shows."

Dragging a folded moving pad from under his seat, he shook it out and tossed it over her. Total blackness surrounded her, along with the stink of mildew and motor oil. Sheryl closed her eyes and prayed that she'd see Harry when she opened them.

She didn't.

When the pad was jerked away, Broken Nose loomed over her once more. His face was a grotesque mask of shadows in the diffused light of the truck's interior.

"Come on, sweetheart," he whined. "You're gonna wait inside. We don't want no nosy Customs inspectors catchin' sight of you in the truck, do we?"

Wrapping his paw around her elbow, he hauled her out of the truck. Pain zigzagged like white, agonizing lightning up and down Sheryl's arm. She couldn't breathe, let alone groan, through the duct tape sealing her mouth.

Broken Nose hauled her to her feet outside the truck and hustled her toward one of the rear doors in a corrugated steel hangar. Sheryl stumbled along beside him, trying desperately to clear her head of the pain and get her bearings. The air she dragged in through her nostrils carried with it the unmistakable bite of jet fuel fumes. The distant whine of engines revving up confirmed she was at the airport.

The moment her captor shoved her inside the huge, steel-sided building, she recognized the cavernous, shadowy interior. She could never forget it! She'd worked at rotation at the airport cargo-handling facility as a young rookie, years ago, and had counted the months until she'd gained enough seniority to qualify for another opening. Palletizing the sacks of mail that came into this building from the central processing center downtown for air shipment was backbreaking, dirty work.

Sure enough, she spotted a long row of web-covered pallets in the postal service's caged-off portion of the hangar. Desperately, she searched the dimly lit area for someone she might know, someone who might see her. Before she could locate any movement in the vast, echoing facility, Broken Nose shouldered open a door and pushed her into what looked like a heating/air-conditioning room. In the weak moonlight filtering through the single, dust-streaked window, Sheryl saw a litter of discarded web cargo straps, empty crates and broken chairs amid the rusted duct pipes.

Her captor surveyed the dust-covered floor and grunted in satisfaction. "Ain't nobody been in since I scouted this place out two days ago."

Roughly, he dragged Sheryl across the room and shoved her down onto a tangle of web cargo straps. She landed awkwardly on one knee. A hard hand in her back sent her tumbling onto her hip. Her elbow hit the concrete floor beneath the straps. Searing pain jolted into her shoulder, blinding her. Tears filled her eyes. She barely heard the snap as Broken Nose pulled another length of tape from his roll, barely felt her ankles jammed against a pipe and lashed together.

She felt the fist that buried itself in her hair, though, and a painful jerk as he brought her face around to his.

"We're gonna be right outside, see? Pickin' up our cargo soon's the lamebrain from Customs clears it. Everything goes okay, I'll come back for you."

His fist tightened in her hair.

"Anything goes wrong, I might or might not come back for you. If I don't, maybe someone'll find you in a week or a month. Or maybe they won't. You won't be so pretty when they do."

Grinning maliciously, he stroked a finger down her cheek. Sheryl couldn't move enough to flinch from his touch, but she put every drop of loathing she could into the look she sent him. Laughing, he left her in the musty darkness.

She lay, half on her side, half on her back, breathing in dust motes and the acrid scent of her own fear. Her relief that they'd left her for even a few moments was almost as great as her discomfort. Her shoulder was on fire. Her elbow throbbed. The metal clasp on one of the web straps gouged into her hip.

She didn't care. For the first time since she'd walked out of the pet store this morning, she was out of her captor's sight. Ignoring her various aches and pains, she twisted and turned, pulling at the tape binding her ankles to the pipe. The metal pole didn't budge, nor did the tape give, but she did manage to generate a small shower of rust particles and bugs. Praying that none of the insects that dropped down on her were of the biting variety, she tugged and twisted and pushed and pulled.

By the time she conceded defeat, she was filmed with sweat and rust and wheezing in air through her nose. For a moment, the panic she'd kept at bay for so many hours almost swamped her.

Where was Harry? Why hadn't he tracked her down? He was a U.S. marshal, for God's sake? He was supposed to be able to find anyone. Where was he?

Gradually, she fought down her panic. Slowly, she got her breath back. Blinking the sweat from her eyes, she shifted on the pile of straps to try again. Another pain shot up from her elbow. The edge of a strap buckle dug into her hip.

Suddenly, Sheryl froze. The strap buckles! The metal tongue of the clasp that connected the web straps had sharp edges. She'd cut herself on the damned things often enough as a rookie. If she could get a grip on one of the buckles, get the clasp open...

Sweating, straining, wiggling as much as her ankles would allow, Sheryl groped the pile underneath her. Her slick fingers found a metal apparatus, pulled open the hasp. It slipped away from her and closed with a snap. She grabbed the buckle again, holding it awkwardly with one hand.

Grimly determined now, she fumbled one of the thick straps into her hand. If she could just pry the buckle open enough...

Yes!

Too excited for caution, she slid a fingertip along the edge of the hasp. Instantly, warm blood welled from the slicing cut.

The thing was as sharp as she remembered!

Her heart thumping, she went to work on the duct tape. She'd freed her wrists and was working on her ankles when a sharp rap shattered the glass in the dusty window. Pieces fell to the concrete. The small tinkles reverberated like shots in Sheryl's head.

An arm reached inside and fumbled for the lock.

With a burst of strength, Sheryl pulled apart the remaining half inch of duct tape. She scrambled to her feet, still gripping the metal clasp. It wasn't much of a weapon, but it was all she had.

Slowly, the window screeched upward. A moment later, a figure covered in black from head to toe climbed through. Even before he holstered his weapon and whipped off his ski mask, Sheryl had recognized the lean, muscular body.

"Harry!"

She threw herself across the room, broken glass

crunching like popcorn under her feet. He crushed her against his chest.

"Are you all right?" he asked, his voice urgent in her ear.

She dismissed burning shoulders and aching wrists and cut fingers. "Yes."

"Thank God!"

His fierce embrace squeezed the air from Sheryl's lungs. She didn't care. At this moment, breathing didn't concern her. All that mattered was the feel of Harry's arms around her. Which didn't explain why she promptly burst into tears.

"It's all right, sweetheart," he soothed, his voice low and ragged. "It's all right. I'm here."

She leaned back, swallowing desperately, and stared up at him through a sheen of tears. "What took you so darned long?"

"It took me a while to convince Inga to talk."

"How…?" She gulped. "How did you do that?"

A small, tight smile flitted across Harry's face. "I got a little help from Button."

"From Button!"

He hustled her toward the window. "I'll tell you about it later. Right now, I just want to get you out of here. Then I'm going after the bastards who kidnapped you. My whole team's outside, ready to move in as soon as you're clear."

"No!" Sheryl spun around and grabbed at him with both hands. "You can't take those two down. Not yet! They're waiting for Paul Gunderson. He's coming in tonight, Harry. Tonight!"

"I know."

His slow, satisfied reply sent a shiver down her back. For a moment Sheryl almost didn't recognize the man who stared at her. His face could have been cut from rock.

Almost as quickly as it appeared, the fierceness left his eyes. In its place came a look that made her blink through the blur of her tears.

"Come on, sweetheart. Let's get you out of here."

Her fingers dug into the sleeves of his black windbreaker. She had to tell him. Had to let him know before he shoved her through the window and turned back into danger.

"Harry, I love you. I...I know it's too soon for commitments and promises and almost-anythings between us, but I—"

He cut off her disjointed declaration with a swift, hard, soul-shattering kiss.

"I love you, too. I suspected it this morning, when all I could think about was getting back to you. I knew it this afternoon, when we found your car." His jaw worked. "I don't *ever* want to go through that again, so let's get you the hell out of here. Now!"

They almost made it.

Her heart singing, Sheryl started for the window once more. Broken glass crunched under her feet and almost covered the sound of the door opening behind them.

"What the hell...?"

Harry spun around, yanking her behind him. Off balance and flailing for a hold, Sheryl didn't see him reach for his gun. Broken Nose did, though.

"Don't do it!" he shouted. Desperation added an

octave to his high-pitched whine. "Your hand moves another inch and I swear to God, I'll put one of these hot slugs through you and the bitch both!"

Harry froze. A single glance at the oversized barrel on the weapon in the man's hand confirmed that it was engineered to fire uranium-tipped cop-killer bullets. The same kind of bullets that had ripped right through his best friend's body armor. Harry was willing to stop a bullet to protect Sheryl, but he couldn't, wouldn't, take the chance that it might plow right through him and into her, as well.

His pulse hammering, he lifted both hands clear of his sides. His Smith & Wesson sat like a dead weight in its holster just under his armpit.

"Yeah, yeah! That's better."

Even in the dim moonglow, Harry recognized the man whose flattened nose and jet-black hair he'd memorized from a mug shot less than an hour ago.

"All right, D'Agustino. Don't get crazy here and maybe we can work a deal."

"Jesus! You know who I am?"

"You and your partner both. You might as well give it up now. We've got this place surrounded."

"I knew it! I knew them guys in the coveralls weren't no wrench benders, not with them bulges under their arms. That's why I come running back for the broad. She's my ticket outta here."

Harry felt Sheryl go rigid against his back. Her fingers gripped his shirt. The image of her pinned helplessly against this killer raised a red haze in front of his eyes. Coldly, he blinked it away.

"She's not going anywhere with you, D'Agustino."

"Oh, yeah! Guess again."

The snick of a hammer cocking back added emphasis to the sneering reply.

Harry started to speak, and almost strangled on an indrawn breath. His whole body stiffened at the feel of a hand sliding around his rib cage. Without seeming to move, he brought his arms in just enough to cover Sheryl's reach for his holstered weapon.

Sweat rolled down his temples as her fingers slid under his arm. Sheryl hated guns! They made her nervous. She'd told him so more than once. She probably didn't have the faintest idea how to use one!

At that moment, Harry figured he had two options. He could throw himself at D'Agustino and hope to beat a bullet to the punch, or he could trust the woman behind him to figure out which end of a .357 was which.

It didn't even come close to a choice. He'd take his chances with Sheryl over this punk any day.

"Think about it D'Agustino," he said, trying desperately to buy her some time. "We know who you are. We know you've been working with Paul Gunderson. I have two dozen men waiting to greet him when his plane touches down a few minutes from now."

"Yeah, well, me and Sheryl ain't waiting around for that. Get over here, bitch!"

Harry could smell the man's fear. Hear it in his high, grating whine.

"You might get away this time, but we'll come

after you. All of us. The FBI. The U.S. Marshals Service. Customs. Better give yourself up now. Talk to us.''

"Don't you understand! I'm a dead man if Big Jake hears I cut a deal with the feds!"

"You're a dead man if you don't."

"No! No, I ain't!"

He knew the instant D'Agustino's gun came up that time had just run out.

He dived across the room.

A shot exploded an inch from his ear.

Sheryl didn't kill the little bastard. She didn't even wound him. But she startled him just enough to throw off his aim.

His gun barrel spit red flame. A finger of fire seared across Harry's cheek. The wild shot ricocheted off a pipe and gouged into the ceiling at precisely the same instant his fist smashed into an already flattened nose with a satisfying, bone-crunching force.

D'Agustino reared back, howling. A bruising left fist followed the right. The man crumpled like a sack of stones.

His chest heaving, Harry reached down and jerked the specially crafted .45 out of his hand. Although the thug showed no signs of moving any time soon, he kept the gun trained at his heart. Over the prone body, his anxious gaze found Sheryl.

"You okay?"

She nodded, her face paper white in the dimness. Then, incredibly, she produced a shaky, strained smile.

"You'd better cuff him or...or do whatever it is you marshals do. We've got a plane to meet."

Chapter 14

"**I**'m not leaving."

Sheryl folded arms encased in the too-long sleeves of a black windbreaker and glared at Deputy Marshal Ev Sloan. He fired back with an equally stubborn look.

"It could get nasty around here. Nasti*er*," he amended with a glance at the two men huddled back to back on the asphalt a few yards away, their hands cuffed behind their backs. Fay and another officer stood over them, reading them their rights.

"I want to stay," Sheryl insisted. "I need to see this."

"This isn't any place for civilians. We don't have time to—"

"It's okay, Ev."

Harry nodded his thanks to the medic who'd just taped a gauze bandage on his upper cheek. He crossed the asphalt to the task force command vehicle, his gaze on the woman hunched in the front seat.

"She's part of the team."

His quiet words dissolved the last of Sheryl's own secret doubts. She couldn't quite believe that she was sitting in a truck that bristled with more antennas than a porcupine on a bad-quill day, watching while an army of law enforcement agencies checked their weapons and coordinated last-minute details for the takedown of a smuggler and suspected killer. Or that she'd pulled out a .357 Magnum and squeezed a trigger herself mere moments ago. Until Harry MacMillan had charged into her life, she'd only experienced this kind of Ramboesque excitement through movies and TV.

This wasn't a movie, though. She had the bruises and the bunched-up knot of fear in her stomach to prove it. This was real. This was life or death, and Harry was right in the middle of it. There was no way Sheryl was going to leave, as Ev insisted, while Harry calmly walked right back into the line of fire.

Besides, she and Harry had a conversation to finish. They'd tossed around a few words such as "love" and "commitment" and "promises" in that dark, dirty storeroom. Sheryl wanted more than words.

She wouldn't get them any time soon, she saw. Having assured himself she'd sustained no serious injury, and having had the powder burn on his cheek attended to, the marshal was ready for action. More than ready. In the glow from the command vehicle's overhead light, his whiskey-gold eyes gleamed with barely restrained impatience. He paused before her, holding himself in check long enough to brush a knuckle down her cheek.

"I don't want to worry about you any more than I already have today. Promise me that you'll stay in the command vehicle."

"I promise."

"Ev told you that we have a U.S. Marshals Service plane standing by. If Paul Gunderson's aboard the incoming aircraft and we take him down..."

"You will!" Sheryl said fiercely. "I know you will!"

His knuckle stilled. The glint in his eyes turned feral. "Yes, I will."

She bit down her lower lip, waiting for him to come back to her. A moment later, the back of his hand resumed its slow stroke.

"I might not get a chance to talk to you after the bust. I'll have to bundle Gunderson aboard our plane and get him and his two pals back to Washington for arraignment."

"I know."

Cupping her chin, he turned her face a few more degrees into the light. He stared down at her, as if imprinting her features on his memory.

Sheryl could have wished for a better image for him to take with him. Her cheeks still carried traces of the rust and squashed bugs that had rained down on her from the overhead pipes during her desperate escape attempt. Her hair frizzed all over her head. If she'd had on a lick of makeup when she'd left her apartment so many hours ago, she'd long since chewed or rubbed or cried it off.

Harry didn't seem to mind the bugs or frizz or total lack of color on her face. His thumb traced a slow path across her lower lip.

"I'll be back. I promise."

Turning her head, Sheryl pressed a kiss to his palm. Her smile was a little ragged around the edges, but she got it into place.

"I'll be waiting."

His hand dropped. A moment later, he disappeared, one of many shadows that melted into the darkness.

Even Ev Sloan deserted Sheryl, vowing that he wasn't going to miss out on the action again. Another deputy marshal took his place in the command vehicle. He introduced himself with a nod, then gave the bank of radios mounted under the dash his total concentration.

Sheryl huddled in her borrowed windbreaker. For some foolish reason, she'd believed that she could never again experience the sick terror that had gripped her those awful hours with Broken Nose and Slick Hair. Now she realized that listening helplessly while the man she loved put his life on the line bred its own brand of terror.

Her heart in her throat, she followed every play in Harry's deadly game.

The game ended less than half an hour later.

To Sheryl's immense relief, the man subsequently identified as Richard Johnson-Paul Gunderson stepped off the cargo plane, tossed up an arm to shield his eyes from a blinding flood of light and promptly threw himself face down on the concrete parking apron.

As a jubilant Ev related to Sheryl, the bastard was brave enough with his mob connections backing him up. Without them, he wet his pants at the first warning shout.

Literally.

"Harry had to scrounge up a clean pair of jeans before he could hustle the bastard aboard our plane," Ev reported gleefully. "The government will probably have to foot the bill for them, but what the hell! We got him, Sher! We got him!"

Grinning from ear to ear, he unbuckled his body armor and tossed it into his gear bag. His webbed belt with its assortment of canisters and ammo clips followed.

"I would've left him to stew in his own juice, so to speak, but then I didn't have to handcuff myself to the man and sit next to him in a small aircraft for the next five or six hours the way Harry did."

"I can see how that would make a difference," Sheryl concurred, her eyes on the twin-engine jet revving up at the end of the runway.

Ev's gear bag hit the back of the command vehicle with a thunk.

"Harry told me to take you home. Fay has to hang around until the Nuclear Regulatory folks finish decertifying the canisters. I told her I'd come back to help with the disposition. You ready to go?"

The small plane with U.S. Marshals Service markings roared down the runway. Sheryl followed its blinking red and white lights until they disappeared into a bank of black clouds.

"I'm ready."

Ev traded places with the marshal who'd manned the command vehicle. He twisted the key in the ignition, then shoved the truck into gear.

"We have to swing by the federal building to pick up the mutt."

"Button?"

Ev's teeth showed white in the airport exit lights. "Harry left him with the security guards when we came chasing out here. As obnoxious as that mutt is, I wouldn't be surprised if one of the guards hasn't skinned him by now and nailed his hide over the front door."

They soon discovered that Button was still in one piece, although the same couldn't be said for the security guards. One sported a long tear in his uniform sleeve. The other pointed out the neat pattern of teeth marks in his leather brogans.

Sheryl apologized profusely and retrieved the indignant animal from the lidded trash can where the guards had stashed him. Button huffed and snuffled and ruffled up his fur, but let himself be carried from the federal building with only a few parting snarls at the guards. After a few greeting snarls at Ev, he settled down on Sheryl's chest.

She buried her nose in his soft, silky fur. The lights of Old Town, only a few blocks from the federal building, sped by unnoticed. The bright wash of stars overhead didn't draw her eyes. Even Ev's excited recounting of the night's tumultuous events barely penetrated. In her mind, she followed the flight of a small silver jet over the Sandias and across New Mexico's wide, flat plains.

He'd be back. He'd promised.

But when?

"Looks like it's going to be next week before Gunderson's arraignment."

Turning her back on the noise of the lively group who'd just arrived at her apartment to celebrate young Master Brian Hart's christening, Sheryl strained to hear Harry's recorded message.

"You have my office number. They can reach me anytime, night or day, if you have an emergency. I'll talk to you soon."

The recorder clicked off.

Frustrated, she hit the repeat button. Except for one short call soon after Harry had arrived in D.C., he and Sheryl had been playing telephone tag for almost three days now. From what she'd gleaned through his brief messages, the man she now thought of as Richard Johnson had held out longer than anyone had expected before finally breaking his stubborn silence. Once the dam gave, the assistant DA working the case had kept Harry busy helping with the briefs for the grand jury. Now, it appeared, he'd have to stay in D.C. until next week's arraignment.

"Sheryl, where are the pretzels? I can't— Oh, I'm sorry, honey. I didn't know you were on the phone."

Replacing the receiver, Sheryl pasted on a smile and turned to face her mother. "I'm not. I was just checking my messages."

"Well? Did he call?"

"Yes, he called."

"Where is he?"

"Still in Washington."

"I want to meet this man. When is he coming back to Albuquerque?"

"He doesn't know."

Her mother's thin, still-attractive face took on the pinched look that Sheryl had seen all too often in her youth. Joan Hancock wanted to say more. That much was obvious from the way she bit down on her lower lip.

Thankfully, she refrained.

She had driven up to Albuquerque from Las Cruces three days ago, after Elise's frantic call informing her that her daughter was missing. She'd stayed through the rest of the weekend, demanding to know every detail about Sheryl's involvement in a search for a dangerous fugitive.

Needless to say, the cautious bits her daughter let drop about the deputy marshal who'd swept in and out of her life hadn't pleased Joan any more than observing Brian Mitchell's growing attachment to his namesake…and his namesake's mother.

The christening ceremony tonight had only added to her disgruntlement. Sheryl and Brian had stood as godparents to the baby. Seeing them together at the altar had rekindled Joan Hancock's grievances against Elise. She was still convinced that the new mother had schemed to steal Sheryl's boyfriend right out from under her nose.

"Just look at her," she griped, pressing the pretzel

bowl against the front of the pale-gray silk dress she'd worn to the church. "The way she's making those goo-goo eyes at Brian, you'd think he'd fathered her child instead of her shiftless ex-husband."

Sheryl's gaze settled on the scene in the living room. Elise had anchored the baby's carrier in a corner of the sofa, where it couldn't be jostled by her two lively boys. They were showing off their baby brother to the assembled crowd with patented propriety. Brian leaned against the arm of the sofa, one finger unconsciously stroking the baby's feathery red curls while he chatted with Elise. Even Button had gotten into the act. Perched on the back of the sofa, he waved his silky tail back and forth and guarded the baby with the regal hauteur that had made the shih tzu so prized by the emperors of China.

It was a picture-perfect family tableau. With all her heart, Sheryl wished everyone in the picture happiness.

She'd told Elise so when the two friends had snatched a half hour alone yesterday. Even now, she had to smile at the emotions that had chased across Elise's face, one after another, like tumbleweeds blown by a high wind. Pain for Sheryl over her break with Brian. Guilty relief that he was free. Disbelief that her friend had fallen for Harry so hard, so fast. Worry that she was in for some hurting times ahead.

Like Joan, Elise couldn't quite believe that her friend had opted to settle for a life of loneliness, broken by days or weeks or even months of companionship. Sheryl couldn't quite believe it, either, but sometime in the past few days, she had.

Joan gave a long, wistful sigh. "Are you sure you and Brian can't patch things up?"

"I'm sure."

Her gaze left the group on the sofa and settled on her daughter's face. "Oh, Sherrie, I hoped you'd do better than I did."

Sheryl's smile softened. "You did fine, Mom."

A haze of tears silvered Joan's green eyes, so like her daughter's. "I wanted you to find someone steady and reliable. Someone who'd be there when you needed him to kiss away your hurts and share your laughter and fix the leaky faucets."

"You taught me to be pretty handy with a wrench," Sheryl replied gently. "And Harry was there when I needed him."

He'd been there, and he'd done more than kiss away her hurts, she acknowledged silently. After her breakup with Brian, he'd driven the hurt right out of her mind. At the airport, he'd wiped away a good measure of her terror and trauma by the simple act of acknowledging her as part of his team.

Along the way, Sheryl thought with an inner smile, he'd also taken her to dizzying heights of pleasure that she'd never dreamed of, let alone experienced. She craved the feel of his hands on her breasts, ached for the brush of his prickly mustache against her skin. She longed to curl up with him on the couch and share a pepperoni-and-pineapple pizza, and watch his face when he bit into one of New Mexico's man-sized peppers.

In short, she wanted whatever moments they could snatch and memories they could make together. Everyone else might count their time together in hours, but Sheryl measured it by the clinging, stubborn love that had taken root in her heart and refused to let go.

Her mother sighed again. "You're going to wait for this man, aren't you? Night after night, week after week?"

"Yes, I am."

Joan lifted a hand and rested a palm against her daughter's cheek. "You're stronger than I was, Sherrie. You'll…you'll make it work."

She hoped so. She sincerely hoped so.

"Come on, Mom. Let's get back to the party."

Despite her conviction that Harry was worth waiting for, Sheryl found the wait more difficult than she'd let on to her mother. The hours seemed to stretch endlessly. Thankfully, she had her job to keep her busy during the day and Button to share her nights.

According to Ev Sloan, she could expect to have the mutt's company for some time to come. He called with the news the evening after little Brian's christening. Just home from work and about to step into the shower, Sheryl ran out of the bathroom and snatched the phone up on the second ring. With some effort, she kept the fierce disappointment from her voice.

"Hi, Ev."

Clutching the towel she'd thrown around her with one hand, she listened to his gleeful news. Patrice Jörgenson/Johnson, aka Inga Gunderson, cut a deal with the federal authorities. In exchange for information about her nephew's activities, she would plead guilty to a lesser battery of charges that would give her the possibility of parole in a few years.

"We're transporting her to D.C. Got a plane standing by. She wants to say goodbye to the mutt first."

"You mean, like, now? Over the phone?"

"Yeah."

The note of disgust in Ev's voice told Sheryl he hadn't quite recovered from his initial bout with Button, when the dog had locked onto his leg.

"I'll, er, put him on."

Perching on the side of the bed, she prodded the sleeping dog awake. At the sound of his mistress's voice, he yipped into the phone once or twice before curling back into a ball and leaving Sheryl to finish the conversation. Somehow, she found herself promising to write faithfully and keep the older woman apprised of Button's health and welfare.

Sniffing, Inga provided a list of absolute essentials. "He takes B-12 and vitamin E twice a week. His vet can supply you with the coated tablets. They're easier for him to swallow. And don't forget his heartworm pills."

"How could I forget those?" Sheryl countered with a grimace.

"Make sure you keep his hair out of his eyes to prevent irritation of the lids."

"I will."

"Don't use rubber bands, though! They pull his hair."

"I won't."

"Oh, I canceled his standing appointment at the stud. You'll have to call them back and reinstate him."

"Excuse me?"

"Button's descended from a line of champions," Inga explained in a teary, quavering voice so different from the one that had shouted obscenities at Harry and Ev that her listener found it hard to believe she was the same woman. "We could charge outrageous stud fees if we wanted to, you know, but we just go there so my precious can, well, enjoy himself."

Sheryl blinked. She hadn't realized her responsibilities would include pimping for Button. She was still dealing with that mind-boggling revelation when Inga sniffed.

"He's very virile. They always offer me pick of the litter." She paused. "You may keep one of his pups in exchange for taking care of him. Or perhaps two, since you work and a pet shouldn't be left alone all day."

"Th-thank you."

Underwhelmed by the magnanimous offer, Sheryl glanced at the tight black-and-white ball on her bed. She could just imagine Harry's reaction if two or three Buttons crawled under the covers with him in the middle of the night.

Assuming Harry ever got back to Albuquerque to get under the covers.

Sighing, she copied down the last of Inga's instructions, held the phone to the dog's ear a final time and hung up. She stood beside the bed for a moment, staring down into her companion's buggy black eyes.

"What do you say, fella? Wanna share a pizza after I get out of the shower?"

Chapter 15

The glossy postcard leaped out at Sheryl from the sheaf of mail in her hand.

Tahiti.

A pristine stretch of sandy beach. A fringe of deep-green banyan trees. An aquamarine sea laced with white, lapping at the shore.

Resolutely, she fought down the urge to turn the postcard over and peek at the message on the back. She'd had enough vicarious adventures as a result of reading other people's mail to last her a while.

She won the brief struggle, but still couldn't bring herself to shove the card in the waiting post office box. For just a moment, she indulged a private fantasy and imagined herself on that empty stretch of beach with Harry. She saw him splashing toward her in the surf. The sun bronzed his lean, hard body. The breeze off the sea ruffled his dark hair. His gold-flecked eyes gleamed with—

"You okay, Sher?"

"What?" Startled out of the South Pacific, she glanced up guiltily to meet Elise's look. "Yes, I'm fine."

"You're thinking about the marshal again, aren't you? You've got that…that lost look on your face."

Sheryl flashed the postcard at her friend. "I was thinking about Tahiti."

Elise pursed her lips.

"All right, all right. I was thinking about Tahiti and Harry."

Nudging aside a stack of mail, the new mom cleared a space on the table between the banks of postal boxes and hitched a hip on the corner. She'd insisted on coming back to work, declaring that her ex-mother-in-law, her parents, her two boys and her regular baby-sitter were more than enough to care for the newest addition to the Hart family. She still hadn't fully regained the endurance required for postal work, though. Sheryl scooped up her bundle and added it to the stack in her hand.

"How long has it been now since Harry left?" Elise demanded as her friend fired the mail into the appropriate boxes. "A week? Eight days?"

"Nine, but who's counting?"

"You are! I am! Everyone in the post office is."

"Well, you can stop counting. He promised he'd come back. He will."

"Oh, Sher, he said he'd come back after the arraignment last week. Then he had to fly to Miami. I hate for you to…"

Buck Aguilar rumbled by with a full cart, drowning

out the rest of her comment. Sheryl didn't need to hear it. The worry in her eyes spoke its own language.

"He'll be back, Elise. He promised."

"I believe you," the other woman grumbled. "I just don't like seeing you jump every time the phone rings, or spending your evenings walking that obnoxious little hair ball."

"Give Button time," Sheryl replied, laughing. "He grows on you."

"Ha! That'll be the day. He almost took off my hand at the wrist when I made the mistake of reaching for the baby before Butty-boo was finished checking him out. Here, give me the last stack. I'll finish it."

"I've got it. You just sit and gather your strength for the hordes waiting in the lobby. We have to open in a few minutes."

Elise swung her sneakered foot, a small frown etched on her brow. Sheryl smiled to herself. Her friend still couldn't quite believe that she would prefer the marshal—or anyone else!—over Brian Mitchell. Despite the long talk the two women had shared, Elise had yet to work through her own feelings of guilt and secret longing.

She would. After watching her and Brian together, Sheryl didn't doubt that they'd soon reach the point she herself had come to this past week. They were meant for each other. Just as she and Harry were.

She'd wait for him. However long it took. Wherever his job sent him. She wasn't her mother, and Harry certainly wasn't her father. They'd wring every particle of happiness out of their time together and look forward to their next reunion with the same delicious anticipation that curled in Sheryl's tummy now.

After zinging the last of the box mail into its slot, she slammed the metal door. ''Come on, kiddo. We'd better get our cash drawers from the safe. We've only got…''

She glanced at the clock in the central work space and felt her heart sommersault. Striding through the maze of filled mail carts was a tall, unmistakable figure in tight jeans, a blue cotton shirt and a rumpled linen gray sport coat.

''Harry!''

Sheryl flew toward him, scattering letters and advertising fliers and postcards as she went. He caught her up in his arms and whirled her around. The room had barely stopped spinning before he bent his head and covered her mouth with his. Instantly, the whole room tilted crazily again.

Flinging her arms around his neck, she drank in his kiss. It was better than she remembered. Wild. Hot. Hungry. When he lifted his head, she dragged in great, gulping breaths and let the questions tumble out.

''When did you get in? Why didn't you call? What happened in Miami?''

Grinning, he kissed her again, much to the interest of the various personnel who stopped their work to watch.

''Twenty minutes ago. I didn't want to take the time. And we nailed the arms manufacturer Gunderson was supplying.''

''Good!''

Laughing at her fierce exclamation, he hefted her higher in his arms and started for the back door.

''Wait a minute!'' Sheryl was more than willing to let him carry her right out of the post office, but she needed to cover her station. "I've got to get someone to take the front counter for me."

"It's all arranged," he told her, his eyes gleaming.

"What is?"

"The postmaster general got a call from the attorney general early this morning, Miss Hancock. You're being recommended for a citation for your part in apprehending an escaped fugitive and suspected killer." The gleam deepened to a wicked glint. "You've also been granted the leave you requested. There's a temp on the way down to fill in for you."

"I seem to be having some trouble recalling the fact that I asked for leave."

"I wouldn't be surprised, with all you've gone through lately." Harry wove his way through the carriers' stations. "You asked for two weeks for your honeymoon."

Sheryl opened her mouth, shut it, opened it again. A thousand questions whirled around in her head. Only one squeaked out.

"Two weeks, huh?"

"Two weeks," he confirmed. "Unless you don't have a current passport, in which case we'll have to tack on a few extra days so we can stop over in Washington to pull some strings."

He slowed, his grin softening to a smile so full of tenderness that Sheryl's throat closed.

"I want to take you to Heidelburg, sweetheart, and stand beside you on the castle ramparts when the Neckar River turns gold in the sunset. I want to watch your face the first time you see the spires of Notre Dame rising out of the morning mists. I want to make love to you in France and Italy and Germany and

wherever else we happen to stop for an hour or a day
or a night.''

"Oh, Harry."

He eased his arm from under her knees. Sheryl's
feet slid to the floor, but she didn't feel the black tiles
under her sneakers. Not with Harry's hands locked
loosely around her waist and his heart thumping
steadily against hers.

"I know you said it was too soon for commitments
and promises, but I've had a lot of time to think this
past week."

"Me, too," she breathed.

"I don't want almost, Sheryl. I want you now and
forever."

He brushed back her hair with one hand. All trace
of amusement left his eyes.

"The regional director's position here in the Albuquerque office comes open next month. The folks
in D.C. tell me the job's mine if I want it."

Her pounding pulse stilled. She wanted Harry, as
much as he wanted her. But she wouldn't try to hold
him with either tears or a love that strangled.

"Do you want it, Harry?"

"Yes, sweetheart, I do. It'll mean less time on the
road, although I can't guarantee I'll have anything
resembling regular office hours or we'll enjoy a routine home life."

Sheryl could have told him that she'd learned her
lesson with Brian. On her list of top-ten priorities, a
comfortable routine now ranked about number
twenty-five. All that mattered, all she cared about,
was the way his touch made her blood sing, and the
crinkly lines at the corners of his eyes, and his soft,
silky mustache and...

"I'm a deputy marshal," he said quietly. "The service is in my blood."

"I know."

"So are you. I carried your smile and your sun-streaked hair and your little moans of delight with me day and night for the past week. I love you, Sheryl. I want to live the rest of my life with you, if you'll have me, and take you to all the places you dreamed about."

A sigh drifted on the air behind her. She didn't even glance around. She didn't care how many of her co-workers had gathered to hear Harry's soft declaration. One corner of his mustache tipped up.

"I thought about buying a ring and getting down on one knee and doing the whole romantic bit," he told her ruefully, "but I don't want to waste our time with almost-anythings. I want to go right for the real thing. Right here. Right now."

He would, she thought with a smile.

"There's a judge waiting for us at the federal building," he said gruffly. "He'll do the deed as soon as we get the license."

An indignant sputter sounded just behind Sheryl. Elise protested vehemently. "You have to call your mother, Sher! At least give her time to drive up from Las Cruces!"

"The judge will do the deed as soon as your mother gets here," Harry amended gravely, holding her gaze with his own.

Someone else spoke up. Pat Martinez, Sheryl thought.

"Hey, we want to be there, too! Wait until the shift change this afternoon. We'll shred up all that mail languishing in the dead-letter bin and come down to the courthouse armed with champagne and confetti.''

"Champagne and confetti sounds good to me.'' Harry smiled down at her. "Well?''

"I love you, too,'' she told him mistily. "I'll have you, Marshal, right here, right now and for the rest of our lives.''

Stretching up on her tiptoes, she slid her arms around his neck. He bent his head, and his mouth was only a breath away from hers when she murmured, "There's only one problem. We'll have to take Button with us on this honeymoon. Unless you know someone who will take care of him while we're gone?'' she asked hopefully.

"You're kidding, right?''

When she shook her head, he closed his eyes. Sheryl closed her ears to his muttered imprecations. When he opened them again, she saw a look of wry resignation in their golden brown depths.

"All right. We'll pick up a doggie-rat carrier on our way to the airport.''

At that moment, she knew she'd never settle for almost-anything again.

* * * * *

The World's Most Eligible Bachelors are about to be named! And Silhouette Books brings them to you in an all-new, original series....

World's Most
Eligible Bachelors

Twelve of the sexiest, most sought-after men share every intimate detail of their lives in twelve never-before-published novels by the genre's top authors.

Don't miss these unforgettable stories by:

Dixie Browning

Marie Ferrarella

Jackie Merritt

Tracy Sinclair

BJ James

RACHEL LEE

Suzanne Carey

Gina Wilkins

VICTORIA PADE

MAGGIE SHAYNE

Anne McAllister

Susan Mallery

Look for one new book each month in the
World's Most Eligible Bachelors series beginning
September 1998 from Silhouette Books.

Silhouette®

Available at your favorite retail outlet.

Take 2 bestselling love stories FREE

Plus get a FREE surprise gift!

Special Limited-Time Offer

Mail to Silhouette Reader Service™

3010 Walden Avenue
P.O. Box 1867
Buffalo, N.Y. 14240-1867

YES! Please send me 2 free Silhouette Intimate Moments® novels and my free surprise gift. Then send me 6 brand-new novels every month, which I will receive months before they appear in bookstores. Bill me at the low price of $3.57 each plus 25¢ delivery and applicable sales tax, if any.* That's the complete price, and a saving of over 10% off the cover prices—quite a bargain! I understand that accepting the books and gift places me under no obligation ever to buy any books. I can always return a shipment and cancel at any time. Even if I never buy another book from Silhouette, the 2 free books and the surprise gift are mine to keep forever.

245 SEN CH7Y

Name _____ (PLEASE PRINT)

Address _____ Apt. No. _____

City _____ State _____ Zip _____

This offer is limited to one order per household and not valid to present Silhouette Intimate Moments® subscribers. *Terms and prices are subject to change without notice. Sales tax applicable in N.Y.

UIM-98   ©1990 Harlequin Enterprises Limited

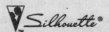

SILHOUETTE·INTIMATE·MOMENTS®
commemorates its

15th Anniversary

15 years of rugged, irresistible heroes!

15 years of warm, wonderful heroines!

15 years of exciting, emotion-filled romance!

In May, June and July 1998 join the celebration as Intimate Moments brings you new stories from some of your favorite authors—authors like:

**Marie Ferrarella
Maggie Shayne
Sharon Sala
Beverly Barton
Rachel Lee
Merline Lovelace**
and many more!

Don't miss this special event! Look for our distinctive anniversary covers during all three celebration months. Only from Silhouette Intimate Moments, committed to bringing you the best in romance fiction, today, tomorrow—always.

Available at your favorite retail outlet.

"You know who I am?" she asked.

Anger swamped Joe's reserve. "What the hell kind of question is that?"

She flinched, though he hadn't raised his voice. "What I mean is, who do you think I am, Mr. Guinn?"

Joe checked the impulse to answer with the phrase, "My ex." He didn't like any reference to the act that had "X-ed" out what had once been the emotional center of his life. The divorce had been her doing. If this was her way of testing his attitude, he wasn't going to make it easy for her.

"Why don't you just tell me why you're here?" he asked harshly.

"Very well." Her chin lifted. "I want to hire you, Mr. Guinn. I have amnesia, and I need you to find out who I am."

Dear Reader,

We've got six great books for you this month, and three of them are part of miniseries you've grown to love. Dallas Schulze continues A FAMILY CIRCLE with *Addie and the Renegade*. Dallas is known to readers worldwide as an author whose mastery of emotion is unparalleled, and this book will only enhance her well-deserved reputation. For Cole Walker, love seems like an impossibility—until he's stranded with Addie Smith, and suddenly… Well, maybe I'd better let you read for yourself. In *Leader of the Pack,* Justine Davis keeps us located on TRINITY STREET WEST. You met Ryan Buckhart in *Lover Under Cover;* now meet Lacey Buckhart, the one woman—the one wife!—he's never been able to forget. Then finish off Laura Parker's ROGUES' GALLERY with *Found: One Marriage.* Amnesia, exes who still share a love they've never been able to equal anywhere else…this one has it all.

Of course, our other three books are equally special.
Nikki Benjamin's *The Lady and Alex Payton* is the follow-up to *The Wedding Venture,* and it features a kidnapped almost-bride. Barbara Faith brings you *Long-Lost Wife?* For Annabel the past is a mystery—and the appearance of a man claiming to be her husband doesn't make things any clearer, irresistible though he may be. Finally, try Beverly Bird's *The Marrying Kind.* Hero John Gunner thinks that's just the kind of man he's *not,* but meeting Tessa Hadley-Bryant proves to him just how wrong a man can be.

And be sure to come back next month for more of the best romantic reading around—here in Silhouette Intimate Moments.

Yours,

Leslie Wainger
Senior Editor and Editorial Coordinator

Please address questions and book requests to:
Silhouette Reader Service
U.S.: 3010 Walden Ave., P.O. Box 1325, Buffalo, NY 14269
Canadian: P.O. Box 609, Fort Erie, Ont. L2A 5X3

FOUND: ONE MARRIAGE

LAURA PARKER

Published by Silhouette Books
America's Publisher of Contemporary Romance

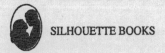

SILHOUETTE BOOKS

ISBN 0-373-07731-9

FOUND: ONE MARRIAGE

Books by Laura Parker

Silhouette Intimate Moments

Silhouette Special Edition

*Rogues' Gallery

LAURA PARKER

A Texas native, Laura recently made a "major" relocation. Her office is now on the third floor of a turn-of-the-century colonial house in northern New Jersey, where she lives with her husband and three children. Laura is often told that she must have the best career around. "After all, my hours are my own. I don't have to get up, dress and commute to work. I'm available if my children need me. I can even play hooky when the mood strikes. Best of all, I get to live in my imagination—where anything is possible."

Chapter 1

The east Texas drawl coming through his cellular phone broke up a little as Joe Guinn's pickup rounded a line of trees.

"... the damn investigation kept quiet! If Lacey's disappearance turns up in print every damn loony between here and the gulf will want cash for a lead. I'm hiring you 'cause you're one of us. I expect you to keep things under control. No damn leaks! Got that, Joe?"

"Yes sir, Mr. McCrea." Joe's tone was that of a patient professional. "I'll need to speak with your wife, of course. I can come by this even—"

"Absolutely not! Too upset. Doctor had to give her a sedative." Exasperation laced McCrea's baritone drawl. "Day or two won't make much difference. That hothead son of mine won't get far without my damn gold card! I've had enough. Gonna stick his butt in a military academy! You come by the bank tomorrow. Give you the details then.''

The line went dead abruptly.

Joe smirked as he punched the Off button on his phone. McCrea was not only part owner in East Texas Ranchers Savings and Loan, but a state senator. He was a man accustomed to issuing orders and having them followed without comment. Not everyone appreciated the treatment. Lacey McCrea seemed to be among them. Sixteen-year-old runaways were so common these days the media wouldn't ordinarily consider it news. But the disappearance of an unhappy son whose father had just announced his intention to run for another term would be of interest. That meant this job could become one big pain in the rear.

Joe reached for the ice-cold soda can wedged between his thighs and took a swig as the radio weatherman predicted that the unusually warm spring weather would bring thunderstorms by nightfall.

McCrea wasn't the only one who mistrusted the media. Two years ago Joe had been the main course in a media feeding frenzy that had savaged his life. He'd moved from New York City all the way back home to Gap, Texas to avoid more. Nowadays, all he asked of life was to be left in peace . . . and for the fish to be biting at sunrise.

He tucked the can back between his legs and reached up to scratch the week's growth on his chin. He'd been fishing down at Sam Houston National Park when the urgent message left by McCrea had prompted him to return today.

He supposed he should be grateful he had been offered the job. McCrea could have gone to Houston or

Dallas to hire big-time professionals. A private detective in a town the size of Gap didn't get many cases. Running down the occasional errant husband or back child-support checks barely kept his lights on and the phone connected. Nearby Tyler offered the slightly more lucrative case of the cheating spouse or bad check writer. But, all in all, no case these last two years promised to pay as well as this one.

Joe shifted gears as he made the turn onto the dirt road that led a hundred yards along a windbreak of oaks to the farmhouse that had been in his family since Roosevelt charged San Juan Hill. Three generations of Guinns before him had sunk roots deep into east Texas soil. The fact that he hadn't set foot in the state between the ages of fifteen and thirty hadn't counted against him with his neighbors when he moved back.

He had overheard a conversation between his closest neighbor, whom everyone called Uncle Liam, and the mailman not long after he arrived. His return was the subject of their discussion.

"The boy ain't a Yankee," Uncle Liam had offered in explanation. "Joe just now figured that out, is all."

Joe was grateful for the backing but he suspected the older man was as curious as everyone else about his reappearance.

No one had dared probe directly into the reason for his sudden and unexpected return to the place of his birth, but he knew people talked and speculated behind his back. The gossip that had dogged him all the way from Manhattan was too juicy to be ignored. One rumor said he had married and divorced an ex-Radio City Rockette. Another whispered that she'd been a rich-bitch society type. Others concentrated on his professional life. It was said he had committed a crime and been forced out or even fired under a cloud of suspicion from his position as a detective of the NYPD. For a few months, those rumors made him the quiet eye of a very lively storm. Joe did not answer them, defy them, or defend them. To do that would have meant he would have to think about the rumors. And thinking was the last thing he wanted to do... unless it was feeling.

Gradually, he had learned to reappreciate the simple pleasures of the pine-forested gentle rolling land of his youth. He had even found an excuse to awaken every day by going fishing. He had learned to put pleasure before purpose and found that life had become bearable.

As Joe rounded a turn, he expelled a rough whisper of vulgarity as he braked hard to an accompanying spray of gravel from beneath his truck tires.

A paper banner stretched twelve full feet across the front porch of his house. In big block letters were printed the words: HAPPY BIRTHDAY, JOE! The fancy banner acted on him like a red flag waved before a touchy bull.

"Lauren," he muttered irritably as he swung open the truck door and stepped out. Lauren Sawyer had been trying for months to "draw him out" as his neighbors would say. He had tried to make it perfectly clear that he didn't want to be drawn out. He couldn't imagine how she found out it was his birthday. He hadn't meant to remember it himself.

He slammed the truck door then leaned against it, thumbs hooking into the belt loops of his jeans. Though he didn't see her car, he suspected she might be inside waiting to surprise him. Behind his shades his gaze narrowed in on the end of the banner that had come loose and snapped whiplike in the brisk wind. He saw now that it contained the day's date: April 1. It was his birthday—but it was also the anniversary of his marriage, and divorce.

The reminder made the old anger and hurt and humiliation roil in his belly like a barrel of snakes.

Since the day of his return, he had had to battle east Texas hospitality. Folks just smiled when he said he wasn't much for socializing and continued to invite him over for fried chicken or barbecue. Occasionally, reluctantly, he accepted. He had a PI business to run, such as it was. Contacts were vital.

Not surprisingly, he often found himself introduced to the unattached sister, aunt, cousin or friend who just happened to be in town. He would smile cautiously, avoid eye contact, and then retreat as soon as etiquette permitted. Occasionally the woman wouldn't take no for an answer. Lauren Sawyer was one.

As tenacious as a burr, she found ways and excuses to meet him in town, at the grocery, in the street, even at the homes of mutual acquaintances. The few times he had relented and they'd gone out had been nice, but only nice. Ending up in bed with her had not improved his feelings of discomfort. The impulse had been a response to a call of nature that she was more than willing to answer. He'd been lousy. She'd been a sport. No strings, she said. Just laughs, she promised.

Had he been any other man he suspected her flattering attention would eventually have made inroads in his reluctance. But he didn't want a relationship with her or any other woman just yet. He liked his self-made hell just fine.

A wicked smile bloomed in the dark nettles of his beard. He hadn't bothered to shower or change clothes since he left home. He looked like a wild man and smelled like something that had washed up on the riverbank and been left too long in the sun. He knew that if he chose he could in five seconds flat have Miss Sawyer running for her jasmine-scented life.

Smiling, he reared away from his truck and headed for his house.

There was no one inside the dim cool interior when he pushed open the front door. As he glanced about the empty living room he felt the sudden letdown of a man cruising for a fight only to find no takers. His gaze whipped right and left, past the plain but well-preserved furnishings nearly a century old, past the more modern additions of TV and stereo, to the dining room. He discovered only one thing out of place. In the center of the crocheted tablecloth sat a slightly melting cake with a single candle sticking up from the middle.

He closed in on it like a member of a bomb squad approaching a ticking package. He glanced toward the open door that led to the kitchen, half suspecting that at any moment a party horn would blare and confetti would rain down cheerfully from a feminine hand. Nothing.

Up close, he recognized the white boiled frosting cake with toasted coconut and pineapple tidbits for garnish as a staple of church socials. He stuck a finger in the stiff marshmallowlike frosting and sucked the sweet glob off his finger. Almost reluctantly he admitted that it was good.

Then he spied the card lying on the table. In a neat swirling feminine hand was written his full name: Joseph Aloysius Guinn.

Joe winced. In a part of the country where boys were given short masculine names like Jake or Chip or Bart or Sonny, his appellation had been the bane of his young life.

He opened the card and his dark brows lifted in surprise. He knew at once she had not purchased this card in Gap. It contained an unexpectedly salacious drawing with an invitation to do more than share a slice of cake. At the bottom she had left the impression of her lips in scarlet with her phone number beneath. He closed it with a rough sigh.

Maybe he was being a little too hard on himself. Maybe the only way to get over the past was to participate in the present. Maybe... if...

He glanced up, accidently meeting his reflection in the gilt frame mirror that hung over his grandmother's buffet. What he saw was a tall man in a burnt orange University of Texas T-shirt. Above the shirt his sun-darkened face was all but masked by bristle and too long thick dark brown hair whipped by the wind. He looked like a mugger or a rapist. No doubt about it, Lauren would have run.

He dropped the card on the table, plowed his finger again into the icing, and then headed for his bedroom. After a shower and a beer he might even change his mind about that birthday invitation. He wasn't dead—just cautious.

It was nearly dark and Joe had gotten no farther than his living room. All he wore was the towel he had wrapped about his hips after exiting the shower. Drops

of water ran from his hairline down the sides of his
face, mimicking sweat tracks. He sat sprawled in a recliner, staring absently at an Australian rules football
game on the TV. It was amazing what a satellite dish
could bring into one's home. Other things weren't so
easily obtained.

After two years' absence he had decided that he really missed only three things about his New York life:
real pizza, all-night Chinese takeout, and...and....
A blur of images swam before his unfocused gaze. The
third thing escaped him.

He took a slow-motion swig of beer from the can in
his hand. The rest of the empty six-pack lay beside him
on the carpet. He would not be leaving his house tonight. He was way beyond the legal limit for drivers.
He rarely drank much. But he had decided to celebrate, after all.

He glanced at the crumbling facade of the birthday
cake sitting on the coffee table next to where his bare
feet were propped. Three tender yellow layers were
exposed where he had hacked away several slices with
a butcher knife. Cake and beer. It wasn't much for
nutrition but it had filled his belly.

There was another place inside him that could not
be filled. The hollowed-out place in his gut carved by
bad luck, bad timing, and bad choices had not been
plugged, paved over, or healed to any real degree by
two long years of regret and self-recrimination.

Halle!

The aluminum can caved in to the pressure of his
hand and then warm beer foamed over his fingers. The
TV image blurred before his gaze. But not from tears.
He had not, could not, shed a tear as long as blister-

ing rage continued to make a wasteland of his emotional terrain.

He had nominally survived the divorce. But at times like this his brain kept tossing up question marks at the end of the positive statements of survival.

Someday he would get over her.

Fine. When would his 'get over' begin?

He would move on.

Good. How long before the pain would end?

He would love again.

Great! Who and when?

He knew the answer. No one and never. He had left something undone, incomplete. He had never had a chance to explain his actions, his mistakes, his regrets to the one person in the world who deserved an explanation: the very ex-Mrs. Joe Guinn.

It did not help one iota to know that she had gotten on with her life. Hell! She'd remarried within a few months of their divorce to the exact type of man she should have married in the first place.

But, sometimes, the self-loathing bled over into rage at Halle. He knew it wasn't her fault that he had not moved forward. He envied her resilience...and hated the memory of her that would not let him get on with his own life.

Joe opened his eyes at the sound of a car coming up the road toward his house. He heard a car door open then the gentle whisper of a female voice.

A lopsided self-satisfied male smile blossomed in his unshaven beard as he rose slowly to his feet. Lauren must have come back. Maybe she had known he wouldn't accept her invitation and decided not to take no for an answer.

He was only mildly surprised to hear the car retreating. She must have had someone drop her off. Was she making certain he wouldn't be able to send her away? Well, this was her lucky day. Her appearance caused him to make a snap decision. From now on, he would fake it until he could make it. His 'get over' would begin tonight, with the woman who walked through his door.

He checked his towel. No need to scare her away.

He heard her heels tapping across the rough planks of his porch as she approached. He imagined that she wore something silky and fluid that would slide off easily under the impetus of his hands. He paused a few feet from his open door and waited until she was an indistinct shape in the darkness beyond his screen.

"Joe Guinn?" Something familiar in her tone. Something Yankee in the inflection. This was not Lauren.

"Yeah, that's me."

"The private investigator?"

"That's right." Joe's amorous hopes evaporated as he retucked the end of his towel below his navel. This was a prospective client. "What can I do for you?"

"I want you to find someone for me."

Her voice backstroked through his memory. He reached for the porch light switch as he asked, "Who?"

"Me."

The yellow halo of light jumped to life, illuminating the very last person he ever expected to see. He sucked in a breath of astonishment. "Halle?"

Chapter 2

A thunderclap right by his ear could not have jolted Joe more.

Halle—pronounced "holly" like the berry bush she told strangers—Halle Shipmann nee Hayworth, ex-Guinn, was staring back at him through the rusted webbing of his front door screen.

Surfacing emotions adrenalized his nervous system. His vision narrowed to a star point of light and then widened so quickly he felt dizzy. His heart expanded like a balloon, pumping as if a sawed-off shotgun were aimed point-blank at his chest.

As his gaze bored into her through the screen she shook her head slightly as if to shake off the daze that had for a second or two bound them both. Riveted by an intensity he hadn't experienced since she walked out of his life, he watched unfamiliar dark tresses shift over her shoulders. That was Halle. When they were married she changed her hairstyle and color with the seasons. She had been a strawberry blonde with a razor cut the last time he'd seen her. She had been two years younger and still Mrs. Joe Guinn the last time he'd seen her. She had still been *his* the last time he'd seen her.

He finally met her gaze, frank and arrested by the sight of him, and every instinct for self-preservation sounded an alarm. He wasn't ready, wasn't nearly prepared emotionally to see her again.

He leaned a bare shoulder against the doorjamb and even managed to sound casual. "Well, well. What brings you all the way out here?"

He saw her eyes widen fractionally. The yellow bulb leeched the green flecks from the well-remembered hazel, leaving them muddy. "I came to—to—"

She frowned slightly. She had always frowned just that way when trying to remember something that momentarily escaped her. Then she smiled the tough-girl tender-woman smile that had hooked him day one of their meeting. "I know this is going to sound strange, but did you just call me by name?"

Joe shrugged, folding his arms across his bare chest. He wasn't going to give anything away until he knew exactly what he was up against. "So what?"

To his surprise she put a hand to the screen and he saw that a swath of surgical tape and gauze spanned her left palm. When she spoke again his gaze lasered in on hers. "How could you possibly know me?" The whispery tone of her question seemed to escape despite the fact that she sounded as if she held her breath.

Anger swamped Joe's reserve. "What the hell kind of question is that?"

She flinched though he had not raised his voice. He saw her fingers curl as if she were trying to cling to the screening. "What I mean is, who do you think I am, Mister Guinn?"

Joe checked the impulse to answer with the phrase, "My ex." He didn't like any reference to the act that had x-ed out what had once been the emotional center of his life. The divorce was her doing. If this were her way of testing his attitude, he wasn't going to make it easy for her.

Yet he couldn't take his eyes off her. For a fraction of a second the professional part of him recorded her in detail, as if he might need at some later time to verify a description of her. She wore a white peasant blouse and gauze skirt. The woman he had married believed in dressing for success yet this was obviously department store discount merchandise. Still, the figure beneath the clothing was as he so achingly remembered it. So was the high curvature of her cheekbones, the blunt tip of her nose that made it look as if it had been chipped, and the wide mouth and square jaw that anchored her face clearly on the side of attractiveness versus prettiness.

Behind his towel, the halfhearted arousal he had been summoning for Lauren Sawyer jumped suddenly to life. It had always been that way for him where Halle was concerned. Even after three years of marriage the mere glimpse of her entering a crowded room was enough to give him the hard-on of an eighteen-year-old. In less time than it took to blink he knew he was in trouble. The reminder reinforced his sense of distrust.

"Why don't we cut to the chase? You tell me what it is you want. I assume you came all the way out here for some reason other than to play twenty questions.''

His tone seemed to brace her. She backed up a step, releasing his screen. He could guess from past experience that her expression accompanied a blush that the yellow light masked. ''Actually I have a perfectly good reason. It's business, as I stated before.'' Again the smile that dared any man to meet it and not be affected. ''It's going to take quite a bit of explaining.''

From the way his body reacted to her smile he knew that he was dangerously close to committing a felonious assault. Or...would she go willingly with him into the sexual heat of desire that was licking at the back of his eyeballs even as his face remained perfectly expressionless?

That had been the most cherished thing he had discovered about her. She had seemed so reserved, so aloof. She did not even like him to kiss her in public. So he had not been expecting the uninhibited amorous woman she had become the first time they made love. Exhausted and exhilarated, he had asked if the reserve was a joke. She had blushed and said it was him—only with him had she ever behaved that way. Only now she was remarried and some other—

''Mister Guinn?'' The sound of her voice snapped him back to the moment. She had opened the screen door several inches but he stood blocking the way. ''May I come in?''

''I don't think so.'' Joe placed his arm across the opening, anchoring his hand on the jamb. He felt the towel tucked at his waist slip but decided he would be damned before he made a grab for it. She wanted to know how he felt about her? She might yet get lucky.

"I'm not feeling very friendly tonight. Besides, it's after business hours."

"It's important." Her voice dropped into a more persuasive register. "Very important."

So that was it! Joe fought the impulse to answer in kind. She had always liked role-playing games. During their marriage they had played Cop and Collar, Stud Service Review, Pickup Encounter and a dozen other very private games that inevitably led to steamy fun in bed. Once he would have joined in the spirit of her game—whatever this was—without a second thought. That was then.

Two years' worth of pent-up anger and frustration surged through him on a sea of beer. *She* had walked out on him. *She* had initiated the divorce. *She* had refused to even meet him during the dissolution of their marriage. *She* had refused to allow him to explain the reasons why and how his world had been blown to pieces. *She* had refused to be there for him at the very time he had needed her most. For exactly those reasons, and half a dozen more, too many emotional risks—all his—were at stake.

He looked at the place where her hand was folded over the edge of the screen door. She was left-handed and he noticed that while she wore a bandage, she did not wear a wedding band. He had never known her to take off her wedding ring while they were married. Something spiteful made him hope this meant there was trouble in her new paradise. Considering the shambles his life had become in the aftermath of her desertion, he was in no mood to be generous.

"Why don't you just tell me why you're here and then I'll decide what I want to do about it."

She looked taken aback but the blank surprise didn't last two seconds. After all, he surmised, she had to come twelve hundred miles from Manhattan to Gap just to find him. He hadn't expected her to simply go away. But she did release his door. It swung closed all but the last inch.

"Very well, Mister Guinn." Her chin lifted. "I want to hire you. At least I did until you began—well, never mind. I was in a traffic accident recently. I woke up in the hospital to discover that everything was intact but my memory." He saw the right side of her mouth quiver but she recovered. "I have amnesia, Mister Guinn, and I need you find out who I am, unless..."

She looked up at him through the smoky haze of the screen, her eyes shining more brightly than before. Jesus! Tears. "Can you tell me who I am?" She asked the question as if it were burdened by the sum total of her emotional life.

Too much emotion. Joe let the contents of her previous statement roll over his head without comment. He was way past trying to figure out why she was saying any of this. All he felt was great resentment that she could find no better way to reintroduce herself into his life than by this cheap trick. So why was the sight of her enough to set loose this thumping, pumping pressure of desire?

The only other question in his mind was how to get rid of her before he lost control. Hell! He was trembling.

"You've lost your touch." His tone was not friendly. "The amnesia story is too far-fetched even for a gullible country boy like me."

He reached out and jerked the screen door closed.

"Once you didn't want anything to do with me. Now I don't want anything to do with you." He shut the door in her face.

She pressed against the screen in anguish as the sound of the slammed door reverberated in the air about her. She rapped her knuckles on the wooden frame. "No! Please! Mister Guinn? Please!"

No sound answered her frustrated cries, though the porch light went dark. He didn't believe her story. That didn't matter. He knew her!

She took a deep breath, trying to steady a heart that had been galloping since the moment Joe Guinn opened his door.

Holly! He had called her Holly. Or maybe he had said Molly. Polly? His speech had been slurred. She did not have to guess the reason. He was holding a crushed beer can in his hand.

She reached up to knock again but her hand never rapped wood because she heard the dead bolt slide home. She might have lost every memory more than two weeks old but common sense told her Joe Guinn was not likely to come to his door again this night. More than that, his hostile stare and posture said that he didn't like her—maybe didn't like women in general. Wonderful. A beer-swilling, chip-on-his-shoulder, woman-hating private investigator might hold the key to her identity. What was she going to do?

Behind her the banner she had read in the headlights of the taxi that had brought her out here rustled in the breeze. It read Happy Birthday, Joe. Her mind conjured up the image of the damp bath towel slung precariously about Joe Guinn's lean hips. It struck her that maybe she had interrupted a very private celebration. That would explain why he wasn't pleased to see her and wouldn't let her in.

She took another calming breath. See? Rational explanations.

She turned from the door and walked a few steps to the edge of the porch before her thoughts halted her. She had even more pressing troubles than the brooding man behind the dead bolt.

With a shock she realized she had not asked the taxi that dropped her off to wait for her. It was obvious to anyone with half a brain that taxis didn't exactly cruise east Texas back roads looking for passengers. Why had that not occurred to her before now? She was a good ten miles from her motel room. What was she supposed to do now?

This time deep breathing didn't deter the anxiety creeping back over her. Though it was a warm night shivers coursed up and down her spine. An overwhelming sense of futility dragged at her courage. Who was she kidding? How could she hope to uncover her lost life when she could not even trust herself?

She felt like a watch with a broken stem: she was ticking all right, but she wasn't set to the right time. The simplest things frightened or disconcerted her, like the fact her face still surprised her each time she looked into a mirror. Yet she had discovered in the hospital that she knew without thinking when to turn on the TV for "Oprah." She didn't remember how old she was or her phone number or her address but she had complained when a nurse parted her hair on the wrong side. Wrong side? Everything about her was off center. There was only one thing about which she had no doubt.

Someone was after her.

A shiver, bringing up goose bumps, hit her. She was on the run, running away. Fear was the first emotion she experienced upon opening her eyes in the hospital. Fear was the dominant emotion she had experienced ever since.

She placed a white-knuckled grip around one of the set of square posts that held up the porch roof. Wood splinters dug into her palm through her bandage but she barely noticed.

She had awakened in the hospital with a terrorizing sense of panic even before she realized she didn't know where she was or even who she was. The doctors had said she had suffered a concussion in the accident. Commercial buses didn't require seat belts and she had hit her window during the collision. They had explained in great complicated detail about impact brain injuries, swelling and pressure causing headache, confusion and rarely transient memory lapses or loss. All she hung on to was the reassuring promise that her condition was not as serious as amnesia would make it seem. And that, in time, her memory should return. They had explained away her anxiety by saying it was perfectly normal for her to have moments of disorientation, claustrophobia, even panic until her memory came back. She had tried, and failed, to believe them. She'd had no form of ID on her person: no driver's license, no credit cards—nothing.

Was this terrible sense of foreboding, the need to find shelter and lie low, real or imagined? Standing on this dark porch in the middle of nowhere beneath a star-sifted night, her fears seemed more real than ever before. They had compelled her to come here in the first place: to find out the truth.

After her release from the hospital this morning, she had decided to discover who she was before whoever it was caught up with her.

She had picked Joe Guinn's name out of the yellow pages. Not that there had been a great deal of choice of private investigators listed. She was definitely in small-town, USA. Yet his name had leaped up at her, not in recognition exactly but with a positive, compelling feeling that he was the right man for the job.

Uncannily, that sense of rightness had increased when he answered his door. Some sense of recognition—no her reaction to him had been more subtle than that—it was more like window-shopping and then spotting the perfect dress that you didn't even know you were looking for.

Certainly he was not the kind of man who at first glance seemed tailor-made to provide a sense of security. With beer can in hand, wild dark unkempt hair and unshaven jaw, he'd loomed in his doorway like every city dweller's idea of a backwoods' nightmare. Despite the towel, she wasn't even convinced he'd lately been near a tub. Yet, for one brief second, Joe Guinn had caused a calming inside her that gave substance to her sense of having chosen rightly.

Then he had blown her sense of security sky-high. He knew her! Knew Holly—Molly?

"Doesn't sound right," she whispered and realized that her voice was being drowned out by a strange roaring.

She put her hands to her ears but the noise was inside her. Panic rushed back into the void left by fleeing calm. She had been assured that the symptoms of her concussion were over. Maybe. But the sudden thought that she might have been walking around all day in plain sight of many people who knew her, of someone who might be after her, was close to giving her a heart attack.

Sensing that she was being watched, she turned to look back over her shoulder. Though she could not be certain she thought she saw the curtain in the window to the right of the door move fractionally. Joe Guinn was watching her.

She deliberately turned to face him, anger making her a little more brave. For better or worse, her need to know the truth had become entangled with the life of the stranger behind that curtain. As if she didn't have problems enough. As if her head weren't throbbing with unanswered questions. As if the roaring weren't growing louder instead of receding.

There was no warning that the world was changing, just a gentle slow slide into oblivion. She went down so smoothly she did not even bump her head.

Joe swore viciously under his breath as he slammed his door on the most tempting woman he had ever known. He hadn't missed the stricken look on her face before the door eclipsed her. He didn't need her beating on his jamb or hear her plaintive voice to know he was being the worst kind of coward. He couldn't help it.

She had gotten to him, gotten to him big-time.

Still . . .

He turned and reached for the knob. Then he thought about what today meant to him, thought about what the date had once meant to both of them. He reached a little higher and shot the bolt home.

Today would have been their fifth wedding anniversary. If he had opened that door a second time, he

would have slugged or kissed her—either way she
would have been in serious trouble.

Turning away, he hurled his empty beer can across
the width of the living room, past the dining room and
through the pass-through window that separated it
from the kitchen. It struck the refrigerator and
bounced noisily into the sink. It was a maneuver he
had perfected during his many hours of unemploy-
ment these last two years. Usually, a successful throw
made him smile. Tonight it was just physical release.
Actually, he was pumped enough to juggle the living
room furniture.

Halle Hayworth had a talent for making dramatic
entrances into his life. The first time he saw her she'd
been bending over a collapsed pedestrian in the middle of Fifth Avenue. Summer on the Texas prairie had
nothing on ultraurban Manhattan when it baked in a
July heat wave. The thermometer had climbed into the
midnineties while humidity percentages of seventy plus
glazed the air. Heat sheered off the surrounding concrete and glass and filled the streets like clear Plexi-
glas waves. It was no wonder an elderly woman had
succumbed to heat prostration. What was amazing
was the fact that an expensively dressed young woman
had paused to help a stranger.

He had been off duty, trudging toward FAO
Schwarz to buy a birthday present for his partner's
four-year-old, when traffic screeched to a horn-blaring
halt in the intersection he was waiting to cross. Flipping open his badge, he had waded into the tangle of
taxis and curious onlookers and announced that he
was a policeman.

He had noted in appreciation the slide of honey
blond hair veiling the Good Samaritan's face and

golden brown shoulders bared by her sundress as he would have the assets of any attractive woman. Then she had looked up at him, her eyes as cool and inviting as damp moss-dappled earth, and he had felt the top of his head lift right off.

He never remembered exactly what they said to one another nor why they were still chatting after the ambulance had taken the unfortunate woman away. Afterward, he could only recall her wide disarming smile so unlike the usual skeptical, prove-it-to-me smirks of most city women. She had even touched his forearm, the briefest of touches, before she had finally turned away.

He had returned to the precinct to announce to Hunter, his partner, that he had just met the woman he was going to marry.

Halle Hayworth—he'd gotten her info for the record—was the most beautiful thing he had ever seen. Maybe not the most beautiful woman, he tried to explain to friends and colleagues, anyone who would sit still long enough to listen to his litany of infatuation. He had seen more spectacular women—or maybe he hadn't. Once he saw Halle he was no longer an objective surveyor of women. He only knew one thing. She had to be his or he would die.

"Dumb jerk!" he muttered. After two long sorry years he was still mired in the hopeless rage of bitter regret.

She, on the other hand, had remarried so quickly he knew how Hamlet must have felt about his mother's marriage to his uncle. 'Unseemly haste' might be an old-fashioned phrase but he was an old-fashioned guy. Toward the end, when he knew he was losing her, his jealous desire had sometimes made him say and do stupid things.

Sometimes he thought he must be a little mad to be still clinging to the memories of a misguided marriage his friends had warned him was a mistake from the start. Hadn't he just promised himself when he thought it was Lauren Sawyer at his door, that he was due a change of emotional climate? Only a masochist would willingly step back into an entanglement that had ruined his life.

Yet he had been an investigator too long. His mind wouldn't let go of the facts surrounding Halle's sudden reappearance in his life.

Forget the crap about her lost memory. He was pacing his living room trying to decide why she had come all this way. After all, no one accidently dropped into Gap on the way from Manhattan to anywhere. What reason could she possibly have for coming here?

And why did she look so scared?

He hadn't missed her frightened expression. He had been a New York City policeman seven years. He had dealt with people in the throes of every kind of emotional turmoil. There had been too much of it in her face for someone in control of her feelings. That catch in her voice was new, too.

Details played over in his mind as he plopped down in his chair and stared at the silent TV. The bandage on her hand bothered him. So did the fact she was not wearing a wedding band. And another thing, the way she stood in his doorway, a little too close, as if she did not just want entry but needed it. She had nearly danced on tiptoe at one point, as if something hostile was at her back. All part of her act? If so, she had become one heck of an actress in two years. He could feel her anxiety through the screen.

He wasn't vain enough to believe he was the cause. Even so, he wouldn't be exaggerating to say she had first looked at him as if he were a six-foot chocolate sundae, complete with whipped cream and a cherry, and she had the only spoon. That was before he had refused to play along.

He rubbed a hand briskly back and forth across his bearded face. Too many emotional spikes for reality. Too many mood swings. She was trying to hide something, cover up something. The only trouble was, after two years of silence, he could not begin to guess what it was that might be upsetting her. Unless it was...

Daniel Shipmann. That was the name of her new husband. He even vaguely remembered meeting him at one of those posh, self-absorbed bashes frequently hosted by the exclusive Manhattan auction house where Halle worked. Tall, lanky, a Harvard man with straight blond hair cut to form parentheses along either side of his chiseled face, Shipmann had reminded him of a high-fashion model: all surface, no substance. He might have guessed the bas— the man would be trouble. Then Halle announced that Shipmann was her new partner at work and he knew it.

She hadn't joined in as usual his game of poking fun at the other guests on their way home. It was rare enough he got the time off to accompany her. It made him feel closer to her to make jokes that distanced them from the people she worked with every day; rich people, powerful influential people who considered him, a detective first class, little more than a grunt on the public payroll. That night she had defended Shipmann, said he was different. He came from money, yes, but she had known him since fourth grade. He was one of the good guys.

Good guys. That left him no room to criticize.

But it left him plenty of room for silent rage and jealous sniping, and other decidedly Neanderthal responses to the man who became Halle's regular after-hours escort to business functions when he couldn't make it. Halle's response to his jealousy was to patiently wait each time for him to cool off. It wasn't that he didn't trust her. He didn't trust Shipmann. But how could he complain about Halle's conduct when he regularly drew assignments with female detectives in some pretty tricky scenarios? He couldn't. But he didn't like it one bit.

Was Shipmann the reason she had come here tonight?

That thought shot Joe to his feet with a surge of perverse satisfaction. If Shipmann had hurt her, was threatening her, he would cheerfully disconnect every bone in his upper-crust body.

He moved toward the door. Maybe she hadn't wanted to launch right into that one. Maybe she had needed first the reassurance that he would help her. Could she have doubted that? Of course she could! He had not said or done anything right that last month they had been together. Still, she had come all this way to find him. The least he could do was open the blasted door.

Latent embarrassment made him move to the window first, just to make certain she was still there.

He saw her jump and whip around as he moved aside the curtain, as tense as a jackrabbit sighting an eagle.

Then she turned to face him, a challenge in her expression.

He smiled and reached for the dead bolt. She had been waiting for him to cool off. Good old Halle. That, at least, he might have predicted.

He was stunned to open the door and not see her standing on the other side. It took only a second but his heart was double pumping by the time his gaze changed trajectory and he saw that she had not run away, but collapsed.

Chapter 3

As Joe gathered his unconscious ex-wife into his arms he had no rational reason for smiling. Touching her, feeling her weight as he lifted her from the porch floor into his arms, made her real for him in a way no amount of staring at her through a rusty screen could.

Seconds earlier he had nearly burst through that screen instead of opening it when he had spied her sprawled on the porch. Years of first-aid training had taken hold as he bent over her. Her breathing had been shallow, her pulse thready and slow yet there were no other signs of physical distress. It seemed she had simply fainted. He decided that she might be reacting to the day's heat though it was not that warm now. Or maybe the emotional trauma of their meeting had effected her more than he suspected.

He had never known Halle to faint but two years could change a lot of things. Perhaps her tolerance for stress had changed drastically since their divorce.

Perhaps she had recently been sick, or not eating right, or maybe the accident she had mentioned was real. Or maybe he was fooling himself. Maybe this was another trick.

He glanced down into her very still face. It would have been hard for her to fake the slack stillness of her features or the clamminess of her skin. He, on the other hand, was sweating from a first-class case of nerves.

He shifted her higher against his chest so that he could reach for the door with a free hand. The scent of baby powder drifted up from the cool skin of her shoulders. He didn't want to think about how good it felt to hold her. He didn't want to remember the feel of her body pressed to his, didn't want the silky drift of her hair across his arm to remind him of how he had often begged her to let it grow. She had refused, saying short hair was all the rage. Had fashion changed or had she simply changed her mind...or had she done it to please Shipmann?

Every muscle in his body tensed at the thought. That's right, he goaded himself. He needed to keep thinking of her husband. It might help him get some perspective on the situation, find a dispassionate position. Once he had been a cop accustomed to weighing people's words against their actions and possible motives. So far, Halle hadn't told him anything he could accept as the truth. No reason to go off the deep end over her reappearance in his life. No reason to be anything else than a detached, disinterested party.

He was halfway across the living room headed for the most comfortable spot in the house when it occurred to him that Mrs. Shipmann might not respond well if she came to in her ex-husband's bed. Not that

he might do any better. Seeing her lying on his grandmother's patchwork spread might snap his control.
He'd spent far too many sweaty nights tangled in his
sheets dreaming about how she would feel if she was
there beside him, beneath him, as he slid into her welcoming embrace. No, definitely not a good idea.

He made a strategic swerve and changed his direction toward the sofa. The living room was at least
neutral territory.

Too bad his body wasn't listening.

By the time he bent his knees to lay her on the sofa,
his heart had formed a conga line with his stomach
and gut. Or maybe it was the birthday cake and beer
doing the cha-cha. Either way, an antacid was definitely going to be his late-night snack.

She moved a little when he released her. Her arm
came up, across his back, not really clutching at him,
but all the same it checked his impulse to draw away.
He knelt down beside her, uncertain of what to make
of her gesture. It couldn't mean anything. She didn't
even know who held her.

Eyes still closed she sighed softly and he smelled
lemon-flavored candy on her breath. She had always
liked lemons, loved to jab a peppermint stick into a
fresh lemon then suck the juice out. It made his jaws
ache just thinking about it, but he'd always made certain there were lemons and peppermint sticks in his
apartment after they met.

"Halle? Do you hear me? It's Joe." He touched her
face. God. Her skin was softer than he remembered,
and so cool. He noticed, belatedly, a dark shadow
edging up from under the wing of dark hair dipping
over her right temple. He reached over and snapped on
the nearest lamp. His gut jumped.

It was a bruise, all right, a big ugly purplish-greenish discoloration that ran from her right eyebrow all the way into her scalp. She had tried to cover the bruise with makeup but the only reasonable explanation for his having missed it before was his own shock at her unexpected appearance and the yellow light cast by his porch bulb.

He gently lifted back her hair and saw at her hairline a half-healed contusion into which five delicate stitches had been sutured.

He drew back his hand with the revulsion of one who had accidently uncovered someone else's nasty secret, uncertain he wanted truthful answers to the police procedure-type questions forming in his mind. She had said she needed his help. He wasn't so certain now that she didn't need help. But his? No. That couldn't be. Not now.

He patted her cheek gently, bending closer as if he could see between her lashes. "Come on, baby. You're okay."

Her eyes swept open and stayed open, no fluttering or tentativeness like in the movies. She was staring up at him and there was only six inches between them. She smiled, a beautiful smile of welcome that made his heart do a back flip.

Her arm, trapped now between his own arm and side, flexed at the elbow. He felt her fingers touch him lightly between his bare shoulder blades. That touch burned. He held his breath.

He doubted she had ever understood precisely what her touch did to him, how it went past every guard of ration and reason an adult male naturally developed to keep himself whole against the onslaught of living in the world. After a while the barrier stayed raised even with those he loved. A man needed his space, his place to be whole and wholly himself. But when Halle touched him the guard dropped—hell, disappeared. There was no holding back, no separate place for him to be. Like a snail removed from its shell, he was all soft and fragile and exposed when Halle touched him. Damn. It still happened.

His body tensed in protest against the slide of her fingers down his spine. He thought he must be wrong about the cause of the sudden widening of her eyes. That intensified green in those gold-brown depths had once meant she was beginning to be aroused. Now it must be a trick of the light. Her softly parting lips must just be a reflex of relief. Her eyes drifting to his mouth couldn't be a signal welcoming the possibility of his mouth on hers. She couldn't really expect him to just bend closer and kiss her and forget two years worth of hell.

He wasn't that easy. He wasn't still in that deep with her. He wasn't—

He jutted his chin out a fraction, testing the waters.

She didn't move. That was her first mistake. If she wanted him to beg, she should have protested, pushed at him, turned her head away, done anything but stare up at him. It was all the encouragement he needed.

In a swooping gesture his mouth claimed the lips he had dreamed about for so long he thought he had made up or embroidered the power of their reality. But his dreams had not lied. The feathering of her warm breath across his lips, the taste of her secret self, the shape of her softer, fuller lips still fit his to perfection. He dug an arm under her shoulders to lift her close as his free hand moved up to cradle her face to his.

Desire jolted him as he dragged her mouth open with his. He knew it was crazy. This was outlawed bliss. But he couldn't stop. Not yet. He was too needy, had been dying by inches for months. Kissing her was like experiencing Saturday night and Sunday morning rolled into one. Halle had the power to lead him into wild abandon and still save his soul. How could he ever let her go when all he wanted was to get even closer?

She moaned. Or maybe it was only a sigh. The spare inarticulate sound of distress got through.

As he drew away, a smile lifted just the edges of her lips. Faint color summoned by his kiss warmed their surface...then she remembered. The sick lost look that had been in her eyes as he closed the door on her returned.

Reality check!

He saw her hazel irises swimming in twin pale oceans of surprise. "What were you—?"

"Mouth-to-mouth resuscitation," he lied baldly as he drew back. Sweet Grief! What *had* he thought he was doing?

A frown puckered her forehead. "What happened?"

Joe sat back on his heels, trying to casually withdraw the arm that had been supporting her shoulders. "You fainted."

"I never faint," she replied in a matter-of-fact tone.

He pulled back farther, easing his butt down onto the rug, but his gaze never left her face. She had kissed him back, dammit! He wasn't going to take all the heat. "Was this just an act to gain entrance?"

"I've never been that desperate." But her voice quavered just enough to call into question her statement on this occasion.

"Whatever you say."

She reached up to smooth her hair back from her face. She threaded her fingers through it, forking it up and away from her head onto the sofa cushion beneath her. As she did so, the underside of her upper arm was revealed. He stared at the smooth flawless skin. He knew it was very sensitive. Once he had liked to kiss her there and other even more sensitive places.

With a coughing sound like that of a man trying to dislodge a crumb from his throat, he looked away. He hoped his expression didn't reveal his thoughts for they were speeding readily along on their own raunchy course.

Dangerous thoughts. More dangerous because she was looking at him again, her eyes wide with speculation of their own. Only there was now the dispassion in her gaze that he wished accompanied his own.

"Tell me about your injuries." He pointed at her brow and then her bandaged hand. "What happened?"

She winced, as if it pained her to even think of it. "I told you before. I was in an accident. The bus in which I was traveling collided with an eighteen-wheeler just outside Tyler almost two weeks ago." She glanced at him, "You heard about it?"

Joe shook his head.

"Oh." She made the word sound very small. "It must have been on TV and in the papers." When he shook his head a second time she said, "Well, it was a pretty bad accident. I'm told the truck driver was killed instantly. He'd fallen asleep at the wheel, crossed the median and struck our on-coming bus. We were forced off the highway into a ditch and then flipped over. I was on the impact side.''

Joe's stomach jumped. She might have died! He only said, ''That so?''

''Yes, that is so.'' she said sharply. ''Matter of public record, Mister Guinn.''

Anger made her sit up. As she swung her legs off his sofa her skirt caught under her hips, hiking up her hem to midthigh. Those legs settled a few inches from his right bicep, their proximity causing Joe to notice how long and firm and tan they were. Where had she been to get a tan in March? She didn't believe in baking under artificial light. Or, had that changed too?

He almost sighed in relief when she tugged her skirt down to her knees. In the lamplight he had seen pale gold hairs shimmering on the surface of her thighs. It had been a while since her last leg wax. That thought unaccountably excited him. An earthy man, he often preferred a little natural variation to artificial perfection. Then he noticed the Band-Aid in the crook of her arm. Results of an IV? Hadn't noticed it before. He was slipping.

''You don't seem to be much the worse for your experience. No serious damage done.'' That was rude and he knew it but he needed to regain control of the moment.

Her composure held. ''I suppose that depends on what you call damage.'' She met his gaze without hesitation. ''I can't remember where I live, my phone number, or even my name.''

He glanced at the eelskin purse slung across her body by a long thin shoulder strap. ''Why don't you just open your purse and consult your wallet?''

She reached for the strap and whipped it over her head then thrust the purse at him. "You look in it. It's what the hospital gave me this morning at checkout."

Joe debated the wisdom of humoring her but he had always been a sucker for an easy play.

Their fingers scarcely touched before she jerked away.

The eelskin felt smooth, oily, almost damp in his hand. He snapped the latch and dumped the contents into his toweled lap. It contained a compact, lipstick, two tissues, a gold pen, a small tin of aspirin, and a matching wallet. No checkbook, calendar, or notepad. No bus ticket stubs, either. He picked up the wallet and flipped it open. There were no credit cards stuck in the spaces provided, not even a gas card or license. He felt a bulk through the soft leather and spread wide the dollar bill section. Inside was a stack of cash an inch thick.

He pulled out the top one, a crisply minted one-hundred-dollar bill so new it felt slightly sandy between his fingers. He pulled out another and then another and then thumbed through the rest.

He stared at it a little longer than was professionally, objectively polite but he had never seen so many one-hundred-dollar bills other than at a drug bust. Mystified for the first time, he looked up. "There must be eight—"

"Nearly ten," she interjected.

"—nearly ten thousand here." He glanced down again. "You win the lottery?"

"I think I have money."

He relaxed for the first time. "I'd say you do."

She didn't smile, didn't even seem to realize that he was teasing her. Her expression was sincere again, passionately so. "I mean I think that money is mine. I earned it, or inherited it."

Joe's face lost its animation. Mention of her trust fund made him uncomfortable. He had refused to touch it when they were married, believing that they should live on what they earned themselves. Evidently, she'd had a change of heart since their divorce. "So, you come from money. Do you have another point?"

She bit her lip. Not that coy kind of bite women use when they want to seem earnest. She bit down so hard he thought she might draw blood. "The police were very suspicious of that money, especially after I couldn't explain it, or even who I was. Then, too, I didn't have any ID to back it up."

"I would be too," Joe murmured . . . if he didn't already know who she was. "They thought you were dealing drugs?"

She sighed and nodded. "Something like that. Do you believe me now?"

"No." He didn't try to temper it. "Your story has more holes than a colander. People don't just lose their minds—" he smirked "—excuse me, lose their memories from a simple tap on the head. As for the rest, you never took a bus in your life. Of course, you couldn't explain how you just happened to conveniently wind up on my doorstep if you'd taken a plane, right?"

She blinked then, the first hint that she was lying or holding back something. "You seem to know a lot about me. Why don't you tell me everything you know."

Danger. The word was a neon red blinking signal in Joe's thoughts. "I told you before, I'm not going to play games with you, now or ever. Got that?"

She watched him a long silent time. He could tell she was calming herself, breathing slowly, weighing her options, trying to find a strategy, desperate despite her denial not to be thrown out on her ear. "Won't you at least hear me out?"

Joe hesitated only a moment. "What the hell. Sure."

He rose from the floor, one hand at his waist to hold his towel closed, and padded barefoot over to his chair. He sat, legs spreading wide out before him. He wasn't about to worry what she could or could not see beneath the gaping edges of his towel. This was his home and he was in no mood to be polite. "All right, let's have it. But keep it short." His expression was not at all one of confidence building.

"I think I may know why I wasn't carrying any ID." She kept her gaze politely averted even though he did not respond. "The police checked my fingerprints through their computers and they didn't come up with anything criminal on me. They said they wanted to print my picture in the paper but I refused."

"Why?"

"I think—feel—that before the accident, I was in some sort of trouble. I believe I was running away." She looked up, her expression almost shy. "Someone may be after me."

Joe laughed, the rude kind of guffaw that jumps out unexpectedly in the middle of an awkward moment.

She pinkened. At least, he thought absently, his reaction was good for her circulation. She had been much too pale for his liking.

"You don't believe me, do you? Don't believe any of it?" She didn't sound angry or surprised, only resigned. "Check it out." She pointed to the phone on the end table by his chair. "All you have to do is call the sheriff or the county hospital."

Joe wagged his head. "I'm ready to call your bluff."

Her chin lifted. "Go ahead."

He sank lower in his chair, his towel inching open. She didn't even glance down. "You don't have a driver's license because you and I both know you don't know how to drive. As for the money, though I never knew you to carry so much you almost always dealt in cash. Many New Yorkers do."

He came to his feet. "Are you ready?"

She looked the long way up to his face. "Ready for what?"

"I'm driving you back to wherever you came from."

She blushed but held his gaze as he came toward her. "Does this mean you'll take my case?"

Joe's expression soured. "No. I'm going to get your cute butt out of here and then forget this night."

She stood up. He hadn't realized he was so close to her until in her rising they nearly touched. But he'd be damned before he backed away. She met his dark brown gaze at less than a foot. "I'll go," she said in the measured tones of a seasoned bargainer. "But only if you answer two questions."

He rested his hands low on his hips, as if he thought that might prevent him from strangling her. "Shoot."

"What is my name and how do you know me?"

He didn't know why he did it, maybe just to get it over with. "Your name's Halle, H-A-L-L-E, pronounced holly like the berry bush, remember?"

She shook her head. "Halle what?"

"Hayworth." He didn't stop to think why he gave her maiden name instead of her married one. Neutral territory, he decided. "Now, is this charade over?"

"How do you know me?"

"God almighty!" Joe gave a terse shake of his head. No, he wasn't going to let her get to him, no matter the provocation.

There was no light, no interest in the chill dark gaze he directed at her. "That's a third question. You said you'd leave after I answered two."

He saw her color rise another notch but she offered him a fetching feminine smile. He caught it like an easy fly ball, at the level of his crotch. "You are *not* a nice man."

"You already knew that."

This time he caught the swift darting look of fear in her eyes, as if she really didn't know that, or anything else about him. Was it possible? Or was she just playing him for some purpose he couldn't imagine? "Come on, you're cutting into my recreation time."

She gave the room a quick glance, spying the birthday cake and empty beer cans in her brief perusal. When her gaze came back to his there was clear derision in her expression. "Celebrating alone? Could it be I'm not the only one who thinks the birthday boy is no great prize?"

He let her have that, but it cost him. He wanted to grab and shake her and make her understand that everything that had gone wrong in his life was somehow bound up in her. But he knew that wasn't true. He had made enough of his own mistakes to cancel out whatever ones she had made. But she was a handy target and he had learned long ago that anger didn't need much of a lightning rod. So he smoldered, practically shimmered with suppressed rage.

She must have noticed, caught a glimpse of the white-hot anger blazing behind his composure because she suddenly turned, practically shouldered him aside, and walked briskly toward the door. He followed more slowly, at a safe distance.

When she turned at the door he was stunned to see tears once more in her eyes. Halle had never been a water faucet.

"I—I really don't want to be alone tonight." She seemed to swallow back something.

Then the meaning of her leading statement smacked him right between the eyes. "You can't stay here!" It was nearly a shout.

She looked at him almost resentfully. "Why not?"

"Why not?" He didn't know why he repeated the dumb question. What was she trying to do, ruin his life a second time? He pretended not to notice the slight quiver of her breasts beneath her cotton blouse. Then she was reeling him into the dappled green depths of her amber eyes.

"You're the only person I've met so far who knows me. You can't know what that means, what it's like to look in the mir—" Again she broke off, swallowing an even larger lump of emotion. He felt a sympathetic lump form in his own throat. Some big bad cop.

"I'll pay you." She looked past his shoulder, as if she could wish herself back into the center of the room. "I can sleep on the sofa. Or, I'll pull a chair out on the porch if you don't like the idea of having me in your house."

She tried to smile but he saw the muscles in her jaws bunch in a near grimace. "I just don't want another night . . . alone.'' The last word was all but lost in a whisper.

Staring into her face, as familiar to him as his own, Joe made himself think of at least ten good reasons why he should just push the screen door open and get this over with. He didn't believe her. He didn't want to believe her. He couldn't afford to believe her. Even if every crazy word she had spoken tonight was the absolute truth, he had no comfort left to give of any kind for any reason.

He gave the idea his last impartial effort. She might be lying. She might be telling the truth, in which case, he *definitely* didn't want to be involved. He had once loved her. Now she was another man's wife. She was not his responsibility. Kissing her had proved one thing. He could not win, no matter what the truth was. She seemed to need him—the biggest no-no of all.

"You thirsty? I need a beer in the worst way."

He turned and headed for the kitchen without looking back.

They hadn't exchanged a word, just stood silently in his kitchen, each leaning a hip against the opposite counter while sharing a silent drink. He'd substituted a diet soda for his offer of beer once he realized that a woman who had fainted shouldn't be consuming alcohol.

The fluorescent light overhead gleamed off her throat as she tilted up the can to drain it. He noticed she held the can with two hands like a child but that wasn't what kept his interest. She had a thing about drinking anything from a can, said it was the height of barbarity. Yet she hadn't even asked for a glass. Their first Christmas she had brought him a set of extravagantly expensive cut crystal beer steins to keep him from having an excuse to drink from the can. They were in the cupboard behind her head but he hadn't offered one to her.

His eyes narrowed on his own half-empty can as he smoothed away with his thumb the condensation that frosted the side. It collected in droplets then dribbled off the tip of his finger onto his big toe. He was no happier now with his decision to detain her than he had been when he'd made it five minutes earlier. Why hadn't he forced her out when she was already moving in that general direction? What was it about looking at the woman he had once loved and lost that filled the sick little space in his psyche that two years of living had not?

He knew she was watching him with equal interest. He felt her shooting tiny glances his way each time he looked in another direction. She was nervous, didn't yet know whether or not he was going to let her stay. But it wasn't only that. She was rabidly curious about him.

Her gaze felt like a touch on his bare shoulders when he turned away for a moment to toss his can in the re-cycle bin. It grazed his waist then probed cautiously the contours of his terry-clothed hips. He knew, with some pride, that he still measured up to the man she had walked out on two years ago. He had made damned certain he didn't go to seed physically even though emotionally he was a mess. Odd jobs that de-manded physical labor and a minimum of conversa-tion filled in the gaps between his career as a PI.

Shipmann, as he recalled, who was a little taller than he but lighter in weight, played racketball at the Har-vard Club to keep in shape. The ivy leaguer's jacket might hang better but in a brawl Joe had no doubt about which of them would be the victor.

"Do you always dress so informally?"

He turned back, startled by her voice which sounded more like the old Halle than at anytime so far this day.

She glanced deliberately at his towel and then her eyes widened in mock innocence as they met his. "I thought a cowboy always wore his boots and spurs."

Desire slammed into him so quickly he didn't expect it. He thought he had plumbed it's depths ten minutes earlier when his mouth was hot and open on hers. He was wrong. Suddenly he wanted nothing more than to rip off his towel, strip off her clothes and ram into her—right here, right now, standing up—to make her remember a need so primitive that sometimes they had both been a little afraid of it.

He amazed himself with his control. He hooked his thumb into the knot at his waist and grinned. "Bother you?"

She shrugged. "Looks a bit drafty."

"Prairie air-conditioning." He flipped the flap open and closed, revealing for a fraction of a second one long hairy thigh and the arc of a bare hip. To her credit she didn't turn away but laughed.

Joe smirked but turned quickly away, pretending to check out the contents of his refrigerator. But the hand he put on the handle trembled. Had she noticed the bulge he'd almost revealed? Or was she just better at hiding her reactions than he was? "Another soda?"

"No, thanks. But if you've got anything to eat?"

Without looking up he said, "Sorry. I've been out of town until today. Fresh out of everything edible."

From the edge of his vision he saw her glance longingly at his refrigerator. "I'd settle for scrambled eggs."

He pushed the door shut. "All I have is beer and birthday cake."

Her voice brightened. "Cake? Fabulous."

Joe turned and reached past her to open the cabinet by her head. He withdrew and then thrust the plate at her. "Help yourself. I've had my fill."

She followed him back into the living room where the cake still sat on the coffee table. When he handed her the butcher knife he had been using she only gave it a wry glance before she knelt down and plunged it into the confection.

"Is April Fool's Day really your birth date?"

Joe winced. She was determined to play out her role to the bitter end, it seemed. It had been her idea to link this date with their marriage. She had turned the birthday party she had planned for him into an impromptu wedding ceremony that was a surprise for their guests. Then, after things fell apart, she had made certain the final divorce papers came through on the exact same date. She had always had a sense of humor. Too bad he couldn't appreciate her final joke.

"Yeah," he said finally. "That's me. The original fool."

"What year are you celebrating?" she asked as she slipped the blade under the generous slice she carved for herself.

"Thirty-two." Joe stood watching her as if she were going to get a grade on her dexterity with a knife. "Don't tell me you forgot."

She looked up, her eyes lingering a perceptible moment on the broad sun-darkened planes of his chest, and then away, as if it had only now occurred to her that she was alone with a half-naked man.

He retreated to his chair as she pinched off a piece of her cake slice with two fingers and brought it to her mouth. "Umm. Good. Homemade?"

Joe shrugged. "A friend made it for me."

She glanced from the cake to him; her gaze dropped speculatively to his toweled hips. "Were you expecting company tonight?"

Mean-spirited or not, he wanted a little of his own back. He rubbed his bare stomach as a slow suggestive smile spread across his face. "What makes you think she hasn't already been here?"

She blushed but said pertly, "I don't see any presents or wrapping paper. Doesn't look like you got much."

The direction of her gaze as it followed his hand's movement into the sleek dark hair fanning out above the towel span just below his navel had him growing hot and heavy again. "I'm a big boy. The present came in it's own unique wrapping."

This time, she did look away.

Definitely mean-spirited. But, hell! She was married to someone else, probably had a kid by now. She—they had always wanted children. They'd just been waiting for things to settle down. Only, they'd never settled.

She finished her cake in silence, curled up on the floor beside the coffee table. Joe concentrated on the TV, Australian football traded for cartoons. Only when the last crumb was gone from her plate did he move. He came to his feet so quickly she started.

"Where are you staying?"

He saw the light go out of her eyes but she didn't protest this time. "A motel on I-20."

"You left your things there?"

She only nodded but he felt her draw even further into herself.

"They should be safe." He shrugged and left the room.

When he returned a few minutes later with a pillow, sheet, and blanket in hand, she was standing by the open door, gazing out through the screen.

She looked so remote, so lonely, so lost standing there with her back to him, her elbows cupped in her palms and her legs crossed at the ankles. Looking at her he could almost believe she felt all alone in the world.

He knew about loneliness, knew what it felt to be so alone that he wanted to stretch his neck and howl like a dog at the moon. So lonely that his stomach clenched and his eyes ached and the blood inside his veins whispered his isolation to the night. But if she felt that way, for whatever reason, it was her own doing.

He dumped the bundle of linens onto the sofa. "Lock up when you're done."

She started at the sound of his voice. Her skittishness was beginning to affect him. His stomach quivered as she glanced at the bedding and then at him, a smile of gratitude brightening the shadowy places in her eyes. "I thought—"

He shrugged off the impulse to smile back. "If anything you've said is true, it will keep until morning."

She came toward him, reaching out to touch his arm before the coldness in his gaze made her it draw back. "Thank you."

Joe turned away without any offer to help her make up the sofa or even a good-night.

He had every right to be angry and defensive and resentful. He didn't want her to touch him again, not for any reason. It made him feel things he was better off not feeling. But as he closed the door to his bedroom, his heart felt a little lighter than it had in a long time. It couldn't be Halle's presence. Could it?

Strange, that he should feel comforted by her presence. But then, nothing about them had ever made sense.

Chapter 4

"Halle. Halle? Halle Hayworth. Hi, Halle!"

Halle stared at her face in the bathroom mirror as she tried different inflections of the name—her name. She watched the mirrored mouth, wide and generously lipped, slowly form the syllables. "Hal-lee."

It wasn't the kind of name that would inspire nicknames. She suspected that anyone named Halle would always be called Halle and nothing else. So why, then, didn't the name sound even the least bit familiar?

She concentrated on her reflection. Average nose, straight but not prominent with an abrupt almost chipped tip. Oval face, average chin, no dimples, no scars if one discounted the bruise fading at her right temple. She was not a raging beauty but neither was she plain. She supposed she would be thought in the middle somewhere; attractive.

Only her large almond-shaped amber eyes with veins of celadon radiating out from the center were vaguely familiar. More than likely that was because she had stared into them often enough this last week, like a newly hatched duckling imprinting on her only friend—herself.

She continued staring a moment longer, as if she might discover some revealing shadow, freckle or expression she hadn't noticed before. Her arched brows were a shade lighter than her mahogany tresses. That struck her as odd. But this time she noticed that her hairline seemed to be disappearing. Well, not disappearing exactly but lifting.

She leaned forward until she was practically nose to glass then combed her fingers through the just-shampooed hair at her hairline.

"It's blonde!" she whispered. There was no mistaking it: the new growth was definitely much lighter than the rest. What blonde would dye her hair darker? Unless, she didn't want to be recognized. Goose bumps rose upon her skin.

"You planning to spend the day in there?" Several heavy thumps on the bathroom door accompanied the shout.

Halle jumped and spun around at the same time, knocking the plastic toothbrush holder into the sink. It clattered against the porcelain, making an awful racket.

"You okay?" demanded the masculine voice on the other side of the door.

"Yes, fine. Nothing broken," she added in afterthought.

As she scooped up the container and placed it back on the sink rim she decided that her adrenal system would soon need an overhaul if she didn't stop jumping at every unexpected sound.

Yet it was more than Joe Guinn's bombastic ~~t~~ that made her nervous this morning. It was his voi The moment she'd heard his voice the night before it's edgy quality had struck a responsive cord in her.

"But of course, it should," she murmured. After all, he knew her. She was the only defective personality operating beneath this roof.

Rattled by that thought, she stripped off the towel she had wrapped herself in after her shower. As she did so she spared the towel bar a rueful glance. Her rinsed out underthings should have dried overnight. They hadn't. After a moment's debate over the discomfort of wearing damp clothing, she simply slipped back into the blouse and skirt in which she had slept. The clothes weren't hers but had been given to her by a friendly hospital pink lady. She would have nothing of her own until she could pick up her suitcase from the sheriff's office where all unclaimed baggage from the accident was being kept.

When she opened the bathroom door a minute later, Joe was lounging against the opposite wall, his thumbs hooked into the belt loops of his jeans.

Though his face was lost in the shadow, a slat of early morning sunlight had partially wedged its way into the hallway. It contoured the planes of his chest and abdomen in golden light. Even at rest the heat and energy of his body was a palpable presence. She suspected he had pulled on jeans as a begrudging concession to her presence because they weren't snapped and only half zipped. Provocation or arrogance?

Like an unexpected breeze on a sultry summer day, a sense of familiarity again brushed her consciousness. Was it possible she remembered his body?

Startled by the thought she followed the narrow path of sleek black hair arrowing from his rugged chest down past his navel as if it were the path to knowledge. It led instead into the V of his fly which the weight of his hands had dragged open to near indecent dimensions. Again tantalizing hints of lost memory shifted beneath the veil of her conscious thought. Just how well had she known this man?

"Don't get too worked up, sugar. I'm not making you an offer."

The rude remark spurred her gaze to make the short trip back to his face where his hooded dark eyes offered no possibility that his words had been said in jest.

"I didn't mean to stare," she began coolly. "It's just that I can't remember..." She cut that off immediately. The excuse that she was only trying to determine if she'd ever seen his body before didn't seem a good idea. How could she possibly think she remembered the pattern of body hair swirling about his navel when she didn't even recognize his face?

For a moment longer they regarded one another in wary silence. Only now did it occur to her how odd her behavior must seem to him. The night before she had felt perfectly safe in this house. She had wanted to throw her arms about him in thanksgiving for allowing her to stay. This morning, the idea that he knew her when she didn't know him made her very uneasy. What on earth had she been thinking to beg a night beneath a strange man's roof? So far, he had behaved with perfect decency if not good grace. Did he dislike her, or was that only her imagination working overtime? She couldn't simply ask him, not when he was scowling at her as if he suspected she had used up all the hot water.

"The water's nice and hot," she said defensively.

"Then why don't you move aside so I can make use of it?"

His hand shot out and caught her by the elbow as she quickly sidestepped away. "Stop jumping every time I speak to you!" he growled. "You're giving me the heebie-jeebies."

"Sorry," she murmured and looked up at him from a much closer angle. Beneath the jut of dark brows his molasses-dark eyes revealed nothing. She felt no corresponding sense of recognition like the night before, no hint of familiarity. This morning, nothing about Joe Guinn's gaze connected in her synapses.

Disappointed, she looked away. Her confused brain was about as useful as a bowl of scrambled eggs.

When he released her, she brushed hurriedly past him down the narrow hall. At the end of the hall she glanced back. He hadn't entered the bathroom but was watching her with a more sullen look than before. Embarrassed to have been caught stealing yet another glance at him, she turned and moved into the living room.

Joe scowled as he watched her retreat. The urge was strong to go after her, grab her from behind, and boot her out on his porch. He must have been closer to being drunk the night before than he had thought. It was the only explanation he could think of for why he had allowed her to stay beneath his roof.

It was bad enough he had tossed and turned all night, unable to settle into anything like sleep while she occupied a room in his house. He should never have kissed her. Even though he had brushed his teeth before going to bed, he would swear he could still taste her. Now this morning he'd had to lie in bed and listen to her humming to herself on the other side of the wall while she took a long hot shower in his bathroom, using his soap, and his towels. Torture. Pure torture.

That's when he had decided to teach her a lesson in provocation. He had set out to be deliberately vulgar, daring her to check out what his zipper barely kept hidden. Wrong move. She had stared at his crotch as if he were a prize stud bull on fair day. To his chagrin, he had become excited under her gaze. Dammit! She was like an itch he couldn't scratch. She had to go.

Annoyed with himself, he turned and entered the bathroom. The first thing he spied were her panties, pale pink satin trimmed in lace, hanging on the bar by the door. The second thing he noticed was her bra. It was lying on the floor.

He picked it up. Halle had a healthy chest, as his father had liked to describe a well-endowed woman. He stuck his fist into the damp half-moon cup and grinned in spite of himself. This bit of elastic and lace wouldn't cover much. It was mostly lace and mostly for show. Too bad she wasn't flat-chested and skinny-shanked. It might have made keeping his mind off her easier.

Hell! Who was he kidding? His passion for Halle had never had much to do with body parts. Not that she didn't have lovely breasts and a rear end ripe enough for his every fantasy; it was just that those attributes weren't separate in his mind from the woman herself. Never had been. He had fallen in love with everything about Halle Hayworth, a woman greater than the sum of her parts.

From the day they married Halle had been forever draping their tiny Manhattan studio apartment with assorted articles of feminine clothing; panties, panty hose, garter belts, slips, teddies, bustiers and more. He'd liked the feeling of having gained access to his very own harem. Had liked her in that lingerie and out of it. But that was another life.

"Women," he muttered and slung the bra across the nearby towel bar. Come to think of it, if her bra and her panties were in here that meant she wasn't wearing—

He quickly twisted the knobs in the tub until the water beat down like bullets and steam rose as if in a sauna. He knew better than to let his thoughts linger on the fact that Halle was sitting in his living room wearing nothing under her blouse and skirt.

Yet, as he stepped into the shower and water sluiced down his body he couldn't block the sudden erotic image of her standing naked and wet in this very spot just minutes earlier. Steamy thoughts fogged his mind like mist on the bathroom mirror. She still sang off-key. Aretha Franklin, she was not. Yet he liked it because her singing reminded him of the times when he would slip in with her and—

"Cut it out!" he muttered to himself. Forgetting her was going to take work.

He banned all thoughts of her while he toweled off. Even so, his body tinged with latent desire. He didn't let himself think about her while he shaved but he still managed to nick himself. He didn't even glance down the hallway as he crossed back to his bedroom.

By the time he began dressing he actually found other things occupying his mind. For instance, how he was going to tackle the McCrea case. He had looked at his accumulated bills last night and knew how badly he needed the job.

He reluctantly pulled a charcoal dress shirt with a cream pinstripe from his closet. After a moment's consideration of a fresh pair of jeans, he reached instead for the charcoal gray slacks he hadn't worn for nearly two years.

Thoughts of Halle slipped in under his guard. She had bought the slacks, the shirt as well, saying he needed to augment his wardrobe which had consisted before their marriage of regulation blues or T-shirts and jeans. Casual chic, she had called the additions.

He'd need every ounce of his dubious charm as he went to talk to the McCreas this morning. After that, he would go by Lauren's house and thank her personally for the birthday cake. Last night had proved one thing. He needed in the worst way to get on with his own life.

He was still tucking his shirttail into the back of his pants when he came out of the bedroom.

"You look nice."

His head jerked up. He saw her gaze travel over his shirt and slacks and then to his clean-shaven face and combed hair. Her approval rankled as did everything about her. "Let me guess. You were expecting the local private investigator to be a potbellied burnout whose only exercise consisted of hoisting a can of beer." He patted his flat belly. "Sorry to disappoint."

She rose from the sofa. The sunlight slipping into the room through the window beyond backlit her. The shadow of long slender legs reminded him that she was naked beneath that flimsy material. He looked away.

"You might want to collect your lingerie before you leave."

"Sorry, I'd thought they'd dry overnight." She looked right and left, anywhere but at him. "I assume you have a dryer?"

"I use the laundry in town." He scowled in her general direction. "You want me to drop them off on my way in?"

"I don't think that will be necessary," she replied primly. "I'll just hang them outside to dry."

Joe shook his head. "Don't have time for that. I've got a business appointment in about—" he checked his watch and though it said 6:45 and he knew Mr. McCrea wouldn't be expecting him a minute before nine he said "—twenty minutes."

"I hope that means you're going to check out my story."

Another head shake. "I've got real business, paying business, to attend to."

"I'm paying business," Halle maintained in a level voice. She had succumbed to hysterics enough to last her a while. "You know I can afford it."

He shrugged, his gaze rising no higher than her chin. "Not interested."

Halle made herself calmly survey him. For the first time she could see all of his face. It was rugged, arresting and downright handsome even if the contours were stiffened by disapproval. His mouth was a hard unfriendly slash. There was an old sickle-shaped scar on his chin and another above his brow. The scars bothered her. Were they badges of a violent nature or had he gotten them falling off a bike, a rock, playing sports?

It didn't matter, she reminded herself. While he had been showering, she'd had a serious talk with herself. She didn't have to like Joe Guinn. She didn't have to recognize him. He was her lifeline and she wasn't going to give that up until he told her everything he knew about her or provided her with another source.

She took a challenging step toward him. "Why aren't you interested, Mr. Guinn? Just exactly what is it you know about me that makes you so reluctant to look me squarely in the eye?"

He didn't answer, just headed toward the kitchen.

Halle made a detour before following him.

Joe was pouring a cup of coffee when she caught up with him, coffee she had made without even asking him if it was okay. It tasted pretty good, which surprised Joe. She hadn't known how to boil water when they met. Kitchen duty wasn't what a woman like Halle learned in prep school. There had always been maids and cooks and caterers in her world.

As she approached, he saw that she had put on her shoes and tucked her damp underwear into the side pocket of her skirt. "I'm ready," she announced stiffly.

He nodded slowly. "Be right with you." He was glad she was going without further argument. He gulped down his coffee, refusing to admit that he burned himself in the process. He just had to get her out, get away, forget.

He banged his cup on the counter, not looking her way. "A bit of friendly advice. Don't wave that wad of hundreds under anybody else's nose. This may not be New York but you shouldn't sell the backwoods short. We have our share of criminals. You could end up a statistic even here."

"Why did you mention New York? Am I a New Yorker?"

He turned quickly to her, crossed the three steps between them and thrust his face into hers. "Don't push me, Halle. I didn't ask you to come here. I don't want you here. In fact, I don't ever want to see you again." He hurled the sharp words at her like a carnival knife thrower. He was so close she could see the red veining in the whites of his eyes, evidence of a bad night's sleep.

His hostility, which she half suspected she had fabricated in the pit of her own personal paranoiac hell, was impossible to miss this time. His anger was real, and personal and aimed point-blank at her. "What have I done to make you dislike me?"

He snorted. "You came back into my life. Until last night you were history. I liked it better that way. Is that plain enough for you, or do you want me to go into the ugly details?"

Halle shook her head. Suddenly she knew she couldn't handle any more bad news before she had had a taste of the good, if there was any good in her life.

She met his gaze. It was as hard and tense and opaque as his expression. So now she knew. They shared a history. But learning its exact nature didn't seem nearly as important as getting out of the range of his temper.

"I'm sorry if my appearance has inconvenienced you." She listened to her voice as if it were a disinterested stranger's. "I hope you'll let me pay you for your time."

He jerked back from her. Only then did she realize he had been holding her shoulder in a tight grip.

"Look," he began, his expression softening a fraction. Then, as if he changed his mind, it refroze in midthaw. "Never mind." He released her. "Let's get the hell out of here."

They rode out to the highway in silence.

She sat so close to the passenger door of his truck that Joe half expected her to jump out before he came to a full stop at the motel parking lot. She didn't. She did, however, reach for the handle before turning to him. To his surprise the expression she turned to him was fully composed.

"Thank you for your time, and the use of your sofa," she began as if spurred on by Miss Manners herself. "I know you don't believe me but I truly can't remember what our past relationship was, Mr. Guinn. Still, I would have thought you—anybody—would set aside his feelings under the circumstances to help someone in trouble. Regardless of your feelings toward me, you owe me the courtesy of checking out my story."

Joe didn't answer.

As she slid from the seat and slammed the door all he felt was great relief. He gunned the engine of his truck, sending it hurdling out of the parking lot. It bucked over the curb and then the ride smoothed out as his tires ate up the blacktop.

He leaned back in the leather seat, slung a wrist over the top of the steering wheel and smiled out at the view through his windshield.

Halle Hayworth had come and gone a second time from his life. This time he'd gotten over her with a minimum of trouble. He had even allowed her to have the last word and not let it get to him. He had handled it well. It was over. There was nothing to fear. Nothing to worry about. He was home free.

Two minutes passed before he saw the flashing blue lights of a highway patrol car in his rearview mirror. He glanced down at the speedometer. He was doing ninety miles per hour. He eased up on the gas pedal but it was too late. He knew then he was running away from that last lost look he had spied in Halle's eyes.

Ten minutes later, he was pulling off the shoulder back onto the highway, a little angrier but a little wiser. He could run but he couldn't hide, not from his conscience nor his feelings for Halle. The price of that lesson was couched in the form of a speeding ticket.

"All right, Halle," he murmured to himself. "I'm going to call your bluff."

He headed off the exit marked Tyler. He was going to get irrefutable proof that Halle was as sane, if more devious, than he. He owed it to his own peace of mind.

Joe leaned forward in his chair drawn up before Dr. Lawlah's office desk. "Amnesia. Caused by a concussion?"

"That's right, Mister Guinn. It's called amnesia or in the vernacular, memory loss."

As the doctor veered off into a long rather grisly account of brain swelling and ruptured and bleeding capillaries to explain the physical cause behind the condition, Joe's thoughts turned inward. He had picked up the trail of Halle's story at the county sheriff's office from a friend. Surprisingly enough there *had* been a highway pileup just outside town two weeks ago involving a commercial bus and an eighteen-wheeler. It had happened while he was in Fort Worth bagging a deadbeat father. Several bus passen-

gers had been injured, one of them a young woman
with a head trauma. The sheriff's department did not
have her name or any information about her because
she wasn't carrying any ID. The hospital had informed them that the young woman in question was
diagnosed as suffering from amnesia but that she
didn't want publicity of the fact. Because she had no
record nor were there any law enforcement bulletins
seeking a woman of her description, they had let the
matter drop. So far Halle's story checked out, but she
could have read about it in the papers or seen the story
on the TV.

Joe told himself he didn't have to figure out why she
was lying to continue to believe that she was. Cops
often worked from the gut. Sometimes it was the only
lead they had. He didn't ask himself why he wanted to
believe she was lying. He just did. Yet, if he was going to call her bluff, he knew he had to go the distance. A good cop checked out every lead. Took
nothing at face value, even his gut reactions.

It had taken him two hours to track down the attending physician, Dr. Lawlah. The doctor was willing to talk to him in generalities about his former
patient, released the day before, but Joe was getting
the feeling he wasn't hearing all he might. "You're
certain she couldn't be faking this."

The doctor looked surprised. "You mean a psy-
chosomatic memory loss?"

"Actually, I had something else in mind. Outright
lying."

The doctor frowned. "Why would you even ask?"

"The woman claiming to be your amnesia victim
has hired me to find out who she is." Joe pulled out
and displayed his private investigator's license. "I deal

with a lot of zanies in my line of work. I have to check her story out."

The doctor smiled. "Of course. Your earlier description of her certainly matches my patient. I can understand why she might seek your expert help. Our Jane Doe was very upset by the fact she could not remember anything useful about her life."

"So you say. But couldn't she be faking it? I mean, people fake illnesses all the time."

"I must assume that you have a reason for feeling she might want to do that. What is it?"

"I don't have a reason, not really." Joe leaned back in his chair, unwilling to admit anything he didn't have to. "You've got to admit it's very suspicious that no ID was found with her belongings."

"Unusual, yes, but hardly criminal."

Joe scowled as if it were the doctor and not himself who was being difficult. "Why did you let her go, knowing she couldn't fend for herself?"

The doctor looked like a man whose resources of patience were being tested. "I did try to persuade her to remain, Mr. Guinn. The bus company is picking up all medical expenses for injured passengers. I pointed out that until her brain swelling subsided during the next few days and her memory began to return, that she would be more comfortable here. But she was adamant about leaving."

"Did she say why she wanted out of the hospital?"

The doctor shook his head. "We had no choice but to release her yesterday, at her insistence. She can been a very persuasive person."

"I know." Something else had Joe stumped. Halle had actually been on a bus. "Did she say why she was in Texas?"

"If she could answer that," Dr. Lawlah replied tolerantly, "she wouldn't be diagnosed as having amnesia, Mr. Guinn."

Joe grunted. Dealing with Halle was making him sound like an idiot. So, she hadn't lied to him. But how much of the rest of what she had told him was real and how much was the result of a hard knock on the head?

"Is there any medical reason why an amnesia victim would think that she was being followed or threatened?"

"Not per se. However, occasional irrational fears would not be an uncommon reaction for someone suffering memory loss, particularly in an instance where the victim was traumatized, as in a motor accident. She is in unfamiliar surroundings among strangers. Certainly there might be cause for the development of moments of panic, inexplicable fears, feelings of isolation, desertion."

"So you're saying she might not really be in trouble or being stalked. It could all be in her mind?"

The doctor leaned forward with a slight frown. "You seem very preoccupied with my patient's motives, Mr. Guinn. More than professional interest would seem to allow. Would you like to tell me why?"

"It's kind of delicate." Joe glanced across the desk at the doctor. It was obvious he was going to have to reveal his hand to someone. Better a physician than the sheriff's department, just in case Halle might really be in trouble. "I need you to hold what I'm about to tell you in confidence, even from your patient."

"Sounds serious. Very well, unless it directly concerns my patient's well-being, I agree to keep your secret."

"Your patient's name's Halle Hayworth. She's from New York."

The doctor's expression did not alter. "How do you know that?"

"I know—knew her once, a long time ago."

"I see." The doctor reached for his pen and pad. "Then perhaps you know some next of kin or if she is married?"

Joe sighed. "She's married."

The doctor's pen hovered over the blank sheet. "To whom?"

"His name's—wait. Halle says she thinks someone may be after her."

Doctor Lawlah's brows drew together. "You suspect that 'someone' may be her husband?"

"Perhaps." Joe aired his middle-of-the-night musings. "A woman traveling through a strange town with serious cash in her purse isn't on what I'd call a regular holiday."

The doctor leaned back and steepled his fingers, pen still in hand. "Would you say you know her well enough to make that kind of judgment about her marital relationship?"

"Perhaps."

"Really?" Skepticism lifted the doctor's brows. "How so?"

Joe stepped across his personal line in the sand. "I'm her ex."

"Ex? Husband?"

Joe nodded. "We divorced and she remarried a couple of years ago."

The doctor nodded. "I see."

"No, I don't think you do. Halle's from a very wealthy family, Manhattan born and bred. She didn't have a driver's license because she doesn't own a car. She leases one with a driver when necessary. She's never been west of Chicago, and then only by plane. The woman I married never even considered taking a bus across town. She sure wouldn't have taken one through east Texas.''

''Maybe she was coming to visit you.''

''It wasn't exactly a friendly divorce.'' Joe shrugged. ''I'm the last person on earth Halle would come to for help if she was in her right mind which, obviously, she isn't. I figure it must have been just plain dumb luck she found my name in the phone book and came to me for help. To tell you the truth, I don't want anything to do with her.''

''I see.''

Joe suspected that what the doctor saw all too clearly was that he was being a bastard in a situation in which another man would have been more gallant. But he didn't owe anyone an explanation of his feelings and he certainly wasn't going to offer an emotional one to a stranger.

He pulled out his wallet and flipped it open again, showing Halle's picture to the doctor. ''Just for the record, this is your patient. Right?''

The doctor examined the picture with a frown. ''My patient has dark hair.''

Joe formed a circle with his thumb and forefinger and laid it over the picture so that only Halle's face appeared in the center.

With a surprised look, the doctor nodded. ''Oh yes, that's her.''

Satisfied, Joe repocketed it. ''So, if she's still ailing, is it safe for her to be wandering around east Texas?''

"Ms. Hayworth was released from the hospital because essentially there's nothing seriously wrong with her. I expect her memory to return gradually over the next few days or weeks."

"Day or weeks? You're certain?"

"I'm reasonably hopeful," the doctor countered.

Joe smiled at his caution. "Okay, doc. All I want to know is, if I give you all the information you need, like the right phone numbers and addresses of friends or family, will you take over her care from here?"

"Certainly. You have that information?"

"I can get it with a phone call or two."

The doctor's gaze sharpened. "I don't suppose you'd consider looking after Ms. Hayworth for a few days?"

"No, absolutely not." Joe stood up. "I told you before, we're history."

"Then why do you still carry a picture of her in your wallet, Mr. Guinn?"

Joe didn't reply, just tucked in his chin. "I need to find a pay phone. Make a few calls."

"Be my guest. There's one in the waiting room at the end of the hall. Ms. Hayworth needs to be with her loved ones at a time like this."

Loved ones. Joe thought about that phrase as he left the doctor's office to go in search of a public phone. Halle had had very few loved ones when he'd known her. Her family had not been among them.

Most children became orphans by losing their parents. Halle had been born into a family where it just seemed as if she were an orphan. Her parents were jet-setters, divorced and remarried so many times to other partners she had lost count of her erstwhile step-mothers and fathers. Neither parent had made a home for her with them during her growing-up years. That had fallen to a cadre of servants who manned an enormous upper eastside Manhattan apartment. During the three years he was part of her life, her parents had never even bothered to visit her, not once. She had done the usual things, sending them birthday and holiday greetings. They responded by sending gifts without cards once a year, as if a message popped up in their social calendars that read, "Send gift to female child. Occasion unknown."

If either parent bothered to respond to Doctor Lawlah's messages, it wouldn't be to bring Halle into either of their homes. The Hayworths would more than likely deposit her in a fancy rest home or private European spa, provide lots of money for therapy, and then promptly forget about her.

Joe's steps dragged a little as he neared the pay phone at the end of the hall. He had always thought story plots in which the heroine lost her memory were just cheap, no-brainer tricks for lazy suspense writers who wanted a convenient way to terrorize the protagonist. But now Halle was the heroine of her own "Home Unknown" and her lost memory was more than an inconvenience. It laid responsibility for her, at least temporarily, squarely at his own door. How was that for irony?

But Halle couldn't be his problem. She had excluded him from her life by divorcing him. As much as he hated the idea, he was going to have to get in touch with Daniel Shipmann.

He dialed information in Manhattan and jotted down the only number he received in reply to several requests.

The auction house where Halle worked refused to give out her home phone number even after he identified himself. He could have simply left a message for Shipmann but jealousy held him back. At the last moment he managed to remember the name of another of her colleagues, Sarah Stuart, and asked to be transferred to her.

"Joe Guinn! After all this time," Sarah greeted him. "I can't quite believe it! Where are you? In the city, I hope."

"I don't have much time, Sarah. This is long distance," Joe replied curtly. In her day, Sarah had been one of his greatest detractors. Her false note of delight grated. "I'm looking for Halle. On business. How can I to get in touch with her?"

"Now that might be difficult. I haven't seen her lately, not since she quit. She'd been through so much. Who could fault her for wanting to take an extended vacation? We all agreed it was deserved, considering the climate in the office these last months. But to leave permanently? That was amazing."

Joe didn't bother to summon any enthusiasm for the tidbit of office gossip she was obviously dangling before him. The trials and tribulations of auctioneering had never appealed to him. "Was she behaving in an unusual manner the last time you saw her?"

"That's the most amazing thing. She was. You know Halle. The auction house was her life. Then she quit, just like that. Said she needed a change of scenery. I suppose it had something to do with Daniel taking another job."

"That so? Where did he go?"

"He got a really cushy job at Sotheby's in London, the kind Halle had been yearning for."

"I see. So then, they're moving to England?"

There was a significant pause on Sarah's end. "Joe, you don't know, do you?"

Something in her voice made his spine tingle. "Why don't you fill me in?"

"Actually, it's probably not my— Oh, it's no secret. Halle left Daniel six months ago, Joe. They're divorced."

Chapter 5

Some Texans toned down their accents after they'd earned their first million. Not Bill McCrea. His was pure LBJ. A paternal depot of the old school, McCrea was known for dispensing cash and orders with equal generosity in a drawl thick enough to spread on cornbread.

"The thing is to find the boy and bring him home before he makes a dam—dad-blame fool of himself!"

"I'll do my best," Joe replied, secretly amused that McCrea was curbing his profanity because of his wife's presence.

"I demand the best effort from my employees, only the best."

"I'm sure Joe knows no other way to do business."

Joe smiled at his supporter, Ella McCrea, who sat on a sofa of golden brocade.

From the outside the McCrea residence looked like a ranch house on steroids, everything oversize and exaggerated but rustic. But once inside, the foyer and living room took their decorative cue from Versailles. Drapes, walls, ceilings and furniture, every surface was richly textured and painted in shades of cream or rose, or gilded. If Joe hadn't already visited Bill McCrea's study with its distressed wood paneling, leather sofas and chairs whose framework was made up of longhorn steer horns, he would have thought he was in the wrong house. McCrea was a short spare man who favored gray suits and bolo ties. Obviously this ornate setting reflected the taste of the lady of the house.

Ella McCrea was a petite woman of a certain age with ash-blond hair piled up in large billowing waves. The heavy gold earrings she wore could be counterweights, Joe thought. Though she was dressed in a man-tailored western shirt and slacks the aura of femininity was undiminished. The shirt was pale yellow and her slacks were the color of mint ice cream. To top it off enveloping clouds of a classic fragrance drifted through the room with her every movement.

"You must understand, Lacey was a late-life child, Mr. Guinn." Mrs. McCrea touched her throat a little self-consciously, drawing Joe's attention to the cluster of diamonds encircling one of her fingers. "We already had three girls. Deirdra, the youngest, was fourteen when Lacey was born. I'm afraid we all spoiled him, treated him more like a new toy than a child."

"That's the gospel truth," Bill McCrea responded. "Fixed it so the boy's spoiled, moody, thinks he should have his own way."

Joe detected tension between the pair but solving family differences wasn't part of his job description. He had found the best way to operate in such an atmosphere was to be matter-of-fact. He pulled out a small notepad and pen. "What sort of things have you and Lacey argued about recently, Mr. McCrea?"

McCrea waved a hand dismissively. "Things every father and son do."

"He means there wasn't much they didn't fight about," Mrs. McCrea added softly.

"The last fight?" Joe prompted.

"Don't remember," McCrea muttered.

"The last one began when my husband told Lacey he was going to enroll him in a military academy, the one down near Harlingen, next fall," Mrs. McCrea offered helpfully.

"Time he became a man." McCrea scowled at Joe as if he expected an argument. "Military school will shape him up before it's too late."

The combative tone in McCrea's voice perked up Joe's investigative senses. "Is there a reason why you're worried about Lacey's ability to measure up as a man?"

"I certainly don't think so," Mrs. McCrea said in a snippy voice. Her husband slanted a quelling look her way but she bristled under it, twitching her shoulders in annoyance. "I think you should tell him just how old-fashioned you are."

"Now, Ella, we agreed—"

"Don't 'Now, Ella' me!" Mrs. McCrea turned a sweet smile on Joe. "My husband thinks Lacey's been tainted by certain influences."

Joe offered her a sympathetic look. As a cop, he'd become accustomed to shocking revelations of every sordid sort. "What sort of influences?"

"Dancing lessons," Bill McCrea muttered under his breath. "The blame thing is," he went on in a louder voice, "the junior high football coach encouraged it. Said it would make him a better quarterback. Only I never heard of Roger Stauback or Troy Aikman taking dancing lessons."

Joe curbed his urge to smile. "It's become pretty common, Mr. McCrea, for male athletes to take up dancing as a method of improving their flexibility and balance. Linebacker Rosie Grier broke the ice back in the seventies by taking up ballet. Then he took up knitting. Said it was more relaxing than meditation."

McCrea frowned at Joe. "That was easy for him, he'd already proved himself a man. By the way, what's Grier doing these days?"

"He's now a minister."

McCrea snorted then glared at his wife. "You see? Dancing turns a man's thoughts away from the field of conflict. No son of mine is going to be a dancer."

Joe's restraint slipped and a smile appeared. "Is that what you fought about? Lacey wanted to take dancing lessons?"

"Took 'em." McCrea's face was set in the age-old lines of parental disapproval. "His mother thought he should have them if he wanted them. Drove him into Dallas every Saturday the first year."

"I did the same for the girls," Mrs. McCrea maintained.

"Was Lacey ashamed for it to be known that he was taking these lessons?"

"Hell, no!" McCrea exploded. "Once he turned sixteen and got his driver's license, he spent more hours after school in Dallas than here. Dam—blamed if he didn't start boasting about the classes to his teammates. Claimed they were a quick and easy way to meet city girls. Lots of would-be models and cheerleaders in Dallas dancing classes."

"So Lacey likes girls," Joe said lightly, mentally scratching off another possible motive for the boy to feel compelled to leave home.

McCrea snorted. "That was never the issue. The trouble is, he wants to drop football and take up dancing full-time. He was going to make the state all-star team this year, practically guaranteed. The coach came to see me almost weeping because Lacey had told him he wasn't going to play. Might as well have aimed a .45 between my eyes, right?"

Joe didn't doubt the coach's distress. He hadn't been back in Texas fifteen minutes before he was reminded that football was taken just about as seriously as religion in this state.

"My husband is a traditional man, Mr. Guinn," Mrs. McCrea added graciously. "The thought of his son performing on stage is anathema to him."

"I hate it!" McCrea concurred. "You ever see a man in dancing tights? Indecent doesn't begin to cover it. Depraved, is more like. Standing on the stage being ogled at like a centerfold. A man should have more self-respect!"

Joe turned his attention to Mrs. McCrea. "Is Lacey good?"

"A natural," she answered with motherly pride. "He's received offers from schools, even scholarships. He danced this past winter in a Dallas-based production of *The Nutcracker*. He was the Mouse King.''

''See what I mean?'' McCrea cut in. ''Mouse King. Lord love us! A mouse!''

''Lacey's been accepted at the Dallas Magnet School for the Performing Arts next fall,'' Mrs. McCrea explained with an injured glance at her spouse. ''He disappeared the morning after my husband refused to allow him to accept.''

''I refused to encourage the boy on the wrong path.'' McCrea turned to his wife. ''Football is good exercise, tests a man's courage, his resolve. It teaches him to be a team player, to take his lumps without complaining. It shows him how to accept victory and loss. What does dancing teach?''

''Poise, self-confidence and self-expression,'' his wife promptly answered. ''You had no problem with our daughters dancing in talent shows or participating in drill team.''

''But did I encourage a single one of my girls to think of it as a career? He—heck no! Told 'em, you got to go to college, get a real education and then a real job.'' He turned to Joe. ''I raised a teacher, a junior high school counselor, and a businesswoman.''

''A clothes designer,'' his wife amended. ''Charlotte Designs is a fashion firm.''

''Charlotte owns her firm.'' McCrea's expression turned pugnacious. ''That makes her a businesswoman in my books.''

Mrs. McCrea offered Joe a little helpless gesture with her hands, as if she had participated in this conversation countless and fruitless times before. ''As you may have gathered by now, Mr. Guinn, this is the source of our family conflict. Lacey ran away after my husband refused to allow him to change schools in order to pursue a career as a performer. It's his dream."

"His delusion, you mean." McCrea shook his head. "Boy thinks he's going to be the next Tommy Tune."

"Mr. Tune is a Texan, you know," Mrs. McCrea said confidentially to Joe. "He's danced on Broadway."

"I don't care if he's danced for the president," McCrea thundered at his wife, who nodded in the affirmative to Joe. "No son of mine is gonna be a dancer!"

Mrs. McCrea's face crumpled a little and for the first time Joe realized she was older that her deceptively taut skin made her seem. "I think the best solution is to wait for Lacey to return." She didn't look at either man as she said, "I'm certain he will be back on his own in a few days."

"What makes you think that, Mrs. McCrea?"

Joe noted that this time she didn't look at him as she spoke. "I just know. Lacey is a sensible boy." She sighed elaborately. "Once he's had a chance to think about things he'll come home, if only for my sake."

For a woman whose husband claimed she had required sedation the day before, Mrs. McCrea seemed amazingly calm, Joe noted. Maybe too calm. He was getting vibes that said she knew something her husband did not.

He flipped over to a clean page of his notepad. "I'd like the name of Lacey's dancing instructor and a list of the students he seems closest to."

"Oh no, I can't do that." She turned in appeal to her husband. "Billy, think what an embarrassment that would be if Mr. Guinn begins interrogating Lacey's friends? It will seem that we've driven out our only son."

"I'd be a little more subtle, Mrs. McCrea. You have no reason to be alarmed."

Joe saw her eyes narrow as if in calculation though she turned a smile on him. In that smile he saw a match for McCrea's bluster. When it came down to a real match between the McCreas, he doubted she lost many arguments. "I'm perfectly sure you're a fine detective, Mr. Guinn—may I call you Joe?—or else my husband wouldn't have approached you. But I simply couldn't endure it if my husband or my son were publicly embarrassed by what is essentially a private matter. Mr. McCrea is about to seek another term in the state senate, as you well know. He cannot afford even the teeniest, tiniest breath of scandal."

Joe saw his bank account head toward tilt as the job slipped away. He rose to his feet. "Whatever you say, Mrs. McCrea."

"What about what I want?" Mr. McCrea planted himself squarely before Joe. "I hired you, not Ella. I don't want a scandal, either. That's why I want you to find Lacey. Now. Today."

Joe glanced between the couple. "Can you give me the information I need, Mr. McCrea?"

"I can get the name of the school. Never went there myself but I signed enough checks." He grinned. "You're an investigator. Should be able to dig up the rest. I'll just check my bank receipts for the name."

When her husband had left the room on his errand, Mrs. McCrea turned an appealing smile on Joe. "You must think me a doting mother, Joe, for that is exactly what I am. Lacey is a good boy. He and his father naturally have their differences. What fathers and sons don't? So, since I can't convince my husband not to pursue this matter, I must appeal to your sense of chivalry.''

She rose and came toward him, her eyes wide with kind appeal but Joe felt the web being spun about him. It was obvious she was just as accustomed as her husband to getting her own way.

''Please, Joe, if you should find Lacey before he voluntarily returns, promise me you'll call me first if you discover anything...sensitive about his circumstance.'' She lay a hand lightly on his forearm. ''Promise me.''

Joe looked into her eyes and the feeling inside him resolved into certainty. She was withholding secrets. He suspected she was covering for her son. ''Is there something you want to tell me, Mrs. McCrea?''

''I— Oh, here's Bill.'' She sounded a bit flustered but her husband did not seem to notice.

McCrea strode across the plush cream carpet and thrust two pieces of paper at Joe. ''Here's the name, address and phone number of the dance school. The check is your retainer. I expect you to get on up to Dallas and get started today.''

Joe glanced at the check and in his mind's eye saw not only a stack of bills marked Paid but a new fishing reel in his future. ''Thanks, Mr. McCrea.''

''I'll pick up all expenses in Dallas, of course.''

Joe folded both pieces of papers into his breast pocket. ''If you don't mind, I'd like to handle this my way. Before I head for Dallas, I need to settle another matter.''

"What sort of matter? You working another job? Cancel it. I'll make up the difference in your salary. I want Lacey back before anybody realizes he's gone."

"The matter is personal and it cannot wait."

The two men eyed one another for several seconds before McCrea shrugged.

Joe knew better than to glance at McCrea's wife as he said, "I've a feeling Lacey's safe enough. It may be just a matter of time before he returns of his own volition."

"Exactly!" Ella McCrea concurred.

"Or he could have gotten himself into deep trouble." McCrea rocked back on his heels. "Ella doesn't like unpleasantness but I can face facts. I'm a wealthy man. A boy alone like that, without protection, he could be kidnapped for ransom."

Joe smiled as Ella rolled her eyes behind her husband's back. "You have no reason to suspect that."

McCrea shrugged. "I had no reason to suspect the boy would light out like he did. Packed a bag and everything."

Joe's gaze cut to Mrs. McCrea. "He packed a bag? May I see Lacey's room?"

A few minutes later, Joe was once again at the front door of the McCrea homestead, as McCrea referred to his ranch house of palatial dimensions. The tour of Lacey's room had been more enlightening than he was willing to divulge to his client.

Runaways seldom took much with them. There were conspicuous vacancies in Lacey's closet and chest of drawers. For instance, not one piece of his dancing attire was there, nor could he find an address book. A dozen CDs were missing from the rack. Lacey's parents volunteered that his CD player and laptop computer were also missing. So then, Lacey had not just tossed a couple of T-shirts and jeans into a backpack and stalked out in a huff. No, a young man that burdened by that many belongings probably had a destination in mind before he even left home. In fact, he'd packed as if he were going to camp, or summer school.

Joe hadn't considered himself to be pilfering when he swiped one of the summer dance school brochures he found tucked in the back of a drawer in Lacey's desk. He needed this paycheck. If it meant pursuing the obvious, he would.

"I just know you will do what's right, what's best for all," Ella McCrea called after him.

"What's best for all," Joe muttered as he stepped out into the bright sunlight of midmorning. He was being asked to make a hell of a lot of ethical decisions this day, and it wasn't even noon.

Halle had left Shipmann.

The divorce became final just a few weeks ago, Sarah had continued. *We all just knew after the first month that it wasn't going to work out between them.*

Joe briefly closed his eyes, hoping he hadn't struck a false note with Sarah when he'd responded.

So, Halle and Dan couldn't stick it out. Any reason in particular?

Other than you, you mean?

Right, Sarah, that's a cheap shot. I wasn't even in the state.

Come on, Joe. Once you weren't so modest. Halle told me about the time near the end of your marriage when you two were fighting constantly and you told her that you had gotten into her blood like a virus and she was never going to recover.

I was wrong. She found the cure. It's called divorce.

Don't fool yourself. Daniel never stood a chance. Not after you, Joe. Halle just never got over you.

Joe swung open the door of his truck and climbed in.

Sarah's words had floored him. Yet he couldn't think of a single reason why Sarah would lie to him. After all, she had sided with all Halle's society friends in thinking that he was little more than a retro Neanderthal dressed in NYPD blue. She had no reason to want to make him feel better now.

To his face Halle's friends had been condescending to the point of snobbery. Behind his back they told her that they understood the attraction—his macho job and working-class charisma were proof positive that he had more testosterone than brains. Sleep with him by all means but then forget him.

Joe stuck his key in the ignition but didn't start the engine.

Had they thought Halle wouldn't repeat their remarks or had her friends hoped their insults would run him off? Halle hadn't understood the depth of his hurt when she told him some of the remarks their relationship was eliciting from her friends. Secure in their love for one another, she'd thought they were hilarious and completely wrong. Despite her lonely upbringing, she was so full of generosity and goodwill she seldom saw the bad in people. Perhaps that's why the seeming betrayal had hurt her so badly she couldn't even face him with an accusation. She had been brought up to ignore unpleasantries and do as she wished. He'd been reared to face reality whatever the price.

A major difference between them. He always tried to be pragmatic and do what was right, no matter the personal cost. Two years ago he had paid a high price for making a mistake about what was right and what was wrong. Now he wasn't at all certain what was right. Basically, he no longer trusted himself to make any decisions that involved anyone else's life.

He put the truck in gear and headed down the McCrea drive toward the highway.

Halle had divorced Shipmann.

If he hadn't cut himself off completely from everything and everyone who had been part of his New York life, he might have known about the breakup before this. But he'd been too badly hurt to risk hearing how deliriously happy Halle might be with her new husband, about how after the first glorious year of marriage they were buying a home in Stamford, Connecticut with plans to convert the extra bedroom into a nursery. If that had been the case, he might have slit his throat.

Now he knew the truth of the relationship. It hadn't lasted until its first anniversary. Though he couldn't say the news made him want to do handsprings, somewhere deep inside him a tiny flame of hope that had no right to do so was flickering to life.

Halle had divorced Shipmann.

So what? It shouldn't make any difference. He and Halle were over long before she looked seriously at Shipmann. The man hadn't come between them. He'd just stepped very quickly into the breach. So why the hell hadn't he stuck it out?

Joe rubbed his palms up and down the steering wheel to stop the itching sensation brought on by the desire to smash something. His dislike of Shipmann wasn't logical or really personal, but it was gut level. What kind of jerk gave up a woman like Halle?

"A jerk like me."

Joe forced himself to relax. He stuck an elbow out the open window and stretched his other arm along the bench seat, absorbing the heat from the sun-drenched leather as he turned onto Interstate 20, heading west. The fact that their marriage hadn't worked out didn't mean he held any animosity toward Halle. He wanted her to be happy. That is all he had ever wanted for her, even if it meant he had to lose her to achieve it. Now he knew she wasn't better off without him.

She was suffering from amnesia. She didn't have a husband or a reliable family to turn to. That pretty much meant she was alone in the world. Logically the thing for him to do would have been to present Dr. Lawlah with the facts and then leave the medical man to take over things from there. No doubt she had been in a delicate emotional state before the accident.

Certainly she had to have been devastated by a second divorce. She was not a coldhearted bitch, no matter what his own friends had thought at the time of their divorce. They hadn't understood why she hadn't stood by her man, right or wrong, in his hour of need. Loyalty often ranked above ethics in police circles. At least he had thought so—until loyalty cost him everything.

He'd had two long miserable years since to reconsider his choice of loyalty to an old friend over loyalty to his wife.

Perhaps if he had confided in Halle at the beginning then she would have understood, or tried to, when his gamble blew up in his face. Maybe then she wouldn't have listened to the attorney she'd hired who advised her not to give her husband a hearing, another chance, or the benefit of the doubt. She might have seen him anyway, given him a chance to explain why his badge was being taken and the possibility of a trial loomed in his future. He knew for certain she would not have believed the rumor that he was seeing someone else.

But things had begun to get shaky between them months before. Small differences escalating into huge fights that became harder and harder to smooth over. Like a chronic hangover, the next bout of fighting seemed the only way to erase the soreness that remained from the last. By the time his professional life cratered, it was too late. They no longer trusted one another. They were adversaries, estranged by differences greater than background and economics.

Joe's hands flexed on the steering wheel as behind his sun shades his eyes glistened. Halle didn't deserve such a fate. It was as if a light had gone out inside her. The radiance that had first drawn him to her was absent when she gazed at him. He was a stranger, as she was to herself.

It seemed as if life had abandoned her. He just could not turn his back on her, no matter what pain it might ultimately cost him. That lost look in a pair of celadon-flecked amber eyes was stopping him from walking away. He couldn't leave her, even if she might one day soon remember how much she hated him. Until then, he was going to stick as close to her as a burr in a cotton sock.

Joe floored the accelerator, causing the wind rushing in through the open window to rustle the speeding ticket he had stashed on the dashboard hours earlier.

* * *

"We were friends in New York City?"

"That's right. Friends." Joe repeated the words with all the warmth of a cop reading a collar her Miranda rights. Keep it neutral, he told himself, matter-of-fact.

He was relieved that Halle didn't overreact, cry out or jump up from her perch on the motel-room bed where he suspected she'd been sitting ever since he dropped her off three hours ago. She hadn't changed her clothes, turned back the bed, or in any way disturbed the pristine vacuousness of the room. It was almost as if her presence didn't leave an impression these days. The dark color of her hair still disconcerted him. Its drabness seemed to shun light instead of filter it the way her fair hair had. Even her posture seemed contrived to hide the woman he had once known.

Only her eyes, enormous now in her too thin face, were familiar. He recognized that expression in them. Was she still afraid, afraid even to leave this room? The uneasy feeling residing in his gut knotted.

When Joe had returned to Dr. Lawlah's office to tell him what he'd learned from Sarah, the doctor had suggested that he not hand Halle all the reality of their past relationship at once. The added information that she was recently divorced for the second time had made the doctor more cautious. The trauma of the divorce might be one of the contributing factors to her amnesia, he had said. If so, she might be unconsciously fighting her memory's return. Only time would tell. He had advised Joe to take things easy, see if his gradual revelations jogged her memory.

"Give her positive reinforcement," he had said. "Make her want to remember."

Joe took a slow breath. He had devised a plan on the way over here. He would tell her who she was and where she was from, all things he thought he could safely supply. If she wanted names and phone numbers, he'd get them for her. *But*, he wasn't willing to hand her the lit firecracker of a detail that they were once married. He would help her remember her past but he wasn't at all certain she would thank him for it when she did. "So, what do you think, Halle?"

Halle looked at him with guarded interest. "Why are you telling me this now? Why not last night, or even this morning?"

He shrugged. "I was annoyed before, because you forgot we were friends."

"I see." Halle sat poised on the end of the hotel bed where she had been sitting all morning long, staring with unfocused eyes at the TV. It passed the time but little else. "How good friends were we?"

"Pretty good." Joe shifted his weight from one foot to the other, jutting out the opposite hip. He debated only a moment before adding, "We were room-mates."

He saw her gaze drop for an instant below his belt buckle and chagrin deepened the color in his cheeks. "I didn't mean we were lovers," he added hastily. Good grief! He didn't want to stir that up yet. "We were roomies, that's all."

"Platonic?" she ventured doubtfully though her cheeks were quite pink.

"Yeah. Platonic. Buddies." His throat tightened on the lie. This was going to be harder than he thought. "So, I was thinking, since you're out here in Texas alone that we might, well...er, become roomies again, until your memory comes back."

Halle rose. "But if you know me, you must know my family, my friends, other people I can call for help."

Joe knew that was coming and so he didn't have to tell an outright lie this time. "I didn't know your friends that well. I never even met your family. You didn't like to talk much about them. They live in Europe."

"Europe is a continent." She cocked a brow. "Can't you be a little more specific?"

Joe smiled a little. Glimpses of the old Halle helped. "Not really. Last I heard, your mother was marrying for the third time. Your dad was already on to his fourth wife." Her expression was one of faint shock. "Look, it was no big thing for you. You once told me your parents weren't exactly reliable or what you'd call steady influences."

"I suppose not." Halle tilted her head to one side, as if she might better hear the tiny voice that had begun whispering inside her the night before. But it had no information to offer about her parents. It only said Joe was not lying about their relationship. And she wanted, no needed, oh so badly, to trust him.

"What's that?" He pointed to the expensive leather suitcase at her feet.

"My things. At least, they're supposed to belong to me. A deputy from the sheriff's department brought them by. By process of elimination with other passengers having claimed their belongings, they determined the suitcase must belong to me."

Joe tensed. "Recognize anything?"

She shrugged and flipped the lid open. "Not really. Everything fits, though. Even the shoes and bras."

Joe bent and picked up a flimsy bit of turquoise fabric which turned out to be a scantily cut teddy. "It's your taste.'' He dropped it back into the bag without making eye contact with her.

He knew he was toeing a thin line. Now that he was determined to take her in, he suddenly wondered if she'd actually go off alone with him a second time, a complete stranger but for his word to the contrary. The old Halle had never been gullible.

''What did you do when you lived in New York, Joe?''

''I was a cop.''

''A police officer?'' she corrected automatically, as he had taught her to when her friends used the more derisive word cop.

''That's right.''

''What kind of policeman?''

''Detective in vice, bunko, narcotics.''

''Sounds dangerous.''

''Someone's got to do it.''

''And so you volunteered?''

His expression sobered. ''I did.''

''Were you any good?''

''The best.''

Joe couldn't quite believe it when she suddenly smiled at him. But he knew by the expanding of her pupils that she was buying his story, hook, line, and sinker.

She stood up. ''Then I should be in very safe hands with you, Officer Guinn.''

Safe hands! Was she joking? If he dared put his hands on her in the ways he ached to, that would result in a major felony.

She tossed her head to clear her face of her hair. Joe found himself following that sweep of unfamiliar dark hair as it swung out and away from her head, revealing one side of her neck and ear.

"Where did you get those?" He pointed a finger at her ear.

She reached up and touched one of the earrings she was wearing. It was a silver loop from which dangled a silver cow with enameled pink udders and chocolate brown eyes. Her finger set its fully articulated legs dancing. "They were in the suitcase. Cute, huh? I must have a sense of whimsy."

"Or the giver did," Joe responded in a tight voice.

Her expression altered as her gaze snagged his and he knew he'd given himself away. "Did you give these to me?"

He could have, maybe should have lied. "Yeah. For your birthday."

They were the first gift he'd given her and she'd worn them for months, even to work. Knowing how much she valued his gift had made him feel like a millionaire though he could only afford sterling silver, not gold, on his salary. And now, she'd brought them with her to Texas. More mysteries.

She glanced at her reflection in the mirror a few feet away. "How old am I?"

"You'll be thirty next month."

"So old?" The arrested expression on her face was worth his admission.

"No, you don't look it." He chuckled. "But over-the-hill isn't what it used to be. I'm thirty-two, remember?"

Her smile lit up that dingy room. He had known it to light up a city block at midnight when the snow was falling soft as sighs around them.

"I do remember." She rose and took a step to close the distance between them. "You told me last night." She touched one earring again, rubbing the silver lightly between her thumb and forefinger. "Cows from the cowboy. Nice."

Joe hissed a sigh of supreme frustration. Things were getting tougher by the second and he hadn't even gotten her home yet. He needed distance, a realignment of judgement, but mostly distance. He grasped at straws. "I'll bet you haven't eaten today. Neither have I. Let's get out of here and get some food."

She caught his sleeve as he leaned down to reach for her bag. For a moment there was an odd little silence in the room while he did a mental backstroke through the dappled golden green of her shady-lake eyes.

Then she leaned toward him and placed a featherlight kiss on his cheek. "I'm glad you came back today. Really glad."

The touch was so brief he should hardly have felt it. Instead, the kiss mark on his skin burned as he watched her bend to relock her suitcase. It burned as he took the case from her and followed her out the door. It burned for old time's sake and present possibilities and for what must never be.

"I'm not ready for this," Joe muttered to himself as he hoisted her bag into the back of the pickup while she climbed into the cab.

He was still too raw, too needy, too likely to take any kindness from Halle as a sign that her feelings for him had softened or, better yet, never gone completely away. No, he mustn't do that to himself, or to her. The fact she'd packed his gift of the earrings was mere coincidence.

They were history.

He bent forward and lowered his head between the arms he'd slung over the side of the pickup and stared at the ground.

Okay, he could at least still think of them as over. Maybe, when her memory returned and she began to regard him with the same wariness with which she had treated him during their final days together, he would finally begin to believe it was over. Really dead-and-buried over. In the meantime, he was going to have a roommate for the first time in two years.

It belatedly crossed his mind that there'd be no way he could keep Halle hidden for long. He'd never bothered to tell people in Gap that he was divorced...or had ever married for that matter. His private life was just that, private. Yet, this was a small rather straitlaced community. He was going to have to deal with gossip about Halle.

A thumping sound caught his attention and he looked up and saw Halle waving and smiling at him through the back window of his truck cab. That smile reached deep inside him and tugged at the roots of his being.

God help him, he thought with the fatalism of a drowning man, if she could still do that with only a smile.

Chapter 6

"I feel as if I have been married."

Joe spilled iced tea down the front of his clean T-shirt. Cussing under his breath, he grabbed a dozen paper napkins from the dispenser sitting on the table of the booth they occupied and daubed at the beige stains. They were having lunch at the local Dairy Queen.

Halle watched his bent head intently, distracted by the thick dark waves of his hair until he looked up and his face was once more visible. Whatever emotion her question had triggered was gone from his expression. "Well?" she prompted.

"Well what?" he deadpanned.

"Why do I feel married?"

His lip curled as he reached for his sandwich. "How the heck does one 'feel' married?"

"I don't know."

Halle glanced down as she repeatedly dunked the crushed ice floating on top of her tea with the tip of her straw. "It's just a feeling, the sense that I was once connected to someone else. Not family exactly. Different. I don't feel quite whole."

She shifted her gaze back to his face. "Does that make sense?"

Too much sense. Joe took a huge bite of his chicken-fried steak sandwich. She was digging in sacred ground and he wasn't going to help her spade over their life together.

Halle watched him chew furiously, as if he had a mouthful of nails instead of beef. "I'm still willing to pay for your professional services, Joe, even if you are doing me a favor by letting me stay with you. I need answers and I know you can supply them. I can handle the truth. I'm not an emotional cripple nor am I delusional. I've made a few observations of my own. For instance, look."

She held out her left hand and pointed at her ring finger. "There's a very faint pale stripe around this finger. That means I wore a ring regularly until fairly recently. That intensified my feeling that I was or am married. I want to know what you know about me. It's only right."

He lifted blazing dark eyes to hers and she felt a flutter in her stomach. That gaze was recognizable, all right, recognizable as potent attraction tinged with an unwelcome admission of fear. He was feeling what she was feeling and trying like the devil to ignore it. Well, that was his problem. "So? Are you going to tell me?"

He chewed a little more and then swallowed. Then he took a long drink of his tea. Finally he wiped his mouth, smearing a blob of white gravy across his top lip. "I may have heard that you were married for a time."

Halle's whole body reacted to his statement. She leaned forward across the table until the edge of it was digging into her middle just below her breasts.

"Really? Whom did I marry?" She grabbed his wrist just as he was about to take another bite.

Joe plopped his steak sandwich back into its plastic basket. She didn't shy from the hard questions. How the hell was he going to get past this one?

He met her inquiring gaze with stony reserve. "I didn't really know him." No outright lie in that. He didn't really know Shipmann well and it was Shipmann's ring that had left the mark. "I mostly heard about him."

She reacted with a dazzling smile and little jump of delight with her shoulders, pleased as a puppy who'd received a pat on the head. "That's a beginning. What's his name? How do I get in touch with him?"

"I don't know." Joe picked up a long spiral of curly fried potato slathered in ketchup and casually stuffed it in his mouth. Beneath his shirt he was sweating guilt like a perp pulled in for the first time. If he'd been a suspect under interrogation, the officer in charge would have known to go for the jugular now. Lucky for him, Halle had never developed killer instincts.

But Halle had a temper which she reined in as he munched. At least he was talking to her. "This is really important, Joe. Tell me anything you do remember about my husband. Surely you remember something, his first name?"

Joe zeroed in on her hopeful yet determined expression. He should have known softpedaling things wouldn't work. He was once a cop. Time he started to act like one. He could face the truth even if it blew up in his face. "First off let me warn you, you're not together anymore. You're divorced. Your former husband's name is Daniel Shipmann."

She looked like a two-year-old asked to pick the red block out of the multicolored pile. "Shipmann?"

He answered her bleat of distress with the objectivity of the few facts in his possession. "Yeah. He's a Harvard grad. Antiquities dealer, specializing in ancient manuscripts. Ring any bells?"

"No."

The word sounded contrite coming from her, as if she felt the need to apologize. No red block this time.

She sucked in her lower lip. "And we're divorced?"

Inwardly, Joe winced. Her expression was way too open, scared, miserable and exposed. No history, no self-awareness. Her vulnerability made him angry at the world. He hadn't thought of all the ramifications of her delicate emotional state until this moment. And he was all she had. Poor Halle.

"What did you expect?" he muttered, the question directed more at himself than her.

A swathe of dark hair swept forward across her shoulder as if on cue, shielding them both from the haunted look in her eyes. "I don't know. I guess I expected something . . . else."

"Like what?"

She pushed the hair back impatiently. "Oh, a frisson of memory, some brush of psychic awareness." She met his gaze with a touch of spirit in her own. "That name, Daniel Shipmann—it feels empty. Flat. There's nothing in it, not like when—"

Joe's gut clenched. "Yeah?"

Halle shook her head. "It's stupid." But then she looked up again, meeting his watch-your-step stare. "Why should your name mean more to me than my husband's?"

Oh God! He didn't know whether to shout for joy or run and hide. He'd felt the attraction from the moment they'd set eyes on one another again. But now she'd admitted it. The connection between them was not severed. How easily she lured off point his own emotional gyroscope.

"Maybe it's because I'm here." He took pains to keep his voice even. She might be forced by her situation into an emotional striptease but he knew better. "I'm real to you because you can see and tou—talk to me. That's the difference."

She stared at him in challenge. "I wonder."

The need to be honest gripped Joe. He wanted to tell her everything, how she had been the first and only love of his life. How, if he hadn't messed things up, they would still be together. Shipmann had been a mistake, a detour, a blind alley. That was why, even without a single memory to bolster or blast her impressions of him, she knew him deep in her bones. The love had never left.

Instead he slid toward the edge of his seat. Retreat and regroup seemed a good idea. "Want a curly top cone? They'll dip it in chocolate if you want."

"No." She stuck out her leg and propped her foot on the wooden seat opposite, blocking his exit from the booth. "Tell me more, Joe. Was Daniel handsome? Smart? Nice?"

He glowered at her and crossed his arms in a pose of manly impatience. He wanted off the hot seat. That meant placing her in it. "He was rich, if that's what you mean."

Halle frowned. "Why would you think I was asking about that?"

His dark gaze accosted her across the width of the table. "You are rich. Rich women think men are only after their money unless the guys they date have more than them."

Halle gave the idea some consideration. "I don't know that I ever thought about it."

"Trust me. You thought about it." His voice remained flat, abrupt, unflattering. "Your friends wouldn't let you think about anything else."

"How do you know?"

He was no longer looking at her. "I told you, we were roommates for a while. You used to tell me things."

"I see." Trying to keep things light, Halle reached for a curly fry from her untouched basket and dipped one end into the tiny paper cup of ketchup before continuing. "So then we sort of compared notes on our love lives, like best friends."

"Something like that." Again that glance, sharp but guarded, ready to pounce but offering nothing.

Halle bit off a small piece of potato. "What was she like?"

"Who?"

"The woman who made you need to confide in me."

Joe suddenly grinned at her and to her amazement a dimple made its first appearance. "What makes you think there was only one?"

Halle chuckled. "All right. So you're not hard on the eyes. And Mr. Personality, to boot."

"Don't forget, a prize catch."

Her smile softened. "Didn't anybody ever catch you?"

Joe looked down at the remains of his lunch. "Yeah, for a while. But I made the mistake of thinking it was permanent and she saw it as a trial run in which I failed to make the grade."

"How did you fail?"

Oh no, he wasn't going down that road. Not now, not here. He gently shoved her foot off his bench and stood up. "It was all a long time ago. I don't spend much effort recalling painful events. If you're wise, you'll follow my example. You and Shipmann went your own ways. Over is over. All we have is here and now."

"It's certainly all I have," Halle said softly.

He tried not to feel sorry for her. He tried not to feel anything. It was so much easier when he didn't connect to her. But it was too late. He reached to still the finger she was stirring in the ketchup cup. "This isn't easy for either of us, Halle. I know what you want from me but I can't hand you back your past like it was a gift to give. Even if I filled you in on every detail of what I remember about you, it wouldn't mean anything because they'd be my memories. Unless the memories and feelings come from you, they don't count. Okay?"

Halle reached out with her free hand and grasped his hand where it held hers just above the wrist. "But that's what scares me, Joe. What if when my memory comes back, the truth doesn't feel any more real than what you tell me now?"

"That doesn't make any sense, and you know it."

She offered him a troubled but brave smile. "Maybe it doesn't. And maybe my life was already such a mess that I blanked it out on purpose when I was whacked on the head."

Joe ducked his head. Contributing factors, the doctor had called the possible stress-related events which might be behind her amnesia. Her divorce from Shipmann? No, he didn't believe a marriage that has lasted less than a year could have that kind of emotional impact of Halle. Something else? Maybe. He'd have to check it out.

"The point is, Halle, it's the past. Now, about that ice cream."

"I don't think I can eat . . ." But he had turned and walked toward the counter, ignoring her.

No one was after her.

Halle sat at Joe's kitchen table hunched over her third cup of coffee, now cold, and concentrated on what Joe had told her the day before. He had taken time to type up the preliminary report he had handed her before they went to bed, she occupying the guest bedroom this time.

According to his inquiries, there was no reason to think that she was in trouble or in jeopardy of any kind. She had lived a rather straightforward life. She was an only child of Valentin and Calvin Hayworth, the millionaire industrialist.

Halle glanced at the diamond tennis bracelet that now encircled her right wrist. It, too, had been among the things in her suitcase. So then, her intuition was right about the cash found in her purse. Money had never been a problem for her.

The rest of the report was equally terse. She was a graduate of Vassar with a degree in fine arts. She had worked for a series of galleries and auction houses in Manhattan, working her way up to one of the premier houses by the age of twenty-five. Her specialty was Native American artifacts, both North and South American. Within the past year and a half she had married and divorced a colleague, Daniel F. Shipmann. Recently she had quit her job, voluntarily. The reason she had given was that she needed time off. No one knew exactly where she intended to go or for how long. Nothing untoward had happened to her before she left New York City. She was simply on holiday until that tractor trailer made scrap metal of the bus in which she was traveling. There was one contact name and phone number on the sheet: Sarah Stuart.

Halle pushed the paper away. The name meant nothing to her. Nor did the facts. It all sounded artificial, as if her past life were too good to be real. As far as she was concerned, Halle Hayworth might as well be a character in a novel. Where were the messy parts, love affairs, broken engagements? Even her marriage and divorce sounded antiseptic. She had come down with a case of marital bliss and recovered. Had she never bounced a check, cheated on an exam, fought with a friend, made an enemy? She was almost certain she felt as if she had. But how did one call a supposed good friend and say, "Hi, Sarah, this is Halle. Can you tell me who I am?"

"That's pretty pathetic," she murmured. The only concretes of her past life so far were supplied by the paper in front of her. If she could trust them.

No one was after her.

Joe said he had checked his New York contacts and that the divorce from Shipmann had been amicable, no threats, no stalkings, no ugly scenes over division of property. No custody battles for children, not even a dog. He was now working in England. That left no reason to contact or fear him.

She should feel reassured. She should be relieved. She should not be shredding her napkin into tiny pieces. She should not feel as if she were holding her breath as she waited for Joe to come back from wherever the devil he had gone before the sun came up. She should not be rattled because three hours had passed and he had not yet returned.

She most certainly should not be terrorizing herself with grisly fantasies of a truck accident, of Joe lying in a ditch by the side of a dirt road, bleeding and alone, with no one to see or help or comfort him. She shouldn't be indulging such nonsense but she couldn't help it. She knew she was motivated by selfish reasons but he was her only link to the past and the present. If anything happened to him, she'd be perfectly alone.

The sound of his truck engine coming to life just before daybreak had awakened her. Before she could reach the door he was gone. She had comforted herself with the thought that he simply hadn't wanted to awaken her so early to tell her where he was going. That comfort lasted an hour. After the sun came up, she decided to make breakfast, in case he returned hungry. In the refrigerator she had found a carton of sour milk, one cracked egg and a tub of margarine that had begun to separate into suspicious layers. He hadn't lied about not having much to eat.

A little more foraging located a can of coffee in the freezer and a mostly empty cereal box in the cupboard. Her breakfast ended up consisting of dry cereal containing tiny marshmallows washed down by black coffee.

Halle shifted uncomfortably on her chair. Now it was nearly 9:00 a.m. and she was watching the clock as if she were timing an egg. She couldn't shake the feeling that for all the things Joe had told her, many important things were missing from the puzzle that had become her life.

He had practically bolted after dropping her off here the afternoon before, saying he had business to attend to. She understood that. He worked for a living. He had returned late, bringing home prepared barbecue dinners yet he refused to sit and eat with her. Claiming his intense interest in a basketball game, he'd eaten his share in front of the TV then mumbled something about work he had to finish and closed himself behind his bedroom door. When he appeared an hour later he had shoved this typed report at her then retreated to his room for the remainder of the night. It was as if he were hiding something from her. Or, was *he* hiding from her?

There was something tantalizingly familiar about him. Not his face or voice. Those were too obvious. Her brain seemed to be operating on nuance not finite cues. The way his boots creaked when he walked, the tilt of his head when he listened to her, even his smell were more compelling than his features.

She hadn't forgotten for one instant waking up in his arms, no, in his embrace. If he'd been giving her mouth-to-mouth resuscitation then she was Whistler's mother! Okay, so her attraction to him was in-

stantaneous. Tall and tan with deeply hooded dark
eyes in a lean face with hard cheekbones, hard mouth
and hard chin, Joe Guinn was the kind of man a
woman might notice and approach only to receive no
encouragement from, and so pass on with a philo-
sophical shrug. Cute but definitely uninterested.
They'd be wrong. He'd been more than kind to her,
however reluctant he had first been about it. It occurred to her that beneath his battened-down self-
containment there probably lay a kind shy human being. Shy?

"Yes!" she said gleefully. That might be the key-
stone to the man. Joe was shy. His uniform of T-shirts
and worn jeans might cover the muscular lean body of
a hunk but as far as she could tell the Keep Off signs
posted in his dark eyes were permanent features. The
results of his stint as a New York City cop? Or, were
they more personal armor? As for his dimple, it was
the last thing she had expected to see when he smiled,
which he had done exactly once. She was certain he
was embarrassed by that extravagant garnish of nature. Perhaps he scowled so much to keep it from
showing. She suspected the woman who wanted Joe
Guinn would have to go after him, build her own
roadblocks, and stop traffic to get his attention. Or,
maybe not. He was interested in her. It was in his gaze,
intense, banked and all the more powerful for the
smoldering reluctance of it.

"Get a grip, Halle!" She stood and glanced about
the kitchen. A fat lot of good it was doing her to be
speculating about how to snag a man. As if she didn't
have enough problems of her own. This enforced
idleness was making her even more nuts than usual,

whatever usual was. She had to do something, anything or she would go crazy.

She strolled into the living room looking for something to read. The furniture was serviceable but old, looking as though it had been placed just so and not moved for a very long time. The surfaces were a little dusty but that was easily explained by the road which led to the house.

There was a painting of a field of blue bonnets hanging over the sofa and another of a bronco rider hung above the TV. Her critical eye automatically weighed the merit of the renderings. One pulled her in for a closer look. Even as she neared the painting she experienced an odd sense of recognition, as if the work was somehow familiar. Had she seen a copy of it before? The sensations intensified as the artist's abilities became clear to her. The bronco buster was museum quality. She didn't know *how* she knew that but the feeling was unshakeable.

But, as she peered at it, she was impressed by the quality of the reproduction. It was an original oil done by someone with talent. The copied signature must be a joke.

An assortment of aging photos filled the interior of an old rolltop desk. She bent closer to peer into faces that she was certain represented Joe's ancestors. Some pictures were sepia toned. One was a daguerreotype in a silver frame. She picked it up carefully for a better look. The man staring back at her stood bandy-legged in worn leather chaps. The leggings were studded along the outer edges with metal medallions sprouting fringe. A dark bushy handlebar moustache and battered cowboy hat all but obscured his expression yet Halle detected in the angles of his face enough similarity to suggest that he might have been a shorter leaner version of Joe. A great-grandfather, perhaps?

Smiling, she put it back in place to search for a picture of Joe for comparison. Yet there were no photos of him at any age anywhere. It was as if the family record had stopped short thirty or so years earlier. Was that because he had not grown up here? She didn't even know if he had been born in Texas. He'd offered her less information about himself than he had about herself. Instead of supplying answers, her perusal was adding more questions to her list. Most homes gave clues to their owners. So far, Joe's offered as great a mystery as her own life. She had accepted everything he told her as the truth but was anyone that honest? Where would she find clues to the private man?

She moved reluctantly to the doorway of his bedroom, hanging on the threshold like a thief with one ear cocked for the sound of an approaching vehicle. Inside was a roomy king-size bed without a headboard covered by a colorful patchwork spread. In one unobtrusive corner a computer and printer occupied a special table. The rest of the furnishings were dark and heavy maple. Like the living room furniture, they appeared to have taken root in place. After a moment's debate, she stepped into the room.

Though she didn't open any drawers or even pause to read the addresses on the stack of mail on his dresser, she felt as if she were being the worst kind of snoop. Perhaps that was because there was so little of Joe on display. No sloppiness in this man. A single brown leather belt draped the arm of the high-back cane rocker near the open window. On the dresser covered by a handmade doily, a glass ash tray shaped like a boot was filled to overflowing with coins. She noticed a few were pesos. Beside it stood a bottle of cologne.

She reached for it and twisted off the cap. The scents of lime and spice reached her nostrils even before she leaned in to take a whiff. The aroma exploded in her senses, setting off quick-cut flashes of fragmented images and sensations.

Palm trees. A tropical beach at night. Shooting stars across a violet sky salted with the Milky Way. The incessant hiss and roar of breaking waves. Warm salt air. A man's caresses. Warmer, stronger, more potent than the dark sea in which they floated. Bodies skin to skin. Wrapped tight around one another. Surrendering to the push-pull rhythm as primal as the ebb and flow of the surf.

Halle snapped open eyes she hadn't realized had fallen shut. But the afterimage remained. She had been thinking of Joe. Thinking? Or remembering?

Sexual heat suffused her body and left her skin prickled with goose bumps. Was sexual attraction behind the charged atmosphere whenever Joe entered the room? He'd said they had been friends, buddies, roommates. But what if he lied? What if they'd once been lovers?

Heart still beating a little quickly, she looked at the label on the cologne and saw that it was from Jamaica. Did they have a past? Did it include torrid nights on a Caribbean beach? She didn't dare ask. Not yet. Not until those fleeting images had knit themselves into more reliable ribbons of memory.

She glanced carefully around the room, her eyes alighting on the framed diploma hanging on the wall by the door. She walked over to it and gleaned the essentials. Joseph A. Guinn had graduated cum laude from NYC with a B.A. in psychology.

Other than his college diploma, his history seemed as curiously absent as her own. What had a Texas boy been doing in New York City?

The stack of books on the bedside next drew her attention. At last, she thought with a grin, something personal. Reading material was a revealing measure of personality.

She picked up the top book. It was a slickly produced history of the Dallas Cowboys football team. Below it was a mystery novel by one of the more literary writers in the genre. She cradled the books in one arm as she continued picking through the pile. Beneath the mystery was another novel, western this. time, a cartoon collection, a dog-eared NYPD procedural handbook, and several copies of a professional psychology journal. On the bottom of the magazines was a half filled-out form for graduate school. She leaned over to study it. Joe was applying for entrance into the doctorate program in psychology at the University of North Texas. No, maybe not. The form was dated October of the previous year. Had he decided against it, or sent in another? Once again the clue she uncovered only led to more questions.

As she maneuvered the stack in her arms back onto the nightstand, a picture fell out of the police handbook. It fell faceup inside the long triangle of light slanting in through the window, the vivid sunlight spotlighting the subjects.

It was a picture of a younger, smiling Joe in a policeman's uniform. He had flung comradely arms about his fellow officers. To be more precise, he stood between a male and a female officer. The man was taller and heavier than Joe, his broad smile and broken nose giving him the pugnacious air of a boxer. Short and seemingly stocky in her stiff, heavy winterweight uniform, the woman with a cloud of curly black hair stood proudly under Joe's right arm. Joe looked straight at the camera. The woman's smiling face was turned up toward his. Was this the lover Joe had once confided in her about?

Halle picked the picture up slowly. Something trembled inside her. Joe in uniform. Laughing, strong, proud, certain of himself and his way of life. The snapshot had captured his joy in the moment. It made her heart swell and her hand tremble.

The dimple was big as life in Joe's left cheek as he grinned generously at the photographer. He hadn't smiled with that ease even once since they'd met, or to be more precise, remet. The Joe she had come to know during the past thirty-six hours was a tall humorless man with deeply hooded wary dark eyes. What had happened to make him so bitter, so cold, so angry?

"Oh, Joe. What is our history?"

What if they'd had an affair that had ended badly? Maybe he had walked out, or perhaps she had left him. He was certainly angry enough the night she arrived on his doorstep to suspect she had been the transgressor in a relationship gone wrong. But how could she judge that when she remembered next to nothing about him...except that his friends called him Jag?

"Jag?" Her spine tingled. Now where had that idea come from? Was it a memory or had she been cued by something in the house? She flipped the picture over but there was nothing written on the back. Only the date had been imprinted by the developer. The picture was five years old.

Inexplicably, tears began to gather in her eyes as she tucked the picture back into the middle of the book. She didn't know who she was crying for, the lost joy on the face of the young man in the picture or her own confused emotions.

Her eyes blurred and burning, she turned abruptly toward the doorway and collided with the figure who was trying to enter.

"Oh my!"

Halle fell back from the intruder who raised hands in a threatening manner. For one wild moment she thought that she'd surprised a thief, or worse. Then her rapidly blinking eyes cleared. She saw a young woman in denim overalls cut off at the top of her thighs staring back at her in equal alarm and surprise.

Chapter 7

"I'm very sorry!" The stranger began backing down the hall. "I didn't know Joe was entertaining."

Halle pressed a hand to her hard-pumping heart and took a few deep breaths. No burglar just a woman. A woman?

She hurried after the woman, who by this time had passed through the living room and was out the front door. Halle pushed open the screen door and stepped out onto the porch. "Wait. Please."

The woman halted on the drive and turned back to her, her tanned cheeks reddened by an embarrassment to match Halle's own.

Halle summoned a shaky smile. "Please, won't you stay a moment?"

The woman tossed back over one shoulder a ponytail swatch of long hair, professionally shaded equal parts ginger and platinum. As she did so, the gap between her hot pink bra top and her bibbed overalls revealed a broad expanse of tanned torso. She was short and sparely built with the muscular thighs of an athlete. Her well-worn muddy sneakers seemed to confirm this assessment. There was a light sheen of perspiration on her attractive face as if she had been out jogging.

"I'm really sorry I startled you, ma'am." She sounded much younger than she looked, with a high, soft, teenage voice. Her expression was another matter entirely. Surprise had given way to the realization that she had interrupted something, something she didn't like at all. "I did knock. Twice. Called out, too."

"I must have been daydreaming," Halle replied, further rattled by the woman's statement. What if Joe had returned while she was snooping in his room? The resulting confrontation did not bear thinking about.

The fact that the woman was rapidly regaining her poise was confirmed when she said. "Where's Joe? And who are you?"

Halle moved forward off the porch and extended her hand. "My name's Halle. I'm sorry but Joe's not here right now."

The woman nodded. "It rained just before dawn. Fish must be really biting and I know how serious he is about fishing."

Halle smile was noncommittal. So, Joe had gone fishing. Why hadn't he left a note? "What can I do for you?"

"My name's Lauren Sawyer." A significant pause followed as if she expected Halle to respond to her name. She hitched a thumb back over her shoulder. "I live up the highway a bit. Joe asks me to check on things when he's away. On weekends I park and jog the last few miles for exercise. I didn't see the truck so I wasn't certain he was back.''

The woman's inquisitive gaze appraised the white cotton T-shirt and sweat shorts Joe had begrudgingly loaned her the night before. The contents of her suitcase, silks and linens, proved that she might have expensive tastes but she obviously knew nothing about packing for southern climes. Because the shirt was so big, she had rolled up the short sleeves and then tied the tail in a knot beneath her breasts. Her hair was pinned up at the crown, the loose ends flopping forward over her brow. There was no doubt that she looked like a woman who had just rolled out of bed—perhaps even Joe's bed.

''Guess now I know why Joe hasn't been by.'' She smiled but it was brittle. ''Where did he pick you up?''

Halle answered the insinuation with a cool reply. ''I suspect you are misreading the situation. I'm not here as a personal friend. I'm a client. Mr. Guinn is doing a job for me.''

''That so?'' Though she didn't add, ''What kind of job?'' Halle could see speculation in the woman's expression as her gaze shifted past her toward the house. She was deliberately reminding them both that she had discovered Halle in Joe's bedroom. ''You aren't from around here, are you?''

Halle debated her answer and decided to keep things simple. ''No.''

The woman scanned her, pausing this time on the diamond bracelet flashing like miniature klieg lights under the sunlight. ''You from Dallas or Houston?''

''Neither. I'm from New York.'' Halle chose her words carefully. There were only so many questions she could respond to before she ran out of adequate answers. "That's where Joe and I met."

She nodded. "Thought you might be a Yankee. So, you're one of Joe's old friends." This time there was no mistaking the reserve in her sharp gaze. "You the one he's been licking his wounds over?"

"I—no." Halle's brain went on alert. So, there was a woman behind the pain in Joe's eyes. "We were just friends."

"I see." Again that weighing judgmental gaze swept Halle as the woman shifted her weight from one sneakered foot to the other. It was obvious to Halle that she didn't want to leave just yet.

"Would you like a cup of coffee, Ms. Sawyer?"

"No, thanks. I really shouldn't stay." Yet she walked toward Halle.

Forced to play hostess, Halle turned and opened the screen door, allowing her uninvited guest to enter ahead of her. As she followed, she looked down and noticed that during her previous entry the woman's sneakers had left mud tracks on the hardwood floor.

Lauren noticed, too. "Lord! Look at the mess I've gone and made." She sidestepped quickly as if that would prevent more damage. "I'll get a mop. I know where Joe keeps one."

"Please, don't bother," Halle replied graciously. "I'll do it later. Once the mud dries, it'll sweep right up."

"You're domestic?" The woman gave Halle the look she might give an exotic animal she had never before seen. "Joe says city women are never domestic."

"We get dust and spills in the city, too," Halle assured her. "Won't you have a seat?"

Lauren shook her head. "I'm a little too musty." She glanced around the living room and then down the hall.

It occurred to Halle that her guest had come back into the house to do a little snooping, as if she had expected to spy Joe lurking somewhere in his briefs. Her curiosity was piqued. So, this was the woman Joe was sleeping with, the woman who had left him tired but—if his temper was any measure—far from satisfied the night she came here.

When she looked back at Halle she said with a false civility only southern women can achieve, "May I ask how well you know Joe? We've been...friends a while now." Her fractional pauses had in them all the subtlety of a sledge hammer. "He's never mentioned you."

"I'm not surprised." Halle mimicked her smile for smile. A bright pink mantle spread across her face. "I don't suppose you two *talk* about much of anything."

Halle felt an instant stab of contrition and embarrassment. She had been caught in a compromising situation. What could she expect from Joe's lady friend? If she had been in Lauren's place and found a strange woman lurking about her man friend's house in his clothing, she would be furious, too. Under the circumstances, Lauren was behaving well.

She tried to make amends. "Joe has mentioned you. You made the birthday cake, right?"

Lauren warmed for the first time. "Joe told you about that?"

"Yes. I surprised him by turning up on his doorstep on his birthday. The cake was very good."

"Joe served you my cake?"

"As I said, I just happened by."

"I see."

What Halle saw was that she had exceeded only too well in stirring up the woman's jealousy and that Joe would have the devil's own time convincing Ms. Sawyer that nothing was going on between her and him. Feeling a little ashamed for having worsened this situation by being found in Joe's bedroom, she swung a hand toward the sofa in a conciliatory gesture. "Joe should be back anytime. I'm certain he will want to see you. Why don't you have a chair. Really."

Lauren again scanned the house, concentrating on the kitchen archway. "So you knew Joe in New York?"

"Yes, we were roo—rumored to be friends." She smiled weakly over her stumble. Jeez! Was she trying to make things worse or what? "What I'm trying to say is that it's been a long time since we last saw one another."

"I see."

That phrase was beginning to irk the heck out of Halle. As Lauren assessed her yet again Halle started tapping her foot.

"Can I ask you something personal, Holly is it? Woman to woman? You don't have to answer, if you don't want to."

Halle folded her arms, her foot tapping double-timing her pulse rate. She didn't like the hint of malice in the woman's expression but she supposed she should try to smooth things over for Joe's sake. "All right."

"Since you were such close friends before, in New York, I thought you might be aware of Joe's little problem." She gazed at the floor for a moment then raised wickedly shining eyes to her. "I mean where relations with women are concerned."

Halle didn't need a thesaurus to suspect that *relations* as Lauren used the word meant *sex*. Otherwise, why would the woman have bothered to preface the question so coyly? "I'm sorry but I have no idea what you're talking about."

"Oh." Lauren cocked her head to one side as Halle began to feel her gaze contained the texture of sandpaper. "I thought you might, being you knew him in New York before the time of his ordeal."

His ordeal. What ordeal? Halle longed to ask but she wasn't about to reveal her own malady to yet another stranger. "I'm sorry but I can't tell you a thing about that, either."

Lauren nodded slowly. "I understand, I do. Joe's a very private man. It's only natural you, being a friend, would want to protect him."

She moved to perch on the arm of Joe's recliner and began fiddling with the fastener that hooked one shoulder strap of her overalls to the bib. "It's just that I've been so worried about Joe. He was the devil's own spawn as a youngster. Into and out of everything like his tail was afire. Practically every girl in the county wanted him as their boyfriend. Even me, though I was too young for him then." She smiled as she demurely lowered her lashes over her eyes.

"Joe was fifteen when his father up and took a job in the north. Didn't hear much from him for years, then two years ago he shows up again, handsome as ever but touchy as a pig with sunburn, if you know what I mean. He isn't the boy I remember. He mostly broods and goes fishing."

Halle shrugged, unwilling to respond when she had no idea what was expected of her.

"He isn't very—well, motivated, is he?" Lauren offered Halle a coy glance from beneath her lowered lashes. "Not that the man has to be the instigator every time. I've read enough self-improvement books to know that's old-fashioned thinking. But sometimes a woman likes to be pursued, even New York women, I imagine. I don't mind lighting the wick, so to speak, especially when the resulting flame is so impressive. Still it's a shame he's so rarely interested. I read an article in one of those men's magazine's the other day entitled, 'Use It or Lose It.'"

Aghast that a stranger was talking to her about her sexual trials, Halle simply stared. This kind of talk-show purging repelled her.

Lauren turned bright red but that embarrassment didn't silence her. "At Joe's age, over thirty, a man has to be extra careful. I suppose he's occasionally desperate enough to accept titillation wherever it is offered. That or else living in the city spoiled him for the gracious side of romance."

"I was under the impression that 'slam, bam, thank you, ma'am' was a western phrase," Halle answered before she could censor her thought. But, really, the woman had all but called her a cheap lay. "Where I'm from it's thought that when a man denies one woman it's usually because there's someone else he prefers."

Lauren blushed again and rose to her feet. "That was rude and I'm sorry." Surprisingly, she did sound sorry. "I know I was speaking out of turn. Please don't tell Joe I asked about New York . . . or anything else. He won't like it. People did enough gossiping when he first came back."

"Joe is a private man," Halle allowed, feeling the need to respond in some manner. "I try to respect that."

Lauren's eyes crinkled at the corners in her first genuine smile, even if it was tinged with the resignation of defeat. "This really isn't your fight. Joe and I, well, at least we had a run at it. I think you're right about there being someone else. None of us local women have been able to draw Joe out of his shell. I thought maybe you were the one he won't talk about."

Halle didn't know how to answer that. "I'm not here to come between you, if that is what is worrying you."

"No. Well, yes. But I don't think there's much to come between with me and Joe. You are staying a spell?"

"A spell? Oh, a while. Yes, a few more days, at least."

"Don't let him run you off." She dusted the imaginary dust of Joe's life off her hands. "Joe's a good man, I don't care what happened to him up north. The way we figure it around here, he wasn't a Yankee only he didn't know it until things went against him. He just needs a reason to move on."

As they moved to the front door, Halle had to bite her tongue to keep from asking Lauren the questions that were bursting to be free inside her. What did gossip say had happened to Joe in New York? Did it involve his job, the police, or his private life? One thing was clear. Joe Guinn's past seemed as much of a puzzle as her own.

"Lauren was here?" Joe's head popped through the neck of the clean T-shirt he was donning as he walked into the living room from his bedroom. "What did you say to her?"

"Hello. How are you? Won't you come in? Standard American greeting phrases." Halle tapped her foot impatiently as she stood with arms crossed. Livid barely described her mood. Joe had returned just before noon, covered in mud and smelling ripe with sweat and fish. Without explanation or apology for his extended absence, he had headed straight for the shower. "What did you expect?"

"That's not what I meant." Joe tugged the skin-tight shirt down over his torso, which was gleaming with a few droplets of water that had fallen from his damp hair. "How did you explain your presence?"

"Oh that," she said airily. "I told her we were sleeping together."

He gave her a hard look from beneath his brow ridge. "That's not funny."

"Why? She thought it was about time you gave some woman more than the time of day."

She saw him pause while tucking in his shirt, his face growing as dark as a thundercloud. "You discussed my sex life?" The question was little more than a snarl.

"She discussed it. I listened."

"Oh yeah? Did you learn anything?"

"Plenty." Halle hadn't meant to mention any of this but he was behaving so arrogantly, so callously. "According to rumor, you don't have a sex life, or at least much of one."

Something changed in his expression, shifting the moody hunk quality into the desperado column as he slicked back his damp hair with both hands. "Never listen to rumor."

"Thanks for the tip."

He turned as if about to leave the room again.

Astonished that he had the audacity to walk out on her a second time, Halle hurriedly stepped between him and the hallway and stiff-armed him in the middle of his chest. "Not so fast, Mr. Guinn. I've waited all morning to hear your pearls of wisdom. Aren't there any others you'd like to share with me?"

"Yeah." A clump of damp dark hair sprang forward over his brow, Elvis style, as he went back to tucking in his shirt. "Don't bother to answer my door in the future. If the visitor thinks no one's here they'll go away."

Halle's mouth dropped open for an instant as he turned away from her and headed for the kitchen. He had thought she was serious. She went after him.

"What about the phone?" she called at his back. "Surely there are house rules for the phone?"

He moved toward the refrigerator and opened it. "Let it ring." He bent into it so his second statement was muffled by the barrier of the door. "I have an answering service that will pick it up."

Halle folded her hands into fists and settled them on her hips. "Let me get this straight. I'm not supposed to answer your door or your phone? Maybe I should just be locked in the bathroom while you're out."

Her voice had risen with her anger but she couldn't keep her resentment from boiling over when he straightened and looked at her in mock innocence, soft drink can in hand. "Oh, another thing. Stop locking all the doors. I almost never lock my doors."

"Doesn't that encourage burglars?"

"This is Gap, Texas. We don't have burglars. What's gotten into you?"

Boy, was she ready to tell him. "You and your asi-
nine behavior, for one. You treat me as if I'm another
piece of furniture or a pet. No, you would at least pat
a dog on the head as you came and went. Me you
barely speak to."

A dangerous gleam came into his dark eyes as he
pushed the refrigerator door shut then propped a
shoulder against it. His toasted gaze tugged every
curve and swell on it's way from her chin to her toes.
"You want me to pet you?"

Halle almost choked. "I want respect. I'm paying
you to help me piece together my absent memory. I
expect service for the dollar, Mr. Guinn, not snide remarks."

Joe popped the top on the can and took a long
swallow to give himself time to think.

Anger made some women unattractive. It changed
Halle's face from mere prettiness into flagrant beauty.
He had been provoked by the best hustlers on the
street, pimps, drug dealers, confidence men and bru-
tal thugs. Only Halle had ever been able to slip under
his professional veneer. Only she had ever made him
afraid of emotions like anger, jealousy and lust. Only
she made him daydream of a sexual encounter just by
crossing a room. Her sarcastic banter was the first
sustained glimpse he'd had of the old Halle and it
made him want to...

He lifted a brow as his heavy-lidded gaze surrepti-
tiously caressed the curves of her breasts. Never mind
what he wanted to do to her. He had to think when she
was around. Relying on his instincts was too dangerous.

NO COST! NO OBLIGATION TO BUY!
NO PURCHASE NECESSARY!

PLAY "LUCKY 7"
AND GET FIVE FREE GIFTS!

HOW TO PLAY:

1. With a coin, carefully scratch off the silver box at the right. Then check the claim chart to see what we have for you—FREE BOOKS and a gift—ALL YOURS! ALL FREE!

2. Send back this card and you'll receive brand-new Silhouette Intimate Moments® novels. These books have a cover price of $3.99 each, but they are yours to keep absolutely free.

3. There's no catch. You're under no obligation to buy anything. We charge nothing—ZERO—for your first shipment. And you don't have to make any minimum number of purchases—not even one!

4. The fact is thousands of readers enjoy receiving books by mail from the Silhouette Reader Service™ months before they're available in stores. They like the convenience of home delivery and they love our discount prices!

5. We hope that after receiving your free books you'll want to remain a subscriber. But the choice is yours—to continue or cancel, anytime at all! So why not take us up on our invitation, with no risk of any kind. You'll be glad you did!

This beautiful porcelain box is topped with a lovely bouquet of porcelain flowers, perfect for holding rings, pins or other precious trinkets — and is yours absolutely free when you accept our no risk offer!

THE SILHOUETTE READER SERVICE™: HERE'S HOW IT WORKS

Accepting free books places you under no obligation to buy anything. You may keep the books and gift and return the shipping statement marked "cancel". If you do not cancel, about a month later we'll send you 6 additional novels, and bill you just $3.34 each plus 25¢ delivery and applicable sales tax, if any.* That's the complete price–and compared to cover prices of $3.99 each–quite a bargain! You may cancel at any time, but if you choose to continue, every month we'll send you 6 more books, which you may either purchase at the discount price…or return to us and cancel your subscription.

*Terms and prices subject to change without notice. Sales tax applicable in N.Y.

If offer card is missing, write to: Silhouette Reader Service, 3010 Walden Ave., PO Box 1867, Buffalo, NY 14240-1867

BUSINESS REPLY MAIL
FIRST-CLASS MAIL   PERMIT NO. 717   BUFFALO, NY

POSTAGE WILL BE PAID BY ADDRESSEE

SILHOUETTE READER SERVICE
3010 WALDEN AVE
PO BOX 1867
BUFFALO NY 14240-9952

NO POSTAGE
NECESSARY
IF MAILED
IN THE
UNITED STATES

"Let's get something straight, Ms. Hayworth. If I didn't tell you where I was it's because it's none of your business."

She accepted that slap on the wrist with all the grace of a poke in the eye. "Not my business? You leave me stranded without food or directions, without any kind of expectation of your return, and then tell me it's not my business to question your actions?"

Joe shrugged off his culpability. He had forgotten about his empty refrigerator but that wasn't the point. She was provoking old feelings. He mustn't allow himself even for a short while to slip into the error of thinking she was part of his life. It would make living again without her that much harder. It might just kill him.

"Let's get this straight. You're a client. Until my office hours begin I'm on my own."

Halle's fists slid down her hips. "What time do you open, Mr. Guinn?"

"It depends." He rolled the soda can back and forth between his palms. "As a rule, it's after I've been fishing. If the fish are biting it could be ten, eleven or noon."

"You can't be serious."

He hunched a shoulder then turned his can up to drain it but the hand that held it trembled. "If you don't like my professional style, you can make other arrangements."

He watched her arms come up to hug her waist in an act of unconscious comfort. "You're tossing me out?"

"Suit yourself."

When she didn't answer in kind after a moment Joe glanced over and was surprised by the look in her

green-gold eyes. That raw needy yet wary look said,
"Don't fail me."

Guilt arrowed through him, spearing the last of his
confidence. What had he been thinking to take her in?
He wasn't about to heed the urge that said he should
try to fix things after all this time. They weren't even
on an even footing. Her defenses, the power to weigh
and judge, were missing along with her memory. He
suspected he could promise her the moon, the Golden
Gate Bridge, and a majority share in Disney right now
and she might believe him. The desperation in her gaze
said she needed to.

He wasn't unaware of her interest in him. She
looked at him as if he were the first man she'd ever
seen. He could probably tell her just enough of the
truth to convince her that she had once loved him as
much as he still loved her. He might be able to manip-
ulate that attraction into seduction and slake his own
need of her. But tomorrow or the next day she would
remember and his world would collapse under the accusation in her eyes. He would have failed her again.

He looked away, feeling like the slimiest slug who
ever crawled the earth." Like I said, if you don't like
my rules you can always go somewhere else."

"Where?"

The word clutched at his heart yet he'd known this
kind of pain before. He would survive it. But he could
no longer look at her. "Home. New York. You want
the address of your old apartment? I can get it for you
easy. One phone call."

"No."

"You sure?"

A little sick sound of distress made Joe turn back to her. Her face was ashen and she was clutching her middle as if she'd taken a punch to the stomach.

He bounced off the refrigerator and caught her by the arms. "Halle? What's wrong?"

Halle shook her head weakly. "My stomach. I think it must be hunger." She pushed against his chest. He felt so solid and so warm. If only she dared rest her head there for a moment and be enfolded in his arms as she had been that first night. She pulled back, afraid of the depth of her need for physical contact, of contact with him. "I think I need some water."

"Sure, Halle, sure." His arm slid around her shoulders as he steered her to the nearest chair. "You just sit down. That's right. If you still feel light-headed, bend forward and drop your head between your knees. Don't be shy. It's just me. I'll hold on to you. Okay. Yeah, that's better, sweetheart. I'm sorry for yelling at you, Halle. I forgot you're not well."

"You mean I'm sick in the head," she said between her knees.

"No." He levered her up by the shoulders until they were eye to eye. "I don't think that. You're not crazy. You're just confused and the confusion will go away."

"Will it?"

Joe put a hand to her cheek. She sounded as desperate as he felt. "You're cold." He pressed a little harder and began massaging her face.

What an ass you are, Joe Guinn. Bullying a sick woman.

The doctor had specifically warned him not to push her or upset her. He'd just done both, and not for the first time.

He added his second hand to the first, framing her face in his hands. How good it felt to touch her. It had been two whole days since he touched her. He ached with wanting to touch her. He hadn't realized how much until this moment.

He brushed a thumb lightly over her lips. He ached with wanting to kiss her, and other things he should not think about. But he knew it was too late. Her eyes were suddenly wide and unblinking on his. She had seen his thoughts reflected in his gaze. All he had to do was move in a few inches and their lips would meet. Lord! He must be going nuts. He couldn't kiss her. He mustn't cheat on her memory of him because he could.

In the end, Halle decided for them both.

He stiffened as Halle placed her lips on his yet he didn't move way. The fingers on her face tightened. For an instant, she thought he would push her away. Then his fingers curved under her chin, lifting her face and drawing her closer as his mouth suddenly opened on hers and she was engulfed in the hot passion of his kiss.

There was nothing tentative or even tender about his kiss. The hard persuasion of the mouth moving over hers stunned her with it's hunger, and need. It seemed as if he thought he could slake his curiosity in a single kiss, but only if it never ended.

She wanted Joe to kiss her. She leaned into the yearning she spied in his dark eyes, her own lids falling shut before the sheer audacity of what she was initiating, but suddenly there was empty space where a second earlier his lips had been.

When she opened her eyes it was to find her gaze on level with his belt buckle. He was still touching her face but he had risen to his feet. Even as she looked up at him with embarrassed desperation, he withdrew his touch and backed a few steps away.

"That was a mistake."

Without any mediating gesture he turned and reached for a glass with one hand while he turned on the faucet with the other.

"You must be thirsty," he had said without even looking over his shoulder.

But she had seen the look on his face before he turned the broad expanse of his back on her. The flush beneath his tan betrayed his need. He wanted her. But he was fighting it. The set of his shoulders, that stiff barrier of resistance, was not only to keep her out but to hold him back. He didn't want the passion or the entanglement their kiss promised. As if to ram the point home, he handed her the water without turning around.

She took a long sip but the heat of his kiss could not be doused by water. She didn't blame him for rejecting her. Well, not rejecting her exactly. He'd nearly set her eyelashes on fire with his response. But how could he want to get emotionally involved with a woman with a gimpy memory?

Abashed, she glanced up to find him watching her with all the intensity of a doctor monitoring a critical patient. In a way she felt sick, burning up with a fever called Joe. But maybe he didn't feel anything. It was hard to tell what the sheen in his dark eyes meant.

Joe held his moody silence with an effort. He hadn't seen Halle fold so quickly in the face of rejection since the time she'd received a couriered letter from her mother soon after she'd faxed each parent that she had married. She had been anxiously awaiting their response to her news. The note from her mother read, "Prenuptial agreement a must. Divorce so costly."

She hadn't cried, she'd just subsided onto the sofa and pulled herself into a ball. At first she wouldn't even allow him to touch her. He'd had to fight her resistance, engulfing her in his embrace then just holding and holding on until she gradually melted against him. And how she melted, all soft and open in her need. He had poured his heart and soul into the lovemaking they shared, believing that this night they had really become one, soldered by a need deeper than desire and romantic gloss. He realized that he was all she had, and he reveled in that need to be needed. It had made him believe that he could provide all she would ever need.

Afterward she had clung to him and whispered, "I've always been alone. Always. That was okay. Until you. Promise you won't ever leave me, Joe. Promise."

But he had failed her, and himself, and their marriage.

So what did he think he was doing just now by indulging in the pretense that nothing had changed when everything had, forever. Oh, but it felt good, Halle felt good. For the few short seconds that kiss lasted he'd felt whole for the first time in two years. It felt now as if the hole in his soul would never heal.

Halle put the glass down on the table and licked her still-dry lips. "Every time I feel like I'm getting close to a memory, a kind of dread comes over me. It's almost as if my mind is trying to protect me from remembering."

His eyes narrowed. "Then you are remembering something."

She shook her head. "Not remembering, exactly, It's more like thoughts suddenly pop into my head from nowhere."

"What kind of thoughts?"

She struggled with the decision to answer. It might only make her seem even more harebrained. But then, that wasn't news to him. "Did anyone ever call you Jag?"

His head whipped around. "Where did you hear that?"

His question made Halle more uncomfortable than she had expected. Perhaps because he was now looking at her with a penetrating gaze, his interrogation gaze. *Lie to me,* it said, *and I will know.*

"I didn't hear it. I just was thinking about you earlier."

His brows arched, skepticism etched in the alignment of every hair. She was making things worse for herself and she knew it. He'd made it abundantly clear he wasn't interested in pursuing whatever it was that had reared up spontaneously between them. She shouldn't admit to feeling, only to fact.

Feeling self-conscious, she reached up to smooth a wing of hair away from her cheek but the strands clung to her damp fingers. She abandoned the gesture. "I was trying to remember, something...anything. That's when it came to me that your friends called you Jag. Am I wrong?"

Joe felt as if the earth beneath him had trembled. That was *her* nickname for him. She was beginning to remember. So soon? The doctor said it would take a week, maybe longer. Now it seemed that it might all come back to her right here in his kitchen. What then?

She disappears and life goes on, his conscience supplied. *Live with it.*

"A close friend once called me by that nickname," he said finally.

"Which close friend?"

"What difference does it make?"

Embarrassment blossomed once more in her face but Halle had begun to realize that Joe Guinn didn't require handling with kid gloves. He could look after himself. So then, she should look after herself. She needed answers in order to piece her life back together. If she had to face down a burned-out ex-policeman with a chip the size of Manhattan Island on his shoulder, she would. "Where did the nickname come from?"

Joe wanted to give her everything she asked for but he couldn't, not and save himself, too. He needed just a little breathing space. Five minutes alone to think. "It's my initials. Joseph A. Guinn. J. A. G."

She smiled. "Of course. What's the A stand for?"

He scowled. "I'd rather not say."

Her smile turned mischievous. "Let me guess. Albert? Alvin, maybe? No, I've got it. Adonis."

"Aloysius."

"Aloysius?" Laughter bubbled out of her. "Oh, I'm sorry—but—that's awful! How could your parents do that to you?"

A smile tugged at Joe's mouth. It was good to see her smile, to hear her laughter. Very good. "It's a family name. I'm half Irish and half Italian. Mom got to name me Joseph after her grandfather, Giuseppe. Pop thought he should get equal time. He had a grandfather named Alabhaois which is Irish Gaelic for

Aloysius. He built this house before the turn of the century."

She gazed at him with wonder. "Really? I didn't think anything west of Mississippi was more than five minutes old."

"That's a New Yorker for you. Never can appreciate that anything west of the Hudson has a history worth seeking out."

"That's hardly fair. After all, you told me my major interest is in Native American art."

Joe leaned into her. "But you never went in search of it, Halle. You just let it all come to you."

She gazed deeply into those rich brown eyes and wondered if *he* had ever come to her. If he had, she was certain she would never in this lifetime have turned him away.

Her hand rose from his forearm to rest on the smooth sun-baked side of his face. Did he lean in closer or was it she who was falling in toward him?

He reared back. "Sorry," he muttered, "but we can't. We can't."

"Oh." Halle looked down at her lap. Twice she had initiated a kiss. How many times did it take for her to accept no as an answer? What did she think she was going to learn from Joe's kiss that made her able to risk rejection twice? Aside from the fact that kissing him proved all her female hormones were in full -working order, very little she supposed.

Yet it was pure female jealousy that prompted her to say in accusation, "It's Lauren, isn't it?"

"Maybe." *Lie big!* "Yeah. Lauren."

Halle studied her fingernails as if she had never seen anything like them before. "I suppose she won't understand why I'm staying here. I wouldn't want to do anything that hurt you, after all your kindness to me. Maybe I should move back to the motel."

Joe shook his head. He had never lied to one woman about another but he didn't want Halle to think he'd been without a steady woman since she left him. She would think that there was something wrong with him. Something was. He was still in love with her.

"You can stay. I'll be leaving in the morning, in any case."

"To go fishing?" she inquired.

"No, I've got another investigating job that's going to take me to Dallas for a while."

"How long?" He shrugged. Evasion. He was leaving her. "I should move out then. To avoid any more misunderstandings."

"Don't worry about Lauren." He glanced away and then back at her. "For the record, if I didn't want you here you wouldn't be."

But Joe found later that night that he couldn't sleep while listening to the sounds of her moving about in the other bedroom.

Was he being a fool to reject her? Since the moment she had stepped back into his life like an apparition out of his most fondly held dream, he had been afraid she would vanish. Was he losing out on the reality of her for fear it wouldn't last? So what if it didn't? They had here. They had now. That was more than he'd ever thought he'd have with her again.

During the past forty-eight hours the sexual tension between them was thick enough to slice and serve. His head and his libido definitely weren't communicating.

Maybe this was that second chance he had given up on when he'd left New York. Fate had handed him the chance to live out that if-only-I-could-start-over scenario almost every shattered romantic partner hoped for but which almost no one ever received.

Maybe, if they could get away from everything, her past and his, they might find again the magic that had brought them together in the first place. Once love had made them brave enough to spurn all of the odds against them.

Maybe...if...then...she might forgive him and...perhaps...learn to love him again.

Chapter 8

As she gazed through the truck windshield into the distance at the ultramodern skyline of Dallas with its keyhole archway skyscraper and sky blue glass hotel flanked by a restaurant shaped like a golf ball on a tee, Halle tried to contain her annoyance.

Joe's invitation to join him on his business trip had been made that morning between his after-fishing shower and the time it took him to shove a few essentials in a duffel bag. Aware that he might only have been being polite, she had said yes and then run to grab her toothbrush and toiletries before he changed his mind. Joe's house was darling but it left her feeling totally isolated and very alone. At least now she had the scenery to look at.

East Texas had been surprisingly woody with large patches of evergreen forest. Near the shoulders of the highway delicately stemmed wildflowers spread out on either side like spilled paint in brilliant shades of red, yellow and blue. Too bad there had been no conversation to go with that view.

Stoic was a polite description of Joe's behavior the past two hours. His gaze shielded by dark shades, he had driven in absolute silence, listening to a series of discs on his CD player by Chris Isaak, Sade and Eric Clapton. The few times she had attempted conversation he had grunted or ignored her entirely. His treatment of her seemed to swing in extreme arcs between solicitude and bare tolerance. He had to be the moodiest man she'd ever known. She then wondered if that was true.

If he hadn't just pulled off at a service station to buy gas and use the lavatory she would have thought he was on automatic pilot. Something was on his mind and so far he wasn't willing to share whatever it was with her.

"Hi!" The appearance of a smiling Joe at her passenger window was so unexpected that Halle jumped. "Want one?" He held up a canned drink.

She shook her head. "No thanks."

"Suit yourself." He walked around and climbed in then popped the top on his can and took a long swallow before tucking it between his legs.

Halle glanced at the can wedged against his crotch. The sweat from the aluminum was greedily absorbed by the faded denim of his jeans. Considering the part of his anatomy that fabric covered she wondered if it didn't feel . . . her thoughts got no further before she noticed that *he* had noticed where she was looking.

His eyes, usually so still and mysteriously dark, flashed with amusement. "Sure you don't want some?"

She glanced away but it was much too late. His not-to-be-taken-seriously sexual tease had roused, suddenly and sharply, her desire. She would give a lot to know what had happened to his mood while he was out of the truck.

The air conditioner roared to life as he turned the key in the ignition, spewing her heated skin with its chilly blast. The analogy to taking a cold shower was a little too obvious. She shivered as her silk blouse absorbed and held the cool against her skin.

As he maneuvered the truck back onto Interstate 20 he said, "I may be able to use you today so I hope you read that dossier."

Halle glanced down at the manila folder she had been balancing on her lap since they left Gap. "I read it."

He had been hired to locate a runaway by the name of Lacey McCrea, son of state senator William McCrea. She doubted she could contribute a single thing to his investigation but she didn't offer that observation to him. She had gaped at his crotch. She needed a change of topic.

"Why do you suspect Lacey McCrea came to Dallas to pursue a performing career? If he was serious, wouldn't he head for New York, Broadway and all that?"

Joe glanced at her, his sunglasses once more shielding his expressive eyes. "How do you figure a seventeen-year-old kid from Tyler would be eager to go it alone in the Big Apple?"

"Why not? You think he'd be afraid to go east?"

"I know he'd be afraid. It scared the bejabbers out of me."

"That's right. You were an East Coast transplant." He had actually made a personal reference without her pushing him. Remarkable. "How did you handle it?"

He stretched an arm out along the back of the seat, his hand resting just behind her left shoulder. "I was with my family, first of all. Second, I was still in school. That kind of forces you to meet people. I joined the wrestling team where I made a few friends. Other than the language problem, it worked out all right."

"What language problem?"

He smiled a slow I'm-going-to-enjoy-this grin. "Anybody who thinks Americans speak the same language hasn't traveled much. First day of high school I felt like I'd been dropped into the middle of a Martin Scorsese film. Tough guys, wise guys, tougher-looking girls dressed all in black with attitude to spare, all talking ninety-to-nothing in that Jersey accent. It was about impenetrable to me the first week."

"What about Texans? A western thesaurus would sometimes come in handy. 'Touchy as a pig with a sunburn' is not the sort of simile that would immediately come to my mind."

He chuckled. "You got that one from Lauren."

"Oh?" Halle responded politely though she was not happy to hear the woman's name mentioned. "Is she partial to porcine metaphors?"

"Whoa! Do I hear the sharpening of claws?"

"No, of course not," she answered primly. But she was thinking unkind thoughts about Lauren and resenting her hold over Joe, however tenuous it might be.

She studiously avoided watching as he pulled the soda can from between his legs and drank a bit more. She already had a head full of images to keep her uncomfortably aware of his attraction for her. And it wasn't just the memory of his searing kiss the day before.

A green reflector highway sign flew by overhead, it's arrow pointing to an exit for Highway 45 north, which he took.

She had dreamed all night long, endless convoluted dreams that began and ended with her in Joe's arms. There had been a soothing tropical breeze, the sound of waves in the warm quiet of the middle of the night, and Joe lying beside her, naked, heavy, and sated yet waiting for her to signal that she was ready to handle another bout of his lovemaking. The mood changed. They were in an apartment in New York, the sound of taxi horns and sirens a strange urban lullaby buoyed by lethargic air currents that wrapped the summer night in its sultry stupor. Heated bodies barely touching, they'd slowly made love that dampened the sheets and slicked their bodies and turned waves to ringlets.

Halle bit her lip as the highway heading north quickly filled with traffic coming up from Houston. There was only one problem. Even in the midst of the dreams she had not doubted their make-believe quality. She'd awakened with damp skin and every nerve singing with the tension of overwrought emotions. That's when she decided the dreams couldn't be reflections of a past reality. They were too intense, too perfectly suited to wish fulfillment. If she and Joe had once been lovers, wouldn't the delirious edge of her desire have been eroded by the experience? In the glare of wide-awake morning she could not say she had remembered anything, only vividly imagined possibility.

So what if she could picture Joe shirtless and pantless, his dark eyes smoked by need? What difference did it make to her that she could shut her eyes even now and imagine the tugging motion of his mouth on her nipples?

Her eyes popped open when an arm struck her dead in the middle of her chest, compressing both breasts as the truck horn blared.

The truck jerked sharply as Joe swerved to avoid a collision.

"Sorry," he murmured. "You all right?"

"Certainly," she answered, but the word sounded smashed by emotion. After a fractional moment he lifted his protective arm.

Halle swallowed and stared straight ahead as his arm resettled on the seat behind her head. She told herself it was only accidental that his fingertips curved over the top so that they brushed between her shoulder blades whenever the truck bounced over a defect in the pavement.

She sipped in a long slow breath. She had no one to blame but herself for her predicament. The dreams meant only that she had an active, fully adult libido. She could control the wistful longing inside her for something she did not know if she'd ever had: the experience of Joe Guinn's brand of loving.

The reality was Joe had a woman friend. The reality was she was nobody, not even a full person. She couldn't with any confidence say from moment to moment what she wanted or needed. When her memory returned it might make a lie of anything she said or did now. She mustn't listen to the voice inside her telling her that she had as much right as anyone to fall in love. In love? Oh brother! She was seriously deluding herself.

From the first moment she saw Joe Guinn she had felt the need to be enfolded in his embrace. It had not been a sexual longing then. The need was more basic, the desire of a frightened female to be consoled by a primal male. He had seemed, no matter the irrationality of her logic, the one man capable of consoling her. Three days later he still fit the bill. But maybe that was because he was the only person in her world who knew her past and present. When she was with him she knew she genuinely existed. With strangers she felt as insubstantial as a shadow, something that only exhibited the shape of reality.

"Do you mind if I ask how close you and Lauren are?"

Joe glanced at her, his eyes concealed behind two smoky ovals of glass. She was beginning to hate sunglasses. "We aren't close."

"But she said—"

"Lauren likes to plan ahead, way ahead." He tucked his pelvis forward and slid into a slightly more comfortable position behind the wheel. The soda can pinged against the underside of the steering wheel but nothing spilled. "Planners don't usually pay a lot of attention to anything that spoils their plans."

"I'd say you were in Lauren's plans big time."

He shrugged.

Halle recognized that gesture as his signature end-of-that-subject punctuation. As long as he was talking she decided to try another subject. "You never said who called you Jag. Was it your wife?"

He sighed. "Why are you so curious to know about my ex-wife?"

Halle plunged in. The only thing she had going for her was honesty. "I'm divorced. You're divorced. That gives us something of a bond."

His profile tensed. "Maybe."

"I'd tell you what happened to my marriage if I knew. If you tell me a little about yours maybe something will click in my head about mine."

"I don't think so. My past life isn't up for grabs."

"Okay. Then tell me something else. Why you left New York and the police force, for instance."

"Too dirty, too crowded, too many criminals."

"No other reason?"

He muttered a curse under his breath and whipped off his shades. The look he turned on her repelled like a physical assault. The moody loner was back. "What did Lauren tell you?"

Halle wondered how the same malleable skin, muscle and bone that made his face so attractive could solidify so quickly into menace. "Not much, really. She hoped I might know something about 'your ordeal,' as she phrased it. Why it made you decide to come back to Texas."

She could see he was thinking about that. "Is that all?"

"I didn't ask for the gory details."

He tilted his head to one side, watching traffic by glancing forward every other second. "Why not? Weren't you interested?"

"Not enough to invade your privacy with a stranger," she answered honestly. "You've been nothing but nice to me. I didn't want to betray that by gossiping about you behind your back."

She waited long enough for the truth of her statement to sink in with him then said, "But if you'd like to tell me about it, I'm about the most unbiased audience you're ever likely to get. As far as my memory's concerned, we're total strangers."

He looked her over carefully. She knew he was judging how much of his truth she could take. "The short version is I got caught in the wrong place at the wrong time holding the wrong thing."

Halle nodded and folded her arms. "That's certainly enlightening."

"Why do you want to know?"

"Why don't you want to tell me?" she retorted. "Are you afraid or ashamed of the truth?"

That got his attention. Color edged up from his collar into the bottom half of his face. "No, I can face the truth. I faced it and the consequences."

"But you feel you never got a fair hearing."

He looked ready to argue the point but then he turned his head back to survey the traffic. "Why do you say that?"

"You resent the gossip so much. You must think it doesn't tell the truth."

He smirked. "Always said you had a good head on your shoulders."

"Would you have told me the truth if I'd been around at the time?"

His head whipped toward her. A long searing glance made her aware that she was daring to cross the invisible barrier Joe Guinn had erected to keep the world out and his feelings in. When he looked away again she felt as if she had scaled an electrified fence. She wasn't yet certain if she had escaped unscathed.

"I would have told you," he said finally, "if you would have listened."

"I'm listening now."

He didn't say anything but he withdrew his arm from behind her head. So that was that, she thought. At least he hadn't rebuffed her in his usual gruff fashion.

She reached up and flipped the visor down to shield her eyes from the midday glare. Dallas must be the brightest city in the country she decided as she squinted against the sharp light. Or perhaps it was just that so much of the uninterrupted sky was on display.

"I tried to help a fellow officer out of a jam."

Halle glanced at him, disconcerted for an instant. Then she realized he was going to tell her what had happened to him. "He must have been a good friend," she ventured.

"The best. We were at the police academy together. We walked our first beat together. For two years we lived in each other's pockets. Later we worked undercover together. When you eat, sleep and live that close, you form some serious bonds."

Halle nodded. "Kind of like a marriage."

He nodded even more slowly. "Exactly. You may pass on to other things but you never forget the old feelings. No matter what comes along."

Halle wondered if he was now talking about his ex-wife. Was he still in love with her? She'd bet the ten thousand in her purse that he was. What a waste.

"About a year after we changed partners Ed's father was diagnosed with cancer. His dad had been laid off a few months earlier and so had no insurance. The bills started piling up but Ed was determined his father would have every treatment possible."

Joe raked a hand through his hair. "Ed went into debt and then he started borrowing. By the time his father died he was up against it with two different loan sharks." He glanced at her. "One thing the movies always get right is how they operate. Ed couldn't possibly pay them back. When he was asked to deal with certain evidence at police headquarters he did it."

"He tampered with evidence?"

"Sometimes. Sometimes he removed it altogether. I won't lie to you. Things occasionally get misplaced. The sheer volume of evidentiary articles collected on a weekly basis by a New York City precinct would stun you. The departments are way understaffed, bound by budgetary constraints that makes perfect record keeping impossible. Ed was careful. He thought no one had caught on. The cases he was fixing seemed so dissimilar."

"But they weren't?"

"They had one name in common. Lazaro Demotta."

"The crime king?"

He nodded. "You know about him?"

"He was once written up as the crime boss so far removed from the source that no charge would ever be linked to him."

"What else do you remember?"

Halle realized with a start that she *had* actually remembered. She lifted a hand to her mouth. "I—I don't... He was finally indicted. The trial was held recently. He was found guilty. Right?"

"Anything more?" His voice had dropped to a deep whisper.

Halle frowned, staring at the star-bright point of light reflected back at her from the bumper of the car ahead. "No, nothing."

Joe shrugged. "Ed came to me in a panic a few days before the mess hit the fan. He'd had enough. He could see he had gotten into a deal that wasn't going to end. He said he wanted to turn state's evidence against Demotta. Only he needed a little help to set up his alibi. He hadn't destroyed the evidence he had stolen. He had kept it as insurance. He wanted help in planting it."

"You agreed to help him?"

"He'd watched my back more times than I want to remember. It wasn't as if he were taking bribes or skimming funds. He'd tried to save his father's life.

"Don't get me wrong. I'm not defending what he did. He broke the law. He knew the consequences. If I'd been doing my job, I'd have turned him in myself."

"Yet you didn't."

"No." It was terse a painful admission. "I wasn't tough enough."

"What happened?"

He turned an annoying glance on her. "What do you think? The night I went with him to plant the stolen evidence we weren't alone. Someone, maybe another cop in the department who was under Demotta's thumb, had tipped off internal affairs. Ed didn't know it but he'd been tailed for weeks. He must have let it be known he wasn't happy doing Demotta's work indefinitely."

"You were caught?"

"We were caught. Arrested and cuffed and taken in."

Halle was silent, thinking about the depth of humiliation that must have caused him. "Did you offer a defense?"

"I was offered an out, if that's what you mean. Rat on Ed and I'd walk away a hero, called a plant who helped set Ed up."

Halle was appalled. "You shouldn't have been asked to make a choice between your ethics and your friend."

"Yeah? The law doesn't see it that way. The law is pretty clear on right and wrong. I wore a badge proclaiming to the world I was one of the good guys, better than the average man even. What I did by going in with Ed sullied that oath."

Sullied. Halle thought about the word he had chosen to describe his transgression. It was a lofty word. He hadn't bent the rules or made a minor transgression, or put it all on the line for a buddy. He had sullied his reputation. The definition was very precise, to tarnish as in his badge, to mar the purity of his oath. Joe was a man who thought in those terms.

Another door swung open on the mystery of the man. He had a code by which he judged things, a higher order than necessity, need, or convenience's sake. What's more, he had tried to live up to that standard in everyday life. That put him a step away from many people.

"What did you do to redeem yourself?"

"What do you mean?"

"Did you testify against your friend?"

Joe shook his head. "Whatever I did wrong I did voluntarily. Because the department wasn't happy about the idea of a policeman with my spotless record going down in flames they offered to accept my resignation instead of pressing charges.''

''What about Ed?''

''He cut a deal. He'd tell what he knew in return for immunity. He was the star witness in the case against Demotta. Been on all the major network talk shows. I hear he's even writing a book.''

''You mean he got the glory after he wrecked your career?''

Joe's profile was grim. ''He didn't twist my arm.''

''I wonder. He traded on your friendship by even asking you to cover for him. He must have known how seriously you believed in loyalty. He must have known it would go against your personal code to betray him. I'll bet he counted on that.''

He slanted a glance at her that revealed that the barrier was back up. ''Why, because that's the way people behave in your world? Oh, come on, Halle. Don't look so shocked. You used to tell me about the dirty dealings and underhanded tricks dealers played on one another to get a sale. Sellers and collectors in some cases are little more than thieves. They'd buy and sell merchandise they knew was stolen, as long as it couldn't be traced back to them. So don't get high and mighty with me about ethical considerations among my friends.''

Halle gaped at him. ''Is that true? Is that the kind of people I dealt with?''

He nodded. ''Every day.''

''Oh.'' Halle pulled in her shoulders and cupped her elbows with her hands. ''I'm beginning to see why you don't think much of me and my life.''

''Life-style,'' Joe amended. ''You were better than the rest of them. At least it bothered your conscience.

You kept saying you were going to get out of the selling end. You wanted to be part of the collecting efforts by museums and other more ethical collectors."

"Why didn't I quit before now?"

He shrugged. "I suppose because you had a real talent for the business. You were a natural with the most difficult of people. The house used you as a front man, front *person*, as often as possible. Your evenings were busier than your days. You'd come home after a big bash with stars in your eyes. You met everybody who was anybody in the art world. You were on a first-name basis with half the A list in Hollywood. I couldn't expect you to give that up."

"Why would you have expected me to do anything?"

Joe looked quickly away. Dammit! He'd almost stepped in a hole again. "I'm just saying you were your own person. You had to do what you had to do."

"Like you, you mean."

He looked back and nodded slowly. "Like me. We made our own mistakes. And we paid for them. Okay?"

"Did we make any... mistakes together?"

A half smile ratcheted up one corner of his mouth. "We're sort of committed here to being together for a few days. Let's be kind to one another and not worry about what might have been. Okay?"

"Might have been or was?"

His hand moved toward his crotch. Halle watched as he slid the soda can free and lifted it slowly to his mouth. "We don't have a might have been," he murmured before he took a swallow.

Joe welcomed the sweet carbonation sliding down his throat. Hell! What did she think she was doing in defending him to himself? How dare she offer him the words of solace he would have given ten years of his life to have heard from her two years earlier. They came to her so easily now that she didn't even remember the love he had for her. No, it wasn't real. What she'd offered was the cheap, easy sympathy one offered a stranger who had just related a private grief. The truth was she didn't believe any of the things she'd said during the last five minutes. She couldn't believe them and treat him the way she had. His suffering was the only reality.

"Tell me about your wife."

"Nothing to tell. It didn't work out."

"Did you love her?" No answer. "That's not what I meant. I meant, did you love her even after it was over?"

"Why do you want to know?"

"I don't know. Maybe because of what you said earlier about loyalty. I gather you feel deeply yet you don't seem the kind of man to be ruled by his feelings. You must have really cared for her to commit to marriage."

"Yeah."

"So you still love her?"

He heaved a sigh. "Look, I don't want to talk about it. It's over. I've accepted that. She even remarried."

"Oh Joe, that must have hurt."

He glanced sideways at her. "What would be your point?"

Halle winced at his rebuff. So, despite their history, he now considered her an outsider, one he wouldn't let into his life in any intimate way.

For the first time Halle began to consider the possibility that they had been nothing more than platonic roommates. If there had been any sexual heat between them she must have been doing all the generating. Had he ignored it or had it ultimately driven them apart? Who then was the man she had turned to for love? "Did you like my husband?"

He shoved the cola can at her. "You look hot. Why don't you finish this?"

Halle took it. It contents had grown lukewarm from the intimate embrace of his thighs. She drank a little of it anyway to be polite.

"My wife walked out on me because she thought I didn't spend enough time with her. After we were separated, she heard I was having an affair which put the squash-you on a reconciliation."

Halle gulped down the warm soda but the bubbles felt like fur in her throat. The bare facts made Joe seem like the typical neglectful husband and unfaithful spouse. Yet, she didn't buy it. Her very unreliable intuition was telling her that she had gotten in too close and he was repairing the breach in his defenses with whatever came to hand. Time would tell.

Halle rose from the molded plastic chair where she had been sitting for the past ten minutes. The dance studio in north Dallas was really a storefront in a strip shopping center that had been converted by the addition of wooden floors, mirrors and ballet bars, and partitioned into a series of studios and offices. Joe was closeted with the manager. Directly across the narrow hall she had been watching through the wall of glass a group of high school girls practice a jazz routine.

Two in particular caught her eye, a blonde and the brunette. The brunette was tall and model willowy with a faintly contemptuous glance and pout that must

"Lacey told that man about me?" the brunette prompted, not one to be easily led astray by other conversational threads from a discussion of herself.

"Well, actually, he was complaining about his father not wanting him to come to the arts magnet high school come fall." Halle leaned forward to impart confidentiality. "I gather his father's not very progressive."

"He's positively retro," the blonde responded. "Lacey was talking about moving out, getting his own place, you know. He's practically eighteen. He can do what he wants."

"It takes money to do what you want, even at eighteen," Halle answered.

"Lacey has money," the brunette interjected. "His father's a banker as well as a state senator."

"Is that so?" Halle said. "But if Lacey decided to tick off his dad, wouldn't he need a job in order to pay for an apartment?"

"He's got plans," the blonde said before the brunette shushed her.

"I would think he must," Halle answered and looked off as if she were more interested in what Joe was doing than in what the girls were saying. "I saw the notices on the bulletin board. Are either of you auditioning for the Six Flags Over Texas summer musicals?"

"I am," the brunette answered. "Worked there last year in the chorus." She sighed and realigned the willowy curvature of her posture for better effect. "I sing as well as dance."

"I'm impressed." Halle glanced again at Joe. "How old do you have to be to work there?"

"Some jobs are open to sixteen-year-olds," the blonde answered. "But the competition is so keen the really good jobs mostly go to college students."

"Lacey may have said something about that. I got the impression he didn't think he was good enough to make the cut."

"Lacey could make it," the blonde answered positively, "if he wanted to."

"Lacey's the best dancer in this school." The brunette flipped her hair back over her shoulder, a habit many women in Texas seemed to share, Halle decided. "And he can sing, too. We share the same voice coach. He says Lacey's got a good clean stage voice. You can hear him all the way to the back balcony of the music hall. We did the Christmas show there last winter, *The Nutcracker*. Maybe you've heard of it?"

Halle decided the girl was not being sarcastic despite her sulky expression. "Oh yes, the ballet with the Sugar Plum Fairy and the Christmas tree that grows."

"We were Sugar Plums," the blonde announced. "Lacey was the Mouse King."

"Impressive," Halle answered. "Oh, here come's my ride. Nice to meet you girls." She half turned away and then looked back. "I'll be sure and tell Lacey you both said hello if I see him again. He's been out of town a while now."

"Then he went—*Ouch*. What are you doing, Paisley?"

The brunette was fuming. "Honest to God, you have the biggest mouth, Shelby!" She caught her friend by the arm and dragged her in the opposite direction without even a glance at Halle.

"That was a great big waste of time," Joe announced as he came up beside her. "The dance instructor admitted that she had written several letters of reference for Lacey but she gave them directly to him to use as he saw fit. The kid could have gone anywhere, including New York.''

"I don't think so. Lacey's off somewhere auditioning for a job," Halle answered.

Joe's brows rose in surprise. "What?"

"Lacey left home to do an audition. I don't think it's for the Six Flags Over Texas Show, though.''

His gaze tracked down to the end of the hallway where the blonde and brunette were engaged in an intense if quiet discussion. "Those girls told you that?''

Halle took him by the arm and steered him toward the main office. "Not exactly. Let's say I finessed it out of them.''

He eyed her with new respect. "I don't suppose you got the details of which auditions and where?''

Halle smiled sweetly. "I didn't want to strain my budding detecting talents. You're the professional, after all. You should earn your salary some way. Ask the owner who in the surrounding states is auditioning summer stage jobs right now and which jobs a boy with Lacey's talents could hope to land.''

Five minutes later, Joe was back in the hallway, a big grin on his face. He walked right up and dropped a kiss on her brow. "You did all right, sweetheart. The Albuquerque Opera is auditioning extras for its summer run.'' He flung an arm about her shoulder and turned her so that they could walk together toward the door. "To prove my heart's in the right place, I'm gonna buy you a great big Tex-Mex dinner.''

"Are you certain this is a good idea?''
"Sure, I eat here all the time when I'm in town.''

Halle glanced around the tamale factory. The long white-painted picnic tables were crowded with customers eating with their fingers hand-rolled tamales right out of the husks. Compelled by the press of Joe's hand in the middle of her back she stepped across the threshold onto the cracked linoleum floor.

"Find us a seat. I'll place our order." He gave her a little push and then moved past her to the end of the line.

Halle stepped aside as several more people entered behind her. After a moment she moved along the wall scanning the tables for two empty spaces. The clientele was eclectic to say the least. There were laborers in hard hats and muscle shirts, men in gimme caps and tooled leather belts that spelled out their names across the back, a quartet of businessmen in suits and ties, two women with infants in strollers, and a young couple who were quarreling rather than eating. The lively polka of a Mexican Mariachi band made the level of voices seem even louder than they were.

The businessmen rose as she reached them, smiled in her direction and pointed to their places as they cleared away the aluminum pans and paper cups. With a nod of thanks she slid into one of the places and lay her purse next to her to hold a space for Joe.

An outburst from the next table drew her reluctant attention to the quarreling couple. The man had risen and was tugging on the woman's arm. Halle tensed as the level of conversation dropped. Everyone sensed trouble. The expectant stillness erupted again as the woman cried out and swung at the man with her purse.

"Let me alone!"

The man reeled off a spate of vile words and wrenched the woman's arm so hard she popped off the seat and careened her into him. As they staggered across the room Halle winced in sympathy and grabbed her purse, ready to flee as nearby customers backpedaled away from their half-eaten tamales.

"Help! Help me!" the woman cried and beat ineffectually at the man as he grabbed a handful of her hair and began hauling her toward the door.

Halle glanced around wildly, wondering why someone didn't do something. And then someone did.

Chapter 9

"I still can't believe you got involved in a brawl!"

Halle stepped into the economy motel room Joe had already booked. As she passed through she dropped her purse and drug store bag onto the king-size bed and then headed for the bathroom sink with the bag of ice she carried. "You could have been killed."

Joe followed at a much slower pace, a handful of damp paper towels held to the cut above his eye. "Did it look like I wanted to get involved? I merely tried to point out that the woman did not want to leave with him. That was her right."

She leaned back through the open bathroom door into the bedroom. "It looked like you didn't mind very much. You didn't back down when he turned on you. Do you always come to the aid of strange females?"

"Yeah. Pretty much." Joe lowered himself slowly into the straight chair by the door. "I don't like seeing anybody roughed up, especially not a man accosting a woman. You think I should have just let him drag her out as he was trying to do?''

"You should have minded your own business and let the police handle it.'' She stepped out of the bathroom carrying a handful of ice in a plastic bag and a damp washcloth. "They were on the spot in five minutes.'' As if she had not already made the point she said again, "You could have gotten yourself killed.''

"Not likely. You forget I was a once New York City cop.''

"You forget you're no longer any kind of a cop.'' She thrust the ice pack at him. "That man had a knife. He might as easily have had a gun.''

He looked at her and smiled. "I know that. Expect the worst is part of my former job description.''

Halle glanced away from the implacable reality in his gaze and found herself staring at the tear at the shoulder seam of his shirt. Three buttons had been ripped off in the brawl. Where the shirt gaped open there was a long thin scratch showing like a thin red river beneath the lacework of his dark chest hair. The knuckles of the hand holding the ice pack to his left eye were scraped and raw. When her gaze came back to his amused one, partially obscured by the swelling shut of one eye, her anger doubled. "You were enjoying it, weren't you?''

"Not exactly.'' Joe shrugged and winced. Something in his midsection was remarkably sore. He remembered staggering into a high-backed chair after the guy's one lucky punch. He reached inside his ruined shirt to gingerly quest out the source. "It's been a while since I had to react so quickly. I'm a little out of practice.''

He found the source of the ache. It was a scrape the width of two fingers along his lower right ribs. He'd look at it later, when he was alone. No need to frighten her any more than she already was.

"The guy never would've gotten that lucky punch in if I hadn't been trying to hold off his girlfriend. Domestic altercations are the worst. Women are so unpredictable." He looked up. "You swing a mean briefcase. Thanks."

Halle blushed, embarrassed by her own temerity. She had grabbed the first thing that came to hand when the fight had turned two to one against Joe. Fortunately the man's briefcase she picked up was as heavy as a brick. Joe's assailant had gone down in a tackled sprawl when it hit him low and from behind. "He had a knife and you didn't. It was obvious that nobody else was going to help you."

It was equally obvious to Joe that she resented having been lured into the fracas but he couldn't keep back a wide grin of pleasure. Halle had come to his rescue.

"Why did you get involved?"

She crossed her arms, drawing his attention to the small rip in her silk blouse where the lace of her bra showed through. "Are you serious?"

"Yeah, I am." He shifted his ice pack from his face to his ribs. "It would never have occurred to you to come my aid before."

"How can you be so certain?"

"Something similar happened a few years ago in the city. I was carrying a shield and a gun in those days. I was off duty and we were out with friends one night when we came across a robbery in progress. You freaked when I stepped in to make the collar.'' He gave her a lazy warm smile. ''Later, you said you'd leave me if I ever did anything like that again.''

''Leave you?'' The air was suddenly as still as glass.

Joe stood up and waited a heartbeat to see if she would say where her thoughts had taken her. But wherever that was, she didn't share it with him. ''I was a cop. That was my job, stopping criminals, even on my days off.''

Halle stared at him, still caught up in the idea that she had once threatened to leave him. How personal a leave-taking would it have been? ''You did what you had to do. Maybe I've grown up a bit because I understand that now.''

Joe moved to and sat down heavily on the bed. ''Yeah, well, maybe I have grown up a bit, too.'' He touched his aching eye. ''Or maybe I'm just not as eager as before to show off.''

Halle came forward and cupped his battered face in one hand, frowning as she surveyed the abuse it had taken. ''Your poor eye. I won't be able to tell until I've cleaned you up but I think that cut over it is going to need stitches.''

''It won't,'' Joe answered calmly and then winced as she gently explored the area around the gash with a damp cloth. ''Soap and water and a few bandages, and I'll be as good as new.''

But he knew that was a lot of wishful thinking. The way it throbbed, he knew his eye was going stay swelled shut for a good twenty-four hours.

He was much more interested in the fact that Halle was standing so close to him that he could see between the buttons of her blouse to the satin skin of her abdomen. He lifted a hand and settled it on her waist as he spread his legs farther apart, allowing her to get closer as she worked. "You smell good," he said and inhaled deeply.

"It must be eau de tamale. We didn't get to have any lunch," she reminded him as she worked carefully to clean away dried blood from his eyebrow and the creases around his eye.

"No, you smell like lemons," he murmured.

"Oh, you're right. That nice police officer at the station offered me a lemon candy while I was waiting to see if you would be charged with assault. I wonder if I've ever ridden in a squad car before?"

Joe wondered what she would do if he reached up and pulled her down onto his lap so that he could lick the lemon flavor from her lips. Would she let him? Would she let him lick all around the edges of her lips and then between them and then sweep the inside of her mouth, taste her tongue and drink her in until the only flavor left was uniquely her own?

His second hand settled on the other side of her waist but she didn't seem to notice. "Are you really mad at me for doing the gallant thing?"

"I suppose not. It's just that what I thought should happen and what did are two different things." She fished surgical tape and scissors out of the drug store bag and began cutting strips to make a butterfly bandage. "Do you think that attorney would really have sued me for scuffing his briefcase?"

Joe chuckled. "You handed him two one-hundred-dollar bills. He looked more than satisfied."

"How did you convince the Dallas police to let you go?" She began applying the strips to draw the edges of the gash closed.

"I gave them the secret handshake."

"What?"

"I told them I'd been a cop. We swapped a few stories. Man to man. Works every time."

"I'm sure the females officers loved that."

"I got a few looks."

As she finished Halle leaned back from him for she had the sudden sensation of being pulled in against him by the waist. "What are you doing?" she asked suspiciously.

"Enjoying the view," he answered, his eyes on a level with her breasts. "You really are a spectacularly arranged woman, Halle."

Halle reached up and laid her hands over his where they rode the narrow curves of her waist. "Joe, you keep saying we need to stay out of each other's way."

"I talk too much." He leaned forward until his forehead was pillowed against her stomach. "You feel good and my head aches so bad I couldn't do much more than hold you anyway. Let me have this comfort, Halle."

A little reluctantly, her arms came up to cradle his head against her. "You'd feel better if you would lie back and take a nap."

"Will you lie with me?" He rocked his head against her middle, his hands flexing to hold her closer. "Lie next to me so that I can rest my head on you. You're so soft, better than any pillow, and you smell like a woman. I like your smell. Always have."

A tiny shock like an electric current zipped through Halle. He was talking to her as a lover might. Did he realize that or had the blow to his head addled his senses? Before she could decide, he leaned backward and drew her with him until she tipped forward over

him and sprawled out along the length of him as he lay
back on the mattress.

For a moment she lay motionless on him, her legs
levered between his spread ones. That position pressed
her hips tightly against his loins. A moment's consciousness of their proximity answered the question of
the source of his interest in her. He was half aroused
and gaining tumescence with every passing second.

She raised up, bracing herself by her hands on the
mattress as she looked down into his face. He was a
mess. The cut over his left eye, which capped a swelling the size of a goose egg, was still oozing blood. His
lashes were meshed into a slit which she doubted he
could see through. The surrounding contused skin was
already turning several shades of red and purple. But
when her gaze dropped to his mouth, she felt the sudden flutter of desire in her middle.

"Halle?" He reached up to cup her head and she
bent to him, sighing as he lifted his head to fit the
shape of his mouth to hers.

Something broke loose from its moorings inside her
as he drew her into his kiss. The hand pressing at the
back of her head ushered her into the welcoming
warmth of his parting lips, pulled her into the surge of
his tongue, positioned her to absorb the rhythm of
their tangling mouths. She knew this, recognized this
moment with a knowing that went beyond mere recorded memory. This was the source of the life force
surging through her, through him, between them. This
was real, true, unforgettable.

She did not know how long he kissed her or even
exactly when she moved or he moved so that she was
no longer draped over him but on the mattress beside
him, so closely fitted to his body that they touched in

one long caress from shoulder to knees. Breasts to chest, stomach and hips fitted like jigsaw pieces, their arms holding the parts locked, they kissed until her lips became so sensitive his mere breath across their surface sent shivers coursing down her spine.

"I could get used to this," he murmured finally, his lips buried in her neck. "I could get damned used to this."

Halle opened her eyes. The light in the room had changed. Had five minutes passed, or an hour? She couldn't tell. He'd only kissed her! Only that. And she felt ravished, afire, burning with the warm steady flame of a kerosine lamp, golden in her glow.

When he rolled away from her an involuntary whimper escaped her. "I know," he whispered beside her. "I know."

Halle turned to stare up at the ceiling. "What? What do you know?"

"That nothing is ever what it seems." How sad he sounded. "Life complicates the simplest things."

"Is this complicated?" she whispered.

"Isn't it?"

"Because my memory's missing?"

"Because mine isn't."

The steady flame inside her wavered in the backdraft of his words. Halle felt like crying, no, weeping. That was that. He'd lit the match, turned up the flow of sexually charged fuel to high, and then blown out the fire. The flameout smoked her eyes, heated her cheeks and burned the back of her throat. "Okay," she whispered. "I understand. No problem."

Yet when she attempted to rise he caught her by the waist and pulled her closer. He lifted his head and rested it on her shoulder as one of his legs shifted up and over both of hers, trapping her. "Just lie with me, Halle. Just do that much for me."

Why? What do you want from me? She tensed to keep from yelling the words to him. Did he think she was some kind of insensitive being because her memory had wandered off? Her mind wasn't missing, nor were her feelings and her needs. The lack of a past seemed an awful burden at the moment.

"Don't be angry," he murmured as he pillowed his face in the valley between her breasts.

"I'm not," she answered. She was furious!

Joe had navigated through traffic with one eye swelled shut before. There was only one problem, he had no depth perception. Highway driving would be hazardous. With great care, he turned into the parking lot of a fast-food restaurant and parked.

He turned and flashed Halle an enigmatic smile. "Come on, let's order. I'm starved."

Halle followed him into the burger place but her mind remained on what had, or rather, had not occurred between them.

Strangely enough they had both fallen asleep on that hotel bed when she would have bet a million dollars that sleep would have been impossible after the kisses they shared. Okay, so she'd survived a heavy necking session. She doubted it was her first taste of sexual frustration. With Joe for a companion, she suspected it wouldn't be her last.

When she had ordered Joe stepped up behind her and said, "We're together. Let's see, I'll have a double burger with extra cheese and bacon, a large order of fries and a chocolate milk shake. No wait, make it a double burger no bacon. Small fries."

His features compressed in lines of irritation. "That's your trouble, it's always been your trouble. You city women think life only happens in metropolises of a million plus. Well, there's life, good decent life, in small average places. There's good in plain average people, too. Maybe if you'd ever bothered to get to know someone besides your designer-clothed friends you would know that."

Gold sparkled in the green depths of her eyes. "What's that supposed to mean? I knew you, didn't I?"

"Yeah. You made me the exception to your rule and you know where that landed you."

Unwilling to be defeated by his shift back into ungraciousness, Halle smiled at him as she reached across the table to wipe a blob of mustard from his lower lip with her thumb. "Actually, I don't remember what happened when I made you an exception on my friendship chain. Why don't you tell me?"

He grabbed her wrist in a grip so tight she gasped. "Don't do that." He whispered the words but they seemed to penetrate the convivial air about them.

Joe glanced right and left and then very slowly released her wrist, one uncurling finger at a time. "Let's get the hell outta here. People are staring."

When she looked around Halle saw that Joe was right. The two high school age waitresses in pink nylon uniforms refilling napkin holders were making no attempt to hide their interest. The middle-aged couple in the next booth were all but craned forward in their eavesdropping. Four young men in jeans and caps were grinning and talking among themselves but every gaze was trained on their table. She supposed they did make a strange couple, a kind of ad hoc Beauty and the Beast, and the beast was growling.

Halle folded the paper over her untouched sandwich and tucked it back into her bag. He waited for her to finish then rose and walked toward the exit, shoving his half-eaten meal into the waste container as he passed it.

The sunset was dying fast. The retreating magenta glow of the western sky cast thick purple shadows on the evening which seemed, by contrast, to be deeper than night. Joe had crossed the parking lot before he noticed that it was his throbbing eye and not Halle's questions that was fueling his temper and his headache. He owed her an apology. He whipped around so suddenly she stopped short as she came up behind him.

The startled look on her face doubled his remorse. She stood five feet away, the Indian gauze skirt she had put on before they left the hotel lifting and floating in the breeze. She stood there straight and slim and hugging a greasy burger bag to her breasts. Such soft warm sweet breasts, breasts he had slept so soundly upon, breasts he longed to touch and kiss.

"I'm damned sorry." The words made three percussive sounds in the late evening air.

"It's all right." Her shoulders shimmied as she shook her head. "I was pushing again."

He took a step toward her. "You weren't pushing. I'm just not good company tonight. Okay, more than usual bad company. It's the eye. Aches like the devil."

He reached up and stretched fingers gingerly over the lump on his brow. "My Good Samaritan routine is going to cost me more than time off the job. To tell you the truth, I don't know if I can see well enough to drive us safely back to our hotel. Maybe we should call a cab.''

She released the death grip she had on her much squashed food bag and let it dangle from her hand. ''I have a better suggestion.''

''Okay.''

''I'll drive.''

Joe chuckled. ''Sweetheart, you can't drive.''

She grinned back. Even with only one eye cooperating and the umber of evening to hamper its efforts Joe knew that smile was genuine. She had forgiven him. He knew he didn't deserve that. But Halle had never been one to hold a grudge . . . until she was convinced he didn't love her anymore.

''I know I don't have a driver's license,'' she said in a conspiratorial whisper. ''But we might cheat just this once, don't you think?''

Joe made an emphatic gesture with his head. ''No. In any case, that wasn't my point. You can't drive because you don't know how.''

She look as insulted as if he had said she wasn't smart enough to drive. ''How do you know?''

''I know.'' He grinned at her. ''Does it 'feel' like you can drive?''

Halle cocked her head to one side. ''I don't know. But, how hard can it be when fourteen-year-olds and ninety-year-olds do it all the time?''

Joe handed her the keys. ''Have at it, sweetheart.''

The truck bucked like an aggravated mule, causing Joe to nearly bite his tongue as the engine died for the twelfth time.

''Oh rats!''

"Try again," Joe said calmly. "You're supposed to give it a little more gas as you let up on the clutch, remember? Both together. A little more gas, a little less clutch."

Halle shook her head miserably. It was now completely dark. She had managed to lurch them exactly six blocks from the burger place and into a deserted school parking lot where Joe said she could practice. But after half an hour of trying, all her confidence had vanished. There was driving and then there was driving. She had not been certain when she got behind the wheel whether or not she had ever driven a stick shift before. Now she was positive she hadn't.

At least she hadn't caused an accident. None, that is, if she didn't count the tiny bump that occurred when she backed into the garbage can at the far end of the pavement. Her hands were sweaty and her nerves were so tightly wound her movements had become as jerky as a puppet's.

"Try again, sweetheart."

With a moan of misery, she leaned her head forward against the steering wheel. "I don't think I can do this after all."

"Sure you can. You just need a little more, uh, practice."

"You mean I need a month of daily lessons." She straightened and looked at the calm man beside her. She had expected him to jump all over her pathetic efforts. "You were right. I don't know how to drive."

He drew up a leg, wrapped an arm casually about it, and braced his booted foot on the bench seat. "Well, then, it's time you learned."

Unconvinced she muttered, "I don't see why."

"It's every American's right to drive. Not to is kind of unpatriotic."

She stared out through the steering wheel and over the dashboard at the pavement lit by her headlights. "I don't feel very patriotic."

"That's because you're feeling crowded by circumstance. But, I ask you. Look around." From the corners of her eyes she saw him make an expansive gesture with his free arm. "Anything is possible here. You're in God's country and don't know it. That's because you're unaccustomed to the wide open spaces."

She swiveled her head toward him. "You mean I've never been to Texas before?"

His white smile glowed faintly in the dashboard light. "Exactly. When I knew you, you hadn't been much of anywhere, not if you discount London, Paris, the Riviera, and Rome."

"Are you serious?"

"It's what you told me. When you were younger your folks would fly you over to visit them for major holidays, or at their convenience. Still, your education in culture is definitely lacking. You've never had what I'd call a proper vacation."

Halle lifted her head. "What would that be?"

"A visit to the Grand Canyon, tour of our nation's capital. Heck, you haven't even been to Disney World."

She fixed on him a jaundiced eye. "And this, to you, is a measure of culture?"

"It's a measure of being part of the great crazy quilt we call America. Regular people go fishing, camping, hiking, tour the country by car. They visit the national monuments and the national parks. You can't judge the real world from the penthouse suite of a grand hotel, sweetheart.''

Halle bristled. ''I'm certain I must have done something average in my life. I must have been camping, at least.''

He guffawed. ''You once told me your idea of roughing it was to take a cab through Central Park.''

Halle laughed with him, pleased to see his dimple on display. ''Was I really that bad?'' He nodded. ''Why then, did you ever agree to be my roommate?''

''Oh, it had its compensations.'' He said it lightly, too lightly for her to miss just how careful he was to keep it light.

She looked in his eyes, his one good eye and the battered, swelled-shut one. ''Joe, I've been wanting to ask you something. Now I think it's time.''

He made no sudden move but the loose-bone quality of his pose disappeared. ''Shoot.''

Halle licked her upper lip which had suddenly become stuck to her teeth. ''Were we ever lovers?''

The truck cab was cradled in a darkness so deep as to make indistinct their features yet she had the impression he blushed. A shy man. Her instincts were right. ''What do you think?''

Halle found she could not draw a decent breath. ''I don't know.''

''What do you feel?'' He reached out and tapped her blouse just above her heart. ''What does this tell you?''

Now that was a very dangerous question. She looked down at where his fingers hovered just above the swell of her left breast. If she moved just a little his thumb would brush the nipple budding behind her bra cup. A sharp jab of hunger struck her low down. But it was useless. He wasn't going to assuage that hunger. He had proved that during the afternoon's debacle. Yet if she didn't want to talk to him about it, she shouldn't have brought it up.

She glanced up straight into one good brown eye drinking her in. "I feel maybe we were."

"And how does *that* make you feel?"

"A little afraid, a little embarrassed." Her lashes seemed suddenly to weigh a ton for her lids drooped over her eyes. "And a little pleased."

"Only a little pleased?"

She glanced up to find him smiling again. "Don't preen. It doesn't become you."

He lifted his hand from the area of her breast to touch her cheek. "Everything becomes you. Only do me one great big favor?"

"What?"

"Stop dyeing your hair. That brown color makes you look, well, tepid."

She smiled, a foolishly happy smile for no reason at all. "What color is my natural hair?"

"Gold with silver highlights and sepia undertones. It's silky as hell and twice as sexy."

His fingers had found and twined in the hair that grew behind her right ear and was filtering through it. The subtle tug of his callused fingers was much like a caress.

"Why do you think I dyed it?"

Joe didn't miss the faint hint of doubt entering her expression. "If you're still worried about someone being after you, you can forget it. When I knew you, you changed your hairstyle as often as the season."

"Why?"

"Beats me. All your friends spent a good portion of their salaries on their looks. Cellophaning, body wraps, facials, massages and so forth. Some of them needed a little help but I never understood why you did half the things you did to yourself when you were already the most beautiful woman I'd ever seen."

Halle let those words sink in, her psyche sucking them up like drops of rain on parched earth. He thought she was beautiful. He thought she was sexy. He thought . . . but he didn't act.

She wanted to grab him by the ears and haul him in for a kiss. She wanted to set his eyelashes on fire and make smoke rise in alarming columns from his ears. She wanted to make him greedy and dizzy and desperate with need. She wanted him to toss aside manners and caution and reserve. She wanted him to get out of control—way out—and take her with him into the blistering heat of mutual desire. Yet she knew the first move must come from him. He knew what she did not. If he thought their past too great a chasm to cross she must accept that, too.

She swallowed disappointment and reclasped her fingers around the steering wheel. "Joe, what are we going to do?"

His hand drifted from her hair down over her shoulder, the touch of his lightly abrading fingers less a caress than a tease. "I don't know. Go with the mood, maybe?"

She stared doggedly forward. No more flirting with aborted desire this night or she'd succumb to dry heaves. "I meant about my inability to drive."

"Oh. I thought you meant this."

He moved very deliberately, gripping one of her shoulders and then the other, turning her upper body to face him. He stunned her with the knowing gentleness of his smile. He understood, no, shared her feelings. In that, at least, they were simpatico.

Halle didn't move, didn't dare think because she knew that what she wanted was impossible. Yet it was so simple. She wanted, simply wanted, him.

His lips found hers and gently pressed their satin surfaces.

Slow sensuous streamers of heat curled up through Joe as he kissed her. This was Halle. He knew her taste, remembered the feel of her beneath his hands, recognized the smell of her. This was the one woman in the world who owned his heart and bore his love, the mate grafted to his soul and psyche in ways no court declaration could ever sever.

The vines of desire branched out, wrapping sensuous tendrils about his mind and heart, creeping up through muscle and sinew, binding and subduing caution in heavy turgid ropes potent as a lover's embrace. He closed his eyes, sheltered by the canopy of verdant green desire.

He was tired of the struggle against his love for her. Just once, to submerge once more in Halle's sweet wet warmth, he asked no more of life.

He knew he wasn't alone. He heard her catch her breath when his lips moved to the corner of her mouth, a gasp as eloquent as any cry for help. He couldn't help her or save her. He could only go with her down onto the narrow bench, holding on to her with a fierce need not to be left alone in the steamy madness of their mutual need.

Halle tasted in his kiss the smoke of bridges burning. She saw in the beauty of his expression, as he moved and lifted her onto her back, the desert trek he had made to reach her. She heard the sizzle of rain upon the vast seared wasteland that had been his life...for how long? Later, her heart whispered. Time enough later to learn the answers. Now there was only his hands on her, moving and removing clothing as they went, seeking out skin to caress and knead and shape in ways that gave pleasure to both of them.

His hands, oh, his hands. How good they felt, on her arms, her breasts, her belly, her thighs. She turned in to meet them everywhere they strayed, unashamed of anticipating the pleasure they gave. He answered her sighs and soft murmurs with deep hard little sounds of hard-won joy, as if he were a little afraid of the pleasure she aroused.

She kissed him wherever she could reach, a bare shoulder, his jaw, the tender spot behind his ear. She licked his wounded eye, murmuring soothing incantations to speed its healing. All the while her body basked in the heat of his, cupping the harder angles, gentling the urgent thrusts, accommodating his possession with a wringing caress of welcome.

The end came quickly. It had been too long, how long she did not know. But much, oh, much too long away from this bliss.

"I remember," she whispered when at last they lay panting, just past the miracle of their own creation.

He stiffened as the miracle shattered. "What do you remember?"

"This." She smiled in the darkness and clutched him tight as a security blanket. "I remember this. Oh Joe! How could I ever have left you?"

Chapter 10

"But you're hurt!" Halle protested as he tried to draw her across his bruised ribs.

"I'll live," he murmured and pulled her fully on him. He licked the column of her neck and then ran his teeth along the sensitive tendon. "As long as you don't stop doing that. Oh yeah, That's it." He shifted his hips to better accommodate her reach. "That's much better."

Halle laughed, amazed by his resilience and still a little shocked at herself. Half an hour earlier they had made love in a truck in a vacant parking lot in the middle of a great big city. Anyone could have come upon them, the police, a caretaker, anyone!

But no one had. Somehow when the world righted itself enough for them to be abashed and amused and thoroughly pleased with themselves, they had managed to make their way back to this motel room. While she gave directions and acted as an extra pair of eyes, Joe had done the driving.

Giggling like teenagers with a guilty secret, they had paused every few feet in their journey from truck to motel room door to kiss and hug and caress. If anyone had seen them, they might have been shocked for Joe Guinn, once roused to action, had no reservations about showing Halle with mouth and tongue and hands just how much he enjoyed touching her. He had pulled her into the darkness of a walkway, dropped to a knee, lifted her skirt and run his palms up the backs of her thighs while licking the fronts. When he rose he whispered between kisses wicked suggestions of things he would do to her once they were inside their hotel room.

Now they were here, stretched out on the bed as he pulled her astride his hips.

"You like this?" he asked, stroking her from the nape of her neck straight down the valley of her spine to the very end which he massaged with his fingertips.

"Yes," Halle purred, arching her back so that her breasts spread out across his darker hairy chest and her hips lifted off his. When his hands slid back up her spine she reversed her arch. Pressing her hips into his hardness she arched up and away so that her breasts rose and swung free as tantalizing fruit before his eyes. He caught one tip in his mouth and pulled strongly on it.

She gasped and giggled, then sighed as his tongue slid all around the puckered crescent before flicking the taut center.

"You're a maniac!" she whispered as he wrapped her arms around her back and pulled her down for a full body hug.

"At the moment I'm your maniac." He smiled up at her, his swollen eye giving him the squinty rakishness of a younger much handsomer Popeye. "Take every advantage of that fact."

"Don't worry." She dipped her head and caught his lower lip between her teeth and gently tugged. It felt so good, everything about him: his taste, his smell, his touch, the way he breathed as he entered her, deep and hard like the sound of a bellows fanning the flames of their passion. All of it aroused and pleased and delighted her.

As he reached down between them to stroke the most sensitive folds of her body, then guide himself home, she sighed and kissed him deeply. Here and now with him, the past and future did not matter. For this while in his arms, wrapped in his need and her need to give, they were perfectly matched. It felt right.

Low down deep where certain knowledge dwells that cannot be uttered as words, she knew that Joe was meant for her and she for him. Whatever else had occurred, whatever memory might toss up on the shores of reality, this would remain true and real and indelible and she would not lose it again.

Joe caught her cries of pleasure in his mouth, enjoying the undulations of her body over his. And when she slumped over him, certain she had no more to give, he gripped her hips hard and began surging upward in hard quick thrusts that wrung the concession of another series of joyous cries from her.

His own release came as almost painful spasms. Too long, oh much too long since he had offered this perfect expression of love for his wife.

Ex-wife

She fell asleep before he did and for that Joe was grateful. He needed to be alone. Not separated from her, but isolated with his thoughts. She lay so trustingly against him. But for how long?

In the past hour he had abandoned every rule he had set up for himself in this arrangement between them. He wasn't sorry but he was wary. Where would it lead?

This! I remember this! Oh, Joe, how could I ever have left you?

His heart had stopped when she said those words in the truck. Was she recanting the anger, pain and rage that had blasted their marriage vows into oblivion? Had she remembered the love and the need, the unity of souls that had brought them together in the first place? Or was it something else?

She rolled against him. Her lips, pliant in sleep, nibbled softly at the underside of his arm. She remembered this much, he thought. She admitted the recall of passion shared, the summation of mutual desire. She said she remembered that they had once been lovers. She admitted that much and no more.

She did not remember the love he had brought her, the only chaste and unsullied emotion he still owned when they met. He had never loved before he met her. He had fancied, coveted, desired, lusted after, yearned for and chased women. But he had never loved a woman before Halle. That loving had conquered all the territory of his heart for all times. It was the reason he had not been able to get on with his life. Without her he was a man without a heart. He could perform all the tasks required to sustain his life but none of it had meaning without her.

Now she was back, absolutely back in his life, the fulfillment of every wish, dream and prayer he had ever uttered these last two years. Maybe she wouldn't ever remember completely. Maybe her memory was gone for good. Maybe they could just go forward, start over, the slate wiped clean. They had this much. His love for her was unqualified, uncompromised, pure and sure. Maybe he could make her love him again.

Maybe.

"You're clutching at straws, Guinn," he muttered as he turned to kiss the top of her hair.

He was nothing but a dirty low-down sneaking coward to let her betray herself this way, in his bed, in his arms. But, God help him, he wasn't strong enough to prevent it.

The only question was, would he survive the explosion when it came? Every muscle in his body tensed as if the anticipated pain would be physical.

The sudden tension in his frame disturbed her. She sighed against him, reached up and stroked her fingers down over his lips, her nails catching on the faint stubble at his chin. "Jag?" she whispered.

The fear redoubled. "Yeah, sweetheart. It's me."

"Hum," she murmured as her hand drifted down over his chest. "I'm glad."

He shut his eyes, scarcely breathing. The end had better come soon or he'd have no defenses left with which to shore up his reshattered life. None at all.

* * *

Her murmuring woke him an instant before she went rigid, her body shuddering beneath the sheet. He rose and half turned to her, laying a hand on her shoulder to jostle her. "Halle? Wake up, sweetheart. You're dreaming."

She shuddered again then jerked once and fell still. Though it was too dark to see her, he sensed she was awake.

"What? What—oh!" She put out her hand and pressed his bare chest. "Joe?"

"Yeah, babe. You were having a bad dream."

"Oh. Yes." She sat up, pushing her cascade of hair from her sleepy eyes as he snapped on the bedside lamp.

"What was it about, Halle? Tell me?"

She caught the concern in his expression but shouldered it aside in her confusion. Random recollections and impressions were raining in on her thoughts like autumn leaves in a stiff breeze. "Nothing. Nothing." She shook her head, again sweeping the hair from her face. This time she held it back with fingers forked through the front. "Silly things. A nightmare."

He leaned in close, kissing the curve of her bare shoulder then propping his prickly chin there. "What kind of nightmare?"

"I don't know, exactly."

She resisted the urge to pull away from him. There were things she needed to think about, alone, before she shared them.

"Tell me about it."

"I'd feel foolish. It wasn't even scary. No monsters or evil lurking."

"Then feel foolish but tell me."

He was touching her, running his palm soothingly up and down her upper arm. Then he reached across and cupped one naked breast.

She hunched away before she could stop herself. "I'm sorry." She glanced in his direction but she didn't meet his gaze. "I'm just feeling a little...touchy. Aftershocks, I suppose."

He shifted a little away but she could feel the tension peeling off of him in waves. He was going to ask her if she had remembered anything. That thought hurried her into speech.

"It was nothing, really. I was dreaming that I was flying. You know the sort of dream where you feel weightless and happy, soaring against a deep blue summer sky. But then I saw these orbs, like gigantic soap bubbles, coming toward me. There were people inside. That's when I realized I was in a bubble, too. I knew their faces—my parents, friends, colleagues. I kept trying to reach them but they didn't see or hear me. Suddenly you were floating by but I couldn't touch you, either. And then you floated away." A rueful chuckle breathed out of her. "Ridiculous, right?"

"Your reaction was real enough." How cautious he sounded, as if he were dealing with a very delicate personality.

She shivered and shook her head. "I felt so alone, Joe. It was as if I were doomed to spend my life looking at things and people I couldn't be with. No connections at all."

"You've had that dream before."

She whipped around to face him. "When?"

His expression was as guarded as an armored truck. "Before we met. You told me you'd had the dream since you were small, each time one of your parents would send you back to New York after a European holiday. It doesn't require Freudian psychoanalysis to figure out that the dream represents separation anxiety and loss. You grew up pretty much on your own.''

She looked down at her hands clasped together in her lap. ''Why should it occur now when we're together? Why not when I woke up in the hospital scared and completely alone?''

''Maybe because you're more scared now.''

His voice drew her gaze his way. ''Because we're together again?''

He was looking at her with a regret and tenderness she couldn't quite fathom. ''The idea scares me a little, too.''

Nodding, she turned away. Beneath the rumpled covers their legs were stretched out side by side like the spines of the Rockies, his upturned feet making higher peaks at the bottom, but together, for now. ''Joe, I need to know about the woman you married.''

''Why?'' Quick caution gusted the word.

''Because what I feel...'' She tried to steady her swirling thoughts long enough to communicate them. ''What I remember feeling doesn't make sense. How could I have felt this way about you and let it all go?''

He was holding his breath, as she was hers. That was the only explanation for the sudden lack of sound in the room.

''What way do you feel?''

Halle heard her expelled breath like air escaping from a punctured tire. ''There have been moments tonight when I've been so deliriously happy that I could float up right off this bed and hover about the ceiling like a helium balloon. Now I could die of this ache so deep down it feels like a toothache in my heart.''

His chuckle surprised her. "You've got the beginnings of a country-and-western tune there. 'Your love's like a toothache in my heart, darlin'!''' he sang in a fairly credible baritone.

She shot him a glance of annoyance. "Don't tease me."

"Why not?" He shrugged elaborately and folded his arms behind his head, leaning back against the headboard. It was the posture of concession or seduction. She could not but admire the masculine torso on display. She hadn't been wrong that first morning to recognize the whorl of hair about his navel. She had dipped her tongue into it this night and tasted sweet memory.

She dragged her gaze away and sat up straighter. Once and for all, even after this miraculous fever and possession, she had to know the rest.

"Tell me about your wife, Joe. I want to know what made you marry her and why you left her."

"I already told you—I didn't leave her." Flat, cold, unemotional. "She left me."

"All right. Then tell me your side."

Joe stared up at the ceiling, away from the well-remembered figure of his ex-wife. He couldn't look at her and talk about her in the third person. For that he needed distance. "It's not easy to talk about. I don't know how to explain how she made me feel."

"Where did you meet?"

A faint smile sketched his mouth. "On a city street. An elderly woman had fainted in the middle of Fifth Avenue and there she was, bending over that woman, trying to offer aid. All she had to do was look up at me and it was all over. I was baited, hooked and hauled in."

"Did she feel the same?"

"She said she did, later. But at that moment it was hard to tell."

"Why?"

"Because I was being a cop and she was a by-stander in an incident. I took down every detail about her I could cram in my notebook. My superior said it was the most thorough report he'd ever seen. But I had what I wanted—her name, her address and her telephone number."

"Did you call her?"

He laughed. "That was the beauty of it. I needn't have bothered. She had taken down my badge number and she called my precinct about an hour later on her break."

"She sounds like a take-charge woman."

"Not in the way you mean. Once I got to know her I realized how unusual that phone call was for her. But I'm glad she called. I might have waited too long and lost my nerve."

"You don't seem the sort to lose your nerve over a woman."

"No. But this was different. I knew, really *knew* she was the woman for me. I was in love before I was in like, if that makes sense."

"Are you certain it wasn't just good old lust?"

"That, too." Joe frowned, absently seeking patterns in the random textural design of the ceiling tiles. "With her I never could separate my feelings for her into their components. She just was and I just felt for her. Whole. Complete."

"You sound like the kind of man who falls in love a lot."

"Never. Never before. Never after." The conviction in his voice anchored the words in her heart.

"So, what did you do? Did you go out on a date or did you just jump her?"

"We had a date and it lasted four days."

"Four days? Are you certain?"

"Positive. Oh, we had to do things like go in to work but those were intermissions between acts in our passion play." His voice was now buoyed by his admission of delirium. "We called each other every free moment. We met for breakfast, lunch, coffee, dinner, midnight snacks, 3:00 a.m. fried egg sandwiches at her place. Wherever."

Halle kept her voice neutral. "So it began as a sexual marathon."

"No." Joe sat up and reached out, wanting to shake her, to turn her to him, to demand that she remember what he could not forget. But he had no right. His arm lowered back onto the coverlet. "I didn't even kiss her the first time we parted. The parting was just too intense. We'd have ended up in the sack and sex would have exploded it. We just needed to *see* each other, to touch and talk and just be in the same place at the same time, to be certain it wasn't a dream, you know?"

She nodded, clutching the sheet to her bosom. "Yes, I think I do."

Joe heard the wistfulness in her voice but it scarcely registered. He had begun a journey of memory that he was loathe to abandon.

"We talked and smiled and laughed like each had at last found a missing part of themselves in the other.

Then I did kiss her. Kissed her until our lips were swollen. Finally we decided that the first date was over so that we could set a schedule for other dates. We agreed to meet for dinner the next night and to not call each other in between.''

''Did you succeed?''

He harrumphed. ''We lasted two hours. I kept getting a busy signal half that time because she was trying to get me.''

''You must have been very much in love.''

''Yeah.'' Husky wisp of honesty.

''So, you married.''

''We married. It happened fast. Maybe too fast, looking back. Everybody we knew thought it was too fast. Between her friends and mine you couldn't have found any subject they would have agreed upon but that one.''

''Your friends didn't like her?''

''My friends never really got to know her. She traveled in vastly different circles from my middle-class friends. Now her friends I met. The stigma of being a cop...'' He released a short sigh. ''It was like being a sanitary engineer. Anyway you dressed it up, my job stank as far as they were concerned.''

''Did that bother you?''

''Sure it bothered me.'' He reached up to massage the back of his neck where tension was building. ''To be held up to ridicule before the one person in the world I would die for? It hurt.''

''Did she know how you felt?''

''I don't think she knew how much I resented them. I tried not to let on because she liked them. They were like her.''

''What does that mean?''

"It means they had money, cachet, knew the right people, haunted the right places, could order expensive wines and get tables at impossible restaurants where they paid exorbitant prices while snotty waiters insulted them. I couldn't even afford the tip. They knew it and they made certain I knew it."

"Did they really seem that bad to you?"

"Sometimes." He nodded in accompaniment to his thoughts. "Towards the end. Yeah."

"Is that why you cheated on her?"

Joe's head swiveled toward her. "I didn't."

He saw her shoulders heave in a sigh then shiver with emotion. "You told me the other day that you had."

The moment of truth, Joe. Tell her the truth. The truth and nothing but the truth. She'll decide for herself, anyway.

His gaze riveted on her back, willing her to believe as well as hear him. "I said she left after someone told her I was cheating on her."

She didn't move, wouldn't look at him. "There's a difference?"

"I never cheated on her. Why would I do that? I loved her."

When she turned to him he met her doubtful gaze head-on. The black pupils had engulfed the shimmering green of her irises. "Why would she believe a lie?"

"Because we weren't getting along." He looked away. It wasn't easier to talk to her face-to-face. He felt raw, as if each answer he gave was stripped from his skin one piece at a time. She deserved her pound of his flesh but it didn't come easily.

"We hadn't been getting on for months. I told you, we married quickly. We hadn't figured out how to live together first."

"What's to living together?" She sounded resentful. "You bring your stuff, she brings hers. You pile it together, sort it out and go on."

"Some things don't sort as well as others."

Joe rubbed his jaw, seeking desperately the right words with which to express himself. "When we were together we could lick the world. Unfortunately we went out alone to meet very different worlds each day. And every day it got harder to see where we fit into one another's lives. We were both overworked, not seeing enough of each other, arguing over money, time and other peoples' intrusion into our lives."

"Who was the supposed other woman?"

He flinched. Instinct told him to deny everything but conscience warned him against the ploy. Sooner or later she would regain her version of the truth. This might be his only opportunity to introduce his. "A female officer at my precinct. Sergeant Maria Garcia. We'd been assigned together undercover from time to time. We went out a few times before I got married, but I realized it wasn't going to work. I guess she carried a thing for me long after I'd forgotten about it. I never noticed until the end."

"What happened between you?"

"Not what you think. I had made the decision not to tell my wife about Ed and what I was going to do for him. I suspected she wouldn't understand why I was risking my reputation. Maybe that's because I wasn't completely convinced myself of the necessity of what I was about to do. As I told you, Ed and I were arrested. When I was finally released I went home but my wife had locked the door. Someone had called her about my jam and she had gotten really scared. She said through the crack in the chained door that she didn't know me anymore and for me to go away until she had time to think.''

"So you went . . . ?"

"To Maria's. I know." Exasperation colored his voice. "Stupid move. But I was scared, in trouble and dog tired. I'd just been hauled into my own precinct on charges of police misconduct. Not many of my colleagues were anxious to be seen in my company. Suspicion by association. Maria opened her door. I went in.''

Halle had to try twice to find her voice. "Nothing happened?''

"Nothing. I ranted awhile, cried a little. My wife had locked me out! Maria listened. Shared half a bottle of whiskey with me. Finally, I slept.''

"How do you know nothing happened? Sounds as if you got drunk.''

"I know.'' He reached out then and turned her toward him. He cupped her face in his hands, that sweetly adored imperfect face more dear to him than any icon of beauty. "I was an ass, Halle, not a rat.''

He felt her gaze reach inside him, deep down where the old hurts and resentments and anger and impotent rage and self-recriminations had slithered in their own bile for two long nasty dark years. He'd let her into that hell of emotions and now waited from her to run screaming away.

"You seem very bitter toward her,'' she said at last.

"Do I?'' He thought hard about that. "I didn't feel that way until afterward. Twenty-four hours later I was looking at divorce papers accusing me of adultery. I went a little mad. I was already on the ragged edge and going down fast. Didn't know yet whether I was going to prison or what. She still refused to see me, talk to me, read my letters. Her attorney came to see me after I made a public scene outside our apartment door.''

He sighed and released her, feeling he had lost more than his physical hold on her. "Her attorney told me my wife, *my* wife, would not allow further contact. If I pursued her, she'd get a restraining order." He slumped back against the headboard, aching all over again.

Halle watched him with conditional sympathy. "She must have been very hurt."

"She had a right. I had screwed up majorly. She had a right to be furious, hurt, afraid." His face swelled with emotion, his mouth severe against the bitterness pouring out of him. "She had every right to shout and rage and maybe even toss me out afterward. But she should not have shut me out."

"How did your wife find out you'd spent that night with Maria?"

"I didn't know the answer to that for weeks. Not until after I'd signed the papers she so obviously wanted me to sign. I'd lost my job, my home, my wife." He looked suddenly smaller, sadder, lost. "Maria told her. I know. I should have seen that coming. I'd been kidded by some of the boys in the precinct about Maria having a thing for me but I never thought she would do something like that. I was married, after all."

Halle admired the simplicity of his explanation. He was married. Enough said. She wondered how many other men viewed their marital commitment just that way. "But your marriage was in trouble. Perhaps Maria thought she might get you if it failed."

He shook his head, not denying but not quite understanding that logic.

"Did you ever try to see your wife, afterward?"

"What afterward? I had no job, a sullied reputation, no friends who would admit to the relationship in public. What could I say to her? 'Hi doll. I know I'm a bastard and near-felon but you've got to believe that I still love you.'"

His bleak gaze rejected any pity his words might have unconsciously engendered. "I had nothing to offer her. Even New York is small-town when it comes to certain things. I was known. Rogue ex-cops aren't popular with any segment of the law-abiding population. Work wasn't steady. After a while I knew I was going to have to leave. About the time I was packing up for good some thoughtful person taped a wedding announcement to my apartment door. My wife—excuse me—ex-wife, was now somebody else's bride."

Halle looked away from the mask of fury and betrayal on his face. "And you never forgave her."

"No, you've got it wrong. She never forgave me. That's what hurts the most, still does."

His gaze found and mated with hers. "She never gave me a chance to explain and be forgiven."

"That's a pretty impressive story," she said after a moment. "It has the sweep and depth of tragedy. Is that how you see your life, as a tragedy?"

Joe raised his hands in a futile gesture. "No. I'm not that important. I've just come to accept that for some people there are no second chances."

Halle looked up into his face, seeing in his expression for the first time the ravages of a man battered and bruised by his experiences with a failed marriage and lost honor. It was awful, the most awful thing she had seen in her sheltered life. She understood now why he had taken her in, in spite of everything. Even with his memory intact, he was more alone than she.

She didn't mean to disturb him, to try to get past the Keep Out sign he had again posted in his eyes. She didn't know if she had the nerve to challenge the bunching resistance in his jaw, or to weather the fury of eyes that dared her to enter at her own risk. She just scooted up the bed on her hips and hands until she was close enough to touch him.

She lay a hand first on his cheek, hot with emotion as if he had a fever. Beneath her fingers the muscles of his face were hard, a man turned to stone by feelings he could not escape. She traced his mouth with her fingertips, waiting and wanting a return of the man who had held her and lulled her and incandesced her with his touch.

He fought her. She could see the effort he made. His lower lip disappeared behind the barrier gate of his teeth. His chin rounded in stubbornness. A muscle twitched in his cheek where the dimple of joy should be. When she leaned closer to add the persuasion of her mouth, he stiffened. But he could not escape. His head was backed against the wall. She rose up on her knees, bracing her hands on the wall on either side of his head, and leaned in to him.

The kiss was so soft Joe thought he must be dreaming. He had not expected this, not to have his confession of sins of commission and omission forgiven in a chaste, perfect kiss.

"I don't expect you—"

She cut him off by deepening the kiss. Deep inside he shuddered not just from desire and relief but from the sure certain knowledge that this was how his life was supposed to be lived, with Halle and for Halle, forever.

He still held one secret from her.

He put a hand on her shoulder to hold her a little away and turned his face to one side. "There's something you should know, Halle. Something every important."

"No!" She grabbed his jaw and wrenched his chin around so that she could kiss him hard. "Later," she murmured against his mouth. "Much later."

"Damn!" Joe dropped the receiver back in its cradle.

Halle paused in smoothing her hair. "What's wrong?"

"Everything." He pointed at the phone. "That was my answering service. Bill McCrea called last night. Seems their missing baby boy has turned up."

"Lacey came home?"

"Not home, yet. But he's on his way. Called his mother last night. Said he'd be home sometime today." He tossed his empty coffee cup into the waste basket. "I had a bad feeling about this. The money looked too good."

"Money again?" she asked lightly.

His eyes cut to her face. "Yeah. Money. Again. Same song, different verse. You got a problem with that?" His expression did not encourage further comments.

Halle raised her hands in a gesture of surrender. As he turned away she stuck her tongue out at him.

Lousy was too nice a term for his mood, she decided. He had awakened looking like a prize fighter the day after a bout and proceeded to act as if everything that had happened between sunset and sunrise was an adult fairy tale: lovely, erotic, but not real.

Halle told herself it was his face. His eye was a little less swollen this morning but it looked painful nonetheless. She could occasionally glimpse a brown eyeball surrounded by angry red inside the puffy folds of skin. There was a four-inch long scrape along his right lower ribs. And there was the pouty fullness of his lips, testimony to their heavy-duty lovemaking sessions. He hadn't gotten much sleep but it seemed that his libido's satiation had made no inroads in his temperament. It was as if he were mad that he'd had so good a time. Knowing Joe, she believed that might be the answer. He was feeling guilty.

She looked down at her breasts which felt heavy and slightly swollen after all his eager attention. She felt guilty, too. But not enough to confess why just yet.

"So, what now?"

He glanced at her. "I go home."

"We go home."

He scowled. "How's that memory coming along?"

Halle bent over to fish a sandal from the floor. "It's coming in little flashes. Kind of like trying to remember someone's name you haven't seen in a long time. You know you know it but you can't quite grab it by the tail as it whips around at the edge of your consciousness."

"You will let me know when you've nabbed the culprit?"

"Will do," she murmured, knowing it was a lie.

Her memory was back, in spades. How to tell him? What to tell him? What to do next? Until she could answer that last question she wasn't about to tip her hand.

"There will be other cases," she offered as she quickly gathered up her things.

"It doesn't matter." He went to stand in the doorway holding the door open with the tip of his boot. "There's always fishing." He glanced back over his shoulder. "Ready?"

"You can't fish your life away," she said a little later as they were heading out toward the highway.

He shot her a smirking glance. "Watch me."

She folded her arms and canted her head to one side, sizing him up as if she were looking at him for the first time. "You must have some ambition."

"Nope."

"Oh, come on. You could work in Dallas as a policeman, for instance."

He shook his head, his gaze steady on the traffic. "Not on the last day I live. I've been a cop. I've seen all the ugliness of life I can stand."

"You have a B.A. in psychology. You could become a counselor."

"Why would I want to do that?"

"You're a natural with people. Look how you took me on."

He spared her a quick glance. "I knew you."

"You were always good with people."

"Your gimpy memory tells you that?"

"Brother! What side of the bed did you get out of this morning?"

He offered her the first smile of the day. "Yours."

She laughed in spite of herself. "Try to remember that when you're speaking to me in future."

"What do you expect? I'm a low-down dirty dude. Weren't you paying attention last night?"

"Yes. I heard every word, Joe."

"Then you know that since I haven't been fishing for two days it's the only unfulfilled wish I have at the moment."

"What about graduate school?"

"I'm too old."

"Try again."

"Drop it, Halle. This is my life. It's all I've got. It's all I want."

"I don't believe you."

He turned slowly, his gaze as steady and as cool as the mirrored surfaces of his sunglasses. "Believe it."

Chapter 11

Halle lay in Joe's bed under the colorful quilt his great-grandmother Mary Maud Guinn had brought to America from County Donegal and thought about her future. To be specific, she thought about her future with Joe or if they might even have one together.

It had come back to her in hard jolts of insight on the drive back to Gap what her life had been like two short weeks ago. Two weeks ago she had been the ex-Mrs. Daniel Shipmann and the recently resigned employee of Manhattan's top auction house. At thirty years of age she had one career and two broken marriages behind her. It seemed she'd begun to accumulate a legacy that would soon match that of her many times divorced parents. It was that horrible thought that she had been running from, her past and her possible future.

Failure.

She had blamed Joe for the first breakup. He had been the one who'd changed after their marriage. He was the one who had become remote, moody, difficult, worried about money, standoffish with her friends, secretive, jealous. It had not occurred to her until Daniel asked her out a few weeks after her divorce became final that she had spent more social time in his company than in her own husband's the last few months of her marriage.

She had chalked that situation up to the fact that Daniel was an old friend, that he worked in the same business, at the same house as she. They had accounts together, mutual quasi-social engagements in common. Naturally it seemed better to go out with a friend to after-hours business events when Joe couldn't join her—which became more and more frequent during the three years they were wed. Daniel was reliable, funny, conversant on many subjects, an impeccable escort just like all the men she had dated before she looked up into the English toffee eyes of Joseph Aloysius Guinn and lost her heart and head.

Joe moved beside her, turned toward her, his arm finding and spanning her waist.

Halle held her breath, hoping this once he would not awaken. Not yet, not until she had decided what to do. She couldn't think rationally when he was looking at her. When he touched her she forgot to draw breath.

It had been that way for her from the first moment. He had not lied or even embellished his remembrances as he had related his side of their story to her in Dallas the night before. He had stated things exactly as she remembered them. He had even remembered that it was she who called him.

What he couldn't know was that she had dialed the precinct three times before she got up the nerve to ask for him. She could not believe she was calling a man so casually met not even in a social setting. A policeman, no less. But he had looked at her, really looked at her, not her setting, her clothes, her body, her name, reputation or any other trappings that gave context to most peoples' lives. He had simply seen her and it had been enough to light up his eyes with the mutual recognition she had felt that here—at last—was the one!

From first glance to wedding vows she had never doubted for one moment that this union was meant to be. Cosmically intersected and soul-mated, they were one.

She turned and watched the pale wraith of lace curtain dance as glib as a shadow in the breeze spawned by the open window. Perhaps if they had been left perfectly alone to work things out they would have found a way to keep the magic going.

Or perhaps, if she had looked realistically at the prospects for failure then she would have spared him the heartbreak of ever-after. What else could she have expected? She was the child of a union so brief neither parent had bonded firmly with her. She was the error neither repeated. For all the stepparents she collected in her diary, she had never been given a stepsibling.

Halle bit her knuckle as a soft-as-a-sigh sob escaped. When she had divorced Joe, so full of the anger and hurt and misery, she was certain it was his fault and his fault alone. But that misery and pain and hurt had followed her into marriage with Daniel. The only difference was that she knew, knew with that frightful clarity that comes in the middle of a sleepless night, that it wouldn't work. She didn't love Daniel. Worse, she still loved Joe. But she had tried to tough it out. She had wanted it to work because the alternative seemed unthinkable; she was replacing the right man with the wrong one.

Daniel said it aloud first. A week after the wedding they were walking on the beach of Half Moon Bay in Antigua and he turned to her, brushed the hair from her face and said, "I'm willing to wait, Halle, until you've gotten over Joe." But they both knew by then that he wouldn't wait forever and that she would never get over Joe.

"Stupid, stupid!" she whispered into the silence modulated by the occasional chirp of a cricket.

She had ruined not one, not two, but three lives. That's why she had come here to Gap, Texas, to Joe, to apologize.

The fear she had had of something or someone being after her was no more than her past, or perhaps she was trying to escape the future. She hadn't counted on Joe drawing her back into his life, of breathing fresh life into old feelings, of resurrecting the possibility of a future in which they both had a stake. Was that possible?

She turned on her side into him, bringing her knee up to rest on top of his thighs as she laced her arms about one of his.

"Love me again, Joe," she whispered in his sleep-plugged ear. "Please, love me again."

"Joe! Thank God you're there!"

Joe came fully awake, half sitting up in bed as he palmed the phone more firmly. "Mrs. McCrea?"

"Yes, that's right. I hope I didn't wake you. My husband asked me to call. I know it's early and all but I do hope you were already awake."

"I'm up, Mrs. McCrea." Joe heard something besides polite inquiry in her tone but decided to follow her lead. "What can I do for you?"

"It's Lacey. He came home last night. He wouldn't speak to either of us. Then, this morning, my husband tried to talk to him but things got all twisted 'round and now, well—" She took a sharp nervous breath. "We have a situation."

"What kind of situation?" Joe kept his voice polite but he glanced at his bedside clock. It was a little past 8:00 a.m. He'd overslept and missed the best time for fishing.

"I'd rather not say over the phone. But you must come. Come quickly!" Joe's attention zeroed in on the woman's voice as she added, "I don't know— I just don't know what to do."

"All right, Mrs. McCrea." Things began to clink into place. This was a plea for help and Ella McCrea hadn't struck him as an easily flustered woman. "I'll be right there. But tell me this. Is there any immediate problem for Lacey or your husband?"

"Ye-es." She drew the word out distractedly. "Bill's in there trying to talk to him but I think he's only making things worse. Lacey's so angry, Joe. So angry!"

The numbers tumbled into place. He'd received similar calls a hundred times as a policeman. "I'll be right there. In the meantime, you call the police."

"No! No police!"

"But, Mrs.—"

"No authorities. My husband was emphatic. He wants only you."

"But I'm not—"

"Come, oh please, come quick!"

"On my way!" Joe hung up the phone and rolled out of bed in one motion.

"Who was that?" Halle strolled in the bedroom fresh from her shower. She was wrapped in one towel and fluffing her wet hair with another. "Joe?" she said sharply as she watched him yank his jeans on over his bare hips.

"Got to go out," he called over his shoulder as he reached for the T-shirt he'd dropped by the bed the night before. "Don't know when I'll be back. Have some coffee. I'll call you when I can." His dark head popped through the neck of his shirt then he wrestled both arms through the sleeves at the same time.

"Something's wrong," Halle said as she reached for her underwear laid out on the back of the rocker.

"Lacey McCrea's back," Joe said as he perched on the edge of the bed to pull on his socks. "He and his dad are mixing things up a bit. Mrs. McCrea wants me to play referee." He tossed her a brief smile as he stood to stomp his foot into a boot. "No biggie."

But Halle had seen that tense look in his eyes too often to believe his facile lie. "I'm going with you."

"You can't." He straightened after wedging his heel into the second boot. "No time." He gave her a short hot glance that scorched her skin as he surveyed her standing there in only her panties. "Sorry."

Muttering a depredation, Halle hurried after him, holding her towel to her bosom with one hand while she trailed bra and his sweat shorts in the other. "Wait! I can dress in the truck!"

Joe half turned at the front door to spare her an exasperated glance. "How am I going to explain it if we get stopped before you're decent?"

"You can tell the patrolman I'm a hitchhiker who overpowered and took sexual advantage of you."

He turned a little more fully toward her as she approached, his arm swinging out to embrace her. "You sure as hell did that, sweetheart." He pulled her tight against him for a quick hard kiss as his free hand found and squeezed a terry cloth covered breast. "Come on. But get in your things quick. I can't afford any distractions at the moment."

As it turned out, Joe had to give up his shirt in order to make Halle decent. No matter the extremity of circumstances, he had to live in this town and he didn't want to deal with having to explain to the state senator's wife why he had arrived in a moment of crisis with a strange woman wearing only a bra and his sweat shorts.

The drive to the McCreas took fifteen minutes. Joe stayed on the back roads where a truck tearing up the blacktop was less likely to draw attention.

"You've got to stop them!"

Ella McCrea's eyes brimmed with tears as she greeted Joe and Halle on the steps of her home.

"It's all right, Mrs. McCrea. I'm here now," Joe reassured her. "Has anything happened since we last spoke?"

"Joe," she whispered, clutching at his bare arm. "He's got a gun."

"Lacey?"

Joe saw her mouth tremble as she nodded once. "A handgun. Smith & Wesson. Bill keeps it in his office drawer."

"Loaded?"

She gave him a look that said "what else?"

The experience of a police officer colored Joe's unexpressed opinion on the subject. It wouldn't help now.

He put a comforting arm about the diminutive woman as he guided her back inside. "Okay, Mrs. McCrea. We're going to get this sorted out."

Inside he paused and turned to his companion. "Halle? Meet Mrs. McCrea. Mrs. McCrea, this is a friend of mine from New York City, Halle Hayworth. She's going to keep you company while I talk to your men. Where will I find them?"

"In Bill's office. Lacey locked himself in there after the fight began at breakfast. Bill got the spare key and went in after him. They put me out when I tried to go in, too."

"How long ago was that?"

"Must be thirty minutes ago by now."

"Okay. You're doing fine." He lightly patted her shoulder to calm her. "Have you heard anything? Voices? Heavy thuds? Gunshots?"

"Raised voices." She shuddered, her bones feeling birdlike beneath his broad palm. "Oh, Joe! You've got to bring them both out of there safely. You've just got to!"

"That's what I intend to do." He looked over the woman's head at Halle. "You and Mrs. McCrea go into the kitchen and have a cup of coffee. I'm going to need a little time."

"Certainly." Halle added, "Be careful" with her eyes.

Joe smiled back at her. "You know it, sweetheart."

"Oh yes, where are my manners?" Mrs. McCrea said but the clawlike grip of her delicate hand remained on Joe's forearm. "You be careful, Joe. Lacey has his father's temper but that doesn't mean he's not a good boy." Her chin rounded in righteous anger. "They're both two bullheaded fools. That's what they are."

Joe waited until the women reached the end of the hallway and then disappeared into the next room before he turned toward Bill McCrea's office. Having been in the house a few days earlier, he found his way there easily.

He knocked, waited a second for a response and then entered.

He hadn't known what he'd find on the other side of that door but the scene before him satisfied him that, for the moment, the situation was still under control.

Bill McCrea sat in one of the pony-hide steer-horn-framed chairs that flanked the desk. Despite his striped bathrobe and slippers he looked anything but rested. His son leaned against the desktop a few feet away.

In profile they seemed two versions of the same man except that Bill McCrea was sweating and Lacey was as pale as a sheet.

Lacey McCrea was even better looking than he appeared in the picture in Joe's dossier. He was medium tall and lithe-limbed with a shock of golden brown hair dipping across one half of his brow. Lounging against his father's desk in a plaid shirt and jeans he revealed a natural grace and lean-cheeked sulkiness women would find attractive. If it hadn't been for the handgun held casually in the youth's right hand, Joe might have thought he had sauntered in on a friendly father and son tête-à-tête.

"Good morning, Mr. McCrea. Lacey."

The teenager's gaze lifted. "Who are you?"

"I'm Joe Guinn." He took a few steps into the room. "I'm the guy who's been looking for a runaway by the name of Lacey McCrea. Only you didn't run away, did you?"

Lacey didn't reply but his gaze skittered toward his father.

Mr. McCrea smiled nervously at Joe. "Howdy, Joe. Glad you could join us."

Lacey came suddenly alert, gray eyes flashing enmity. "You sent for him? Why?"

"I figured we could use a mediator," his father answered.

"We don't need a mediator. This is personal."

Keeping his stride slow but easy, as if his stroll into the room were the most natural occurrence in the world, Joe walked toward the windows, placing himself in the glare and Lacey in stark relief. "Your coming back sort of ruined my plans to pay my bills but, hey, I can live with it. Do you mind if I sit down?"

Joe didn't actually sit but propped himself against the edge of the Spanish commode placed beneath the windows, ready for quick action if required.

Lacey watched him, chin tucked. "Like I said, this business is between me and my father."

"You always do business with a gun?" Joe inquired pleasantly. "I once did but that was because it was part of my job description."

Lacey's suspiciously swollen eyes widened. "You a cop?"

"*Was* a cop. NYPD, like the TV show. Only I never dressed as well nor spent as much time behind a desk."

Lacey lifted a leg and hitched a hip over the edge of the heavy desk. One bootheel plowed into the plush wine-colored carpeting as he braced himself with a stiff leg clad in denim. "Well, this isn't police business."

"In that case, you won't mind putting that handgun away. It's not a very good conversation starter. Somebody could get hurt."

Some new emotion moved through the teenager's expression. "That's the point."

"Don't smart mouth an ex-cop, son," Mr. McCrea said derisively. "He's not easily impressed."

"You shut up!" Lacey snarled suddenly and Joe understood why Ella McCrea was worried. Lacey had a temper and it was far from under control.

Joe flexed his hands in anticipation of action. If he could just shove McCrea out of the line of fire... McCrea was five feet from him. Lacey was seven, maybe eight feet on the other side. His chances of beating a bullet to Bill McCrea weren't good. He sincerely hoped it wouldn't come to that. So far there seemed no reason why it should.

"Suppose you tell me what started this, Lacey?"

"He started it." Lacey gestured at his father with his empty hand. "He never listens to me!"

"You run off like some delinquent and then come home and expect me to take your insults when I want to know where you've been?"

"You don't care where I've been!"

"Now, you listen to me—"

"I'm always listening to you!" Lacey roared back, drowning out his father's bombast. The gun in his hand twitched. "You talk and talk and talk and all I get to do is listen. No more!"

"Damn fool! You're just embarrassing yourself to no purpose. Nobody's going to take you seriously if you don't start acting like a man."

"You see?" Lacey gestured toward Joe with the hand holding the gun. "He thinks he knows what a man is. He thinks he knows everything. I wouldn't put it past him to have bribed that opera company not to take me."

"I might have," Mr. McCrea retorted, "if I'd known where the blazes you'd gone. Like I said before, maybe your not making the cut was a sign that you're not supposed to be a dancer."

"Oh?" Joe interjected, having calmly waited for an opening. "Did you win your first election campaign, Mr. McCrea?"

The man scowled at him in annoyance. "No."

"Then, according to your way of thinking, you should have quit politics right then and there. Like you're telling Lacey, maybe it was a sign you weren't supposed to be a state senator."

Joe could see that McCrea did not like the comparison. "It's not the same thing. Anybody in politics can tell you that there were factors beyond my control during that campaign. My opponent was an incumbent, had connections, resources, his share of powerful friends. Joining that campaign was only meant to make my name familiar to the constituency so that the next time out they'd know my face." He smiled. "They did, too. I won."

"I see." Joe only half heard Mr. McCrea's defense. He was much more interested in Lacey's reaction to it. "How many professional dance auditions have you gone out for, Lacey?"

Lacey hunched his shoulders. "None, before Albuquerque."

"Did you embarrass yourself, fall or anything like that?"

"No."

"I hear you sing, too. Did you sing for them?"

"Yeah."

"Crack a high note? Miss your pitch?"

"No." He glared at his father. "The others said I did really good. Better than most."

"Were you the only one who didn't make it?"

Lacey grunted. "Not hardly. There were fifty of us and only five positions."

"That's pretty steep competition." Joe spared a glance at Mr. McCrea. "Lucky thing you never had to run a campaign in a field that broad, isn't it? Might have taken you half a dozen primaries to have become known."

He looked back at the teenager. "Sounds to me like you made a respectable showing for your first time out."

Lacey motioned with the butt of his gun. "Tell him that! Not that that was the point. I needed that job worse than the others."

"Why worse?" Mr. McCrea prompted. "You got everything you could ever need and then some here with your mother and me. When did I ever not give you what you needed?"

"I need my freedom!"

That sudden piercing wail of pain shot up Joe's spine and reversed his position on the situation. Lacey might look in control but he was sitting on a keg of emotional kerosene and his dad was, however well-intentioned, tossing burning matches his son's way.

"I tell you what. Since you and I don't see eye to eye with your dad on this, why don't we excuse him? You can leave us, Mr. McCrea."

The older man gripped his chair arms as if he thought Joe might try to physically eject him. "I'm not going anywhere until Lacey comes to his senses and puts that damned gun away."

Lacey puckered up. "Not until I've made my point."

"What point are you trying to make?" Joe asked smoothly.

Lacey plowed a hand through the hair hanging over his brow, lifting it up and away to reveal a widow's peak. "That I can make a decision without him."

Joe's heart rate doubled as Lacey pointed the gun barrel in the general direction of his father. "That gun have a safety, Lacey?"

"Yeah." He grinned. "It isn't on. I checked."

"Don't smart off!" his father began only to fall silent as the barrel steadied at his chest.

Joe didn't move. "You know, Mr. McCrea, I think Lacey's got a point. You give a lot of orders for a man who doesn't like taking them himself."

He rose slowly as if he only needed to stretch his legs. "My dad was a lot like you, laying down rules and issuing orders like he was a drill sergeant in boot camp. Mostly I answered 'Yes, sir,' and then did as I pleased." Joe smiled as if in memory and came up behind the elder McCrea. "He hated it like everything when I disobeyed him but he could never say I wasn't polite.''

The tightness in his chest eased a fraction as Lacey smiled and the gun in his hand sank back to rest along the length of his thigh. ''That's good, Joe.''

Joe nodded amicably. ''I'm not saying a son doesn't owe his father due respect. I'm only saying there comes a time when respect and obedience aren't the same thing. People agree to disagree all the time, don't they, Mr. McCrea?''

''I suppose. But Lacey's my son—''

''And so due your respect,'' Joe cut in, wanting to gag the man. No wonder his son was feeling desperate. So was he.

He moved in to stand directly behind the senator and lay a heavy hand on his right shoulder. ''Why don't you do some of the talking, Lacey. Your father and I will listen.''

Joe's grip on McCrea's shoulder tightened significantly as he felt the man gather himself to speak.

''Go on.''

Lacey shrugged. ''This is stupid.''

Joe stood motionless and silent.

Lacey glanced up after several seconds. ''You want to know what I feel? I feel like dirt! Less. Marcie's the eldest, can do no wrong. Charlotte runs her own business. The family success story. Deirdra's given him four grandkids. I wasn't supposed to be. I was the afterthought, the mistake.''

He glared at his father, teeth bared in primitive aggression. ''I hear you and Mama talking. 'Thank goodness the caboose was a boy,' you always say. That's my place, right? Last. No possible use but to carry on the family name. Big stinking deal! I don't want it. First thing I'm going to do when I get out of here is legally change my name!''

Joe's grip nearly snapped the man's collarbone but Mr. McCrea would not be quelled this time. ''That won't change who you are,'' he thundered. ''You'll still be my son.''

''I know,'' Lacey said bleakly. ''That's why I'm thinking about something else.'' His gaze dropped to a contemplation of the gun weighing down his hand. ''There's ways of beating you, old man. Ways.''

''Like running away?''

Lacey glanced up in surprise as if he had forgotten Joe's existence. ''No. He'd just send you or someone like you to find me and drag me back.''

Joe shrugged. ''So what? You'll be eighteen in a few months, right?''

''So?''

''So, he won't have any legal right to send someone after you. You'll be free to do what you what.''

Lacey shook his head. ''You don't know him. He's got connections, knows people. He thinks I'm going to a military academy but he's wrong. I won't go there.''

''Then don't.'' Joe shrugged. ''What can he do? You're a little large to tuck in his vest pocket. He'd look pretty stupid carrying you hog-tied to the front door of the school. The media would have a field day. He's up for election. I don't think it will come to that, do you?''

''No.'' Lacey stared at his father. ''I was thinking about making it so he can never get to me again.''

Joe's second hand came down heavily on the father's shoulder. ''That's a consideration. Dead is an option. It certainly makes a statement. Just about every young man with an overbearing father figure has thought about it. You know Hamlet?''

"The movie with Mel Gibson?"

Joe smiled. "Yeah. That one. Remember how he thought about offing himself but then decided that he'd rather have revenge?''.

"He died anyway," Lacey said contemptuously.

"Exactly. Everybody dies anyway. That's the point. So why not go after what you want from life first? It's not like you're going to miss out permanently on the experience we call dying.''

Lacey half smiled and set the gun on the desktop. "You're weird."

Joe smiled back. "Look, I'm not saying living with your dad's a piece of cake. But you've got options, Lacey.''

Lacey glanced at his father. "Six months and I'm out of here. And I'm not going to Harlingen in the meantime.''

Mr. McCrea shook his head. "You don't have to, son. However, I do think we need to talk about things.''

"But not now," Joe said crisply and moved to the desk to scoop up the gun. As he pushed the safety into place he said, "You need to go and tell your mother the theatrics are over, Lacey.''

"She knows!" Ella McCrea burst through the door and hurried over to throw her arms about her son. "Lacey, Lacey, my baby! You know I love you!''

"Listening at keyholes?" Joe asked in an aside to Halle who came up beside him.

"Absolutely." He saw that her eyes were shining with unshed tears. "You were brilliant. Absolutely brilliant!''

Joe hugged her with his gaze. "I was lucky. That kid has something he wants to do really badly. When dealing with a person with a gun, it helps if he has a reason to want to live."

Mr. McCrea came up to Joe, looking every one of his sixty-plus years. He held out his hand. "You just did a fine job, Joe. No need to fret about your bills. You'll find my generosity equals my thanks."

Joe shook his hand. "I won't accept anything more from you than this handshake, McCrea. You were lucky just now. There's a lot of accumulated hurt and rage in your son. I advise you all to seek family counseling. If you don't work it out now you may never see Lacey again after his eighteenth birthday. You've got to ask yourself if keeping him off the stage is worth that."

The older man bit his lip and wagged his head. "Until today I never knew he hated me so much."

"He doesn't hate you. He wouldn't have come back if that was the case." He waited until the man's eyes had come back to his face. "Lacey's tired of failing you, Mr. McCrea. You need to make it possible for him to make you proud."

"On the football—"

"Anywhere, McCrea. You need to be proud of him anywhere he is, doing whatever he's doing."

McCrea nodded. "You're right. I suppose it wouldn't kill us if he went over to Dallas to attend that arts magnet high school. But it's hard, you know. Men in tights!"

Mrs. McCrea eyed Joe suspiciously as she approached. Reaching up, she captured his chin between her thumb and forefinger. "What happened to your face? Joe Guinn! Have you been in a fight?"

"Joe's been busy earning his Good Samaritan badge this week," Halle offered for him. "He saved a woman in Dallas from assault and another one from incurable loneliness."

The look he gave her curled her toes.

Ella McCrea nodded as she studied Halle with wise eyes. "I suspect you've had something to do with his sudden change about. I don't think I've ever seen him smile before today. You must come 'round for lunch one day soon, Ms. Hayworth." She glanced at the two men in her life with maternal indignation. "I should like the opportunity to erase the impression that Tyler folk have no manners."

"I'd like that," Halle answered. "If I'm still here." She turned quickly to Joe, a plea for escape in her expression. Regardless of how the McCreas felt about it, she was acutely uncomfortable to have met them under these circumstances.

Catching the drift of her feelings, Joe nodded. "I'll be in touch, Mr. McCrea. Mrs. McCrea? Lacey?"

A little shamefaced, Lacey came over and offered his hand to Joe. "Thanks. What you said about things, it helped."

Joe's steady law enforcement gaze zeroed in again on the teenager. "What you did this morning was damned foolish. No more theatrics or next time I'll see to it personally that the authorities are called in. You'll find yourself in a controlled environment talking to professionals in hospital coats."

"Jeez! I hadn't thought—" Lacey turned bright red, the first indication that what he had done was done on impulse and for effect rather than as a committed statement of extreme mental anguish.

Feeling a certain responsibility to see that Lacey felt he had a lifeline, Joe asked, "You fish?"

Embarrassed by his embarrassment, Lacey shoved a hand through his hair. "Used to. Been a while."

"Come fishing with me tomorrow morning. I'll pick you up at first light."

The teenager shifted on his feet. "That sounds kinda early."

"It is kind of early. Be ready on the front step at five-thirty. And another thing. Your dad's got some good points. You must finish school. After that, what you decide to do is your own business. While we fish, I'll tell you some stories about me and my old man. In the meantime, I've got to get my lady home."

Lacey glanced at Halle, a warmly appreciatively male glance. "I can see why you're in a hurry."

As they stepped out onto the McCreas' drive, Halle caught Joe by the hand and thrust her fingers through his to give them a small squeeze. "I'm so proud of you. You were wonderful with that boy."

He turned to her, smiling in a way that made a dimpled canyon in his left cheek. "Lacey just needs a little more of his father's silent support and a lot less of his opinions."

"Do you think he'll get either?"

Joe shrugged. "McCrea can now see the need for change but old habits die hard. They really could use a referee."

Halle turned suddenly into him, halting their trek toward his truck with the cushioned barrier of her body. As his eyes widened in surprise she recalled how she had watched him early this morning, his black lashes lying along his cheeks when he slept. She basked in those dark eyes that seemed to drink her in, losing no refraction of light that contained her image. She trembled at the sight of his hard mouth, badge of his uncompromisable standards, that she knew could suddenly soften with laughter or hot wet kisses.

Reaching up on tiptoe she kissed him and tasted the sweetness of this morning's victory, won at a cost that made it's satisfaction all the more prized.

As he responded by wrapping her hard and high against his length, the accumulated emotions of five long years rolled up through her in alternating waves of bitter and sweet. They rose from her womb, belly and chest, surrounded her heart and then rose higher to inform her brain. This was the man she had loved from the beginning, the one soul in the universe who matched and complemented hers. She had once felt soul-welded to him. Looking up in his beautiful face at this moment, she knew she had never stopped loving him.

Now, finally, in the last days she had come full circle. At the brink once again. But sail off into the ether again? She did not dare. Not for her own sake, but for his.

She settled back on her heels reluctantly, and he was equally reluctant to release her. His arms held her against him a little longer, until their lips came slowly unsealed.

"What was that for?" he asked a little breathlessly, half aroused already.

She gave her head a tiny shake against the pleasure promised by his smile. "We need to talk, Jag."

His head jerked in response to what she knew he saw in her eyes. Her memory was back.

He released his hold on her, as if the temper of his embrace were going to make the difference in how she responded to him. "Okay. Talk."

"At home," she answered softly as she again reached for his hand. But he lifted it, eluding her touch. She looked away, fighting down the ripples of panic his action caused.

Chapter 12

Having led the way, Joe turned to her five feet inside his door. The animation of personality had drained from his face. All that remained was the smooth-as-glass impenetrability of a former member of the NYPD's finest. "Why don't we get this over now? I've got things to do today."

Halle had expected him to be defensive but the breadth of his hostility surprised her. He looked as if he'd had a whiff of the sulfurous River Styx and she was the source. It hit her that despite the speech she had silently composed during the drive here, she wasn't at all prepared to deal with his present mood. She needed a little time.

She glanced past him into the living room. "Can we sit down and discuss this?"

"No."

Halle saw in the glare of his gaze that he was ready to do battle and that she should be prepared to defend herself. She nearly smiled but thought better of it. He was preparing for the worst, preparing to say goodbye.

He might have been on target if she hadn't spent the last few days in his company. But she had all her old memories of Joe back, as well as the new ones. As difficult and stubborn as he sometimes was, she knew with the certainty of memories that were her own that he had once loved her. The past two days proved he still cared. Those feelings were her hope and the source of his fear.

She crossed her arms and set her jaw in a reflection of his own stance. "All right. If you insist, we'll talk here."

He dipped his head, eyes slipping out of her range. "How long have you had your memory back?"

"Why?"

"How long?" The tether on his temper slipped a notch.

She weathered his hostility, amazed that he did not know that his very volatility was giving away the depth of his feelings. "A little while."

He looked up, backing her against a wall with his gaze. "A little while as in a few minutes, a few hours...or a few days?"

"A day." She pushed right back with the force of dappled green. "Yesterday."

His lids flickered. "Yesterday. Did it come back while we on the drive back to Gap?" The color of his eyes changed, growing dark with begrudgingly remembered passion. "Or when we were making love?"

The reminder lifted her heart up on tiptoe. "Why should the exact moment matter?"

"Because it does." His expression remained hostile. "When, Halle? Tell me when, exactly."

Flushed by the cross signals he didn't even realize he was delivering, Halle turned away from the thwarted passion shimmering off the surface of his impelling gaze. "Early yesterday, before daylight. When I awakened from the nightmare."

"Don't you think you might have shared this recovery with me sooner?"

She waved a hand in defense. "While you were explaining the history of my dreams these images began to flash through my mind, disjointed at first but with other thoughts attached. They were playing off one another like a ball in a pinball game."

She was surprised then as he grabbed her arm and swung her back to face him because she hadn't been aware that she was walking away from him or that he was following.

He looked mad enough to throttle her. Why, she wondered in confusion, was he so angry? "Don't spare me, Halle. What's the verdict?"

She gazed up at his scowl and understood. He wasn't applying any of the patient logic he'd used to ease the situation between Lacey and his father to their own case because he stood to lose on a more personal level. Only he didn't know, the fix was in. "I don't know what you mean."

But they both knew she lied.

Joe looked down at his hand where his fingers were making bloodless impressions on her skin. "You let me talk to you about our marriage last night without any defenses in place. Why did you do that to me? Did you need that victory to make your revenge complete?"

Genuine surprise colored her voice. "What revenge?"

"Oh, come on, Halle." He released her, backing off as if he hadn't just minutes before tried to stop her from distancing herself from him. His face was realigned into angles of weariness. It was only 9:00 a.m. but the round with the McCreas had taken its toll. She had been wrong to assume otherwise.

He slumped down in his leather chair and slid a hand down his features trying, it seemed, to wipe away his exhaustion. "We both know how pointed your ironies can be. You did everything in your power to destroy me when we separated. I thought making certain I was served divorce papers on the third anniversary of our marriage was the worst thing you could do to me . . . until you married Shipmann."

Halle flinched. "I want to explain that to you. I want to explain, oh, so many things."

He shook his head once. "No. I don't want explanations. If you're going to walk out of here you might as well do it now instead of an hour from now."

"Why?" she challenged, unwilling to be brushed off or dictated to. "Can't you stand to let me bare my soul to you the way you did to me these last days?"

He stood suddenly still. "Dammit, Halle. I turned myself inside out these last days trying to take care of you. You got your revenge, I'm gutted just like a fish. Go home."

"No." She reached out and pressed him back into his chair when he would have risen. As the flame of his temper rose she brought her face down, level with his, just as she had once seen him do to a belligerent drunk who was disrupting a party they were attending.

"You're going to stay and hear what I have to say because you owe it to me."

He looked a little dangerous as he reached up and grabbed the wrist of the hand she had planted in his chest. "I owe you?"

"Yes." She nodded in the affirmative once. "I listened to you. You can damn well listen to me."

When she would have released him he held on to her wrist and pulled her forward so that their noses almost collided. "Don't push me, Halle," he whispered.

The heat coming off of him made her shiver with the thrill of flirting with danger. She didn't know whether to quail or kiss him. "Why? Can't you take it on the chin anymore?"

His face darkened with a flush, accenting the purple-and-blue rings about his wounded eye, and she wondered how far she could push him before he relented or walked out of her life for good.

He released her and lifted both his hands in mock defeat. "All right, sweetheart. Give it your best shot. But, understand, I will fight back and I know how to fight dirty."

"Very well." Halle straightened and rubbed her hands on her shorts, amazed that they were clammy despite the spring warmth. She stopped when she noticed Joe staring. His experienced eye didn't miss much.

"Remember the other day when you told me that you couldn't hand me back my past as if it were a gift to give? You said that even if you filled me in on every detail of what you remembered about me, it wouldn't be my memories but your memories."

"I said that?"

"You also said that unless the memories and feelings came from me, they didn't count. Well, I needed time to think when the memories came back because, frankly, the feelings that came with them were not what I expected."

"You remembered how much you hated me."

He was staring at his boot tips with the intensity of a bird dog sighting a quail. Did he really think she had set the stage only to berate him with past transgressions? Didn't he know that she wouldn't have wasted the breath if that was all she had to say to him? No. It struck her as fresh insight. He did *not* know that.

She moved to perch on the sofa arm opposite his chair. His gaze shifted for an instant to the length of her bare legs. The expression he could not quite hide was one of longing and bitterness and sorrow.

She swung one leg to keep his gaze focused. "I remembered how much you'd hurt me, betrayed me and then given me up without a fight."

His gaze lifted, snagged hers and held. "Without what fight, Halle? There have to be two people in the ring for there to be a fight. I was boxing my own shadow from the night you locked me out."

"You went to another woman!" she said, preempting the lead-in to her confession.

"Right. And my explanation that nothing happened isn't one you believe."

"No, I'm not saying that." She sought help in his grim expression but did not find it. "I'd never heard your explanation before last night."

He reared back in his seat and crossed one ankle onto the opposite knee. "You want to tell me why you wouldn't hear my explanation before now? Because I sure as hell knew I wanted to give it to you."

The accusation was fairly leveled and she tried to meet it with equal honesty. "I was scared, Joe. I had never had anyone to call my own before you. Then you walked up to me that afternoon on Fifth Avenue and I fell so far and so fast and so hard I don't think I ever caught my breath. I gambled everything in marrying you. Even when no one else thought I was right. That scared me. When it started to go bad it seemed that they were right. I had gambled too much."

"So, you stuck your neck out?" he countered. "So did I. I married you, Halle, knowing that no one who knew you before me thought I was good enough. Your parents didn't bother to recognize my existence except as a possible future alimony collector. We both gambled equally."

Her spirit meter dropped as she realized that he wasn't going to help her. The sudden pain in her chest was the familiar pang of loneliness that she had known all her life but never quite gotten accustomed to. She quelled the eager answer that rose up in her that she had gambled more because she had so much more to lose. When she lost him, she lost the only person who had ever loved her, unconditionally. Instead, she chose his argument.

"Your friends didn't like me, either. They thought I was stuck-up and class-conscious. I couldn't help the fact that I was wealthy yet it seemed as if you were ashamed of it."

Joe wagged his head. "I wasn't ashamed. I just didn't want people to get the idea that I had married you for your money. Your friends all thought so."

"What difference did it make what they thought? I loved you." She had to catch her breath behind that sentence. When she did she said, "That should have been enough."

She saw his mouth tighten and the narrowing of his eyes as he considered the possible answers he might give. In the end it was simple enough. "It was enough, Halle. It was."

"Then why did you pull away after our first year?"

He sighed. "I didn't pull away. You just got so caught up in your job it seemed that way."

"You were never home." She could hear her voice climbing the scale but the memories accosting her were a little more raw than she had expected.

"Crime doesn't punch a time clock, Halle. I sometimes worked undercover, pulled night shifts, or had to track down leads. You worked eighty hours a week if you include all the after-hours functions you attended."

"I had to attend them as part of my job. It was how I made contacts and brought in business."

His expression soured as his hands tightened on the chair arms. "Yeah, you worked real hard at cocktail parties at Trump Tower and dinners at Tavern-on-the-Green with Shipmann."

Her chest hurt badly now. Each breath seemed to sear her lungs. "I stopped asking you to come with me because you said you hated the crush and the people. You thought they were snobs."

"Most of them were," he groused.

"Then so were your friends!" she retaliated.

For a moment they stared at one another, hearing the echo of a dozen other long-ago arguments on the same subject.

He recovered first, shaking his head sadly. "You see? Nothing's changed."

"I've changed." She wanted to tell him that he had been the first and only love of her life. Turning to and marrying Daniel Shipmann had been a mistake, a detour, a blind alley. That was why, even without a single memory to bolster or blast her impressions of him, she had known deep in her bones that they were connected. The love had never left. But that seemed a great hurdle to jump without at least a little explanation.

She stood up and began pacing. "You're right about some things. The mistakes between us were mostly mine. Once I decided we should divorce, I was so certain I held the high ground. The moral indignity of being betrayed by you made it easier not to see you."

Joe didn't say anything about his innocence this time. He was struggling to view things from her point of view. "I've turned things six ways from Sunday, Halle, and all I can come up with is that you owed me at least one hearing. One."

She paused and turned to him. "I agree. It wasn't until afterward that I knew that I had let my attorney railroad me. He said that if I let you back into my life even for a night, you would gain grounds to demand more of me than if I completely shut you out."

"Demand what, Halle?" The answer reached his eyes before he said, "I only wanted you."

"I know that now," she said in a small voice.

"The attorney thought I wanted your money." Joe didn't make it a question. He had known all along that this was the crux of the problem. "I told him I wanted nothing. He didn't believe me. But you, you should have known better."

"I did know better." She came toward him again, braving the effrontery of his unwelcome expression. In the depths of his eyes was another, very different emotion struggling to escape. "I was afraid of something else. I was afraid that you would talk me out of the divorce altogether."

"That fear should have helped us. Why didn't it?"

She paused just short of her right kneecap brushing the boot tip of his crossed leg. "I was furious that you had backed me into the position of considering divorce. My parents may not have taught me much but their example made me certain I didn't want to follow in their footsteps collecting exes and alimony. Our marriage was supposed to be my only marriage." She gazed down into his beautiful battered face and jackknifed right into the golden pools of his eyes. "You were supposed to love me forever, Jag, just as I loved you."

She saw the sudden thaw in his eyes but his brain was still in charge.

"I ask you again, Halle. Why didn't you stay and fight for our marriage?"

She hunched her shoulders. "Because I thought I'd lose. You keep a picture of Maria at your bedside. Why?"

His expression altered. "You went through my things?"

"I didn't open any drawers or read any mail. I didn't touch anything but the stack of books by your bed. The picture fell out by accident." She made herself ask again. "Why do you still have a picture of Maria?"

"I have a picture of Ed," he said flatly. "It reminds me of a time when I was happy, before I learned that loyalty should not be confused with pride. I should have known better than to think I could fix things for him.''

"And Maria?''

Joe shrugged, conceding her point. "Another lesson in caution. I never touched her after you and I met. Never. We had parted weeks before you and I ever met. She knew I wasn't coming back. It never occurred to me to wonder how far she'd be willing to go to see to it that I paid for moving on.''

Halle nudged his boot by flexing her knee. "She made it plain to me the day we met that she considered you hers and that I was poaching. She wanted you back. She said she would get you sooner or later.''

Joe's mouth hung slightly ajar. "You believed her?''

"Not then, not for a long time. Not really until the day after I locked you out and she called to tell me that, in future, if I wanted to find you, I should call her apartment.''

"You fell for the oldest trick in the book.''

Halle thought about that. If it had been her only mistake, she wouldn't be here now. "It was my greatest fear. The pain made me sort of crazy. I loved you so much.''

"You got over it.'' She watched his expression as he emotionally climbed the barrier of defense one more time. "You married Shipmann six months later.''

Halle winced. "Big mistake number two. When things began to change in our marriage I was bewildered, stunned, unable to act or think. My friends said I had asked for it, marrying a man too different from myself. I didn't know how to handle the fights between us or how to stop my sense of loss each time you walked out in the middle of one.''

He looked as if she had inflicted a wound. "Couples fight, Halle. My parents occasionally had some real set-tos. But they got over it. They cooled down, came back together and made it work. They did whatever it took, compromised, revised their plans to accommodate mutual needs. That's what couples do."

What couples do. Not what couples did, past tense.

Was he still thinking of them in some parallel world where the past was part of their present? Hope began to palpitate within her compressed chest. If he could imagine that, she could hope.

Halle tried answering his grimness with a smile though it made her shiver. "You haven't asked me why I came to east Texas."

His gaze slipped down from her face, past her torso to her long, long legs. "Did you have a reason?"

"Yes. And I was right. There was someone I was running from."

His gaze skipped back up to her face, the policeman on alert. "Who?"

"Myself. The day final divorce papers arrived in the mail for the second time in my life, I felt like a complete failure. It brought home to me what I feared most. That our breakup wasn't your fault. It was mine."

She knelt suddenly before him, balancing herself by placing her arms on top of his crossed leg. He didn't pull away or seem to mind her touch. "I took everything out of my purse that had the Shipmann name on it—my ID card, credit cards, checkbook, everything. I felt this urgent need to be free of all trappings of that marriage. I withdrew cash from my bank account and set out—in a real sense running away—to find you."

His gaze met hers, deepening with the emotion he had tried so hard to hold back. "Why?"

"I thought our marriage failed because we were too different. But I'd failed a second time with a man all my friends thought was perfect for me. I had to conclude that it was my fault both marriages failed. I wanted to know what was wrong with me. I suspected you could tell me. No matter what happened between us, I've always believed deep down that I could trust your judgment. Now that I've been with you again I know my second marriage failed because I never got over you."

He shut his eyes as emotion spasmed across his face. "That's easy for you to say now."

"You think so?" She shook him lightly with her crossed arms, causing him to look at her. "I think it's the hardest admission I've ever made. I didn't tell you the truth about my returning memory because I had discovered a man so different from the one I divorced."

"What's that supposed to mean?"

"It means that you are strong, reliable, confident, if not happy—all the things our turbulent marriage had leached away. And then I saw in your eyes that you still had feelings for me. I didn't want to spoil the possibility that we were falling in love again."

"Is that what you think was going on here, resuscitation of a corpse?" He was backsliding, trying desperately to find footing, and feeling only shifting sand beneath his feet. "Did I look that needy to you?"

"Yes," she whispered. "I was, am, as needy as you. That's why I've stayed."

"Don't do me any favors. You tricked me into saying things and having feelings I'm not at all certain I want." His voice was little more than a whisper but she knew he meant every word. "Loving and losing you once was painful enough. You were part of my past, a past I wanted to live down."

Halle understood that. Even before her intuition began feeding her fragments of memory she had felt the need to protect herself from them coming too quickly and overwhelming her. "Do you remember Jamaica?"

Joe started. "Our honeymoon? What about it?"

"Your cologne brought it back."

He glanced toward the bedroom door. "I don't wear that cologne anymore. Haven't for years."

"Because I bought it for you. Like you gave these to me." She reached up and touched one of the silver cows hooked through her ears. She saw his gaze go there, linger on the bits of metal while emotion tugged at his mouth.

"I've changed, Halle," he said, spacing his words with little silences. "I'm more cautious. I don't want to be hurt again. I still believe that the past is the past."

She rubbed a palm along the smooth surface of the leg of his boot. "Does that include us?"

He shifted uncomfortably. "You're trying to get me to admit to feelings I don't trust."

She tilted her head to one side but her gaze never faltered. "You wanted me. Last night. The day before."

He shook his head. "It's not about sex. It never was about sex with us and you know it. When you look at things realistically, we're right back where we started, in paradise as long as real life doesn't intrude."

"You mean as long as we're in Gap, Texas."

"Right." He nodded. "If you want to know if we have a second chance, stay in Gap with me."

Halle shook her head. "I don't think so. You aren't living in Gap, you're hiding from life here. If we are going to have a chance, we have to do so in the real world."

He slumped deeper in his chair. "I'm not going back to New York, if that's what you're leading up to. I guess I can't expect that you will want to spend much time in Gap."

"So what are you saying?"

Joe thought about his answer. Thought hard. "I'm saying it's been nice. Fate or random chance has given us a chance to get back what we lost two years ago." He reached out and caught her hand, enfolding it inside the embrace of his. "Our memories aren't tainted anymore. We should consider ourselves luckier than most and move on."

Halle smiled. "I never thought you were a coward, Joe Guinn."

Amusement tugged harder at his mouth. "Maybe you overestimated me. I'm a realistic coward. I'm the guy who goes fishing every morning. I have nothing to offer you."

"Is that a reason or an excuse?"

"It's a fact. I never tried to be anything I'm not. I could never compete with your friends but when I met you, I had a job. I was respected. I was doing what I loved. I was satisfied with my little corner of the world. Everything has changed."

"Everything? Your feelings, too?" She could see the pitched battle of conflicting emotions in him and knew, because she knew him, how he would answer.

"You can't live on nothing."

She turned her hand under his and squeezed his fingers hard. "You've been thinking about going back to school, do that."

He sighed and rested his head against the chair back as if his struggle were over. "I've been daydreaming about a lot of things. But it takes cash to go to school and I can barely feed myself on what I make. I'm not complaining. I'm just saying that the way I live is living for one. One only."

"I see." Her gaze shifted past him for an instant. "I don't accept that. Your financial status is something that can change." She rose to her feet. "If you want it to."

"Don't you think—?" He shook his head and clamped his lips as if he had been about to give away the secret password to an outsider. "At least we've settled the past. That's something."

"Yes. Our past was something. Something good."

He looked at her with the anguish of a man who feels he's receiving a punishment he doesn't deserve. Yet he was willing to accept it. "I suppose there's nothing else to be said. I suppose this is goodbye."

Halle could cheerfully have kicked him. Two years ago, she would have railed and wept and wounded herself with accusations which he would meet with his stony refusal to back down. This time, she held herself together with spit and nerve and hope. "Will you let me pay you for your services?"

"If you—" He caught himself. "No."

"Okay," She nodded, thinking more quickly than she ever had in her life. He had shown her the door. He felt backed in a corner. He wouldn't back down.

It wasn't his nature. "Then there's only one thing I want from you."

He didn't even ask what it was. Was he that afraid that it might be himself?

"I want to buy that picture from you." She pointed at the bronco rider hanging above the TV.

His expression became suspicious. "Why?"

"I like it. Western and native American art's my forte, remember? How much?"

"It's not for sale. It belonged to my grandfather. He bought it at a farm auction in the thirties."

"You're just being stubborn. I bet you don't know what color shirt the bronco rider is wearing." She bent and quickly placed her hand over his eyes before he could glance at the picture. "I'll bet you that picture that you can't name his shirt color."

Joe hesitated. "Red."

"No, gray. Red bandanna." She removed her hand and smiled cockily up into his face. "I win."

"You always did," he muttered.

"I'd like to pay you—"

He cut her off. "Halle, don't make the last thing I say to you a string of four-letter words. Take the damned picture. It's yours."

"I might consider it a loan."

"Consider it a farewell gift."

"I'll do you one better. I'll give you free appraiser's advice. Take that picture to Dallas and let someone tell you exactly what it's worth." She grabbed a handful of his hair. "You've got a future, Joseph Aloysius Guinn. It's been staring you right in the face all the time. You just didn't see it."

She released him and straightened up. One thing she had never done was sell herself cheap. If he wanted her he was going to have to come after her.

"Now I'm going to take a shower, dress and then call whatever passes for a cab in this part of the country. I'm going to Dallas and then I'm going home. You know where to find me if you decide to rejoin the world."

Joe watched her walk away, half in fear and all in love, and his guts twisted into pretzel shapes by his need for what he couldn't have.

"This was really nice of you to drive me into Dallas, Lacey," Halle said as they sat eating yogurt at a Dallas-Fort Worth International Airport terminal.

"You don't have to keep doing that, thanking me," Lacey replied. "I can use the money and like my dad said, we owe Joe a couple of favors."

"Your parents were very kind to put me up last night. I really didn't expect that."

"You don't know my mom or you would have expected nothing else. She thinks hospitality is the only form of civilized behavior left. I'm surprised she didn't insist you stay a few days."

Halle twirled a lock of her newly styled hair. "I must send her a thank-you for steering me to that salon. They did a remarkably good job."

"I'll say." Lacey grinned. "If you weren't already Joe's lady I'd give him a run for the money."

Halle smiled cryptically. She had tried to put a good face on her exit from Joe's house, claiming when she called the McCreas on advice about how best to get to Dallas that Joe had had to go out of town on short-notice business. The truth was he was gone when she came out of the shower. When he hadn't shown up three hours later, she decided to take matters into her own hands.

The McCreas had been more than understanding, they'd been gracious. As for Mr. McCrea and Lacey, they'd already been to see their pastor and Mrs. McCrea said they were going to have a counselor from Dallas in to see them.

"That's your flight they're calling," Lacey said as the loud speaker interrupted the canned music.

"I think you're right. "Let's go." She rose, picked up her one bag which Lacey immediately took from her and turned to walk toward the gate.

Joe took the stairs two at a time. He had had trouble finding a parking space and cut it too short.

He lifted his battered straw cowboy hat from his eyes as he entered the terminal. The security line was thankfully short. Even so, he was loping toward the gate as the the final boarding call was announced. He was going to be too late. Hell!

At first the glare from the picture windows by the gate made it impossible for him to see any of the boarding passengers distinctly. And then he saw a figure standing at the back of the line. A woman, tall, slender with ash-blond hair drifting about her shoulders.

Joe had never begged anyone for anything in his life but he made bargains with every deity and form of fortune he could conceive of as he hurried toward her to let that be Halle.

She looked surprised when she noticed him coming toward her but then she turned fully and smiled.

He practically stepped on her toe before he halted in front of her. Yet his first words weren't romantically conceived to please. "Your hair!"

Halle put a self-conscious hand to the fall by her left cheek. "I went to a salon here in Dallas. They stripped the darker dye off."

Joe nodded and swallowed. "It's . . . nice."

"Thank you," she said primly. "What brings you here?"

He grinned at her and his dimple had never looked better. "Unfinished business."

He wanted to hold her, squeeze her, drag her away and tear their clothes off. He merely devoured her with his greedy eyes. "You got any idea what a Remington goes for these days?"

Her eyes lit up. "I have a ballpark idea."

"I didn't. Jeez! And to think that fortune's been hanging on the wall these fifty years collecting dust. Several parties are interested and the broker I'm dealing with has advanced me enough money to take the edge off my economy living plan. I can even afford to apply for graduate school tomorrow or the next day. Soon."

"Oh, Joe, I'm so glad." She bit her lip. "Really."

"I've got more news. I've been offered a job." He smirked. "Mr. McCrea offered it. I'm going to run his Dallas campaign headquarters. It will be temporary. But it's a beginning."

"Sounds like you've sorted a few things out."

The thick-as-syrup heat in his brown eyes drew her like a fly. "I am beginning to." He leaned in close to her until their bodies were all but touching. "Some things I've put behind me. Other's I've tucked away in memory as lessons learned and wisdom gained."

She swayed against him, her breasts brushing his shirtfront as she lifted her face to his. "What else is there?"

"Hope." The fire in his eyes was melting her loneliness and lighting up every dark corner of her soul.

She fought for breath. "That's a mighty dangerous word in this day and age."

"Many people don't believe in it," he agreed.

"I'm not so worried about what other people think anymore," she said as she reached up to rest her hand over his heart. "I think I've gotten past that."

"Good for you."

"Yeah," she said, mimicking his western drawl of the word. "Good for me. I've also gotten past my prejudice about living in Texas. I've found quite a few things I like here. If I stayed, I might find a few more." She smiled a sassy smile. "I've got my past back and you've got your future funded. There seems to be only one question left to be answered."

His hands came up to frame her head, winnowing through the wheat blond hair as he found the shape of her skull with his fingers. "What would that be, sweetheart?"

"Oh, if you want to fit an ex-wife into your new life."

His lazy-lidded gaze wandered over her face to her lips. "I can see the immediate benefits. But the long run..."

"The long run is the only race in town worth running." She leaned up and placed her lips so lightly on his that they scarcely touched. "Haven't you figured that out?"

His lips lifted at the edges, brushing sensuously against hers. "You got your sneakers on?"

"Always."

The last sound Halle heard—before the roar of her heart caused by his kiss drowned out everything else—was Lacey's applause.

*   *   *   *   *

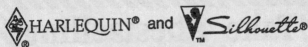

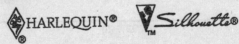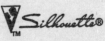

Take 4 bestselling love stories FREE

Plus get a FREE surprise gift!

Special Limited-time Offer

Mail to Silhouette Reader Service™

3010 Walden Avenue
P.O. Box 1867
Buffalo, N.Y. 14240-1867

YES! Please send me 4 free Silhouette Intimate Moments® novels and my free surprise gift. Then send me 6 brand-new novels every month, which I will receive months before they appear in bookstores. Bill me at the low price of $3.34 each plus 25¢ delivery and applicable sales tax, if any.* That's the complete price and a savings of over 10% off the cover prices—quite a bargain! I understand that accepting the books and gift places me under no obligation ever to buy any books. I can always return a shipment and cancel at any time. Even if I never buy another book from Silhouette, the 4 free books and the surprise gift are mine to keep forever.

245 BPA A3UW

Name	(PLEASE PRINT)	
Address		Apt. No.
City	State	Zip

This offer is limited to one order per household and not valid to present Silhouette Intimate Moments® subscribers. *Terms and prices are subject to change without notice. Sales tax applicable in N.Y.

UMOM-696   ©1990 Harlequin Enterprises Limited

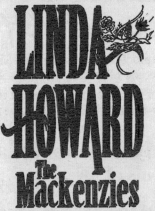

As seen on TV!
Free Gift Offer

With a Free Gift proof-of-purchase from any Silhouette® book, you can receive a beautiful cubic zirconia pendant.

This gorgeous marquise-shaped stone is a genuine cubic zirconia—accented by an 18" gold tone necklace.

(Approximate retail value $19.95)

Send for yours today...
compliments of ▼ *Silhouette*®
™

To receive your free gift, a cubic zirconia pendant, send us one original proof-of-purchase, photocopies not accepted, from the back of any Silhouette Romance™, Silhouette Desire®, Silhouette Special Edition®, Silhouette Intimate Moments® or Silhouette Yours Truly™ title available in August, September or October at your favorite retail outlet, together with the Free Gift Certificate, plus a check or money order for $1.65 U.S./$2.15 CAN. (do not send cash) to cover postage and handling, payable to Silhouette Free Gift Offer. We will send you the specified gift. Allow 6 to 8 weeks for delivery. Offer good until October 31, 1996 or while quantities last. Offer valid in the U.S. and Canada only.

Free Gift Certificate

Name: _____

Address: _____

City: _____ State/Province: _____ Zip/Postal Code: _____

Mail this certificate, one proof-of-purchase and a check or money order for postage and handling to: SILHOUETTE FREE GIFT OFFER 1996. In the U.S.: 3010 Walden Avenue, P.O. Box 9077, Buffalo NY 14269-9077. In Canada: P.O. Box 613, Fort Erie, Ontario L2Z 5X3.

FREE GIFT OFFER
ONE PROOF-OF-PURCHASE

084-KMD

To collect your fabulous FREE GIFT, a cubic zirconia pendant, you must include this original proof-of-purchase for each gift with the properly completed Free Gift Certificate.

084-KMD

You're About to Become a *Privileged Woman*

Reap the rewards of fabulous free gifts and benefits with proofs-of-purchase from Silhouette and Harlequin books

Pages & Privileges™

It's our way of thanking you for buying our books at your favorite retail stores.

✂

PROOF OF PURCHASE SIM-PP163

Offer expires October 31, 1996

Harlequin and Silhouette— the most privileged readers in the world!

For more information about Harlequin and Silhouette's PAGES & PRIVILEGES program call the Pages & Privileges Benefits Desk: 1-503-794-2499